THE MOMENT BEFORE AN INJURY

ISBN-13: 978-1-937677-71-8
Library of Congress Control Number: 2014936512

Fomite
58 Peru Street
Burlington, VT 05401
www.fomitepress.com

Cover Image - Kat Laranger — http://katlaranger.com/
Author Photo - Carolyn Zuaro

THE MOMENT BEFORE AN INJURY

JOSHUA AMSES

FOMITE
BURLINGTON, VT

For my parents

Monday

"Even folks that have lived in Acheron for their entire lives have trouble explaining how to get here."
— Cordelia Swan, local historian, and assistant director of the Acheron Free Library

"...Vermont's best kept secret!"
— Releaf Tours promotional brochure, authored by Oliver Himmel, copyright Acheron Ventures, LLC, 2011

1.

ACHERON, VERMONT (pronounced 'Ah, Sharon' if you're from here), is a town of 7,855 souls bracketed between Burlington, the largest city in the state, and Montpelier, its capital. It is too large to be considered 'quaint,' too small to attract the sort of investment that will help it grow, and too far from I-89 to serve as a stopover between the two more prominent cities. If it were not for the eponymous college sitting like a sentient fortress atop Aornum Hill, it is possible the town would merit little attention from the mapmakers of greater America.

Acheron's reputation as a 'foliage gateway' is of recent manufacture. Before the town began appearing in guidebooks, the only tourists it hosted had either become lost, or confused the apse of Holmes Hall (part of the college) with the golden dome of the State Capital building in Montpelier. Though similar in shape, they are disparate in both color (the basilica of Holmes Hall is an indistinct slate gray), and iconography. While Ceres occupies the State House's peak with a vestal magnanimity, Hermes, the household god of Acheron College, is jailed atop the dome of Holmes Hall by a circle of phalli. The administrative staff refer to these as 'minarets' during campus tours, but alumni, of which I am one, know better.

I graduated from Acheron College over a year ago, and since

Jeremiah Castle (the man semi-responsible for the phrase 'foliage gateway') offered me a job, I had no reason to leave. Though it has little of the bourgeois craft fair exclusivity of Woodstock, or the ski town by day, gallery by night waspish polarity of Stowe, I'm fond of the thumbprint Acheron's student population has left on the town. Time not used in serving the Castle household is spent among the bookshops, coffeehouses, and microbrew salons lining Clamence Street (Acheron's answer to Nevsky Prospekt). Mr. Castle's real estate company, Acheron Property Management, holds the leases on these, as well as two gas stations, three Laundromats, the town's only hotel (the Herrenhof Inn on Loomis Street), a pool hall that does not serve alcohol, another that does, a video store, a pharmacy, and several apartment houses beside the Castle Memorial Recreation field on the town's outskirt. They likely own more, but it's been some time since my last review of APM's contracts. The only establishment apparently beyond Mr. Castle's reach is the college on the hilltop. But since Cornelius Castle (Jeremiah's younger brother) holds the position of president there, the family's interest is represented.

Last week, APM acquired Le Champo, the art-house cinema on College Street, and as I pass the marquee going toward Clamence Street, I notice the cinema has just begun showing a film of Tosca with a fascist leitmotiv (on my recommendation). If I were not on my way to meet Isidore (Mr. Castle's son), I might stop in for a matinée -- though it really makes no difference when I go, since they wouldn't dare charge me admission. And I'm already running late, which is Isidore's fault.

When we spoke last night, he agreed to meet me 'on set' (as he called it), which I understood as the location I'd scouted beside the slope of Mt. Abandon ten miles outside of town, an abandoned house set deep in the woods. But after spending an hour alone at the location, with the dilapidated home glaring from across the driveway, I received the following text message (from Isidore):

where r u henry sg 10 minuts

I haven't replied, because he won't check it. Even if he did, there is no guarantee he'll be at the coffee shop ('sg') when I get back into town. Language historically fails Isidore. When we were classmates at the college atop Aornum Hill, our professors found it easier to pass the local landowner's son than correct him. His family hasn't done much better. And now, he is as rudderless and benign as Russell's galactic teapot caught in an asteroid belt. An old story.

It's the final week of October, meaning the academic term opened a month ago. Directionless students cushion the mid-morning pedestrian traffic on Clamence Street, with an especially large cohort occupying the benches outside Sacred Grounds: Coffee & Tea. The trees lining the thoroughfare are at peak color; the buttery yellow, burnt orange, and a sharp, warlike shade of red like an autumnal oriflamme above my car as I ease into a parking space outside The Scriptorium: Books, New & Used (most shop names in Acheron contain a colon). Whether or not Isidore is here, I anticipate a quiet morning.

But just as I'm about the turn off the ignition, a beige van with 'Releaf Tours' printed across its side speeds past my parking spot in the direction of town hall. I shift the car back into drive, and leave the parking spot in pursuit. I'm driving a relatively new Audi sedan, and it doesn't take long to get close enough to the van for the driver to hear my horn, see my flashing headlights, and hear the music blaring from my stereo ('The Fan and the Bellows' by The Chameleons). The van turns off Clamence Street, stops beside a Methodist Church on Cliff Street, and the driver gets out as I'm pulling in behind him. From beneath my seat, I remove a thick, alphabetical notebook, and open it to 'T,' scanning the pages until I find the proper entry.

"Good morning, Tyler," I say, rolling down my window, and closing the notebook in my lap. Tyler Moskovitz (the driver) approaches the window slowly, scratching his head beneath a woolen watch cap, and trying, though failing, to smile. He's a gaunt, lazy, good-natured slob missing one tooth for each year he is my senior.

"Mornin', Henry," he says, cautiously. "Something I can do for you?"

"Taillight's out on the van."

Tyler doesn't realize I'm kidding. He begins to diligently examine the rear of his vehicle.

"Tyler, it's a joke," I say. "The van is fine. What I really want to know is why it's nearly 10:30, and here you are, talking to me, when you're supposed to be out back of City Hall, picking up leaf peepers at 9:45."

Unsure whether to laugh at the joke about the taillight or appear serious, Tyler's face becomes a theatrical mask, diametrically representing both grief and joy.

"I'm sorry, I really am," he says, with a countrified gravity. "You see, my rotty just had pups, and since then, she ain't been so well, and I gotta help them little ones find the…uh…her teats, is basically what I'm describing. I guess I forgot to figure that into my morning routine, but I just couldn't let them dogs starve."

"I see. So you were late to work because you had to milk your dog. That right?"

"Uhyut…I guess so," says Tyler, scratching frantically beneath his cap to avoid my eyes.

"You know," I say, opening the door of the Audi, and stepping into the street. Tyler takes a few steps back. "Releaf Tours is a small business, and a new business. Those things are difficult to launch. I'm sure you can appreciate that."

Tyler nods. I continue.

"A business that is both small and new depends on two things, Tyler. The first is service, of course. Now, let me ask you, if you spent fifty bucks per head for a tour of some colorful trees, you expect the tour guide to arrive on time, because that's the service for which you paid. Correct?"

Tyler nods. I remove a folding knife from pocket, and open it.

"The second, of course, is honesty. We want Acheron to be known as the foremost foliage gateway in the green mountain state, and when that succeeds, Releaf Tours won't always be small. I know you're only guiding right now, but if you do your job well, there's plenty of room for growth. You perform your duty honestly, and Releaf Tours will reward your hard work. That's only fair, right?"

Tyler nods again, watching the blade in my hand, as I squat beside his van, and begin using it to remove stones from the rear tire.

"Now, you have puppies at home, I say keep those dogs fed. 'Compassion for animals is intimately associated with goodness of character, and it may be confidently asserted that he who is cruel to animals cannot be a good man.' Do you know who said that?"

Tyler's head oscillates. I continue picking at the tire.

"Doesn't matter. The point is that an honest fellow like you should see to his house. But you don't live at any of those apartments out by the rec field, do you?"

"No, sure don't. I'm out by Quim Crossing, near the railroad bed."

"Then why," I ask, extending the hand holding the pebbles I

picked from the tire, "is the gravel we dropped yesterday evening in the parking lot of those apartments out by the rec field stuck in your tires? You keeping your dogs there?"

"I just stopped there this morning. On my way here."

"What I think," I say, dropping the gravel at his feet, and brushing my hands on my pants, "is that you got a girl at those apartments. If remember right, June Bones lives out there, and she has some dogs, and I'm sure I've seen her with a Rottweiler. In fact, I'd swear it was pregnant the last time I saw it. Of course, that was months ago. Also, you have toothpaste on your finger."

Tyler raises his hands to examine them.

"Don't worry, Tyler. She may not let you use her toothbrush, but you're nursing her puppies. That's a sure sign things are becoming serious. Speaking of serious, her husband just died, didn't he? Yes, I remember now. Rudolph Bones, killed in a hit and run out by Quim Crossing, of all places. In fact, weren't you the fellow that found the body?"

"What are you sayin'?" whispers Tyler.

"What I'm saying," I begin, folding my knife, and returning it to my pocket. "Is that Mr. Castle likes a man he can trust, and he wants to like you. I think it's awful nice of you to comfort a grieving widow, and assist her with pet care. Just between you and me, there's no shame in that, unless it makes you late to meet those nice people out back of city hall. Consider this advice, not a warning. We clear?"

I extend the hand that formerly held the knife, and Tyler takes it across what feels like a nautical distance.

2.

By the time I return to Clamence Street, Isidore is absent from Sacred Grounds (assuming he made it there in the first place). I order a coffee, and ask the barista if she's seen him today, but she doesn't understand what I mean. She is my age, likely new to town, and a student at the college up the hill. I introduce myself, and try to better explain what I want.

"The person for whom I'm looking is about my height, slightly taller, but thinner. His hair is black, and carelessly cut. He likely ordered something fatuous, a Pumpkin Harvest Latte, or Soy Gravy Shake. It's also possible that there was a man with him suffering from rhotacism."

"Rhota what now?" she says, handing me a paper cup, and taking my money.

"Rhotacism. He can't pronounce the letter 'r'. He would have ordered a 'dawk woast,' or a 'cawamel fwappaccino,' for example."

"Oh, yes! They were in here about a half hour ago. The one with the bad haircut ordered a…"

"Thank you," I interrupt, dropping several dollars into the tip cup beside the register, and walking back outside to my car. Morning has transitioned to early afternoon, and sunlight sieved through branches of the trees above the street casts a strange Mithraic pattern on the sidewalk, which is littered with damp, fallen leaves, and feels spongy beneath my feet. A cool wind arriving from the direction of Mt. Abandon to the north meets another rolling down from Maybrick Peak to the south, each drawing with it an insuperable chill that settles like a tablecloth across the valley containing Acheron. Though it's still early in the season, the brisk suggestion of snow hangs in the air like the photograph of a bird. I raise the collar of a business-like pea coat I've taken to wearing while on the clock (so to speak), which provides an intimidating, vampiric aspect to my comportment, the collar being proportionally similar to the frill of a *Chlamydosaurus kingii.*

"I am a lizard," I announce to my reflection as I settle into the driver's seat and start the car, because of all creatures roaming the earth, this is the one I regard as my avatar. It is only after I'm on the road, heading toward the base of Mt. Abandon, that I seriously return to it (my reflection). The thin, high-boned face in the rear view mirror glares ambiguously through eyes the color of tarnished, deep ocean copper (my driver's license describes this color as 'hazel'). No, I am not a lizard, but a man, a young man, twenty-five years old, brown haired, hazel eyed, six feet tall, one hundred and seventy pounds. In stature, I resemble a human gallows, my torso slim, and my shoulders broad. I suppose I'm handsome. Women seem to think so (or enough of them to settle the question). But it's unimportant. As my mother used to say, "If people don't like you, they're obviously fucking idiots."

As I pass the recreation field and the apartment houses where Tyler spent the night, I notice the bumper of a police cruiser nosing out of a logging road up ahead, neither obvious nor hidden. Whether or not a motorist can see the vehicle matters little, since Sheriff Blivet's (French Canadian. Pronounced: 'Bleevay') pendulous arm extends from the driver's side window, the appendage terminating in the red, snake-like mouth of a radar gun pointed directly at my car.

I have no idea what speed is posted in this area, but as the needle on my speedometer inches above sixty miles per hour, I'm confident I'm exceeding it. As I pass the police car, the arm holding the radar gun retracts, and reappears, the hand open and empty, the palm like a catcher's mitt facing me in a bit hail-fellow-well-met that I return, my hand waving foolishly toward the Sheriff as if the two of us are friends, which is not a possibility. The Sheriff is a useful man with the mind of a peasant and the moral imperative of a war criminal. He knows me as all the employees of Jeremiah Castle know me, which is to say, not at all.

3.

A HALF MILE UP the access road to Mt. Abandon, Isidore's van (recently appropriated from the Releaf fleet) is parked in the same place I waited earlier this morning. Purvis Blivet (Sheriff Blivet's son) is already removing equipment from the van when I turn into the driveway, and he waves the same way his father did twenty minutes earlier when he notices my car. Purvis is obviously cast from the same mold that cursed the world with the sheriff. Both are large, sloppy men who need to be told what to do, and lately, Purvis has come into his own as a uniquely lumbering Hindenburg of a person. But after I began working for Mr. Castle, Isidore needed to find a new playmate, and Acheron is not a large town.

"Good mowning, Henwy," says Purvis, as I exit my car. He's standing behind a clumsy barricade composed of plastic boxes containing cameras and microphones, and milk crates holding cables. Emblazoned on each piece of equipment is the motto 'PROPERTY OF A.P.S.' The acronym has also been added to the side of the beige van.

"I think you mean, 'Good afternoon," I reply, eyeing the house. "Isidore inside?"

Purvis bobs his globular skull.

"Suwe is. How'd you find this place?"

"It's been here forever."

"No, I mean, how'd you find us?"

"I don't understand, Purvis."

"Well, we was supposed to meet you hewe this mowning and I told Isidowe that we didn't have time to get the van painted, but he said something about this being a fledgling investigation and us having to have a logo if we'we going to film, and then when we got it painted, we went fow coffee, and I guess we kinda fowgot we was supposed to meet you, so I reminded Isidowe, and he sent you a text I guess, but then he didn't wanna wait, so we just came up hewe and figuwed we'd meet you back at…"

"Thank you, Purvis," I say, leaving him with his igloo of film equipment, and walking toward the house. It's a typical three story Victorian, with a broad porch that seems to exhale when I mount the stairs leading to it. The surrounding yard is littered with shingles blown from the mansard roof by the wind from Mt. Abandon, and bits of drapery and wallpaper torn from within. Perhaps a hundred years earlier, the residence was quite handsome, and as it rots in the shadow of the mountain, amid the Greek fire of autumn, a remnant of bereaved pulchritude remains. If it were captured on a canvas, and sold in a ski town, patrons would fight over it. Instead, it's another playground for Isidore, who appears at the head of the stairs when I enter the foyer.

"Henry, glad you made it. Thanks for finding this place. How'd you do it?"

"It's been here forever."

"First I've seen of it."

A digital camera snaps in his hand as he descends the staircase, his head nodding beneath a baseball cap with 'A.P.S.' stitched across its face, his ungainly torso cloaked in a black utility vest.

From one of its numerous pockets, he extracts a decal bearing the same logo as his hat, and offers it to me.

"Here you go. One for the bumper of that sweet little ride you got."

I thank him, and pocket the thing, figuring I'll dispose of it when I get back to town. Before I can avert my eyes, Isidore notices me staring at his hat.

"Oh, don't worry. We got one of these for you, too. There's a whole box out in the van. I got a call they was ready right after we got the logo painted on the side. It's why we couldn't meet you here. P. explained it probably."

"He did. In detail."

"Come here, I want to show you something."

I follow him up the staircase, which seems ready to collapse beneath our combined weights. He turns right on the upper landing, down a dismal, tunnel-like hall barely illuminated by the gray light entering through a broken window at its end. The entire second floor has a sad, inoffensive smell like cold wood.

"You know who owns it?" asks Isidore stomping ahead.

"The Mt. Abandon Conservation Society. They own the land."

"So, it's Dad's," he says, disappointed, as if finding a portion of the township in which his father has not yet inserted a finger might constitute a triumph of some kind. Though I've seen no indication of a rivalry between Mr. Castle and his child, I've witnessed many occasions during which the latter has tried to impress the former, and failed. As I watch his initial excitement fade to resignation, betrayed by a nervous scuffing of his shoe on the wooden floor of the house that was ideal only a moment earlier, I almost feel pity. Any son, no matter how wayward or profligate, wants his father to be proud of him. But I say nothing, and adjust the frill of my pea coat.

"Maybe in the future," says Isidore, pushing open a door, "you could try and find something beyond his purview. If possible."

"If you want this to be a local project, that might be tricky."

"Take a look at that," he says, gesturing at a white wicker standing bassinet occupying the center of the otherwise bare room. "Isn't that the creepiest shit?"

"It certainly is," I say, trying to sound as though I've never seen the thing. The truth is that I found it in an antique shop in town two days earlier, and dragged it up here after Isidore said he was interested in seeing the house. The proprietor threw in a generous and alarming collection of period toys, probably as glad to be rid of the bassinet as Isidore is in finding it.

"You think that's bad," says Isidore. "You should see the fucking jack-in-the-box I found in the cubby under the stairs. Did you find anything about the history?"

"Yes, I did," I lie. "The house used to be a home for unwed mothers in the eighteenth century, and the proprietress was one Amelia Sutpen. She was a nurse who ran what was called a 'baby farm' in the nineteenth century. Pregnant women would come here, give birth, and then, for a small fee, Nurse Sutpen would see to the child's welfare. Of course, it was much cheaper to bank the money, and dispose of the infant. And this is what she did."

"That explains the bassinet."

"Sure it does."

"How many did she..."

"Kill? No one knows. She operated for years. Some say over four hundred, many of which are rumored to be interred on this very property."

"What does 'interred' mean?"

"Buried, Isidore. Put in a hole."

He appears disturbed, and I wonder whether I've overdone it.

Mr. Castle instructed me to 'ham it up' for Isidore, but I'm not an artist. I'm an apprentice without a master.

"Why didn't them women just have their babies somewhere else?"

"Giving birth back then was considered bad manners."

"I could use some air I think," he says. We walk out of the house, and I stand on the porch while Isidore rocks mordantly in a swing suspended from it, the creaking of its chain the only sound aside from the occasional hollow noise of Purvis setting equipment by the front door. I've completed my tour, and I'm waiting for Isidore to recover himself before I leave. The sun is setting, and I assured his father that I would stop by A.P.M. and pick up some papers on Le Champo.

"We got a shovel?" asks Isidore (of Purvis).

"I believe so."

"Get it. You and I might have to do some digging later."

"What fow?"

"Dead babies."

"Naw."

"Just bring the shovel up here on the porch. Henry, you want in on this?"

I make an appealing gesture, and explain about the errand for Mr. Castle, and Isidore nods, continuing to rock sullenly in the porch swing as the outer dark of the fall evening settles in.

"Sure, I understand," he says. "Maybe some other time. I can't thank you enough. You're really the best location scout anyone could ask for, aren't you? I mean isn't there nothing you can't do?"

"Be late to deliver the theater papers to your father."

"Uhyut. But wait a second," he says as I reach the yard. I can see my car, so close, but apparently beyond my reach. "Purvis. Get Henry one them hats out of the van before he goes."

"I'll get one later, Isidore."

"No twouble. Got it wight hewe," says Purvis from behind me. He clamps the baseball cap on my head, twisting the bill like the handle of a valve until he judges it straight. "Thewe you go! You look like one of the team!"

I thank him, and begin silently hating myself for the time I must now spend helmeted by thing for the sake of my job. I manage a smile, bid them both good evening, and walk stiffly toward my car. It is only when I'm on the road, heading back toward town that I remove the headgear, and jam it between my seat and the console, as the earlier promise of snow gives way to patient rain.

4.

THE OFFICES OF ACHERON PROPERTY MANAGEMENT are above
The Scriptorium, and on my way to the second floor, I pass the
former owner of Le Champo on the stairs. He, Wilbur Erlanger,
nods his ice gray head at me in a sort of greeting. He isn't happy
about having to sell the theater to Mr. Castle, whom he suspects
of a design on its integrity.

"The new film did well?" he whispers, meaning the Tosca
production now showing at the theater. He stands too close, his
breath like wind blown from the door of a distillery.

"Sold out," I say, flapping my hand between us to disburse the
odor of fresh alcohol. "People find new things amusing. You'd
know that if you switched reels more than every three months."

"I suppose they do," he says, touching my arm. His hand
begins to claw at the sleeve of my pea coat like a harrow, pilling
the black wool. "I remember your mother took you to see the
children's showing on Sunday afternoons."

I glance toward the bottom landing. Helping him to it would
only require one gentle push, and a call to Sheriff Blivet. He was
drunk. He fell down the stairs. How sad.

"That's enough of that," I say, withdrawing my arm and continuing up the stairs. It's a shame, I suppose. Wilbur adores film,
but, like many people who ruin what they enjoy by trying to sell

it, he can't see that with the proper management, Le Champo could turn a generous profit. Though it was obvious he couldn't pay the distribution company for anything new, Wilbur claimed that the townsfolk hadn't 'absorbed' the films shown at Le Champo ('Yojimbo,' for example), and thus, further cultural privation was requisite.

Behind a plate of frosted glass (bearing the logo, an ironical, unmanned Mercury from the pinnacle of Holmes Hall) separating the lobby from the office, Acheron Property Management is a warren of activity, even at 4PM. Two rows of desks line the opposing walls, with a pert, young broker at each, tapping a keyboard or using a telephone. A station occupied by two secretaries sits athwart these, both of whom greet me as I pass through the glass door separating their post from the lobby. I explain my purpose (papers, for Mr. Castle, on Le Champo), and while one scurries to fulfill it, I ask the other if I might use a telephone.

"Certainly, Henry," she says (I insist that everyone use my praenomen). "Dennis left early, if you want to use his desk."

"Did he? Do you know why?"

"He was meeting a client at the Winchester House apartments. Would you care for a drink? A coffee?"

I decline, and allow her to lead me to Dennis' desk, which sits against a window facing Clamence Street. A tree branch nods in the wind outside as I dial, cradling the phone with my shoulder, and logging into Dennis' computer while it rings. Jo answers.

"Are you coming to dinner?" she asks, somewhat breathlessly.

"I'm not sure. Something just came up," I say, scrolling through Dennis' calendar. I already know that he doesn't handle the accounts with Winchester House, but I see no appointments today in his planner, or none that necessitate leaving early. "I'm just calling to find out if the paperwork on Le

Champo needs to come to the house, or whether I should deliver it to Huld directly."

She withdraws from the phone, ostensibly to ask her husband, but I can still hear her breathing.

"Bring them here," she says after too few seconds. "As soon as possible."

"When is dinner?"

"Around six."

"I'll be there afterward."

I hang up. Allowing Jo to lie to me is acceptable, but only when it does not intrude on my schedule. If she wants me to come to the house, I'll come to the house. But I won't permit her to choose the time of my arrival. The only person allowed to do that is her husband, who thankfully has a good-natured approach to his wife's little deceptions. Or what he knows of them.

As I return Dennis' computer to its former somnolence, and gather the papers the secretary laid at my elbow while I was on the phone, a small, balding man holding a clipboard appears beside me.

"And what do you do here?"

Behind a pair of round-rimmed spectacles, his owlish gaze flits between my face, the telephone, and the clipboard.

"It's...Dennis, isn't it?" he asks. "Was that a personal call?"

"In a way," I reply, unsure of what to make of this bean counter.

"Do you make many while at work?"

"That depends."

He makes some sort of note on the clipboard. Though I volunteered for the job, Mr. Castle insisted on hiring an outside efficiency expert for the office because he wanted me to focus on amusing Isidore. I was not present for the screening of this individual, but I assume the officious person confusing me with another employee is working in this capacity.

"And what do you do here?" he repeats. I momentarily lose myself in trying to conjure a simple answer to this question. My position is without a name. I perform many occupations, but am tethered to none. I have no specific duties, and no oversight. I am a creation of Mr. Castle, who, one year ago, asked me to work for him. When I asked what this would entail, he said only that he needed someone to ask questions. I asked what sort of questions. He said the sort that seem easy at first, but become more difficult the longer they are considered.

"I am a lizard," I murmur at the efficiency expert, readjusting the collar of my coat to better convey this. He tilts his head over his left shoulder, looking at me.

"You're a what? Did you say 'a lizard'?"

"I did. Your name please."

"Norman Bashmachkin. But 'Mr. Bash' is fine."

"I'm not who you think I am, Norman."

"If you're 'a lizard,' that's probably true."

"Ignore that, please. I'm not Dennis. I am using his desk."

"Do you work here?"

"Occasionally, but…"

"Then I need to speak with you as per my obligation to Mr. Castle."

"That won't be necessary," I say, but Norman persists.

"I'm afraid it is. Your name?"

"Norman…"

"Mr. Bash, please."

"Norman, listen…"

"Mr. Bash!"

His exclamation attracts the attention of several brokers, all of whom watch me, rather than Norman, to see what I'll do next, like we're primitive hominids arguing before the mouth of a cave.

How little it takes for modern man to descend to year zero. I stand up, my height placing the austere fallowness of his skull at the level of my chin, and gesture toward the lobby.

"Outside."

And rather than waiting for a reply, I gather the papers beneath my arm, and walk out of the office. And since Mr. Bash is the sort of person to chase a penny down the throat of a lion, he follows. I wave to the secretaries, and hold the door for Norman as he stumps after me.

"That's an interesting hat," he says, as the door closes, leaving us alone in the lobby. "May I ask what it means?"

I silently curse myself for not removing the hat from my head when I entered the office. I suppose the interaction with Wilbur, and the matter of Dennis distracted me. This means I've been wearing a black baseball cap with 'A.P.S.' stitched on it since exiting my car an hour earlier. I suppose it's my fault. I had no umbrella when I arrived, and the cap was only meant to keep my face dry during the walk from the car to the front door.

"Acheron Paranormal Society," I say without thinking. Norman purses his lips, as if this confirms some private suspicion.

"I see. Is that what you do here? Chase ghosts? Have you caught any?"

"I urge you," I reply, "to consider your words carefully."

"Do you?"

"Yes," I say, removing the hat, and placing it over his bald spot as though snuffing a candle. "Unless you want to receive a phone call later this evening, ending your employment with Acheron Property Management, and all other businesses associated with Mr. Castle. You're a consultant, and the compensation involved is considerable, I'm sure. I can easily take that away from you. Now, I have two questions, and one request. Are you ready?"

He doesn't respond, but removes the hat, as I speak.

"First, do I appear to sell real estate?"

"No. I wouldn't say that."

"Do look I like a paranormal investigator?"

"I've never met one, but…"

"My request, Norman," I continue. "Is that you wear this hat that I have left in your care whenever you're in this office, or any other office, place of business, or professional environment associated with your contract. Is that understood?"

"Surely, you're joking."

"Before I leave, I will speak with the secretaries, and one of them will watch you to make certain you're complying with my request. If you do not, your contract will be terminated."

"I want this in writing," he says, glumly positioning the hat on his head.

"You'll have it," I reply to his back, as it retreats through the office door. I follow, and explain this new sartorial requirement to the secretaries.

"Please call me if Mr. Bash removes the hat for any significant period of time."

"What do you mean by 'significant'?" asks the dimmer of the pair.

"Anything aside from a routine brow mop, or spectacle adjustment. Do you understand?"

They nod sympathetically, though whether they sympathize with my having to direct such a punishment, or with Norman for being punished, is unclear.

Once I'm back in the car, I remove the notebook from beneath the seat, and open it in my lap. I make additions to two entries under 'W' and 'D,' and add a new entry under 'N.' Once complete, and I replace the notebook, and start the car.

5.

IF IT WERE MY DECISION, Dennis would work at one of the gas stations, or perhaps as custodian of the non-alcoholic pool hall. But Mr. Castle has a sentimental interest in keeping the former athlete afloat. Though his work for A.P.M. is embarrassing, his record at Acheron Union School is excellent. Dennis began coaching shortly after I was hired, and since that time, the Reapers have made the statewide championships each year (in both boys soccer, and girl's lacrosse).

Thus, Mr. Castle allows him to hold a position for which he is incompetent, and collect a paycheck he has not earned. Whenever I try to broach the topic with my employer, I'm given a long, fireside retelling of an amazing touchdown Dennis made during the last game of his senior year at Acheron Union School, and of all he would have achieved if he hadn't torn his ACL whilst performing a celebratory jig in the end zone immediately afterward. His scholarships deserted him like rats fleeing a burning house, and since the college on the hill didn't have a sports team, there wasn't anything for Dennis to do except hold a sinecure at A.P.M., where his only responsibility is showing up and leaving on time.

But today, he has failed to do the latter, which is why ten minutes after leaving the office, I'm parked across the street from Dennis's bungalow on Vine Street, waiting for him to arrive.

There are no lights on inside, and when I knocked, no one answered, so I'm assuming that whatever errand required Dennis to shirk his non-existent duties is still in progress. No matter. I have time.

A text arrives from Jo:

dessert@9 plz

It is now 8:30PM, and as Dennis' porcine silhouette wanders into the yellow white purview of a street lamp at the head of the block, I accept her offer. This shouldn't take long.

He's dressed entirely in black, a utility case of some sort hung around his neck, and walking with an urgent lope toward the door of the bungalow. If I didn't know better, I'd say he's been exercising, but the scrabbled bit of flora attached to his ankle spins another tale. He shakes it off on the front steps, enters the house, and a light switches on in the front room. I exit my car and cross the street, knocking patiently on the door until an overhead light blinks above me.

"Henry. Hello," he says, nervous, and bloated in the doorframe. The loose flesh of his neck spills over the cuff of a black turtleneck, encircling his throat like a girdle, and his thin, oily hair is pasted across his low forehead by a slick residue of sweat. His small dull eyes travel my deportment like insects preparing to feed.

"Evening, Dennis. Mind if I come in?"

"Why no, I mean, will it be for long? You see, I was just..."

"No."

He waddles to the side, holding the door for me. I've always found him revolting. Even in high school, when he was thin, and relatively handsome, beloved by the teachers, even though he couldn't do their assignments, and the students, though he was dull and categorical as a technical manual. Even then, I didn't understand why the community united in allowing this manchild to skate through it. A kettle whistles from the kitchen, and his wide hips bump me into the wall of the foyer as he rushes toward the noise.

"Sorry, Henry," he says from the kitchen. "You want some tea?"

I decline, and enter the living room to look at his collection of trophies and awards. The oldest are from middle school, while the most recent are a result of his coaching. There are photographs of Dennis posing with his teams, a few more of him in a white suit, with a woman I recognize as Sharon Buchenwald, his high school girlfriend, and adulthood ex-wife. They were married shortly after Dennis' sporting career exploded in the hanger, because in one photograph, a knee brace bulges beneath his trousers, and he's favoring the opposite leg. Sharon looks hopeful in the photograph, likely because she thought she was marrying an athlete rather than a small town real estate broker.

Dennis enters the room clattering a tray, setting a pot, two cups, and a plate of biscuits on a low table standing between the couch and a large, flat television mounted on the opposing wall above the fireplace. It's the sort of hypermodern living arrangement that makes normal people even more normal.

"I know you said you didn't want any tea," says Dennis, wiping his hands on an apron I'm amazed he can tie around his waist. "But I made enough so if you change your mind…"

"Thank you. That's considerate," I reply, watching his hands slop tea from the pot into his cup.

"So, what can I do for you, Henry?"

"Do you miss Sharon?"

"Well…Sure. Yes, sure I do," he says cautiously, watching my hands now as I help myself to a small cup of tea.

"How long has it been since she lived here?"

"About...three years, I think."

"That's a long time to be alone. You two still communicate?"

"No. I mean I would love to know how she's doing."

"Do you ever get lonely?"

"Of course."

I walk over to the wall of photographs, and remove one, a picture of Dennis with the lacrosse team from last spring. I resettle on the couch beside him, and place the photograph on the table between us, pointing to one of the girls, a strong, sturdy blond, with ruddy cheeks and a lantern jaw.

"Who is this?" I ask, tapping the glass. He sips nervously at his tea, burning his mouth.

"That's...Lisa, I believe," he says, squinting theatrically at the picture. I lift the photograph closer to his smacking lips with one hand, and switch on a lamp beside the couch with the other.

"Is that any better? Lisa who?"

"Lisa...Holzer. Yes, that's her. Strong center, good on the wings, too."

"Pretty girl."

"Well...Sure. I suppose you could say so."

A drop of sweat descends his dewlap, and drops onto the glass of the photograph, as I set the frame in Dennis' lap.

"She got a scholarship, right? Someplace in..."

"Massachusetts."

"She must be leaving soon."

"She left today."

"Is that why you left early? You went over there to say goodbye?"

"Yes. Sorry," he says, accepting the excuse I've provided, and embellishing it. "She was one of my star players. It wouldn't be right..."

"But a minute ago, you had trouble remembering her last name."

He doesn't reply or look at me, but his lips smack as he takes another sip of tea, his eyes traveling the room as if it contains an escape, his burnt mouth smiling manfully at its reflection in the television. I glance into the kitchen to check the wall clock and discover that I'm already running over. Jo will be waiting. I return to Dennis, who is still sitting like a demented English-woman in the living room, his teacup balanced in his moist hand as he gnaws cow-like on one of the biscuits from the tray.

"Dennis," I begin. Aside from the mechanical motion of his jaws, nothing moves. "This town doesn't ask much of you. It never has. I think you know that. And there are only two things we require of you at Acheron Property Management. The first is that you show up, and remain at a desk for the duration of your shift. A half hour lunch, two discretionary breaks of fifteen min-utes each. That's an entire hour out of an eight-hour shift. I'd say that's generous. Wouldn't you?"

He bobs his head, still chewing.

"Good. Now the second requirement is that, as an employ-ee of Mr. Castle, you don't do anything that might cast asper-sions on his business or reputation, both of which, I think we can agree, are staked in you at the moment. You are in a place you don't belong because of him. Now, would I be here if both these requirements were being upheld?"

"No," says Dennis, spraying crumbs on his shirtfront.

"No, I don't think so either. So what's my problem?"

Dennis ponders this for a moment, stirring his cooling tea with a thick finger, his eyes angled toward the ceiling.

"You're angry because your mother disappeared, and every-one in town thinks you did it?"

"Did what?"

"You know. Killed her."

I'm not a violent man, but in the minute after Dennis hazards this guess, I imagine the sound of the teapot colliding with the side of his head, a hollow noise followed by the sharp clatter of the lid falling to the floor. I see him blubbering on the couch with a towel pressed to the side of his skull, while I call first an ambulance, and then Sheriff Blivet, to explain that there has been an accident.

But instead of doing this, or saying anything, I leave Dennis in the living room, and walk outside to retrieve the bit of brush he left by the steps, a coiled, thorny tendril of a rose bush. I grab the utility bag he carried earlier on my way back inside, and return to the living room with these items. I place the bit of rose bush on the tea tray, and set the bag (a camera case) on the floor by my feet.

"You remember this of course," I say, pointing at the branch. "It was caught on your pant leg when you came home. Looks like it belongs to a rose bush."

"A lot of people keep roses," he says blankly.

"That's true. They do. Gloria Holzer, for one."

I open the bag between my feet, and remove a digital camera, which I also place on the tray.

"Now, if I turn on that camera, what am I going to see?"

"I just wanted to see her."

"Then you call, and ask if you can visit after your shift is finished at the office. Or just do what you normally do."

"There wasn't time."

"There's always time. You haven't had to leave work early to go play 'Cry of the Owl' in the bushes before today."

"She's leaving forever," says Dennis, his eyes finally meeting mine. "Wait. You knew this entire time?"

"Mildred Hammett, Daphne Cousteau, Lillian Greenleaf, Marjorie von Trapp," I say. "Your star players, one per season.

You must have quite an archive."

He leans forward, and withdraws an orange prescription bottle from the camera bag, but his hands shake, and he can't remove the lid. I take it from him, and unscrew the top, glancing at the label.

"Hillbilly heroin?"

"I have a prescription," he says, tipping his head toward his damaged leg. "Why didn't you say anything before now?"

"Because," I say, standing up. "It wasn't interfering with your work."

"I got my dates mixed up. I thought she was leaving next week. It's my fault there wasn't time. It won't happen again."

"Good."

I walk into the hallway intending to leave, but as my hand closes around the doorknob, I hear Dennis from the living area.

"You won't tell anyone, Henry?"

"No one needs to know," I say over my shoulder, as I open the door. "Sharon is married to a maple syrup baron in Quebec. If you want the number, I'll give it to you."

"That would be nice."

Outside, the rain falls steady and irregular. I draw my frill around my while I run to the Audi parked across Vine Street, my phone vibrating as I settle in the driver's seat with another text from Jo:

YOUR LATE

Yes, my late. The clock above town hall reads quarter after nine as I pass it on the way to Castle Road.

6.

THE CASTLE HOUSE SITS ON A BARREN RIDGE a half-mile up the access road to Maybrick Peak, and from this position, commands a view encompassing the portion of the town laid against the now dark mantle of Mt. Abandon. Some (many) speculate that it was built as a counterpoint to the college, which occupies the opposing hilltop across the valley, the two vantages thus representing the twin pillars of the community, Jeremiah and Cornelius, the political and academic, monitoring the settlement below from their fortresses above. But a man's house is both his castle and his tomb, and it always seemed to me that Mr. Castle, like any suzerain, enjoys watching his empire from a distance. He hasn't been down the mountain since hiring me after commencement.

And if Mr. Castle wished to wage a cold war of private and public works against his brother, the house on Castle Road does not belong on the first line of advance. The home's inelegance only becomes more pronounced when compared with the neo-classical architecture of the campus across the valley. In shape, the house resembles an ambitious ziggurat, though this is somewhat offset by the cantilevered roof jutting like an overbite from each of its three stories. These stories contain all the comfort associated with vulgar plenitude. In the language of Acheron Property Management, this means: eight bedrooms, five bathrooms, two kitchens, a dining room, a breakfast nook, three living areas, a gaming parlor, a theater (of sorts), a solarium, and an art gallery. The garage has space for four cars, and the grounds contain several recreational outbuildings, an edenic garden, a shooting range, horseshoe pits, and a greenhouse. But it is the choice of color that draws the eye from its normal business, to the house looming above Acheron, a jaunty ochre which complements only the fudge-like brown of the roof (or roofs), but clashes with the natural tone of each season, and makes the domicile as conspicuous as a severed head in a fruit basket.

As the access road levels, meeting the ridge on which the house is planted, I nose the car into the cul-de-sac beside it, and turn off the engine. Each window burns bright as the eye of an alcoholic rodeo clown, and from one in the first story, I notice Jo's full silhouette, parting the curtains to see who has arrived. The residence's color, shape, excess (and every other attribute which has made it a local monument to poor choices) are her doing.

When she married Mr. Castle (shortly before he hired me), he offered Jo a new home of her own design as a nuptial gift, a choice for which he has never expressed regret, regret being just another expression of the bad taste in which he lives, because Mr. Castle is (essentially) a spare man. As long as he is able to hunt, fish, and read his newspaper on the rear terrace (when the weather allows), his surroundings make little difference. One could house him in a wine cask, provided it was within strolling distance of Kranion Pond (three miles up the road).

I'm midway between my car and the front door when Aloysius, the house chef (and a valet or handyman, of sorts), appears on the front steps, watching me approach with a disdain so palpable, it seems to ply the darkness of the yard like the prow of derelict freighter. I can't recall why it is that we don't get along. I'll have to check the notebook.

"Evening, Al."

"They're in the sun room having cake."

"Who is in the sun room?" I ask, goading him, because whatever the reason for the derision, it's been constant since he arrived shortly after Jo's marriage to Mr. Castle. What cannot be ameliorated must be fed.

"I don't need to answer that," he hisses, turning toward the entrance to lead me inside as if I've forgotten how to work the front door. Even though I've lived with the family for as long as him, chef Aloysius continues to treat me like an unwelcome guest. "She sent me out here to tell you they're in there."

"And what are they doing?" I ask.

"What I said they were. Don't keep asking me to explain it."

"Well, hold on. Let me just see if I have it right," I say, pausing beneath the portico, and counting the clauses my fingers. "Mr. and Mrs. Castle are…in the…the sunroom? And they…you said they're having…cake? Is that correct? And they want me to…"

"I don't have to listen to this horseshit," he says, throwing the door open and rushing inside. I follow, and find no trace of him in the foyer as I remove my coat, but I know he's nearby, because Aloysius is never far.

"Al," I say to the empty room. "Speak to me like I live here."

A rustle of obsequity rasps from the darkened living area to the right, where Aloysius has sequestered himself to regroup.

"I know you can hear me, Al."

By closing my eyes, I'm able to conjure the memory of the section marked 'A' in the notebook beneath my passenger seat, and though the image is indistinct, I recall why it is that Aloysius doesn't like me. Last fall, while reading through the family's mail (a habit of mine when I have the house to myself), I noticed Al's phone bill was unusually high. Since Aloysius works closely with the household, his cell phone, like mine, is included in a company plan. But the bills for the past several weeks were certainly odd. Al was receiving between five and ten calls per week, all out of state, each for fewer than ten minutes, and when I asked him about it, he outlined what has now become Releaf Tours, and used the somewhat lumbering phrase 'gateway to the foliage' while describing it. He said he'd already taken a number of deposits, and he now had enough to rent a few vans, and hire some college kids as drivers. I explained how a Ponzi scheme worked, and that asking people to pay for a service that did not exist in order to provide them with that service in the future was possibly criminal, and certainly stupid. He said it was real, because he had a website, and asked me not to tell Mr. Castle, who, like any bucolic capitalist, is sensitive to undercutting.

I said I wouldn't, but asked for a list of the people he'd booked on his apparent tour, and took this to Mr. Castle, changing the tagline to 'foliage gateway,' and outlining Aloysius' business plan without mentioning its author. I said that we had 'sent inquiries' to people, and already had a list of them ready to book the tour, and if we acted fast, we might be able to serve them. It would be a short, hasty season, but it would provide an idea of whether Releaf Tours was a good investment. By the end of the week, we had four repurposed vans, and a significantly improved website (Al's was a splash page with a stock photograph of a Canadian landscape, and a phone number). Aloysius fumed, but said nothing, even when I sent him to the university to recruit drivers and a secretary to book reservations.

In retrospect, it was a small thing. But unfortunately (for Aloysius), I traffic in minutia, and if he could only see how much trouble I saved him, he might thank me. But it's one thing to be lucky, another to be skilled in recognizing luck.

I closet the pea coat, and pass a large staircase branching into the partially exposed second story on my way the sunroom, feeling exposed without my frill. No matter. I'm as much a part of the machinery of this house as Aloysius, and thus beyond suspicion. The confidence invested in me is great enough to eclipse treachery, because the human animal is unimaginative, and assumes smothering it with trust can obviate any potential disaster. And most often, this is correct. How absurd.

The solarium encompasses the entire rear portion of the house, and is large enough to hold a school bus. Instead, it holds numerous potted plants, philodendrons, acanthus, spiderwort, a croton here, a dracaena there, and a solitary, morose bonsai installed in the northwest corner on an ionic dais. Lounge furniture is scattered about as well, and at an unnecessarily long shaker table in the center of room sit Mr. and Mrs. Castle, she one side, he on the other.

The seating arrangement looks odd until I realize the couple is playing chess. Since Mr. Castle sits facing the entrance, he notices me first, and his greeting causes Jo to turn feverishly in her chair as I approach the table.

"Please," she says. "Sit beside me, won't you Henry?"

I do this because this is her house, and in it, she gets her way. Aloysius appears from apparently nowhere, and places a wicker chair beside Jo. She pats the cushion, and I sit obediently, but as I do, she gets up, and leaves the room.

"I received an interesting call from Mr. Bash a moment ago," says Mr. Castle speculatively. "Something about a hat. He claims you told he must wear a certain hat or be fired? Is this correct, Henry?"

His mild voice betrays no emotion. Neither does his face, but the gray, philosophic beard guarding his features is partially to blame. His small hands are neatly folded in his lap beneath the table, the top of which sits just below the tip of his beard. From behind a set of round, gold-rimmed spectacles, his dim eyes watch me with a categorical interest, while the stray hair crowning his tonsure sways like seaweed in a breeze from the deck door. Speaking with him in this way is like being interrogated by a gnomish cobbler.

"Yes," I say. "That's correct."

"Why would you do that?"

"A punishment. He humiliated and insulted me in front of the real estate people."

"So you're making him wear Izzy's hat?"

"Yes."

His eyes wander to Jo, who appears with a plate from the kitchen, but return to me as a soft chuckle emerges from within the beard.

"Funny," he murmurs. "Bash said he wanted something in writing."

"Yes," I say, accepting the plate, on which sits a rather forlorn bit of Linzer Torte.

"Get Huld to do it when you give him the Le Champo papers in the morning," he says. "Did you not have time to leave them with him tonight?"

I hesitate, feeling the urgent heat of Jo's body beside my own, and, remembering her earlier imprecation, tell a lie.

"I forgot."

"I don't think so," says Mr. Castle, returning his attention to the board. "You don't forget anything. But I'm assuming that whatever you did instead was important. Your move, lady."

His penultimate sentence may be a warning. Jo checks him with her right hand (a good move using her rook, while the queen remains at a safe diagonal), while the other strays to my crotch beneath the table. She squeezes, and I take a bite of the confection marooned before me.

"This is good," I say, meaning the dessert, though Jo assumes I'm speaking to her. Mr. Castle nods, examining the board. "I need a title."

"A title?" he says. "What for?"

"I suppose for people like Norman…Mr. Bash. He asked what I do. I didn't have an answer."

"Do you want business cards as well?"

I can't tell if he's joking, so I don't reply. Jo's hand silently releases the zipper on my trousers.

"It might not be a terrible idea," she says. "Operations manager? Executive assistant? Public relations coordinator?"

"If you want to print a set of lies on business cards, go ahead," says Mr. Castle, trying a move. Jo shakes her head, touching the spire of her queen. "We're expanding each day, and if things continue to move forward with RT, you'll be dealing with more people like Mr. Bash in the future. Ask Al for the number, and spend what you need to feel official."

"Thank you," I cough, as Jo's hand wriggles within my pants and begins a gestural tug, a movement likely honed during the many fly-fishing (an entendre, that) excursions taken with her husband, who sits pacifically across the table, attempting to rescue a lost game. I set my fork down too heavily on the plate.

"Is something wrong?" asks Jo, discontinuing her massage, and squeezing me far too hard to punctuate the question.

"Not at all!" I reply loudly, seizing my fork once more, and continuing to plow through the desert I do not want in an effort to appear normal, the lower of the two competing appetites having already triumphed.

"I believe you've won," says Mr. Castle to Jo, tipping his king. "I'm off to bed in a moment. Henry, would you mind coming outside with me?"

"Absolutely," I say, happy to leave the dessert and Jo's hand (which, in perhaps reading the inflection in her husband's voice, has already withdrawn to it's proper place by the time he asks me to accompany him on the deck) behind. I tug my sweater down over my gaping fly, and follow Mr. Castle out into the night.

Below us, the minimal lights of Acheron inform the solitude of the home's location like the stars guiding the voyage of a ship. Mr. Castle places a hand on my shoulder (which requires the near full extension of his short arm), and for a moment, some atavistic part of me worries that he's finally noticed Jo's more than professional attention to me, and means to end it here, by casting me from the porch, onto the stones and bracken fifty feet below.

"You're not cold are you?" he asks me. "You were getting pretty red-faced at the table. I thought you might want some air, but I didn't want to say anything in front of Jo. You know how she is."

Indeed I do. I shake my head, and draw up two chairs for us. From somewhere, Mr. Castle produces two short and fragrant cigars, one of which he plants in his beard, while offering me the other. I decline, and it disappears from wherever it came.

"I have what might seem like a small problem," he begins. "But it's bugging the fuck out of me."

Mr. Castle introduces 'small problems' this way; before bed, over cigars, and beyond the purview of his wife (though Jo discovers everything eventually). The 'large problems' (like Dennis) are not introduced at all. They're for me to discover and solve without involving anyone I can afford to leave out. Could this be my title's taproot? Despotic Custodian. Human and Material Resource Overseer. Keeper of Provident Secrets. Explaining my duties requires a business card the size of a wine list.

"You know the swamp next to the road between here and Kranion Pond?" says Mr. Castle, exhaling hot smoke and cold breath out into the darkness. I nod. "Well, the trouble is that for the past few weeks, some shitbird has been throwing trash in it. I didn't notice until Izzy told me. I guess he was out there with Purvis looking for ghosts in one of the camps. At any rate, we put up a little sign at the fishing access that was either too small or the shitbird just ignored it. At any rate, I got garbage in my swamp, and I need you to solve that."

"What kind of garbage?" I ask, removing a small notepad from my rear pocket. Though it's de rigueur to use electronic tablets and telephones for this sort of thing, I appreciate the indelible quality of ink bleeding against paper, as if each task I record is a compact between those involved, and myself.

"Beer cans. Cheap shit. Sometimes a sandwich wrapper. I was going to have one of the kids from AC clean it up, but I'm thinking it might be easier to shoot the legs out from under this thing."

"I understand. How many times has it happened?"

"Four or five that I know of. Once or twice a week."

"During the week?"

"What do you mean?"

"I mean, during the business week. Monday through Friday."

"That would be my guess. That's when the shit seems to appear, and that's when Izzy first noticed it."

"So, whoever's doing it is either unemployed, or they work nights, maybe weekends."

"That's enough. I don't need to know any more," says Mr. Castle, standing up and tapping his cigar in a standing ashtray between us. "If there's one thing I don't like, it's a fellow without a sense of his place in all this beautiful order."

"Just one more question," I say, as he gestures at the woods girding the property, and the mountains bookending it. "I may need to use Blivet. Is it important that he know why I need him?"

"You know Blivet is at his best with minimal information," says Mr. Castle, walking to the deck door. "Just figure this thing out before the end of the season."

"I'll take care of it by the weekend."

Mr. Castle doesn't hear me. He's is already inside, walking to his bedroom with Jo, leaving me alone with Al, who turns briefly from the clearing the table when I come in from the deck, looking me up and down, the plate holding the dessert I did not finish shaking in his hand.

"Barn door's open," he says, turning to leave the room.

"So it is," I say, glancing down at myself. The clatter of a plate rising from the darkness of the hall is the only response.

7.

THOUGH I LIVE IN WHAT WOULD BE CONSIDERED the pool house if the Castle home had a pool (this was apparently where Mr. Castle drew the line during the design phase), the truth is that I preferred living in town. When I began working for the family, I lived in my mother's house on Town Hill Road, the street that encircles the hilltop supporting the college. The home is similar to the Sutpen house, an elegant Victorian with three stories, and a mansard roof, but better kept. When I was a student, I walked from it to class, and after graduating, I sat on the home's broad porch in the evening, watching students walk to town from campus. My mother had been gone for nearly a year, and during it, I had slowly removed most of her belongings and decoration from the house until it became the sort of place I could entertain guests without seeming as if I was hosting them in her tomb.

I don't know why I thought she was dead. When I began bringing bags of clothing to the Methodist Church (beside which I met Tyler earlier today), the deacon, who knew my mother, suggested that I was being hasty. She might come back, and if she did, she would want her wardrobe. I ignored him, and switched to the Episcopalians on Cliff Street, where the deaconess continued to accept donations, but did so with a malignant silence, a silence that I eventually associated with the rumor (or rumors) that I had either killed my mother, driven her away, or I at least knew more about her disappearance than I had shared with Sheriff Blivet.

But the truth was that we all had the same unhelpful information. My mother managed the Herrenhof Inn on Loomis Street, and left work around 6PM on Friday evening, October 31st, 2010. She was walking, and alone, or at least the staff didn't see her leave with anyone, although Blivet (during a moment of uncharacteristic creativity) suggested she might have met someone on her way home. In any case, somewhere between the hotel on Loomis Street, and the house on Town Hill Road, she was absorbed into cold evening of Halloween, and never seen again.

Disabusing myself of useless information is one of my talents, and when I say I don't remember much of what happened afterward, I'm sincere. I was twenty-three years old and a senior at Acheron College, so there was little anyone could do but suggest options, and offer to help. I recall a flurry of concern, which transitioned to a prim, embedded suspicion (presaged by the deaconess) when it was refused.

Though the house was mine, everyone said I should sell it, and move to a smaller, more neutral domicile. I was told it would be too hard to remain there without her. But I said I hadn't seen much of her when she was alive, since managing the hotel occupied most of her time, and in a way, I had always lived alone, even come to enjoy it. Whether or not this made sense didn't matter, because I began noticing the attention of those to whom it was addressed halted at one word, a word which I eventually stopped using when speaking about my mother to other people, and that word was 'alive.'

All of this is to say that shortly after I began working for Mr. Castle, Jo took an interest in my work, which dovetailed into an interest in me. While I could easily avoid the meddling of the townsfolk regarding my living arrangement, her suggestion that I move from the 'large, gloomy' house on Town Hill Road to a more 'cozy, and appropriate' accommodation in the pool house was not so easily ignored. By the time it reached Mr. Castle, and became an order, I was already packed.

The arrangement is pleasant. The pool house is set at enough of a remove from the main house that I don't feel like a servant, and its compact foundation laid in a grove of white pine, which is close enough to the ridge to afford a view of the valley below. If moving here had been my choice, I might be proud of it.

As I enter my quarters tonight, I consider whether referring to them as a 'pool house' is inaccurate. It's really more of a guest cabin, four rooms tastefully (for Jo) arranged in order to comfort a recreational tenant, which is essentially my purpose in occupying them (as far as the lady of the house is concerned). I suppose I think of the place as a pool house because of the associated fable of the pool boy at work, and the lonely dowager taking the sun, each casting their net in search of disparate quarries.

Through the windows above the kitchen sink, the lights of the main house are like the feral eyes of a prowler (Here, I remember Dennis). I wash my hands though they are not dirty, and as I dry them on my shirt, I realize I've left my coat hanging in the closet at the main house. The front of my pants is still open, the fly gaping like the mouth of a Venus flytrap. I unbuckle my belt, and allow the pants to fall to the kitchen floor in clatter of keys and loose change, and walk past the living area and 'study' (as Jo calls it) to my bedroom at the rear of the house.

I'm behaving like a nervous person, because this is what I am. Jo was reckless tonight. Al could have seen something. But why am I worried about him? Her husband was sitting across the same table. It's happened many times before, both under the table and above (while his back is turned), but tonight was the first time she had actually undone my pants in his presence. It's almost as if she wants to be caught. And what good would that do either of us? I'd like to attribute her disregard for our mutual wellbeing as a harmless (for now) manifestation of the infinite, potentially destructive, boredom of someone who does not know what makes her happy, and lacks a day job to obviate the effort in discovering this. Jo has no passion to explore during her endless free time, so she slaps my penis around while beating her husband at chess. Maybe she requires this to feel alive. But I suspect something deeper behind her behavior, though right now, I can't say what it might be.

As I settle into bed, I select a Simenon novel, *The Widow*, from a small pile of books on my nightstand and try to read it. But a bloodstain the size of a monocle on the flyleaf distracts me. It's a library book, and I have no idea how it might have got there. Foul play seems unlikely. If a townsperson were to commit the sort of murder that splashes blood everywhere, why would they return the stained library book? I can't imagine such a lapse in judgment, but then, I've never killed anyone. Why must I always remind myself of that?

I set the book aside, turn off the light, and in the calm autumnal darkness of the house, I wait for Jo, who arrives like one of Isidore's dark entities an hour later. I've drifted between layers of sleep, but the apprehension of remaining duty keeps me semiconscious, and aware enough to hear the front door open and close, the clunk of two shoes kicked free, and the whisk of her bare feet across the kitchen floor. She pauses to retrieve my pants from the kitchen floor with an unmusical jingle of loose change, and a louder jingle as they are tossed on a decorative chair beside the bedroom door.

"You're awake?"

She asks this question each night and whether or not I answer the result is the same. She removes her clothing, lifts the far corner the sheet, and rolls her body against mine. Her hand finds me as it did earlier (beneath the table), her mouth navigates my neck, chest, and face like some territorial probing, until we fuck with the desperate boredom of cell mates, and she returns to the main house. Unless Jo is in the mood for talk afterward, I usually sleep between five and six hours an evening, which I've come to regard as an occupational condition. But she is particularly loquacious this evening, so I'll probably get three hours (at most).

"He's been angry lately. The new medication isn't working, or, actually, it's working too well, which is why I've been here so often. You don't mind, do you? You didn't seem to mind. Are you tired?"

"No," I lie. Jo claims Mr. Castle's blood pressure pills make him impotent. I'd prefer to remain ignorant of her husband's medical history, but most of what she tells me is probably false.

"I'm still a young woman. I have needs, as you know."

This is half true. Jo is forty-one. Her husband is seventy-two. According to her, the medication has been an issue since their wedding day. As for her 'needs,' they became apparent the first time we met, shortly after they were married. Mr. Castle asked me to dinner at the new house, to meet his new wife. This was during Jo's domestic phase, a period in which she tried to master the (still) unfamiliar skills required in the operation of her new home, and so she was doing the cooking (badly), while Aloysius assisted. At some point, we were left alone together in the kitchen, where I had planted myself in a naïve impression of a well-mannered guest, periodically offering to help. She asked me taste some hideous decoction simmering on the range, and beckoned with a spoonful of it. I obliged, and allowed her to feed me with one hand while the other raised the mini-skirt she wore pantie-less whilst cooking. She asked if I 'liked it,' and I agreed to whatever she meant.

"He's become obsessed with roadside garbage. I know he told you. I think it's because he's been out on the pond so much. That's where he goes whenever he can't get it up. I call it 'swapping tackle.' "

I say nothing, trying to remember if there was ever a time when Jo praised her husband's virility. I can't recall anything, but it doesn't matter. Everything with Jo began so early in my employment that I now it consider part of the job, though we're no Jean and Tati (to return to Simenon). Jo is a beautiful women, warmly aged, who is aware that her physical appearance is her foremost superlative, and so has become very good at taking care of it. Her limbs are tautly muscled from the hours she spends amid a regiment of exercise machines in the basement of the main house. She often smells not unpleasantly of sweat. Her dirty blonde hair is cropped in a fashionable, military cut because it got in her way while working out. She is short, hard, blue-eyed, and the sort of woman it is difficult to imagine as ever appearing girlish.

"I sometimes wish he would die. Is that awful?"

"I suppose that's normal for married people," I say foolishly, while a bit of the dread from earlier, when I nervously washed my hands in the sink, returns. I think of her strong, careless hand diddling me beneath the table in the solarium, and Aloysius noticing my pants unbuttoned. Jo scares me far more than her husband, because, other than Sheriff Blivet, I am his only vehicle for serious enforcement. If he discovered my liaison with Jo, he couldn't expect me to punish myself, and he certainly can't punish me with information regarding my employment. He knows none of what I do because he doesn't want to know. That's the arrangement. I suppose he could try to have Blivet run me out of town, or something similarly anachronistic. But I can handle Blivet. I have no idea how to handle Jo.

"Can you fuck me again?" she asks, the full bulb of either breast warm against my shoulder as she raises herself in bed, propping her skull on her hand.

"I suppose I could try."

"I want you to fuck me in the ass," she says, turning over, and positioning her flank against my hip, and parting herself like a set of drapes.

"Why?" I ask. This may be the wrong question, but in the time we've spent sleeping together, she hasn't asked me to do this.

"I want to feel something new," she says. "Just do it."

I oblige as best I can. It's a difficult passage to negotiate in the best of times, and doing so while fatigued and nervous from the break in character is an ordeal. But she grunts, writhes and bucks anyway, pumping her pelvis against my own as if it's all the same while crowing untruths into the dark bedroom of the pool house like a retrograde Eumenide, until she comes mightily, and I weakly, and we separate. She rolls onto her stomach, breathing as if she has just stepped from a treadmill, and I lay on my back, with my eyes closed, transitioning into sleep as though struck with a narcotic dart.

"Sometimes I want to kill him," she says, mopping herself with my sheets. The points of her body depress the mattress as she shifts to the edge of the bed, and begins dressing herself.

"I am a lizard," I reply.

"We call this here 'The King's Woods' because you know who owns it. Nice of him to let us fish the pond, but get caught dropping a beer can, and that's a visit from the other you know who. So just don't get caught, I guess."
— Anonymous litterbug and habitué of Kranion Pond

"Take It With You"
— Sign affixed to a noticeboard at Kranion Pond boat launch and fishing access

1.

THE NEXT MORNING, there are four trucks parked at the fishing access beside Kranion Pond, and four boats with one man in each occupying the pacific surface of the water mirroring an uneven battery of summer camps on the far shore. I say 'uneven' because some are well-kept (Huld's, for instance, a hulking faux-log cabin with large polygonal windows facing the pond), while others are abandoned (Wilbur's, a palsied shanty listing over the water as if preparing to dive in). The bridle of reddish foliage surrounding the pond frames the disparate structures like a communist postcard. The condition of these summer homes is an accurate visual index of whether or not the owners of them are in good standing with the Castle family. Mr. Castle owns most of the land, and, as can be expected, parcels it selectively to those he favors, thus joining the inner circle, or outer shore, that is Kranion Pond's summer community. But favor is naturally mercurial, and as it fades, so too do the structures representing its bestowment.

Morning on the lake is suitably gray and chilly for the job I've come here to perform: locating the person dumping beer cans in Mr. Castle' swamp. I'm parked perpendicular to the four trucks with empty trailers, and have just finished recording the numbers of each license plate in the rear of the notebook lying open in my lap. With one hand, I dial Blivet's cell phone, while the other roots through a plastic sack of garbage I earlier collected from the bog between the house and the pond. It's mostly beer cans and sandwich wrapping, and as the sheriff answers, I remove one of the cans, and set it on the dashboard like a totem.

"Good mornin', Henry," barks Blivet, his voice like the sound of a pumpkin rolling down a tin roof. I place my cell on speaker-phone and set it beside the beer can on the dashboard.

"Morning, Blivet. I have a few license numbers. I need a name and address for each."

"Uhyut, sure, just let me get a pen."

There is a chaotic rooting sound from the other line, as if Blivet has only one pen, and it's hidden beneath a tarpaulin concealing empty paint cans and cordwood. On the pond, a fifth boat has joined the others, debarking from Wilbur's dock. Blivet returns, breathing like a musk ox. I give him the numbers, spelling each twice.

"Uhyut, I'll have these for you in a few minutes, if you want I should call you back, or…"

"I'll wait."

"Sure, no problem, Henry, but let me just ask for …for internal use…is this here some official business?"

"Are you asking whether it has to do with our friend up the hill, or some personal affair of my own?"

"Well…yes, I suppose that's what all I'm asking, you see, we like to keep our …records current, and…"

"Would you like me to help you with that?"

"With what, Henry?"

"Your records," I say, retrieving a pair of binoculars from the floor behind my seat, and raising them to my eyes. "I'm very good with organizing documents, and making certain paperwork is in order. If you need someone to come down there, and make sure that you're not including anything unnecessary, like this phone call for example, that can happen. But the thing is though, Blivet, I'm pretty busy, and I don't know what our friend might think if he heard I was spending my time doing your job rather than my own, especially when he's told you numerous times that part of your job is to help me do mine. So, when you ask me why I need something 'for your records,' you're essentially telling me to help myself, which, as I've just explained, isn't part of the arrangement. Now, do you need help with your paperwork?"

"No, I supp..."

"Good. Call me back in five minutes."

I hang up, rather than waiting, because what I see through the binoculars captures my attention. The fifth boat, a canoe, contains a familiar young woman in a scruffy down vest, but I can't place her. She paddles with a serenity so insular it's almost irritating, her sharp chin raised as the oar dips into water, her arms spinning it like a mill wheel. Dark hair escapes from beneath the cuff of a greasy baseball cap planted on her skull, and the smooth angularity of profile has something in common with that of the loon breaking the surface in her wake, and following it for a short distance before dropping back beneath the surface. Where have I seen her?

The phone rings, and I set the binoculars on the passenger seat, as Sheriff Blivet reads four names and addresses with the halted diction of a functional illiterate. I cross-reference these with my notebook (accounting for them all), and folding the corner of the page containing each entry for later use.

"Anything else you need, Henry?" asks Blivet.

"Actually," I say, staring at the beer can on my dash. "If I was going to buy six to twelve cans of Lowry's Volcano Ale, where would I do that?"

"I wouldn't."

"Wouldn't what?"

"Buy it, I mean that shit'll skin you from the inside out."

"So it isn't popular?"

"Nope, in fact, Grover's Market over ordered some of it way back in June, and it's been on special ever since, because they can't give it away, even to the college kids, why just the other day, I was..."

I hang up again, closing the notebook, and returning it beneath the seat. Before I pull out of the parking lot, I raise the binoculars to my eyes once more, scanning the surface of the pond for the woman in the canoe, but she's gone.

2.

GROVER RATLIFF IS A MILD, TERRESTRIAL MAN, average in every aspect aside from intelligence. He stands somewhere around five feet, eight inches. His brown hair recedes above a chinless, pleasant face, doctored by a pair of Bakelite spectacles that give him the appearance of a Nazi accountant, though he is in fact the owner and manager of Acheron's only grocery store, Grover's Market. We're about the same age, and attended college together, which is how I know that he is far smarter than his occupation and appearance might suggest. In classes, he performed his work with a methodical thoroughness now reflected in the spotless interior of his store, the shelves of which are tastefully arranged with all manner of local and exotic organic provisions.

As Blivet promised, the only incongruity herein is a pyramid of Lowry's Volcano Ale established at the head of aisle five, with a sign suspended above it. The missive 'SIX CANS FOR THREE DOLLARS!!!' is printed on it in the sort of subdued calligraphy customarily used to advertise English caved-aged Cheddar or sulfur-free Turkish dried apricots. I'm examining this when Grover approaches, offering his hand while using the other to gesture at the display.

"I know it's embarrassing," he says, somewhat sadly. "We ordered this crap accidentally, and then the company was bought by a conglomerate that is currently repackaging the brand, and they refused to take it back. In that way, this is now a collector's item. Perhaps I should put that on the sign…"

"If you help me, I'll take the lot," I joke, releasing his hand. "Do you guys deliver?"

"Well…in that eventuality, we would certainly take steps to…to…see that you were provided with proper…um…assistance?" says Grover. He looks relieved at the prospect of getting rid of the beer, but appalled at the thought of a person like me possibly having a use for so much it, a surprise I find flattering. "I honestly thought the college kids might snap it up, but none of them are that desperate. We never were. What can I help you with?"

"I'm thinking some of these people may have bought some Volcano Ale earlier today," I say, handing him a list of four names from the vehicle registrations given to me earlier by Blivet. "Would you remember that?"

"I wouldn't," says Grover. "But let me speak with cashiers. I'm afraid they're terrible gossips. If someone bought beer, especially this beer, on a Tuesday morning, at least one of them will remember."

He leaves with the list while I remain in front of the beer fort, considering the nature of proof. In particular, I'm wondering if this is the best way to prove whether any of the men currently angling on Kranion Pond are responsible for littering in the swamp. Even if Grover returns with a hit, that doesn't necessarily mean whoever bought the beer this morning is the culprit. What's that old chestnut about correlation and causation? Certainly I could have camped out in the woods above the bog, waiting for someone to drive past and fling trash into it. That would be the most empirical of my options. But it would take all day. I consider my time more valuable than that. And do I really need proof, when the most effective sort of punishment is indiscriminate, and inexact? It's not my responsibility to foment a sense of justice in the population of Acheron, Vermont. They're all guilty.

"Morton Downing," says Grover, tapping the list with a finger as he returns it to me. "Apparently, he's related somehow to one of the check-out girls, an uncle or step-uncle, but estranged. At any rate, he bought two six packs this morning around 9AM. Do you know him?"

"No," I say, though this is only partially true. I've seen him around town, ogling the college girls along Clamence Street, or making a nuisance of himself in the alcoholic pool hall, but I don't generally keep track of the local ne'er do wells unless they have some dealing with Mr. Castle. Morton only merited an entry in the notebook because he delivered several cords of firewood to the family camp last winter, and seemed vaguely drunk the entire time, though it never became an issue. He tends to drop in and out of view depending on the season.

I thank Grover, but as I turn to go, he asks me if we can speak privately. He leads me into a minute office to the left of check out, and closes the door, seating himself at an orderly desk on which a laptop is surrounded by a palisade of product catalogues and promotional information. Through a sheet of one-way glass, the clerks idle at their posts, two reading, one texting, and one staring out the window beyond her conveyor at the gray sky above the parking lot.

"Listen, it's good you came by. I have a small problem with a few tour groups."

In addition to running the grocery store, Grover is also an interim manager of logistics and press for Releaf Tours while I ostensibly cast about for someone regular, though I'm considering raising his compensation in the hope that he might remain in the position permanently. He's one of the few residents whose name has not yet made it into my notebook.

"What's the problem, Grover?"

"Well, I'm not certain it's something we can do anything about," he says. "But even so, it's been a consistent complaint for the past week. Tyler took out three groups yesterday, and one this morning, and they all said that they expected the leaves to be… How can I put this? …The leaves were not bright enough. They expect more from the 'foliage gateway.' "

"I see."

"Personally, I think it's a bit silly. We can't possibly satisfy the subjective expectations of all and sundry. But the consistency bothers me. This is the age of the internet, and if we send tourists home disappointed, our online presence will suffer. We both know it's a short walk to better leaf-peeping."

"Are the folks who complained still in town?"

"I believe so. I'll have to check the Herrenhof."

"Do that," I say. "Get in touch with them, and offer another tour, on us. Blame 'pigment attenuation' for the crappy color."

"How will that do any good?" says Grover, looking authentically puzzled. "We're basically admitting that we failed to provide the service advertised, and offering to fail them a second time to make up for it. These people want pictures."

"I agree. Except, we're going to offer them a new route. You're taking the vans up the mountain road toward Maybrick Peak, and you end it looking out over the town, right? So, take them up the Mt. Abandon access road instead, and make sure to get them a good photo op on backside of Aornum Hill."

"You can't see any of the town from there, and they won't get much of the college other than the dome on Holmes Hall. And is the foliage back there any good? I haven't checked."

"I'll worry about that. Just make sure to tell them you have a new route, with better color, and you'll take them for free whenever is convenient. But make sure you get them on the back of Aornum Hill. And I wasn't kidding about the beer. It looks like I might need it. I'll call you in three hours with a location for delivery. Can you put that together on short notice?"

"Try to give me an hour, if possible."

We shake hands again, and he dials the Herrenhof, cradling the phone against his head and nodding in my direction as I exit the office, past the idling cashiers, and through the sliding doors to the parking lot. I draw up my frill against the wind, and eject my tongue, and onto it falls a snowflake, a remnant of the rain the evening before.

In the passenger seat of my car, I dial the number for Olaf Contracting and ask to speak with Elmer T. Olaf, a friend and occasional hunting and fishing partner of Mr. Castle. After several minutes, he wheezes onto the line.

"Mr. Olaf," I say. "I have a strange request. I'm hoping you'll be able to help."

3.

Boris Huld is never in a hurry, and I suppose it's just bad luck that when I arrive at this office to deliver the papers on Le Champo, he's immersed in the closing act of a large meal (oysters on the half shell, French fries, a neglected salad). Eating tends to slow the lawyer's phlegmatic pace to that of a funeral procession caught in a sandtrap. If I didn't need Huld to draft the agreement regarding Mr. Bash's new hat, this wouldn't be a problem.

"And you want him to wear this thing…why?" he asks, though I've already explained it, and I'm certain Mr. Castle provided at least enough detail to draft the document with little contribution from me.

"Because," I say, watching his large, moist hands as they sift the shells on his plate. The entire office smells briny. "He insulted me, and this is his punishment."

"Interesting," he muses, nudging his salad as if it's hiding something. "And when do you need it?"

"Now would be fine."

"I see."

Of course he does. But will it move him to act? In the large window behind his desk, a window braced by two bookshelves built into the wall, each containing an unwelcoming library of textbooks on jurisprudence (or I know not what), I can see the sun drawing itself down the slope of Mt. Abandon. It will set in a little less than two hours, and I still have to return to Kranion Pond, and locate Morton Downing. Much depends on promptly getting what I need from Huld, who is apparently in need of company.

"I'm nearly finished with my meal," he says, placing the wilting salad on a tray with the oyster shells, and depressing a button on a desktop intercom. "Why don't you come with me to the faggy student coffee place, and I'll buy you a cup. What do you say?"

What do I say? As I anxiously watch the sun retreating down the mountainside behind his head, I remember that Huld has been with Castle family far longer than I, and, as a result, his influence is greater than my own. Though I would like to tear the bib from his dewlap, draw him to his swollen feet, and march him to the outer office to find a clerk who might prepare the papers for Mr. Bash, I know that leaving Huld with anything other than the impression of a calm, patient, and (above all) friendly young man would be imprudent. So I agree to get coffee.

A clerk enters from the outer office, and begins clearing the tray, while Huld provides instructions for the paperwork. The clerk listens while using a small comb, the sort used in restaurants, to rake debris from the desktop onto the tray, bows, and withdraws.

"He'll deliver the agreement to Mr. Bash this evening," says Huld, standing up. "Shall we?"

He is an ungodly walrus of a man, not just fat, but quite tall (over six feet) and broad in the shoulders, with a bald head like a bejowled planet rotating in the firmament of the paneled office. His suit is like a parachute made of wool, the wingtips like the noses of two submarines surfacing from beneath the oceanic cuff of his trousers, and his necktie like the patterned tongue of Leviathan. He always smells like food, and as I watch him rise from behind his desk, and lumber to the door, I feel as if I'm following the shadow of Mt. Abandon itself down Clamence Street as I walk with him through the cool of early evening toward Sacred Grounds.

"So Jeremiah still has you tormenting the townsfolk?" he says, as we enter the coffee shop and take our place in the queue. Whether this remark is meant to kindle a jocular rapport between us, I cannot tell.

"Do you want to do my job?"

"No I don't," says Huld, his bulbous head examining a glass case of baked goods. "I prefer things as they are. Or as they appear to be. On the surface, where I can see them. No surprises. Makes for good business."

"Occasionally, a shortcut is helpful. You know that."

"I do know that. But the key word of course is 'occasionally.' You're a merchant of shortcuts. That worries me."

"It need not."

"It does. We create the world we inhabit, but this creation occasionally informs the world of others. You're a person of gravity, Henry. Consider the example of several items, we'll say marbles, arranged in a circle on a mattress. There they sit doing nothing in a circle. But if you were to press with a finger in the center of this circle, these marbles roll inward, toward it."

"What happens next?"

"A gift or a plague, depending on the hand to which the finger is attached."

"While I admire your dialectic," I say, touching his arm and pointing toward the counter as the line shifts. "I'm having difficulty applying it to my circumstance."

"Dialectic? You flatter me," he says, lumbering forward. "But I suppose a lawyer is just a failed philosopher. Occasionally though, it's nice to open the curtains, as it were. My point, Henry, is that I wonder if you won't eventually put yourself out of work by doing your job too well."

"I still don't understand."

"Yes, you do. I'm trying to appeal to your pragmatic side, since I'm not certain there is another. Suspicion is its own fuel. Consider the example of Iago. I like you, though I don't understand why, and I hate to see you waste what I imagine is a generous talent on the punitive micromanagement of simple people, who, if left alone, will eventually do the correct thing because that's what makes us human. A long string of fuck-ups followed by an epiphany when all else is exhausted. Your shortcuts undermine basic biology."

"I do what I'm told."

"You do more than you're told. Much more. We both know that. You seem bored to me. Are you bored?"

"It doesn't matter. People want to be controlled."

"Only after they believe they are respected," says Huld, swiveling his body like a yardarm to place an order with the barista. "Coffee. Black. Free of ephemera."

The barista looks at me for a moment as if Huld is my responsibility. He drums his fingers on the counter while she leaves to fill his order.

"Consider the example of Octavian Augustus. You know your Roman history? No? Doesn't matter. He ascended the throne after the collapse of the second triumvirate, and over the course of many years, created the pretense of a free republic while essentially remaining a military dictator. He was a subtle despot, and rather than the emperor he was, he assumed the title of *princeps civitatis*, or First Citizen, and died loved by his people. His reign is considered the beginning of the Pax Romana. Ah, thank you, dear."

Huld accepts his coffee, but doesn't leave the line, and is obviously expecting me to sit with him and continue this conversation. I tell the barista what I want, and then stand beside him, considering my limited chance of escape. If I lie, he will find out, and if I tell the truth, it will only strengthen his point. So I remain at the counter, as he continues holding forth.

"...And his people loved him because they believed that he respected them. Whether or not he actually did is immaterial. We are certainly credulous fuck-ups, and we want to be told how to do everything, but gently, you see."

But just as my coffee arrives, his phone rings (lord be praised). He withdraws it from his pocket, glances at the number, and then at me (obviously performing a sort of cost benefit ratio), before answering.

"Hold on," he says to the phone, before cupping one of his massive hands over the receiver and returning to me. "I been waiting for this shitcake to return my call all day. We'll continue this later. Remember Augustus, and don't make trouble. Find a girlfriend. Get a hobby."

With his free hand, Huld pats the top of my head like the withers of a favorite stallion, a hand that is only free because the coffee he ordered remains steaming and widowed on the counter as he disappears out into the coming night. I am released.

"No fwappacino today?" asks the barista as I pay for my coffee, and I look at her for the first time since entering the shop with Huld. I realize two things. The first is that she waited on me yesterday morning, and her remark is related to my explanation of Purvis's disability. The second is that she is also the lovely, serene woman I saw earlier today, paddling a canoe across the wine dark water of Kranion Pond.

"No...no, thank you," I say, offering the wrong sort of reply (this would have been the place for a joke of my own to validate her humor), and following it with an overcorrection. "Your name please?"

"Denise," she says, her earlier familiarity fading to caution. She seems to think I want to report her to management or something. I try to make up for frightening her by introducing myself, but my right hand is holding my coffee, and the other my wallet.

"Denise, I'm Henry," I say into what feels like a vacuum. Why do I find this young woman so unsettling? "Nice to meet you. Did I not see you earlier in a canoe on Kranion Pond?"

"I was there," she says, relaxing somewhat. "Where were you?"

"In a car. On shore."

"You saw me from there?"

"Well, no, I had to use binoculars," I reply without thinking. Her slim shoulders inch toward her ears. A defensive posture. I'm doing no good with her, and only a moment ago, I was in a hurry. I foolishly drop twenty dollars in the tip jar beside the register, hoping to smother my embarrassment with absurd generosity, but this only seems to make her more nervous.

"I was watching the loons," I say. "With the binoculars, I mean. Anyway, thanks for the coffee…Denise. See you."

I leave the queue mortified, quietly hating myself until I reach my car outside Huld's now closed office. She's obviously a student, and normally, I know how to speak with them, having been one recently myself. In fact, I'm terribly good at convincing young, female undergraduates that they like me, that I'm not like the other men around campus, and that my company will be interesting, rich, and mature. It's never complicated. At root, all men are pigs, but most in their early twenties haven't learned to conceal it. If I act asexual, and bait my hook with a cursory knowledge of Godard films, and the paintings of Egon Schiele, I'm rarely without company (though Jo's needs often get in the way). Perhaps some part of watching Denise this morning, plying the calm surface of the pond in her canoe, confident and content, unseated my own confidence and contentment in my abilities. It may take more than a passing knowledge of *Les Chants De Maldoror* to interest Denise. But am I even attracted to her? No, not yet. For now, I'm interested.

4.

THIRTY MINUTES LATER, I find Morton Downing asleep in the stern of a flat-bottomed aluminum boat anchored in a remote cove of Kranion Pond, and even at a distance of thirty feet, I can smell alcohol. I lower the throttle on the motor launch borrowed from Mr. Castle's camp, and allow the boat to drift beside Morton's.

A fishing rod braced beneath a seat extends from the bow with a diminutive sleigh bell fixed to the tip, and it rings gently as the slack line is pulled beneath my boat. Morton doesn't stir from the nest of beer cans (Lowry's Volcano Ale, of course) in which he slumbers. I'm unsure of the best way to wake him, and I'm unwilling to climb into his boat from my own. I call his name several times, grading the volume, but this does nothing. Above us, Maybrick Peak hunches like the back of a deranged giant as the sun slips behind it. I don't have time to waste on manners, or anything else.

I stand gingerly (I'm not at home in boats), and retrieve a bail-ing bucket dangling from the gunwale by a nylon rope, and dip this in the water. Once full, I draw it up, and sit down with it between my knees, allowing my boat to drift closer to Morton's before emptying it over his head.

He comes to life as though electrocuted, sputtering and curs-ing in a clatter of beer cans, and plangent knocks as his limbs flail for purchase on the boat. He coughs, spits, and pukes into the water, gasping with his head over the side, until he finally turns around, and looks at me.

"Do I know you, faggot?"

There's a certain medieval regality to Morton. A wild Arthurian beard obscures the weakness of his face (doubtless hollow cheeked and chinless beneath it), and makes his jaundiced eyes appear to glare from the interior of disorderly gray hedge. On his head, a greasy, camouflage baseball cap is disarranged (a strand of vomit clings to the brim), and on his body, the clothing (bruised duck and denim so worn it shines like a suit of armor) hangs as if he lives suspended from a gibbet. The only part of him suggesting softness is the protuberant gut hanging over his belt like an animal trying to escape from inside his shirt.

Morton isn't large, but he's crazy and proud, and this is enough. As he stands unsteadily in the hull I worry he may either leap into my boat, or fall overboard, and ruin my plans. There is no chance of my fishing him out. At most, I'll call Blivet, and have him come with his pole hook.

"I know you, faggot," Morton confirms, straddling the seat in his boat facing me, and combing through the empty cans for (I presume) a full one.

"You have a problem," I say. "I'm here to help."

"It's you who got problems. I'll show you what I mean as soon as I..."

"What are you going to do with all those cans? You recycle them?"

"What do I look like? Some sorta incense burnin' college boy?"

"Nope. Reason I ask is because of your problem. You see, we been finding a lot of these cans over in a swamp up the road. We clean them out, they come back. Real annoying, and I'm sure an outdoorsmen like yourself can appreciate all this beautiful order."

Morton pauses in his rooting, and regards me with his red-rimmed eyes.

"Lotsa folks drink beer, you pretty shitstain. A few cans in some swamp's a dog fart in a hurricane. Don't mean nothin'."

"That would be true," I say, raising my frill, and gesturing at the cans. "Except I don't know any folks who drink that toilet town pilsner of yours. Neither does your niece down at Grover's. She says you're the only person who buys it."

"That ain't proof."

"And this isn't a courtroom."

"You came all the way out here because of littering?"

"Partly."

This seems to amaze Morton, as much as Morton is at risk of amazement. He readjusts his baseball cap, spits over the side of the boat, and resettles himself on transom, jerking the cord on his motor.

"Fuck this shit, and fuck you too, you wiseass bisexual. I'm leavin'."

The motor doesn't start, but he continues yanking on it. I reach into my coat and remove my cell phone, which I hold up in the fading light so that Morton can see it.

"One call," I say. "I make one call, and your life becomes far more difficult. I figure you know how a Breathalyzer works. Right, Morton?"

He pauses in brutalizing the motor.

"What are you trying to say?"

"I'm not trying to say anything. What I'm succeeding in saying is that we both know someone with an inadequacy problem who doesn't have much to do. I'm not talking about you. You want to keep your fishing license, you want to keep your car, and I imagine you want to hold onto that piece of shit boat too, right?

So I need two things from you. The first is no more leaving your garbage where it doesn't belong. Have your beers, but take them with you."

I pause to see if this has penetrated the haze of insanity that seems to surround Morton like a swarm of inebriant flies. He settles back in his seat, facing me, and seems to be listening.

"What's the second, faggot?"

"Stop calling me faggot. The third thing I need-"

"You said there was only two things."

"Two just became three. Now the third thing is that I know someone who has a job for you. You know Elmer T. Olaf?"

"Uhyut. I think I did some work for him once."

"I can't imagine that lasting long."

"What's that mean, faggot?"

"It means your fishing license just became a thing of the past. But the good news is that you can still save your car, and your boat. Let's return to Mr. Olaf. In about forty minutes, you're going to meet his people around the backside of Aornum Hill. They'll have some equipment...do you know how to use an industrial paint gun?"

"I suppose I might," says Morton, removing a satchel of chewing tobacco from his shirt pocket, and jamming a furious plug in his cheek.

"If you don't know, tell them, not me. It's a big job, and you made need help. You seem like the sort of guy who has plenty of unemployed friends. If you want to call them, feel free."

"And what am I supposed to say?" asks Morton. "Come on down to Aornum Hill to do who knows what for some fag...for some guy who ain't even payin'? What about compensation for my valuable time?"

"Your time isn't valuable. You're doing this, so you can keep that," I say, pointing toward his boat. "But you can tell them there will be as much beer as they can drink. Tuesdays in Acheron don't get more exciting than that."

"Just paintin'?" asks Morton, appearing oddly pacified by the arrangement.

"Just painting."

"What we painting?"

"The trees."

"The what?"

"The trees. Elmer's people will show you what to do. I think that about concludes our business. I'm going to leave now, and expect you'll do the same. And I hope I don't need to emphasize that keeping this to yourself would probably be best. But tell your friends."

I start the engine on Mr. Castle's boat, and am about to steer it back toward port (so to speak), but Morton begins waving his arms and shouting at the sound of the motor. I cut it once more, and wait for him to speak.

"Listen, I'm...uh...," he begins. "I was wonderin'..."

"Out with it, Morton. It's getting dark."

"I'm out of gas," he says, as if the statement is a flag of surrender. "Can you give me a tow back to the fishin' access?"

He throws me a line, and I loop it around the gunwale of my boat, start the engine once again, and begin dragging Morton and his craft across the now deserted plane of the pond. Before we reach the fishing access, I call Grover, and give him instructions for delivery of the surplus of beer languishing in his market.

"They're all at the Herrenhof," he says, 'they' meaning the disappointed leaf peepers. "I booked them for tomorrow morning at 10:30, Tyler driving, and lunch included. Champagne picnic. What are you doing exactly?"

"I'm not doing anything. Morton and friends are going to spend the evening correcting the pigment attenuation I mentioned earlier."

"Sounds like a long night," say Grover, thoughtfully. "I'll throw in some sandwiches with the beer."

"That's considerate. You might also include a few wool blankets. I doubt anyone is going to be driving home."

"Does Blivet know?"

"Not yet. Would you call him? I'm in a boat."

Grover agrees, and hangs up as I reach shore with Morton in tow.

5.

Earlier I received a needless text from Jo explaining (or perhaps apologizing) that she and Mr. Castle will be seeing a musical rendition of 'Equus' (written and composed by an MFA student at UVM) in Burlington this evening, and that I shouldn't expect to see her until quite late ('if at all,' as she put it). I would find Jo's attempt at withholding herself depressing, if it was not couched in the promise of an empty house, and evening to myself. While the heavy petting last night beneath the table in the solarium, and later foray into alternative penetration are new (and alarming), Jo's stabs at coyness are not. But there is very little sense in playing hard to get when I can see the lights of her bedroom from my kitchen window. Perhaps she wishes to preserve some of the mystery that normally retreats after two people sleep together four or five times. Or is the uncertainty meant to be psychologically unsettling? Does Jo imagine that the question of whether or not she will make her way across the yard tonight to molest me in the pool house plagues me in the moments we are apart? Or maybe it's simpler than this. As Huld said earlier, we create the reality we wish to inhabit, and I am just another marble rolling toward her finger. Some might call this cowardice, but I consider it pragmatism. At an indistinct (but existent) meridian, the two are identical.

But whichever it may be doesn't matter, because tonight, I'm free of her and Mr. Castle, at liberty to roam the halls of their palace, opening drawers, sifting through medicine cabinets, overturning rocks in the garden, or whatever I please, free of scrutiny. Other than Aloysius, of course, who will probably be occupied concealing himself behind a curtain or something until his master returns. But having the attention of the household distilled into him alone is as good as I can expect, and as I approach the house with a puerile glee, the sort of reckless pleasure a child feels the first time they are permitted to act as their own babysitter, I'm already basking in the glow of the downstairs fireplace as I sift through the week's mail, or a book from the (somewhat limited) Castle family library, a sandwich and a beer at my elbow, and my feet swaddled in pair of slippers lined with rabbit fur (I keep a pair at the main house for nights such as this), like a landlord in czarist Russia.

It's fortunate that I am not a child, because a child would be incapable of absorbing the holocaust of inner disappointment I feel at the mouth of the driveway when I notice the A.P.S. van parked at an oblique angle to the house. For some abstruse reason, I expected Jo and Mr. Castle to take Isidore with them to Burlington, but it seems I was wrong. And wherever Isidore is, Purvis is likely to be found, so it is no surprise to hear the two of them bellowing from the downstairs living area when I enter the house, the room in which I had only a moment earlier, imagined I would spend a quiet evening to myself.

Since the living room is off to the right of the main hall, I have to pass the entrance if I want to get myself something to eat from the kitchen, and thus risk exposure to Isidore. Though part of my job is assisting him with his manifold hobbies, I've had a long day, and I'm reluctant to reassume the mantel of work when Mr. Castle isn't home to notice. This is the problem with working in relative autonomy. Some might call it freedom, since I have no regular 'shift,' and my day isn't confined to some bleak retail establishment or entropic desk job. But I also live with my employers, meaning I'm always on call. For me, work is home, and my apparent liberty is a duck blind for restriction.

The only way to avoid being seen by Isidore is to go back outside and around the house, and enter through the rear (different than with Jo), a route I consider for a only a moment before I'm spotted by Aloysius. He stands at the bottom of the main staircase with a coil of cables in one hand, and flat screen monitor beneath his arm. On his head is a hat identical to the one I left with Mr. Bash yesterday evening (A.P.S. embroidered in red). As our eyes meet, I shake my head, and mouth, 'no' and 'please,' but this does no good. A smile like the opening of an old wound partitions his face, and I know I'm caught.

"Isidore," he anounces. "Henry is here."

He knows I'll remember this, but the damage is done. A bumptious scuttle followed by a crash and a curse (at Purvis), heralds Isidore's head and shoulders appearing around the entrance to the living room.

"Henry, come in here!" he says. "You have to see what we got today!"

"Yes, Isidore. I'll be there in a moment."

I remove my coat and shoes, and walk up the hallway toward the kitchen to find something with which to indemnify myself for whatever is coming. But I'm stalled by Aloysius crossing my path. He walks into the living room, grinning his necrotic grin at me over his shoulder as he sets down the cables and monitor amid a collection of similar equipment on the floor. Purvis is on his hands and knees behind a wooden cabinet containing electronics (a cable box, DVD player, and audio equipment), the furniture pulled away from the wall to accommodate his girth. A massive, flat-screen television broadcasts a wash of static light across the couch before it, on which Isidore sits wearing a pair of headphones, his attention kidnapped by a laptop glowing on the coffee table.

"We want it in wed or yewow?" asks Purvis. Since his head is hidden behind the cabinet, the sentence seems to emerge from his undulant hindquarters.

"Try both," says Isidore. "Al, can you give him the A/V cable?"

Aloysius crosses the room with the cable, but before he can hand it to Purvis, the room is engulfed in a wash of extremely loud static roaring from the surround sound. Isidore tears the headphones from his skull, and Al drops to the floor, covering his head like a schoolchild in an air raid. The reverberant noise ends as quickly as it began, yet Al remains on the floor until Purvis speaks from behind the cabinet.

"Sowwy," he says. "Wong one."

"I'll say," says Isidore, reapplying his headphones, but shifting one phone to the space behind his ear, which makes his head appear lopsided as it swivels in my direction. "Know anything about running a computer through a TV, Henry?"

I say no, and excuse myself before he can ask anything else, heading toward the kitchen though I'm no longer hungry. But I need a moment to myself before hastening unto the breach of whatever madness Isidore is configuring in the living room, and a kitchen is a place from which I derive a certain tranquility, similar to what I imagine the pious find in church, or Mr. Castle feels while alone with his fishing pole on Kranion Pond.

A psychologist would assume it has something to do with my mother. Our limited time together was mostly spent in the kitchen of the house on Town Hill Road, with her hustling through a meal on her way to or from the hotel, and my sitting with her as she ate. We rarely ate together. Watching her shovel food into her mouth while still in her work clothes, a telephone vibrating every three minutes beside her plate, and the concealer around either eye doing nothing for the penumbra of fatigue hanging like the blade of Poe's pendulum beneath it, defeated my appetite then as surely as midwifing Isidore's hobbies does now.

While the kitchen in which I watched my mother eat was a dignified period setting, with a scarred porcelain sink, a clanking range, and a woodstove that burned like an engine of rapine during the long months of winter, the room where Aloysius prepares the Castle family meals is rather different. It's larger for one thing, with a somewhat ovoid island dominating the center of the cooking area. Above this, a collection of stainless steel pots and pans is suspended just far enough from the floor to make using them inconvenient. The stove cowers beneath a martial hood, the sink is narrow and deep as the mouth of a well, and the refrigerator looks like an astronaut's coffin. The counters are the granite of a tombstone, and the cabinets a sanguine pine. Aside from a large picture window with a pointless view of the side yard, the Castle kitchen is as passionless as the rest of the house.

I'm considering taking my business (or whatever remains of it) to the solarium, or even back to my apartment in the pine grove, and just pretending I forgot my promise to Isidore. But I realize how bad a lie it would be when another burst of electronic noise from the living room reaches me in the kitchen doorway. Shouting (Isidore at Purvis), and further braying from the mishandled equipment follow this. With the racket he's making, there's very little chance of convincing Isidore I've forgotten anything, thus I remain a handmaiden to the mercurial passions of a manchild.

A recall a bit of advice my mother gave me during one the meals we did not share: "If you have to do something unpleasant, make sure to eat first. It'll be one less thing to think about."

From the refrigerator, I remove a beer and a plate of wilted pierogi, which I place in the microwave beside the stove. While the dumplings rotate to a proper temperature, I twist the cap from the bottle, and take a long drink before allowing it to fall from my hand, and shatter on the tiles. The microwave beeps, and I step over the puddle of froth and glass, and set the over-warm plate on the island to cool. I return to the refrigerator and get another beer, a jar of horseradish, and a squeeze bottle of mustard (I enjoy mustard with pierogi). I spoon a bit of the horse-radish onto the plate beside my meal, and when finished, I tip the jar on its side with one finger, and roll it from the counter onto the floor. I don't see it break, but I hear the sound of it hitting the tiles as it drops below the granite lip. I pop open the mustard, and squeeze a bit of this beside the horseradish, allowing the nozzle to wander from the plate onto the island itself, whereupon I use the condiment to compose a short missive in shaky yellow text on the countertop: VAE VICTIS.

The living room is less bellicose when I return with my meal. Isidore remains on the couch, his headphones disarranged, while Purvis kneels on the floor, wearing a set of his own (properly). They're both watching the screen of the overlarge television against the opposing wall that formerly showed only static, but now broadcasts a mute interior tour of the Sutpen House. Aloysius is lurking to the right of egress, neither watching the film, nor ignoring it, and as I pass him, I raise my plate in sort of salute.

"I'm afraid there is a terrible mess in the kitchen," I say, nibbling a bit of his food, and gesturing at it. "These are good, by the way."

Even in the dim light of the screen, I can see his former conceit fade to uncertainty, as the smugness uniting his features repatriates them in a sort of worried rictus.

"A mess?" he asks. "What sort of mess? What'd you do?"

"Better go check," I say. "Before someone notices."

"You...you..."

"Yes. Me," I say, drawing unnecessarily close to him. "I am a lizard."

He scuttles from room, orphaning pronouns all the way to kitchen. Isidore and Purvis haven't noticed me arrive, and they don't notice Al leave. Their normally unfixed attention is captured by whatever is unfolding on the screen, and in the headphones, which Isidore removes as I settle beside him on the couch.

"Oh, good. You're here," he says. "We're just reviewing EVP footage from the nursery."

"The nursery?"

"The room with that creepy-ass bassinet."

"Oh. Right."

"I figured that considering the house's history, that would be a good place to start," he says, offering me the headset. "Want to help us listen?"

"I'm eating," I say, rather formally.

"Oh, right. Sure, what am I thinking? Dads got surround sound in this bitch. Purvis! Pull out, and crank up the volume a little."

Purvis hauls himself to standing, and waddles over to the cabinet behind which he spent the earlier part of evening, and begins twiddling the controls until his voice on the video becomes audible from the speakers deployed around the room.

"Is there a spiwit here?" he asks the empty house on screen. "Can you give us a sign of youw pwesence?"

"He's only a junior investigator," says Isidore conspiratorially to me. "But I wanted to let him do one just to get a feel for it."

"Is thewe a spiwit hewe?" repeats the recorded version of Purvis, who, on screen, is standing beside the bassinet I installed in the house. "Pwease shake this baby cawwaige to show me you awe wistening."

"It's not a baby carriage," says Isidore from behind the camera. "It's a bassinet."

"A what?"

"A bassinet."

"Alwight," begins Purvis, somewhat suspicious of the new word. "If you awe with us now, pwease shake this...this thing hewe...fow me...pwease."

"What we're listening for are voices," says Isidore beside me on the couch. "Electronic voice phenomena. You know, anything below the normal auditory spectrum that shouldn't be there."

"Sure," I reply. "Apophenia."

"Right, spirit voices," agrees Isidore, turning back to the television. "It's a good thing Aunt Jo isn't here. This stuff here tends to spook her some."

"Uhyut," I agree, though for a different reason. I have trouble thinking of Jo as anyone's aunt, but it's easier than imagining her as a mother. Though this issue is probably inverted for Isidore (if it troubles him at all). His mother (Lenore) died in a car accident six months before my mother disappeared (during his sophomore year at Acheron College), and the following April (when I graduated), his father married Jo, Lenore's sister. The wedding left a morbid impression on the townsfolk, though their yardstick seems to naturally incline toward the ghoulish. They suspected me of murdering my own mother (or driving her off, at the very least) simply because I didn't wish to cocoon myself with her clothing. And certainly Mr. Castle marrying his wife's sister so soon (it seemed to them) after Lenore's untimely death would have consigned the newlyweds to pariahhood if Acheron were not a fiefdom, and he its lord. The unlikely benefit (for me) of all this was that the disappearance of my own mother soon after Lenore's death drew Isidore closer to me, which led to my employment with his family.

But even when my mother worked for his father, Isidore and I were never friends. When I was very young, she occasionally brought me to business meetings with Mr. Castle, where I was thrust upon Isidore as a playmate (then as now) while our parents talked about the hotel. This never went well. What Isidore lacked in imagination, he remunerated by way of exuberance, and I, being an inward, somewhat somber, child had little to offer in return (no matter how baseless, people of any age want their excitement matched). Thus, when our parents came to reclaim us, it was normal for Isidore to be arranging furniture into a ponderous fort, while I sat reading a book on the floor (because he had taken all the chairs). As soon as we grew old enough to babysit ourselves, we saw no more of each other.

But after Lenore hit a patch of black ice on I-89 somewhere between Middlesex and Waterbury (she was returning from some charity event at the historical society in Montpelier), Isidore suddenly remembered these former playdates fondly. When my own mother disappeared, he began approaching me on campus. It was obvious that he wanted to talk about them (our mothers), but didn't know how. For my part, I couldn't believe I was the only person in the entire municipality Isidore believed was capable of mirroring his grief. His inducements for coffee, a movie at Le Champo, and, when these were parried (by me), dinner with his landed, remaining parent (Mr. Castle) left me feeling something between courted and polished. I say 'polished,' because strong emotion tends to seek similar company for comparison. Though my mother wasn't technically dead, Isidore wished me to be his looking glass in which he might find the ghost of his mother occupying some Elysian domestic plane beside my own. And so, I was buffed.

I finally agreed to have dinner with Isidore when he mentioned that his father asked after me, and wanted to know how I was doing. I mistook this for a warning, but I realized later that it was part of why he approached me to begin with. He must have been aware of the rumors regarding my mother's disappearance, and the invidious brand marking my relations with the townsfolk. Yet by virtue of his own social position, he was also an outsider (which is the terminus of communal pillarhood, no matter how gentle or despotic). Whether he recognized this in himself, or simply felt it, like the gentle tug of a bowel movement, who can say? What's certain is that in me, Henry Hoffmann, he saw not only a chance to match his grief with a childhood friend (fiction), but a common ostracism (nonfiction, biography, or memoir).

So I went to dinner with his father, whereupon it became clear that Mr. Castle had been watching me for some time, even before my mother disappeared. The evening meals became a weekly occurrence, and I began staying up late afterward, speaking with him (Mr. Castle), offering advice, and suggestions (when solicited), and sometimes remaining overnight in a spare bedroom. And one year later, I'm living in his house (nearly), sleeping with his wife, and entertaining his son. Perhaps this is progress, but as a poet (whose name escapes me) once said, "Everything changes, and nothing changes."

6.

THE KITCHEN IS SO STERILE that when I enter it to return my plate, that I can't bear to leave the crockery unwashed in the sink, and thus ruin the Sistine Chapel Al has made of my mess. The floor shines, the fixtures gleam, and were it not for the fruit bowl (which Al likely produced as both a capstone to his typhoon of good housekeeping and a 'fuck you' to me) centered on it, the island could probably be used for outpatient surgery.

As I arrange my plate in the dishwasher, and deposit my empty bottle in a recycling bin beneath the sink, I wonder if Al may have missed the point, and whether he believes he has won some definitive skirmish by reclaiming the kitchen. Does the bowl of fruit symbolize vengeance to come, or triumph earned? There is no translation for this sort of thing. A solitary apple (symbolically rich food) shines amid the cornucopia as if Al polished it before arranging the fruit. I withdraw and raise it to my nostrils, inhaling the sweet, autumnal odor certainly, but above this, the chemical scent of the floor, cabinets, and counter. Yes, polish he did. Was I meant to see this as I have seen it? Is this The Last Temptation of Henry Hoffmann, or perhaps, The Passion of Chef Aloysius? Does Al realize it was probably a pomegranate that caused the fall, since, at the time, apples were native to Kazakhstan, which wasn't Kazakhstan then, but

Scythia, home to Indo-Iranian pastoralists, good on horses to the point of impotence?

I've unfortunately burrowed so deep inside myself to retrieve this information, that I don't hear the excited noise from the living room (or rather, I do hear it, but it makes no impression), or the rapid footsteps approaching from the hall, until Isidore appears in the kitchen doorway, and catches me impishly sniffing the apple as if I've pilfered it from a Flemish still-life.

"You gonna eat that?" he asks cautiously, my apparent weirdness having momentarily sentenced whatever news he's come to deliver to the back seat.

"I may," I say, placing the apple back in the bowl. "But later, I think. Is there something you wanted to tell me?"

"We got one," says Isidore, his excitement returning.

"One what?"

"A voice. An E.V.P. You gotta hear this."

Purvis has graduated to the couch when we return to the living room. Both his hands are cupped around the headphones he's wearing as though he fears their escape. He doesn't hear us enter, and Isidore taps him on the shoulder.

"How's it sound?" he says, nodding at the laptop on the coffee table. "We get anything else?"

"Not yet," says Purvis, handing the headphones to Isidore. "But it's a good one. I used a computew pwogwam to enhance the audio. Check it out."

Isidore dons the headphones, and Purvis taps a key on the laptop.

"Shit, nice job, man," says Isidore, after several seconds. "That's clear as...something. It's real clear. Can you loop it?"

"Suwe can!"

Isidore listens, nodding to himself, while Purvis grins vacantly, waiting for someone to pay him a compliment. My thoughts

are still with Aloysius, and the possibility of his plotting or en-
acting some minor revenge as I sit here, watching Isidore listen to
what is probably displaced fragment of a radio broadcast thrown
from a nearby tower.

"I'm hearing 'help me,' " says Isidore, removing the headphones and handing them to me. "You mind giving it a listen to
confirm that, Henry?"

"That's what I heawd too," says Purvis. "It's a woman's voice,
I think."

"Yes, it's definitely a woman," agrees Isidore, nudging my arm
with the headphones, which I apply to my skull because I'm too
busy trying to remember the last time I saw Aloysius, and what
this means, to think of an excuse. I make an affirmative gesture
at Purvis, and he touches a key on the laptop.

What I hear in the headphones is a foolish conversation between Isidore, and the emptiness inside the Sutpen house.

"Is there a spirit here?"

Purvis burps in the background, and Isidore shushes him
before continuing with his interview.

"If you're here, please give us a sign of your presence."

This earns no answer, and Isidore veers in a more personal
direction with the questioning.

"Are you sad that you died?"

This is followed by several seconds of silence, and just as
Isidore begins speaking, a smaller, garbled, yet certainly feminine voice joins him, and, despite myself, I immediately wave at
Purvis so I can hear it again. He loops the clip, and as it runs over
and over, shadowing itself and becoming neither voice nor noise,
but a sort of invocation, the clarity within it suddenly yawns (not
like a living creature, but like something that wouldn't be expected to yawn, a lake, or a mountainside perhaps), and I'm instantly

so terrified that I tear the headphones from my head, and drop them on the floor.

"Sorry," I say, more to myself than either of them, and nearly knocking heads with Isidore as we both stoop to retrieve the fallen equipment.

"You hear it?" he says. " 'Help me,' right?"

"Yes," I say, edging toward the door. "Yes, definitely a cry for help. Absolutely. Say, do either of you want a beer? I could use a beer."

Purvis says 'suwe', and Isidore asks for a grape soda instead, and with these orders, I amble from the room, down the hall-way, but pause halfway to the kitchen because I feel like I may collapse. I steady myself against the wall, all thoughts of any-thing that I considered important, Denise in her canoe, painting the trees on Aornum Hill, Morton Downing's compliance, Boris Huld's warning, Denise again, beautiful in her work clothing, and most recently the vengeance of Aloysius, all of this is gone because it seems like nothing compared with what I heard on the recording. I've read that during panic, the human brain will jet-tison all unnecessary information, and revert to utter clarity, and so here I am, in a manifold cerebral poverty, my memory of the day eclipsed by the last ten minutes. It's just me, and the voice on the recording now, a female voice which did not ask for help, or anything at all. Rather, it beckoned, or perhaps enjoined, though it offered no further instructions as it had for Isidore and Purvis when it said 'help me.' No, for me, in a voice that may resemble my mother's, though it's been so long since I heard her speak, it only pronounced my name, 'Henry.'

7.

Half an hour later, I'm standing amid the pine grove, wondering whether the lights glowing from the front window of the pool house mean Jo is home early from the theater. It seems unlikely. I didn't see Mr. Castle's palsied Ranger in the driveway when I crossed the lawn, and she wouldn't come here until after he's in bed. And I'm not the sort of person who forgets to switch off lights before I leave the house. So who or what is waiting inside my apartment?

I'm also not the sort of person who has the experiential capital to invest in a serious threat of violence. Without my notebook, I'm not equipped to defend myself against an opponent with even an elementary understanding of physical punishment. Even so, or perhaps as a result of this, I unfold the knife from pocket, keeping it low and close to my leg as I thread my key into the lock that isn't locked. The door falls open without a sound, and I don't bother closing it as I step inside, my attention held by a domestic noise originating in the bedroom down the hall. I don't know what I expect to find. Perhaps a chimera comprising the body of Aloysius, the head of an apple, and the voice of my mother. And as it turns out, I'm one third correct. It's been the sort of evening that seems perfectly designed to preempt madness, but I'm neither shocked nor afraid when I enter the bedroom, and find my mother shaking out the top sheet. I'm actually relieved that it's only her, and not something worse.

"Hi, mom"

She pauses in making the bed, regarding me with an older iteration of my high-boned face, and eyes the color of copper sunk deep in the ocean. She's a very pretty woman, with a dark, nearly black, mantel of thick hair cut at an understated angle just above the blade-like set of her jaw. I've never seen her not dressed for work, and even now, her broad shoulders, comparatively narrow hips and conservative bosom are caparisoned in a tweed blazer and matching slacks, an outfit that I always thought made her look like a lesbian folk singer. But other than the clothing, it's like looking at myself in a wig.

"I heard you tonight," I say, watching her wave the comforter as though signaling a rescue ship.

"No you didn't," she says. "That's why I'm here. Ghosts don't exist. And don't let a village idiot like Isidore convince you otherwise."

"You never made my bed before. Why are you doing that?"

"Well, I made plenty of other people's. Even when you were a kid, you were never as helpless as most of them. So, old habits, I suppose. Where you're living now doesn't seem very comfortable. It reminds me of the hotel because of that. And I was tired of waiting for you to come back."

"Where did you go?"

"I didn't go anywhere. I was promoted. It doesn't matter. We need to talk about your job."

"I'd rather not. I'm bored with it."

"Yes, I know. Everyone knows. That's the problem. Jo will be here soon, so I need you to listen."

"It's just a job, mom," I say. "Work is just what people do so they don't have to think about what they could do. I'm comfortable with that. But I don't understand why it matters to you."

"If it was just a job," says my mother, "do you think I would be here? Think about it."

"I need a glass of water," I say, turning toward the kitchen. I expect her to say something parental to guide my attention back to the conversation that seems so important to her. "I'm sorry, Mom."

I don't know why I'm apologizing, but I feel penitent, even as two bare arms enfold me from behind, touching my chest, my stomach, and deliberating near the waist of my pants, as calm in this work as they were in making the bed.

"Are you asleep?" says a mouth beside my ear, and, if I was, I am no longer. Jo shifts the comforter aside, or has already shifted it aside (I can't tell which) in the inner dark of my bedroom. The time is a mystery, and I make the mistake of asking her because I'm still partially dormant, and thus she is figmentary, the raw corporeality of her descending like a curtain of soft tissue across the stage of my back.

"It's time for you to either fuck me or talk to me. We need to talk."

And here, despite the imperative (the talking we must do), I am gently relieved by the possibility that tonight I have what passes for a choice, and Jo seems inclined to talking (which for me means listening). She is naked beneath the comforter, her parts rasping my own in a sort of injunction meant to foster attention in place of desire. But when has she ever entered my small house and retained her clothing? Have we even been here together in daylight? Once, when she opened the house to it to show me, the two keys chiming like dog tags in her hand as she passed them into mine (her prisoner in this, our war) after I offered hollow approval of the property, with

Mr. Castle appearing all the more elderly and ill-proportioned beside her on the morning one year ago when I was informally evicted from my home on Town Hill Road and installed in the pool house.

"How was the show?" I ask the darkness in which Jo is forever a denizen.

"Abysmal. A naked man singing about torturing horses because his dick doesn't work. Can you imagine anything more embarrassing? Of course, Jeremiah loved it. I'm sure he identified. How was your evening?"

"I think your nephew is channeling the spirit of my dead mother," I say, hoping to scare her, but she either thinks I'm joking, or doesn't hear me.

"Oh, don't let it bother you. I told Jeremiah not to buy him all that ridiculous equipment. He even let Izzy take one of the Releaf vans. Did you know that? It's a damned creepy business, but they already had t-shirts made so I suppose it's too late. I mean, I understand why Jeremiah is doing it. It's better to have him out looking for haunted houses than knocking up one of the girls from the pool hall. That's the fate of the landowner's son. I know you've read your Faulkner. Someone 'forgets' to take their pill on the right day, and the whole estate comes apart."

"I was under the impression that Mr. Castle enjoyed seeing Isidore happy and occupied."

"Well, of course, but there are other considerations here, Henry," she says, her hand navigating from its emplacement on my chest to the space between my navel and groin. "You know that. You're the duke of other considerations. Jeremiah realized a while ago that the best he can do for Isidore is keep him comfortable, and occupied, as you said. It's you and I who are going to manage things when he's gone. You must know that."

"It hadn't occurred to me," I say, the hand (Jo's) now beginning to absently twiddle me. "I think with time, Isidore will...-"

"Isidore is a fool," says Jo plainly, continuing to deploy her limited charm beneath the sheet. "He isn't capable of what needs to be done, and while I admire your refusal to admit what we both know, I worry that doing so means you aren't either. I need you to start thinking about Jeremiah like he isn't there, because someday, he won't be and I can't be here alone with that simple boy, I won't do it. Is something wrong?"

I nearly answer honestly before I understand exactly what Jo is asking. And though I can't see her face, I'm certain it's inclined toward my groin, where her hand has tented the sheet absently gnawing my penis like some befuddled river fish. I try to trick myself, imagining the rigid sound of keys in her hand the day they were imparted, and the flat metalloid runes cold against her skin. But there in the foreground of this recollection is Mr. Castle, as though he were airlifted in for the occasion from some Lombardian annex, his flat gray hair and beard like the flat gray of the counter in his kitchen (which is to say the color of a tombstone), and the polite gold-rimmed spectacles doing little to obviate the simple barbarity of his comportment. They sat on the bridge of his gnomish nose with the suggested violence of a saddle on a Manticore as he wandered the veranda beneath the pines, testing a loose brick with the tip of his boot like the unhinged jawbone of a vanquished enemy, while Jo gave me the keys and asked if I needed anything else.

"What's wrong?" asks Jo once more, a hysterical chord not struck, but shadowed in her voice. And though it sounds like a question, it is more an acknowledgement of shared failure, not in the manipulation of her hand, or the withering of my stubborn part, but the unmet necessity of whatever was foreshadowed yesterday evening beneath the table in the solarium. And later when she asked me to fuck her in the ass. And now, when she seems to have remade the disparate impulses at war only yesterday into something resembling a plan, but a plan to do what? I've reached the limit of my intuition.

"No. I'm sorry. Nothing's wrong," I say, hoping it is true. "Why are we talking about this?"

"Talking about what?"

"Mr. Castle. Like this."

"Because I want your help. I need your help. I said that."

"To do what?"

"I said that too."

"I don't want to be part of something I don't fully understand."

"That's your job."

Can I argue with that? I suppose not. It's the same problem I encountered with Mr. Bash. I lack a title, and therefore a definition. Since I have no contention, I cup my hand between Jo's legs in tactical desperation, hoping that by laying hold of what I understand theoretically, my body will follow. She emits a burlesque moan as I introduce a finger, remembering the keys once again, but hoping or praying (if there is a difference) with the manic, insane positivity of a corsair walking a plank, that whatever I do now will eclipse or stifle whatever happens later.

"Kiss me, you faggot," barks Jo like some feminine capitulate of Morton, her ragged mouth chewing the skin of my shoulder. "And fuck me. Like you did last night. Right now."

With the memory of the keys of course, Mr. Castle arrives once again, kicking loose paving stones on the rear patio the day I moved in (the only day that Jo did not remove her clothing in the house), his limited vision bobbing across the foreground in search of something to alter. It isn't guilt that defeats my desire for his wife. That albatross dropped from the sky long ago. And it isn't shame, because in these situations, that is left to the help-meet. And it isn't fear, because Mr. Castle can't manufacture this by himself. He needs me. But I'm afraid, even so, because when I remember him now on the veranda one year ago, or even last night on the terrace, or his simple face above the table as Jo fondled me beneath it, I realize that I am no longer the only person who recognizes his vulnerability.

"What are you thinking about?" asks Jo, and when I don't answer, a flat white hand like the yardarm of ghost ship emerges from the darkness of the bedroom, and collides with my face. Jo may not know her own strength, or she may know it very well and simply not care, but the blow lands on my jaw, hurting less than a blow to the nose or eye, but painful enough to stun me, and powerful enough to turn my head toward the bedroom window (through which I see a penumbra of light from the main house). What I don't feel when my head snaps back is anger. It's a calmer and more dangerous emotion, with something of the collected animal about it. A vengeant poise. I reach blindly into the gloom, and clamp one hand on an ankle and with this as a polestar, find the other.

"Do it, you fucking coward," says something, it may be Jo, though the voice is not her voice, but the oblique growl of a demoniac in heat. I can tell that she is lying on her back by the shuttering of the mattress as she props herself up on one elbow to lean forward and take another swat at my face, which I don't see coming, and thus don't dodge, but absorb as I jerk her toward me by the ankles. I wrench her thighs apart like the pine boards of a coffin in which someone has been buried alive, and plunge myself into her backside.

"Take off your bonnet and hurt me!" she shouts, demonstrating what I suppose she wants by throwing an actual punch that glances off my jaw. "Come on, cake boy!"

And rather than considering the sort of compact this might represent, I lean forward and slap her face once, and then again, and then once more, accidentally coordinating these sorties with my pelvis as it swings into her like the tongue of a bell. Her mouth catches and begins to gnaw one of my fingers, and her hand stirs my hair into a hold, yanking my head downward. Her teeth fasten on my cheek, and I try not to scream because I know doing so will only make it worse.

"You slap like an English lady," she hisses through a mouthful of my skin. "Are you challenging me to a duel? Hit me like you hate me, faggot!"

That sounds easy enough. At this point, it's partially true. She releases my face from her teeth, and I rear back, swinging my arm in a wild career (like the slamming of a door) toward the moist sound of her breathing. But her legs bind me from the rear, and as I release my hand out into the darkness, I'm hobbled and collapsing toward her. I'm reluctant to make a fist, which matters little, since it is the bony knob of my elbow that collides with the side of her face. Her jaw clicks, and she grunts, and I almost apologize. But the hand rotating between her legs (as if removing a stain) pauses for only a moment before resuming its orbit with a renewed furor. The canal in which I am interred contracts, and I ejaculate despite myself as Jo corners a second orgasm.

"Stay!" she shouts, her back arching, her heels crossing against my spine, and her unoccupied hand drawing my mouth against her own in a kiss that tastes of blood. Her body seems to deflate beneath me. I roll over, trying to guess which of us is more wounded, but figuring that it's probably best to just ask. "If you're confused, that means you're not curious enough." Another quote from Mom.

"Are you...alright?" I venture, unsure of whether the evening's savagery has receded enough to accommodate a condition report.

"Thank you," says Jo, pillowing her nudity against my own. "But..."

"What? But what?"

"Use a real fist next time, please."

"Next time?"

"Yes. You know. When it happens again."

However terrifying the thought of repeating what we have just done, I say nothing, allowing her to settle quietly across my chest, even pressing my lips beneath her hairline in a pantomime of affection. The loyal employee. Mr. Bash would be proud. But my terror is not limited to the promise of further violence between us. I'm more concerned with what exactly this violence means, and why it has appeared now as a mordant herald, like standing on a beach and watching the surf retreat only to see its collected mass rearing on the horizon and racing toward shore. I think (I hope) it is still early enough to retreat from what's coming. The water has scurried over the sand and away, the tide pools have emptied, the boats lay anchored in shoals. Now, I await the surge, or, in this case, whatever Jo is planning, because there is certainly some design unspooling in the blond skull resting in the crook of my shoulder. But what is it? Perhaps I'm not curious enough.

"What are you thinking?" I ask. This seems like a normal question.

"We're very good together," she says. "You can't hit, but you can fuck. And you can learn to hit. I like us together. I really do."

"I'm sorry it took me a moment to...get started," I say, not meaning a word of it, but hoping that foolishly apologizing for what turned out not be a problem might curry the sort of sympathy that leads to oversharing. It's a long, desperate shot, but at this point, I'll try anything.

"You always do what you're told," she says, patting my crotch. "That's why I like you."

While I don't consider obedience one of my virtues, I allow the subject to rest, perhaps proving myself wrong by doing so. Jo lapses into dormancy rather than sleep, from which she'll wake us both in an hour to return to the main house. Her hair smells like saliva, and the room smells like a bat cave. And no matter where I place my hand on the bedspread, it touches moist fabric. Perhaps to escape these singularities, I return to Mr. Castle, pacing the veranda on the day I moved into the pool house, and realize that the reason I find this image so comforting is that it was the last time I saw Jo pay any sort of attention to him. When he finished patrolling of the terrace, he walked around the house with his bootlace trailing him like a thin red snake loyal to his shambling gait, and he met us (Jo and me) in the front yard like that, the keys to the house cold in my hand, the house on Town Hill Road a memory. But Jo noticed the lace, and without saying anything knelt and united the loose strands as he stood there, watching her with what might have been complacence had he not touched the top of her blond head with his hand, and had she not taken this hand and walked with it curled in her own back to the car I borrowed from them to transport my things.

WEDNESDAY

"I taught at a school in Julian Falls [Ohio] that had a nature preserve nearby, and the students said the same stuff about bodies being found in the forest or whatever. They never actually decorated the place with cadavers, but I guess what I'm saying is undergrads seem to have a morbid sensibility for woodland. Make of that what you will."
— Martin Bastarde, Phd., vice chair of the English department, and campus ethics officer at Acheron College

"While not the most family-oriented of Acheron's many foliage-related attractions, all in the mood for a good scare are welcome to join students and lifelong residents on Halloween night at the Aornum Hill Haunted Forest! Entrance is free, costumes are encouraged, and the event is BYOB (Bring your own body!) ..."
— Releaf Tours promotional brochure, authored by Oliver Himmel, copyright Acheron Ventures, LLC, 2011

1.

AT 8 THE NEXT MORNING, I'm watching the barren surface of Kranion Pond from the front seat of my car. Steam rises from a canister of coffee resting in the console, as if in symmetric homage to the bank of mist drifting above the water. Beyond this, a dark circlet of naked trees and the vestigial shadow of one or two summer homes stand guard. And above it, a flat, blank sky, like a page reserved for a notice of quarantine. And from the stereo, the disembodied voice of what may be my mother speaks my name every ten seconds. Before leaving for the day, I woke Purvis from a nest of A.P.S. equipment in which he had made his bed, forced him to make me a recording.

I suppose after my brush with it the evening before, I wanted to defeat, or at least understand my initial fear. And I'm no longer afraid of the small, female voice pronouncing what now sounds like gibberish after two hours of listening to it. Certainly, it could be my name ('Henry!'), or it could be a request for help ('Help me!'). It could also be a clinical verdict from beyond ('Healthy!'), or a locative, followed by a question of clarity ('Hell, see?'). Part of inflicting the odd little voice on myself is meant to produce doubt, because I don't want to spend my limited idle time worrying that my mother's spirit is attempting to contact me through the dubious medium of Isidore and Purvis (in this context, I consider them as one). And in point of fact, I don't believe in this sort of thing. And neither does she, apparently, according to what she said last night during my dream of her making the bed. I'm comfortable thinking of it as a dream, because what else could it be?

In order to distract myself, I watch the mist through my binoculars, and assuring myself that I'm looking for loons rather than Denise.

"I like birds," I say aloud, examining the vapor as if I expect her to emerge from it standing naked in the gut of her boat like some outdoorsy reimaging of Botticelli. "Yes, I like birds very much."

Why do I find this young woman so fascinating? It's a good question, and one I can use to distract myself until I leave to meet Grover at 9AM. I lower the stereo, and immediately, the aspect of morbidity cast over the morning lifts allowing the problem of Denise to pitch camp. She isn't classically beautiful, tall and spare. Her chest is likely flat, and her rump somewhat bony. If she wore her hair short like Jo, she would probably look like a boy, especially with the kind of roughneck clothing she seems to favor. From a distance, Morton could have sired her. But something in the angular pitch of her nose, or similarly sharp cast of her chin and jaw mark her as distinctly patrician (lapsed, most likely), though a well-mannered variety. She wasn't afraid of familiarity when she served me at the coffee shop. And even when I implied that I consider watching girls with binoculars a hobby worth sharing, she didn't make a scene. Instead, she became cautious, and observant, waiting to see what I would do next, which is exactly what I would have done. Perhaps this similitude is part of why I'm here, watching the empty water of Kranion Pond, when I should be out back of Aornum Hill.

A tapping on the driver's side window startles me, and the binoculars fall, bouncing off the passenger seat onto the floor. And as I turn around, my elbow rolls the volume nob on the stereo, amplifying the odd recording as I lower the glass, which frames a pendulous, khaki gut ferruled by a utility belt.

"What is it, Blivet?" I ask the thorax blocking my window.

"Nothin', Henry, I was just…Say, you mind lowerin'… whatever that is?"

"Is there something you want?" I ask, turning off the stereo. The sheriff leans down, laying a meaty forearm across the door, and replacing the khaki torso with a bejowled, roseate face like the ass of a baboon.

"What you listening to?"

"Capuchin chanting. From Italy," I reply, assuming a man of his type has likely marked anything European as uninteresting and homosexual. "Why are you here?"

"Well, I was just coming up to check a fishing license or two, but I didn't see anyone on the pond, so I figured I'd head on back to town, but then I saw your car parked over here and I thought I'd come over to say good morning, and…"

"Good morning then. Is that all of it?"

"Well…No," says Blivet, suddenly becoming conciliatory, a wolfish grin dividing his face like a mood-reliant halberd. "I actually been tryin' to get in touch with you for a day or two, but I guess maybe your phone was off."

"It was on."

"Oh, I see. Well maybe your ringer there wasn't …engaged?"

"It vibrates when I have a call."

"Well maybe you ain't got my new number, here let me…"

"I have it, Blivet," I say. "I also have an appointment in twenty minutes. Tell me what you need or I will leave."

"Oh sure, I see, well, I was hoping we might have a talk about Dennis."

"Dennis what?"

"And I thought you were in a hurry," says Blivet. "You know, Coach Dennis, he's one of yours by way of A.P.M, so…"

"Alright, yes, I know him," I say. "What about Coach Dennis?"

"Well, the thing is," replies Blivet, leaning in so close that the car actually tilts, and I can smell his breath (also like the ass of a baboon). "If it was just some regular creeper from the pool hall or a place like that I'd have taken care of it myself, but seeing as he works for a friend, I figured I better run it by you first, but it's a bad business, because he's got a pretty good reputation with the people around here, what with the time he puts in with them girls, and I hate to see a good man suffer because of one mistake but that fact is…"

"Blivet," I say. "You're telling the story backwards. Start from the beginning. What about Coach Dennis?"

"Oh. Sure. Well, I got a call the other night from Gloria Holzer saying she thought maybe someone was in her flowerbeds, and I figured she's just a little nervous, you know her daughter Lisa leaving for school and all, but I went over anyway, and had a look with the flashlight, and what do you know? I find a patch of dirt looks like a man's been lying in it under one of her rose bushes, so I guess sometimes women know what they're talking about."

"And other times?"

"Well," he begins, scratching his head beneath a harassed-looking Stratton. "I suppose they talk as much sense as anyone else. Except for…"

"For…?"

"You know…when they're bleeding…down below."

"Menstruation?" I say, watching him cringe.

"Yup, I guess that's what I meant, anyway, it looks like when

Dennis was belly down in that dirt, he maybe forgot that his belt buckle his name on it, and I ain't no scholar, but I can surely read backwards."

"Dennis has his name on his belt buckle?"

"Why sure, it was a wedding gift from Sharon as I recall, and I guess he must still miss her if he's wearing that."

"I guess so."

"And I know Jeremiah has a soft spot for the kid, I mean, we all do after what happened, but listen, Henry: I can't have no creeps in my town, and that's why I come to you with this, so how do you want to handle it?"

Revealing to Blivet that I've already taken care of Dennis is more than the sheriff needs to know. On the other hand, if I allow him to deal with it on his own, my name might come up, since Dennis has no need to keep secrets if he's caught. No one is more honest than a condemned man.

"I'll take care of it," I say, starting the car. But Blivet's shank remains on the window.

"Well, that's just fine and all, but I'd like to be involved," he says, possibly apprehending the limited chance of this. "I mean, I at least should ask him some questions."

"Not necessary. I'll take care of it."

"But see that?" he says, pointing to the badge crookedly ad-joined to his manbreast. "That means I got a duty, not that I don't trust you, because you know I do, but I need to see some part of this for myself, because that's my job, and I won't have no perverts in Acheron."

With a speech like this, it's easy to mistake Blivet for a noble lawman, an image in which he may invest the lion's share of his confidence and identity. But there are several facts standing between him and this caricature. A relative on the college grounds staff sells marijuana confiscated from students by Blivet back to them. I believe they split the profit evenly. It's the wont of the small town sheriff to sell pardons for anything short of a murder in broad daylight, and as payment for this, Blivet accepts not only cash, but cars, major appliances, and, in one perhaps not exceptional case, a tumbledown three bedroom shitshack by the gas station, which he now rents as subsidized housing for a tax break. He knows that I know about this. The entirety of what passes for an underbelly in Acheron is aware of Blivet's 'reason-ability' (as he calls it). What they don't know, and what he doesn't realize that I know, is that a month or so after my mother disap-peared, an eighteen year old Purvis was caught having consensu-al sex with a fifteen year old girl in the driveway of her parents house, which in Vermont is statutory rape. I wasn't keeping track of things of this sort at the time, and I only discovered it much later (Isidore told me indirectly), after Blivet had either paid off the parents, or intimidated them into not pressing charges. Either way, they left town a month later.

But for my purposes, he is essentially a thug on Mr. Castle's payroll, useful when obedient, but not unwilling to present some form of the duty-bound, noblesse oblige constable argument when he feels his mirage of authority threatened. Naturally, the tension between us is sustained, if not mounting by the day. For the moment however, he needs to be reminded (once again), that his job is a front for interests beyond his own, and if he wants to keep it, he'll do the nothing I ask regarding Dennis.

"That," I say, pointing at the badge. "Doesn't mean what you think it means, in this context. Shall I explain why?"

"Shit, Henry, what happened to your hand?" asks Blivet, ig-noring the question, and focusing instead on the finger I've used to point, a scab yet unformed on the raw knuckles reddened with an areole of infection where Jo gnawed them nearly to the bone five hours earlier.

"A dog," I say, withdrawing my hand. "A bitch. I was attacked by a bitch."

"You know who owns it?"

"No one owns it."

"A stray?"

"Of a kind."

"Well, I can't have no savage mongrel running around town biting who it wants, so tell me: where'd you see it last?"

"See, now this is the problem," I say, nudging his ham from the car window, and preparing to explain why a tin star is not a certificate for meddling, and what sort of trouble I'll make for him if Blivet continues misunderstanding the terms of his employment. But before I speak, I realize I've accidentally created a fine phantom for Blivet to chase rather than bothering with Dennis. All it needs is an embellishment or two.

"What's the problem?" he asks, braced for abuse.

"The dog," I say, and he relaxes. "I last saw it out back of Grover's, rooting through the trash. It is blonde, compact, without a definite pedigree. It appears to be domesticated, but don't be fooled. I made the mistake of allowing the cur to approach me, and when I tried to pet it...Well, you've seen the result. She's a cunning, duplicitous beast."

"Why'd you try to pet it? You shouldn't try to pet strange dogs."

"I didn't have a choice."

"Okay..." says Blivet, standing to adjust his belt and apparently accepting this, his gut reframed in the car window. The fly on his trousers gapes like a sideways mouth filled with minute, metallic teeth. "How'd you know it was a...a girl dog?"

"A vagina was apparent," I say, raising the volume on the

stereo to discourage a reply from the sheriff. "See that you find her, Blivet. She's a menace."

He makes an agreeable gesture in the rear view mirror as I swing the Audi toward town, touching his mitt-like hand to his Stratton, and holding it there, as if releasing his pinch on the brim might dispel the mythology directing the gesture. The stereo suggests the possibility of my name as the sheriff is drawn below the vanishing point of the declivity down which I descend toward the morning grid of Acheron.

2.

Forty minutes after sending Blivet to apprehend the dog that did not bite me, I'm walking alone across the backside of Aornum Hill, in a dense patch of old-growth forest known as the Aochegahara among the students. The word is a portmanteau, a blending of the town's own appellation with the Japanese phrase Aokigahara, meaning 'Sea of Trees' (the 'o' was either kept from this, or included to mirror the name of the hill itself), the name of a similarly thick, fourteen-acre patch of woodland bearding the northwest base of Mt. Fuji, popular both with hikers and those wishing to unmake themselves, the latter leading to its western reimagining as the Suicide Woods (of Mt. Fuji). Apparently, the two favored methods are overdosing on drugs, and hanging.

This ghoulish rechristening of Aornum Hill is attributed to an Eastern Studies student who supposedly attended the college during the seventies (a period of deep mystery among people my age). The story is that he became possessed by the originless, yet malevolent spirits occupying the woodland behind the school, and began referring to the place as the Aochegahara before descending into it the day of commencement to commit seppuku (obviously). No one can remember his name, or even what year he attended, but it takes very little for campus legends of this kind to root themselves beneath the fecund skin of the student body. And so, the demon forest of Aornum Hill has since birthed numerous sub-legends, continuing to claim at least one fictitious victim per school year. When I was a student, the most popular story was a brazen falsity involving a professor of Tibetan Conflict Resolution who immolated himself in the forest after being denied tenure.

In truth, the forest is no more or less spooky than any other in Vermont, and perhaps the student body realized this shortly after the legend of the Aochegahara was introduced. Since leaving my car on the lower road, I've seen three bodies suspended by the neck from branches, two more lying in cradles of bloodstained leaves, and the feet of another extending from the unzipped entrance of a tent pitched beside the trail. And I know I'll see others on my way to meet Grover.

These are not real bodies of course, but dummies or mannequins constructed and deployed by the students in preparation for Halloween. As the holiday approaches, the woods become a sort of pastoral morgue, with more grotesque tableaux added each day as their authors attempt to outdo one another. On All Hallows Eve, the students and more adventurous members of the townsfolk tour the woods (in costume), usually with alcohol and whatever controlled substance Blivet has sold them, mocking their own credulity by using the legend as an opportunity for a peripatetic masquerade shitshow. The tradition is known by the somewhat unwieldy and low-achieving name of Aochegahanarama, and is not recommended for families.

Grover is standing in the center of a small clearing collecting empty beer cans with a trash pick and dropping them into a black garbage bag when I appear at the trailhead. The ground shows signs of recent activity; trampled swatches of fallen leaves, the depression left in the soft earth by what was likely a portable generator, and the stray ends of cigarettes ground into bootprints collecting water.

"They tried to clean up," says Grover, gesturing with his stick. "But after working all night, I honestly felt bad holding them. And I realized after a short time that it was easier to do on my own."

"A man on the edge knows no leverage," I say, grabbing a stick, and using it to knock cans toward Grover's spear. "The leaves look fine."

"I don't know how you thought of it," he says, looking at the canopy around us, which has a distinct, singular brightness to it. "I talked with Elmer when he came up to pack the generator and lights away. He said that it isn't paint so much, more like a dye."

"Organic, if that matters. He said it would fade naturally."

"We actually drove up the access road to have a look. Elmer was curious. It's a little patchy, but better than not doing anything. I told the hotel to give them a complimentary Mimosa or two with breakfast. By the time Tyler picks them up, they should be good and credulous."

"I take it the beer helped Morton and friends through the night?"

"Well, it got the job done. And I no longer have to look at it in my store."

"Did Morton behave?" I ask, taking a step backward. The dangling foot of a dummy lynched from the tree behind me touches my shoulder, and a tortured, papier-mâché visage shining from a paraffin treatment frowns down at me as I look up.

"He didn't like those much," says Grover, watching me watch the dummy. "In fact, he wanted to cut that one down because he felt like it was watching him. A few of the other fellows went off to take a piss and got spooked by the decorations, but men like that will go to a picnic in a volcano if there's free beer. So it worked out."

"Good," I say, dropping a can in Grover's bag. "Thank you for helping me make this happen."

"Don't mention it, Henry. Though, I should be honest. When I finally understood what you wanted to do here, the potential schadenfreude was too much. How could I pass that up?"

"You assumed I would fail?"

"No. I assumed you might. Occam's Razor, Henry. When customers at the market are unhappy with the Alaskan Sockeye Salmon, I don't fish a basket of Pickerel out of Kranion Pond, and sell it as Nordic Spotted Codfish. I give them a gift bag and send them home. I wonder if you aren't bored..."

"Why would you say that?" I ask, jettisoning any pretense of helpfulness by tossing my stick into the bushes.

"Because you're taking unnecessary risks to prove a point," says Grover. "Though to whom, I can't say. The Greeks might have called it 'hubris.' But you're essentially godless and pragmatic, so even when you act out it's calculated, and purposeful. Normally, people react to what they see as inescapable monotony by swimming with sharks or climbing a clock tower with a high-powered rifle."

"Acheron doesn't have a clock tower," I say, weary of Grover and his familiarity. At what point did I indicate that I was opening up the conversation to include my motives? I drift toward the trail back to the road, as he continues collecting his jetsam from the clearing. "Thanks again for your help."

"My pleasure. I'd rather have the chance to participate in a world-ending failure than a mediocre success."

"Provided the responsibility for it belongs to someone else."

"Of course. That's why I own a grocery store and you do what you do."

"What I do?"

"What you do," he confirms, wandering into further into the clearing, and perhaps deliberately beyond the distance at which I might respond without shouting. Is this a tactic? Forcing me to rejoin by raising my voice? I can't remember the last time I yelled at anyone, and this town provides many opportunities.

As I navigate the trail of dead back to my car, I'm unable to decide whether or not Grover is right. Am I dangerously bored? What was it my mother used to say?

"He had been bored, that's all, bored like most people. Hence he had made himself out of whole cloth a life full of complications and drama. Something must happen -- and that explains most human commitments. Something must happen, even loveless slavery, even war or death. Hurray then for funerals!"

No, that doesn't sound like her. She was more succinct. And perhaps it doesn't apply, although 'loveless slavery' is an accurate footnote to my relationship with Jo. And of course, something must happen, but as long as I control it, what's the harm? I imagine the view from the clock tower is terribly lonely. But as I sit in the driver's seat with my notebook opened to 'G' in my lap, my pen hovers over the page unable to commit anything useful. I may have accidentally made a friend, but I'm struggling to remake him as an enemy, which may prove him correct. I close the notebook without adding anything, but before I can replace it beneath the seat, another tap on the window startles me. But where earlier I found only the contour of Blivet's paunch, I see instead the steady, boyish, and somehow comforting face of Denise.

"Good afternoon," I say, glancing at the digital clock beneath the stereo terminal, which reads 10:28AM. Still morning. How embarrassing. Inability to differentiate between times of day could either indicate eccentric flaneurism or a career of pathological indigence, both unattractive. I chuckle falsely, and over-correct. "I mean, morning. Sorry, I was up late. I had trouble sleeping. Not because I was doing anything peculiar. I actually got up early as well."

"Are you following me?" she says, as if I'm a stranger (which I suppose I am) she is asking for directions (which I suppose she is). Which way is the place farthest from you, Henry, and how do I get there?

"I was here first," I say, becoming defensive, and thus territorial. But her voice is so earnest that I feel like I'm wearing a sandwich board with 'Predatory Liar' emblazoned on it. Perhaps I am a creep. No, it isn't true. Even if I did scan the lake earlier, hoping for a glimpse of her through my binoculars, she doesn't know that. There were also the loons ("I like birds...I like birds very much"). Yes, I was interested in their movements. Had I known she would be here, I would have planned for it. But I can't tell her that either.

"Okay...What are you writing?" she asks, inclining her head toward the notebook in my lap as her body retreats, one step, then another, making no attempt to conceal her curiosity while cautiously moving beyond my reach. As if I might at any moment seize her hair and drag her through the car window, subdue her with a syringe of Phenobarbital, and drag her immobilized body into the forest, to be violated and never seen again.

"Poetry," I lie, trying to appear poetic. I adjust my frill.

"Oh. Are you a writer?"

"Possibly."

"That's interesting," she says, taking a step blessedly closer to the car. "I ask because I'm a writer."

"Yes," I confirm, seizing this chance to appear common. "I am a writer as well."

"I'm actually studying it at the college. Writing, I mean. Part time."

"That's interesting," I echo, unsure of what else to add. "I studied there not long ago."

"You're an alumnus."

"Yes. I graduated a year ago."

"And you're still here?"

"I'm from here."

"I see. Well, I didn't mean to interrupt you. I just wanted to make sure I didn't have to start checking behind my curtains."

"I'm more of a Svidrigailov sort. Peeping through keyholes, that king of thing. I rarely make it indoors."

"Wasn't he suspected of murder?" asks Denise. But she's laughing, and her pale, finely boned hand actually rests on the doorframe, absolving me, I imagine (I hope).

"I...I can't remember. And there's no need to leave. I'm finished...composing...as it were."

"Would you read me something?"

"Would I read you something?" I say, trying to appear accustomed to sharing my non-existent work. I open the notebook, and flip at hazard to an entry for Dennis (strange augury, that). I clear my throat. "Certainly, yes...Huffy Henry...hid the day... unappeasable Henry sulked..."

"Are you testing me?" interupts Denise, looking disappointed. "You might have at least chosen something from later in *The Dream Songs*. How do I know you've gotten past page one?"

"Good question. Is that your pram, over there?"

Behind her, an industrial Victorian baby carriage with a torn, black hood like a disheveled bat wing is parked on the opposite side of the road. I suppose I was so occupied with appearing unlike a stalker that I didn't notice it until now.

"Why, yes," says Denise proudly. She crosses the road to retrieve the stroller, which emits a plangent, tortured noise as she wheels it toward the car, and of course, it is not empty. The tattered awning shelters a rather subhuman-looking doll swaddled in the pram's belly. It is dressed in drab set of pajamas, the glass eyes plucked from its bald porcelain head, and the vacant sockets each drooling a dark tear of red nail polish. "What do you think? I found it in some junk shop in Waterbury. I was going to find a spot for it in the Aochegahara. For Halloween."

"It'll fit right in. The forest is full of atrocities."

"Oh, you've already been? Is that where you go to write?"

"No, I had business in the woods," I say, only realizing how creepy this sounds after I've said it. "I mean I had to meet someone. For work."

"What do you do for work?"

That question, once again. Perhaps I should direct her to Grover. He seems to know the answer. On the other hand, she probably doesn't care. She's just being polite. Make something up.

"I'm the operations coordinator for Acheron Property Management. We're thinking of buying a stretch of the hillside, and I had to...inspect it, so to speak."

"Oh. They're the people who own my uncle's camp up on the pond."

"Whose your uncle?"

"Wilbur Erlanger. Do you know him? He used to own the movie theater."

"Yes. I mean no. Vaguely," I say, struggling for a change in subject, and settling on the grisly pram. "If you like, I could help you find the perfect place for that...that display you have there."

"That would be nice, I think. Yes, why don't you come along?"

I lock the car, and help Denise lift the pram over the drainage ditch separating the forest from the road. And once settled on the trail, we make a strange, domestic burlesque; a young couple pushing an abused stroller containing a mutilated infant through a temperate, autumnal forest in which bodies hang from trees like the uncollected fruit of some seasonal and eccentric terrorism. And yet, we appear calm and happy, laughing, and mostly agreeing, as we install the carriage on an escarpment overlooking a bend in the trail, and return to the car, where we depart after she gently refuses my offer of a ride to town (revealing a bicycle stashed on the far side of the road), but returns it with an invitation later that evening to do something around 7PM. We leave the activity undecided, because the entire point, I suppose, is to continue the conversation.

3.

Rather than resembling his older brother, Cornelius Castle looks more like a deflated facsimile of Boris Huld, but this could be a result of context. His office in the tower room beneath the apse of Holmes Hall is a similar in position and shape to the dome of Monticello (or the Chiswick house). It is cornerless and ovicular, but with panels of dark wood cobbling the walls containing sunken bookshelves, and square windows in place of the portholes favored by Jefferson. Were it not for balistrariae windows set between the ribs of the umbrella dome forming the ceiling of the office, the room would be dark as a catacomb. Instead, they cast a pious, church-like illumination into the room's geometric center, where Cornelius has chosen to place the broad wooden desk across which he watches me with an incredulous boredom.

"Let me understand this," he says. "You're worried about Jo. You have a…what was the term you used?"

"It was a phrase," I say from my uncomfortable seat, a high-backed Queen Anne chair that looks like a cake decorator designed it. "Premonitive sense of unwell."

"Did you read that somewhere, Henry?"

"No, I just can't explain why I'm worried. And I didn't want to tell your brother because he relies on me for certainty. And I'm not certain about this."

"What am I supposed to do?"

"Tell me what to do."

"About Jo?"

"Yes."

"Are you fucking her?"

The question is delivered calmly, without the sense of corroboration that might indicate Jo and I are caught, or the locker-room masculinity that might simply be curious. His mouth is calm as a portcullis, and the light reflecting from his small, shaved head forms a sort of Orion's Belt as it joins with that of his golden cufflinks, his hands touching the sides of his head, the fingers rotating the against the temples, his thick, black spectacles bobbing onto his forehead with each revolution. He pauses, reaching into the maroon lining his a gray woolen suit to retrieve a packet of Dunhill's, offering me one, which I decline.

"No. I'm not fucking her."

"Liar," he says. "You should come see me more often. Then you might know what I know."

"You know nothing, and you don't like me. Why would I come see you?"

"No one likes you," he says, smiling through a porous cobweb of smoke. "Except Huld. He won't tell me why."

"You're wrong. I made a friend today. Two, actually."

"More lies."

"It isn't a lie, Cornelius. And your brother likes me."

"Jeremiah thinks he needs you. It's different. Friendships don't appear from necessity. Are you fucking her?"

"I don't understand why you keep asking me that. I came here because I'm concerned. Something is changing, and Jo is part of it. She treats him like she hates him, and that worries me. Shouldn't it worry you?"

"You've never been married, Henry. Marriage is measured in small hatreds."

"I don't respect you enough to agree with that. But we both know that she is in a position to get everything if anything happens to your brother. And she knows it too."

"What about Isidore?"

"She said he can't handle any of it. And she's right."

"She said this before or after she asked for your help 'managing things'?"

"Before. I suppose it was a kind of preamble."

"Were you in bed together?"

"I'm leaving," I say, standing up, and walking toward the door. "Have an awful day, Cornelius."

"Henry, sit down," he says, his voice calm and impenetrable as an oceanic trench. "I didn't mean to imply anything. I guess with all the tin weasel fuckups around here I forget that some of us are still professionals. Please, sit down."

"I know that you and your brother don't get along," I say, furling my coat around my shoulders. "In fact, you know I know that, which makes this entire performance all the more pointless. I'm not paid to tolerate your nonsense, or listen to the uninformed half-truths that govern your pestilential relationships with the people unlucky enough to enjoy your company. I'm also not a bodyguard. If something happens, you'll have to live with it because you're a family member. I'm an employee."

"If you worked for me, I'd like you more," says Cornelius, tapping ash into a stray coffee cup on the desktop. "You could work for me, you know. I could see you in admissions. Or financial aid. I'm kidding, of course. But I could certainly use you for bullshit repellent if nothing else. You know your worth of course, but I don't. How much is Jeremiah paying you now?"

"I'm paid in smiles, laughter, and conjugal rights to his wife," I say, buttoning my coat. "But you already knew that. I'll have you secretary convert it into pieces of silver on my way out."

"Your new car is nice."

"It's six months old. It's not new."

"All is vanity."

"Goodbye, Cornelius," I say, opening the door.

"What do you want me to do?" he asks. "Come back. Sit down. Tell me what you want me to do because I honestly don't know how to handle this."

"You could tell him," I say, returning to my seat without removing my jacket, the collar standing at attention around my face like a woolen fortification. "But I wouldn't do that."

" 'Jeremiah, I know we're not really friendly, but I just stopped by to tell you that I heard through the grapevine that your wife might be plotting to kill you,' " says Cornelius, more to himself than me. "No, I don't see it. We'd have better luck if you told him."

"I'm not doing that. He wouldn't listen, and it would end up rolling back on me, especially if she found out."

"Isidore?" suggests Cornelius, shaking his head as soon as the name leaves his mouth. "I don't know why I said that. We'd have to make him understand the entire thing first, which is just working backward. Would you mind turning down your collar, Count Fuckula?"

"I think our best option," I say, ignoring him. "is to watch, and wait. Jo won't do anything rash, but subtlety isn't one of her gifts. She's more calculating than passionate, and if she's plotting something, I'll notice it."

"Because you're fucking her," says Cornelius. I stand up. "Oh, sit down, come on. I'm just trying to lighten up the fucking conversation. Talking to you makes me feel like I'm on the short bus to Treblinka. Should we tell Huld about this?"

"For a lawyer, Huld has a remarkably intact ethical imperative," I say. "He would demand honesty, even if it compromised my position, and his client's marriage. On the other hand, you're a liar, and a coward, and because of that, you recognize gray areas. Blessed are those who exist in the outer dark."

"I don't know what that means."

"It means you won't say anything because you have nothing to gain, but you'll help me if it comes to that, because as much as you hate your brother, you need him to retain your position here."

"That's less true than you might think. I've been the best candidate for five years. The search committee obviously recognizes that," says Cornelius, somewhat embarrassed. "And I'm very well respected by the board. But you have my word that I'll help you if you need it."

"I don't want your word. I want your telephone number."

He says a number that I punch into my phone, and another phone rings on a small table between two leatherette armchairs sentenced to unfilled tenure before the cold fireplace at the rear of the room. I stand up again for what I hope is the final time, and Cornelius joins me, buttoning his suit, and adjusting the cuffs as he extends a manicured hand from one sleeve. I take it reluctantly in my own, stepping into the circle of light downcast from the dome.

"I know you're not fucking her," he says, imprisoning my hand as he attempts to apologize. "But you can't tell me you haven't thought about it, right? She is gorgeous. What I wouldn't give to wear her like a hat, you know what I mean? She has the body of one those Romanian gymnasts. Like she spends all day…hanging from things. What are those bars called?"

"You're telling me that you want to put your penis in the same woman as your brother, Cornelius?" I say, yanking my hand away, and walking toward the door.

"Well...not when you put it that way," he calls after me. "Jesus Christ, Henry. It's always bloody diarrhea and the siege of fucking Leningrad with you. No wonder you have no friends."

"I told you -- I made two friends today."

"I'd better call the elementary school. See if any kids are missing."

"Good luck touching dicks with your brother."

"Out of my office! Be gone, Count Fuckula!"

On the way out of the office, I nearly trample the secretary entering it, a wan, tubercular graduate student with a cup of weak coffee clattering in saucer.

"He told me to bring you this," she says, steadying the cup with a thin, diaphanous hand. "But...you're leaving?"

"I am," I say. "But I'll take it to go. Thank you."

Before she can reply, I relieve her of the saucer, and balance it one hand while guiding the other along banister on my way down the two flights to the entrance. On the broad granite stairs fronting Holmes Hall, I take a dignified sip overlooking (or outerlooking really) the quadrangle of the campus, bookended to the east and west by the red brick edifices of Burke, and Hare Halls, the former a dormitory, the latter a warren of classrooms and administrative offices. Opposite Holmes Hall is the H. Fish Building, a newish, and rather harsh, modular structure containing the cafeteria, and more classrooms. It was recently and unnecessarily united with the library via a kind of winding, umbilical parapet hooded in glass. If a snake were transformed into a greenhouse, the result would be something like this new addition. I can see one contoured elbow of it across the quad, shuttling students between meals and study like an incorporeal Brutalist vein, reflecting not the sun from the sky, but the promise of a snow. The design won an award for which Cornelius appropriated most the credit, it being his idea (or so he said). I don't trust him, but in this circumstance, trust is a bonus rather than a sine qua non. A happy household is important to us both.

I descend the stairs, and stroll through the grassy quad, passing beneath the withered foliage of several large Maples, and few solemn Oaks, their leaves so dry that they seem to shatter beneath my feet like the translucent brown glass of a broken bottle. I pinch the saucer between my thumb and the knuckle of my index finger, sipping daintily from the matching cup as I wander past the mostly empty picnic tables scattered around the common lawn like a duke touring his garden. I always enjoyed the compact visibility of the campus. There is a place for eating, a place for class, and a place for books, all within reach of each other. Navigating between them is integral to the experience of each. I suppose this is why Cornelius' crystal sausage casing seems so unnecessary. Small inconveniences are part of an education, and attaching a house of learning to a house of eating is like placing a cat's food bowl beside its litter box. What would my own education have been without the commute between classes, and the house on Town Hill Road? A hypothetical is a bastion of dialectic flotsam, and in conversation, I avoid them. But in private, questions of obsolete possibility run like riderless horses across the prehistoric steppe of my inner world. I pride myself in not mistaking this exercise for regret.

At the campus gate, I hand the security guard the cup and saucer through my car window, which he accepts with a somnolent goodwill.

"Some of the president's crockery," I say. "See that he gets it?"

The guard, another graduate student, in anthropology or environmental science judging by the cut of his jib (youngish, learning to grow a beard, fundamentally uncomfortable in his uniform), waves me toward the gate without a word. Good enough for me. Cornelius won't notice the courtesy, but perhaps his secretary will include me in her prayers.

I'm just beginning to plot the remaining portion of my afternoon when my phone rings, the number familiar but surprising. Mr. Castle rarely calls me during the day unless it's important. Since my responsibilities are deliberately vague, he falls on the generous side of things, and assumes I'll fulfill them without a reminder (which is mostly true). So a call at 3PM is unusual, and though I anticipated having the remainder of the day to myself, I answer it anyway.

"I don't mean to disturb you," he says in a voice like a mendicant.

"I'm not disturbed."

"Where are you?"

"Approaching town," I say. There is no reason to tell him that I'm near the college.

"I was wondering if you would be willing to...Well, if you meet me at the house, I'll explain it. Are you in the middle of something?"

"I'm between things, at the moment. Is everything all right?"

"Yes, everything's fine. I don't mean to cryptic, it's just...It's embarrassing, Henry, and I'd rather embarrass myself in person, if that's alright."

"I understand," I say, though I don't. "Can you give me half an hour?"

"Sure. See you then."

A strange conversation. But whatever Mr. Castle needs, it probably has nothing to do with Jo. After my time with her yesterday evening, and the repeated, mocking accusations from Cornelius, I've had enough of her at the moment.

4.

The Acheron Free Library sits beside the church where I waylaid Tyler a few days earlier, (and where the deaconess silently accused me of matricide) and if he hadn't distracted me, I might have remembered to return my books after our discussion. But part of my job is suffering fools with the appearance of grace, and as a result, I now mount the steps fronting the library's classically revived façade with three overdue books beneath my arm. I have to meet Mr. Castle in twenty minutes, and though it would be most simple to dump my burden in the drop box nested between two of the four Corinthian columns bolstering the portico and pay the fine later, I can't do it. As others cannot bypass private litter without transferring it to a public trashcan, or leave a dirty dish lingering on a stranger's dinner table, so I through some inner failing cannot allow library fines to accrue in my name. Ethics are a result of luxury, so I suppose it makes sense that their particular tug be felt at an odd and inconvenient time. Mother, have you any thoughts on this? "It's the little things that eventually kill you, Henry. Get them first."

I attended high school with the librarian occupying the front desk in the building's atrium, and she greets me while I'm still in the lobby, eyeing the drop box through the window with an aspect of grief.

"Henry. Always a pleasure."

"Hello, Cordelia. I'm afraid I have some overdue books."

"Well, you better come on over here and pony up before we pull your card."

I find the goofy banter nauseating, but Cordelia Swan is the sort of person who will continue it with or without my consent. And since I use the library regularly, reducing her amity to ashes would be imprudent. At one time, when were both much younger, she may have nursed a longing for me that I politely ignored, and when romantic tension fades, contempt is the remainder. I suppose I should be grateful that she's made the best of it.

I try to appear humble as I neatly stack my three books on the counter separating us. Why did I never acknowledge Cordelia's interest in me? She's rather nicely broad in the hips and shoulders, and warmly blond, with a smooth skin the color of honey, and a bluish clear-eyed gaze settling officiously on my books as she opens each volume to expose a barcode fixed to the flyleaf. Cordelia is an example of the sort of Viking femininity favored above and slightly below the Arctic Circle, and the carbon opposite of Denise, who I appear to be chasing. But why run, when I can stay put? Because Cordelia was clumsy. Her overtures were too obvious. And I was too young to know the value of winning without having to try.

"You owe me fifteen cents," she says, the final volume beeping as it passes beneath the scanner. It's a comforting noise in this context when compared with a grocery store, for example. "Couldn't let it wait could you? You just had to make it right."

"I have a problem," I reply, delving idly into the pocket of my pea coat for the coins, the small uncertainty of the movement allowing me a second to glance at the books open on the counter, and notice once again the rust-colored bloodstain on the interior page of the Simenon novel. It is the size of the quarter I fish from my pocket and hand to Cordelia.

"You sure do," she says, accepting it with a perfectly aligned smile. "You're beyond hope."

"No, I mean it. I actually do have a problem. This book," I say, tapping the Simenon with a finger. "You see…It's a bit odd, but would you be able to tell me the names of the people who have checked it out?"

"No," says Cordelia flatly. "And why would you want to know that?"

"It's a personal matter. I'm rather embarrassed to talk about it."

"Try."

"Well," I begin, trying to compose the perfect fable that will engage Cordelia's sympathy while preserving my dignity. "Several years ago, a friend of mine left something compromising between the pages of this book."

"What was it?"

"I'm afraid I can't say, but when I saw this friend recently, she noticed me reading it, and revealed that ever since she returned the book with the item forgotten between its pages, she has received erratic, author-less letters, threatening to reveal the secret which, by its very existence, this item implies."

"Your telling me this friend of yours was using a naked picture of herself as a bookmark?"

"You're in the neighborhood, Cordelia. But I promised not to reveal more than necessary to find an answer to her problem."

"Sounds like bullshit, Henry," says Cordelia, snatching the book from hands, and stuffing onto a cart behind the counter. "Why should I help her? Or you?"

"No one deserves to live in fear," I say softly, with a limpness meant to imply that I see the answer as obvious. Why wouldn't she want to help my fictional friend? But I see no sign of vicarious empathy on her wide, Nordic face. Failure is imminent, so I opt for human sacrifice. "If you like Cordelia, I can explain it in further detail over a meal? My treat, of course."

"Food? With you?" she says, and for a moment, I worry that she might whisk my offering from the altar and refuse me. I have no tertiary plan, and in terms of satisfying my curiosity regarding the bloodstain, it would be catastrophic.

"Yes. With me, your friend and former classmate, Henry Hoffmann. Is tomorrow evening…possible?"

"Did you concoct that absurd story just to ask me out?" she asks, her glibness returning.

"No. I actually need the list."

She appears to balance this contingency with an internal set of weights and measures. In one pan sits her job, and the integrity and professional expectations therein. In the other, I sit, or the promise of me, a simple man really, who long ago slipped her baitless hook, only to circle back now, a decade later to gnaw it with the hapless, ichythoid greed that a raisin-sized brain makes possible. Once again, I'm reminded of Jo chewing my finger raw the previous evening, and I shudder.

"Meet me here around 8PM?" she says, and as I agree, her finger taps a key, and from somewhere beneath the counter, I hear the sound of printer ejecting sheets of paper. She bends down to gather them for me, and folds them in half before passing them across the desk. "They only go back two years. That's when we went digital, and we're still catching up with the old records. I hope your friend's secret is true, because if you tell anyone about this, I'll do my best to make sure they find out about her."

"They won't. I mean, I won't."

"Good," she says, her gelid eyes thawing as they meet mine. "I look forward to catching up, Henry."

I should wait to review the paperwork. It's already 3:20PM,

and I'm going to be late to meet Mr. Castle. But what man isn't a slave to curiosity? When no one is watching, I have the patience of an autistic child. Perhaps to remind myself that I am an adult (of sorts), with responsibilities, and other adults to meet, I start my car as I sit in the passenger seat, shuffling between the five pages Cordelia provided. Nothing interesting. Apparently, Simenon is not a popular author in Acheron. Perhaps the list would be longer if the book featured Inspector Maigret (a hypothetical). I'm reading the list in the order it was given to me, backward, and finding very little of interest aside from my name, appearing first. But I have no idea what I seek in the names and dates, the bulk of which are familiar, and without utility, though I'm surprised to see that Morton Downing shares my interest in the roman dur. Apparently, he borrowed the book January of last year. Have I misjudged him? I never assumed he was illiterate, but I certainly wouldn't have guessed that whatever form his literacy took might direct him to apply for a library card in service to it. If things go well with Cordelia, maybe I'll request his record next.

I'm growing bored, and scanning through the index quickly, my hand already shifting the car into drive when I notice two names toward the end of the list that give me pause. The first is Winifred Hoffmann, my mother, who checked out the book on October 28th, 2010, three days after Mr. Castle ('Jeremiah H. Castle' on record) returned it, and three days before she disappeared from the known world. But according the list, the book was returned on November 5th, 2010. Of course, it doesn't say by whom. Maybe her ghost (another hypothetical), or a bibliophile involved with the investigation (not Blivet). Is there someone whose job it is to search the homes of the recently deceased or disappeared for library books?

"I don't like this list," I say to no one, but preserve it anyway, folding the pages along the seam made by Cordelia and tucking these inside the cover of the notebook beneath my seat. My life has suddenly become more complicated. Or has it? How much thought should I devote to unraveling what is likely a coincidence? Perhaps Mr. Castle recommended the book to my mother. Maybe she saw him reading it, and placed it on hold. Maybe they never spoke about it at all, and she just happened to choose it from a shelf. But my mother didn't read many mysteries, or suspense novels. The stack of books on her bedside table. What were the titles? *Annals of a Former World. The Lives of the Later Caesars. Gone With the Wind.* It doesn't make sense that out of all the books at the Acheron Free Library, she would select a hurriedly written pamphlet by a Belgian philanderer. But supposing she did, that still leaves two problems. The first is the identity of the person who returned it after she was no more. The second is the stain on the flyleaf. Could it be my mother's blood? I want to say no, but the only logical answer is yes. It could.

5.

When I arrive to meet Mr. Castle, Aloysius is in the front yard of the house bedeviling a shrub. A forelock like the tail of a small, neglected pony is decoupaged to his forehead with sweat, giving him a needlessly urgent appearance when he intercepts me at the door.

"He's on the deck. Waiting for you," says Al. I'm so deep in my hypothetical trench that, for a moment, I forget we're enemies.

"Is he angry?"

"What do you think, Henry?" he asks, his eyes traveling the length of my body twice, and settling on the top of my left hand. "Why'd you write 'penis' on your hand?"

"It doesn't say 'penis,' you subhuman," I reply, somewhat remembering myself. "It says 'Denise.' Ask me why."

"Why?"

"None of your business," I answer, pushing past him into the house, and straight down the main hallway toward the solarium. I stop outside the kitchen and examine my hand, and yes, the inscription could possibly be read as a sort of male advertisement, rather than a personal reminder. I wrote it while driving, my pen wandering from its purpose with each bump in the road, hence, the stem of the 'D' stretched past its normal terminus, and the final 'e' distantly appended (or floating, more accurately), like a launch dispatched from a flagship. I try to wash it off in the sink, but the mark only becomes more obscene as the remote 'e' fades to almost nothing, while the rest of the letters remain. How is that possible? I jam my hand in the pocket of the pea coat, using the other to raise the frill in the hallway mirror.

"I am a lizard," I whisper. It seems a while since I've reminded myself.

Mr. Castle puffs a cigar on the deck with his back to the door, and doesn't turn around when I open it. A rifle leans at a dangerous angle against the railing beside his chair. He's dressed in a tattered woolen jacket, green crosshatched with black, a pair of similarly disheveled logging trousers girding his legs above large, practical boots that appear purposefully cobbled for kicking shit. Even if the gun were not part this deportment, it would be obvious that he intends to go hunting.

I apologize for my tardiness, and take a seat beside him, relieved as I notice a calm smile appear within the gray foliage surrounding his mouth, and a kindly wrinkling in the corner of his eyes behind the golden rim of his spectacles.

"It was short notice. I'm sorry to pull you away from...whatever you were doing."

"Are we...hunting?"

"In a way," he says, standing up, which puts him slightly above eye level with me, sitting down. "You want a gun?"

"I don't understand how they work."

"It's simple technology," he says. "You point it at whatever you don't like, and it disappears."

"You know I don't know how to shoot."

"Only because you won't let me teach you."

"I don't see how this is embarrassing," I say, ignoring the offer, and attempting to change the subject. "On the phone, you said you were..."

"How about we get going?" he says, shouldering the rifle. "We're running a little short on daylight. I have a flashlight, but I'd rather not come down the mountain in the dark."

"We're going up Mt. Abandon?"

"If we hurry."

I follow him around the side of the house, and through the front yard. Aloysius is nowhere in sight, and as I pass my car in the driveway, I check to make sure I've locked it. Dinner isn't for several hours, and there's no telling what sort of villainy he might get into while I'm waylaid with our employer on the mountaintop.

Mr. Castle crosses the road in front the house, and mounts a crude footbridge across the drainage ditch running beside the road, beyond which sits the trailhead. He waits for me at a break in the woodline beside a sign he had printed in town, and fixed to the tree himself several years ago.

Please use this trail with all the freedom and responsibility that once made America great. Reset an example.

Mr. Castle doesn't own the entire mountain. Stowe Mountain Resort holds the deed to the opposing side. But the slope above Acheron is part of a land trust that includes Kranion Pond and the subalpine woodland around it, with Acheron Property Management as the trustee organization, and the population of the town as the beneficiary. This was accomplished with almost no publicity, and few of the townsfolk know anything about it other than what suits their prejudice. Around the pool hall, the land area surrounding Mt. Abandon is known as the King's Woods, because hunting here is prohibited.

"I'm embarrassed because I'm old," says Mr. Castle as we begin ascending the trail toward the summit through the florid, yet silent, forest. The canopy above our heads and the trail beneath out feet are embossed with the emollient ochre of the season. Expired leaves fallen, and the braver among them suspended like rufescent coral in seawater, and attenuated only by a stray evergreen.

"You're not old," I say dumbly. It isn't true. Like a whiskered cheese, my employer ages by the day (a tautology, but so are many unpleasant topics. Death, the father of age, for example).

"I used to enjoy this," says Mr. Castle, ignoring me. "Everyday, I was out here, doing what we're doing. Alone."

"Hunting?"

"That's what I tell people if they ask. It easier than explaining why I'm going up the mountain."

"What's the actual reason?"

"I don't know," he says, resting his gun on a tree trunk to fuss with his coat, but it's obvious by the moisture wicking his brow that after a somewhat inclined quarter mile, he's tired. "I suppose a man's business gets confused with what he does for work. Maybe he's even good at it. I'm good at making money. That's my work. But I think my business is walking around the woods with a gun. That's why I'm embarrassed."

"This is hard for you," I venture, leading him a bit as I remove a canteen from his gamebag, and offer it.

"It isn't getting easier. That's for sure," he replies, splashing water from the vessel into his beard. "The doctor said with my heart and all, I should have someone with me if I'm going up the mountain. Jo used to come, but not so much anymore. I always knew she was more the indoors type, and we've been married long enough to stop pretending we enjoy everything about each other. But I can't say I'm not disappointed. And Izzy's got his spook hunting, which means I barely see the kid. But he's enjoying himself. I don't want to pull him away from that. So, I called you, because I need this time, and there wasn't anyone else to ask. I mean, I took Al once, but that was just…not right."

"I understand."

"I think he needs a girlfriend, Henry."

"I agree," I say, thinking he means Aloysius. "Though I can't imagine who would want to date him."

"I don't think it's as bad as that. I mean, Izzy won't ever be an early fucker, but he's got an essential kindness. And he's comfortable. We could all do worse, especially in a town this small."

"I'm sorry, I thought you meant Al."

"Good lord no," scoffs Mr. Castle, realigning his gun on his shoulder, and unconsciously handing me the gamebag as we start walking again. "I wouldn't wish that man on a corpse. A fine cook, and a decent gardener, but probably the creepiest damn fellow not under lock and key. If Jo wasn't so fond of him, I would have put him out long ago."

"So Izzy won't be an 'early fucker,' " I say, offering my arm as we cross a narrow, rocky rivulet dividing the trail. "What does that mean exactly?"

"Well, like most animals, a human life is pretty simple," he says, ignoring my arm, and sloshing his way across the brook. "You want your food, your fucking, and maybe a nice place to sleep it off. But I always thought it was good to have a head start on the fucking. Life is full of mysteries, but there isn't much uglier than an adult man afraid of women. I lost my virginity to a young woman named Beryl Ferry in a rowboat on Kranion Pond when I was fourteen. She asked me to teach her how to fish. It was only when we got out on the water that I realized she didn't give a hoot for fishing. Granted she was experiencing her time, as it were, but she had me take the back channel, so I think it counts. Smart girl. Point is, I didn't see any more of Beryl, but I saw some other girls. By the time I was old enough to send to war, I had seen more girls naked than most of the adults I knew, even though I wasn't pretty, or tall, or any of it. But I figured out how to talk because I got a head start, and if you know how to talk, you don't get lonely. And it wasn't until later that I realized the fucking I did when I was learning how to talk was the best I'd ever have. Later it becomes about other things. You're either doing it before something else, or in between things. I guess I liked having my head empty, and a man's head is never emptier than when he's fifteen. What I'm saying is there are plenty of people without the benefit of learning how to talk when they're as young as I was, and I guess the difference is that they're unhappy because they're still looking for it. They're the late fuckers. Maybe they didn't get laid until college. Maybe it was prom night. Maybe one of those Asians at that pay to pull massage place in Burlington. They came late to the party. The world is still a puzzle."

"You're talking about confidence?"

"That's part of it, sure. But any fool can be confident. It's a question of what he does with it. If I hadn't gone fishing with Beryl, I probably wouldn't be good at making money. If you look at the most successful man, you'll see an early fucker."

"Hitler was successful too," I say. "And he had part of his penis bitten off by a goat. I think he was trying to pee in its mouth."

"Are we speaking German? There is a difference between success and compensation, Henry. But that's the point I'm trying to make. Whatever you're doing, fucking is usually the reason. It's a question of whether you've had enough of it to take your time, or are in a hurry to figure it out. If Hitler was an early fucker, he wouldn't have spent Christmas Break in Russia. Same with

Napoleon. Late fuckers don't know restraint, because they didn't learn how to talk instead of act. So they substitute experience with charisma, and burn out early. I look at Izzy's excitement with his ghosts, and I worry. He's putting together a pilot for television, and he might just get what he wants. But personally, I think he just needs a woman."

"Even if it's already too late."

"It is too late," he says, as we pass a sign indicating that we are a quarter mile from the top of Mt. Abandon. "But I still want him to have a good life. And I don't want other early fuckers to look at him and see what you probably see. You're an early fucker. Am I right?"

"Eleanor Crow. In her friend's attic, 1998. I was thirteen," I say, taking the rifle from Mr. Castle as he pulls himself up a steep portion of trail. "I can't remember the exact date. But it was Free Cone Day at the ice cream stand in town."

"I figured as much. I don't suppose you can think of any nice girls? For Izzy, I mean," says Mr. Castle, taking the rifle from me, as I climb after him toward the summit. The verdure has thinned to a sparse brocade of lichen and scrub pine, and the trail faded to a general direction across patches of bare sedimentary rock. "Unofficially, of course. I know this isn't your job."

"I only know one at the moment," I reply, thinking of Denise. "And I'm not even sure she likes me."

"He misses his mother. That's a hard sell," he says, standing above me, as I pull myself over a final boulder onto the austere, moon-like pinnacle of Mt. Abandon. The pellucid view encircling the summit of a sunless Acheron below seems to cower in the shadow of Maybrick peak across the valley. Beyond this, Camel's Hump and Mt. Mansfield hang suspended in an undulate, cadmium topography beneath a sky the same color as my companion's head, as the diminutive body supporting it settles on a striated bench of stone overlooking the town. Mr. Castle removes a wedge of cheese, and several apples from the gamebag, setting the meal on a blaze orange handkerchief between us as I settle beside him. It is the perfect moment to take a risk.

"Jo spoke to me about Izzy, too," I say, chewing a slice of apple. I'm not hungry, but I want to appear casual. "She seems worried."

"Yes, she said she talked to you," he says. "I hope it wasn't overwhelming. She means well, I think, but she isn't the most delicate lady."

"Yes," I reply without understanding what he means. "She sure isn't."

"But she's right, Henry."

"How so?"

"About you needing to handle things. If something happens to me. It's only you and her. Izzy can't do it. We all know that. You're young, and you have a lot of choices to make still. But whatever happens, I'd like to know that you'll make sure everything is in good shape before you move on."

"If you're not around."

"That's right."

"I can't believe we're having this conversation," I say, and I mean it. What was Jo's motivation in sharing our conversation with her husband?

"Well, you've been a part of this family for long enough, Henry, in one way or another. It had to happen eventually. Funny, I never figured you for the sentimental type."

"I just seems...preemptive. That's all. We just climbed a mountain."

"And I feel every inch of it. I already outlived my father. He was gone before Beryl took me fishing. Death is mostly genetics. You get what your parents got, give or take."

"I didn't realize Jo and I were having a serious discussion," I say. A red-tailed hawk bobs in an updraft originating in the valley before us, static, yet remarkable in the landscape for it being the only part of it appearing undoomed.

"I can imagine her not introducing the topic at the best time," says Mr. Castle, a crumble of cheese disappearing into his beard, with the raptor's anti-career reflecting in the lenses of his gold-rimmed spectacles. "But I'm grateful that the two of you are close enough to talk about it. She needs someone other than me. I know that."

"Happy to oblige," I say idiotically, focus the bulk of my attention on everything aside from the earnest man beside me. I can't look at him, and yet, I don't feel guilty. We are master and man, but amid the cheerful sorrow of the former is couched the inclement conclusion of the latter (me). Unless he knows more than is polite to reveal, though I can't imagine that after holding forth on early v. late fuckers, Mr. Castle would find the topic of Jo's infidelity indecorous. Either that, or he approves of it. But I can't ask, so I don't know.

"Looks like we're losing light," says Mr. Castle, standing up. "It'll be dark soon."

As he bends to gather the remnant of our meal in the handkerchief, a gurgle emanates from somewhere inside his coat causing him to pause. I hear it again; a moist, unintelligent warble with a quizzical intonation, like the sound of a puzzled, morbidly overweight housecat.

"You all right?" I ask as he totters past me, the rifle precariously disarranged on his shoulder, the gamebag hung like deflated bladder from his hand.

"We should get going. I don't want to go down this goddamn mountain in the dark," he says as another enigmatic bubbling issues from his gut. "I can't believe this happening right now."

"What is it?"

"The heart pills that fucking witch doctor gives me," he says, dropping the rifle and the bag, and unbuttoning his coat. "I'm sorry you have to be here for this, but I need a place to take a shit."

"Well...You seem like the sort of guy whose done his share of crapping in the woods," I say, trying to sound cheerful as Mr. Castle glares around the mountaintop, searching for some crevice or recessed place to use as a toilet.

"You're not wrong," he says, trundling past me. Another oddly intoned warble issues from the left side of his gut, and he touches it with his hand, as if trying to forbear the ineluctability brewing there. "But I'm not much of a squatter anymore. Climbing a mountain is one thing, but my hips...My mother couldn't even walk when we she was my age. Death and genetics, like I said. Jesus, is there nowhere on this goddamn shitting whoreson mountaintop for an old man to take a dump?"

I following him at a distance as he leaves the boulder, and patrols the outward edge of summit, moving quickly, yet with each passing moment, becoming more bent in his movements, until he is nearly doubled over. He stops, and I stop, keeping my distance, unsure of how to help him, but assuming that if I was in his position, saddled with the need to evacuate, yet incapable of doing so without befouling myself, I would rather suffer my dyspepsia alone.

"Not even a tree to grab," he murmurs, his body forming a right angle with the ground. "Goddamn alpine fucking growth patterns."

"Maybe lean your back up against a rock?" I suggest.

"Same problem as squatting. Hips, knees, death, and genetics," he growls. "I know I said I was old. But I didn't think it was diaper time just yet."

"Give me your hands," I say, walking toward him. "No, wait. First, take down your pants. Then give me your hands."

"Are you...serious?" he asks, the formless shape of his head swiveling toward me in the dim light. "I can't ask you..."

"You're not. I'm volunteering."

He straightens up a bit, undoes his belt, and lowers his pants as much as possible without bending his legs. I step closer, and take his small, wet hands in the coming dark, allowing his weight to hang from me. And in this way, Mr. Castle is able to void his bowels on the mountaintop. I try to imagine what the red-tailed hawk must see, suspended in the updraft to the north. Here we are, two hominids, one standing with legs spread to accommodate the weight of the other, who is bent in an angular, hook-like shape, his pants swaddling his thin ankles, his pale backside exposed, and his head dropped forward on his chest in a universal semaphore of shame. Yes, here we are. To the hawk, it must look like we're engaged in a scatological tug of war, though a penitent one, as Mr. Castle will not stop apologizing, and since, at the end of this very long day, I remain his employee, I keep telling him that it's fine, even normal.

"I'm so sorry, Henry," he blusters toward the ground.

"It's fine," I urge, though it isn't. "Let me know when you're through."

I've turned my head to one side for the sake both our comfort, and try my best to completely revolve it like an owl when I hear a sound like someone tossing a bowl of soup into the bushes. A splash, punctuated by a rude, equine fart, followed by precarious silence, and in this way, we wait. I try not to breathe, and wish I remembered to wrap a handkerchief around my nose. But how much more comfortable would I be (hypothetical)? Is there a position downwind in a place exposed on all sides? Another fart, like the air horn of a tugboat bleats from Mr. Castle.

"I think…I think I'm…It's done," he says. I walk him a few shuffling steps forward away from his mess, still holding his hands.

"I'm going to let you go now," I say. I release his hands, and turn away. Behind me, I hear the jingle of his belt as it's drawn up and refastened.

"I suppose I should give you a raise," he says, his voice jocular, but defeated, and the joke too obvious to dispel the awkwardness.

"That isn't necessary. It's over."

"Thank you. Don't tell anyone I didn't wipe."

"We should go," I say, ignoring the second, more obvious joke, and removing the flashlight from the gamebag. "I still have something to do tonight."

"Work or play?"

"I'm meeting the girl who doesn't like me. Yet."

"A student?"

"Yes. Writing, she said."

"Isidore and Purvis are going to be out at the Sutpen place. Would you mind stopping by to check on him before or after?"

"No. I can do that."

He thanks me, and we continue down the darkened ridge of Mt. Abandon, the rifle and gamebag hung from my body, the flashlight bobbing in my hand, as Mr. Castle breathes heavily behind me. It's only when we reach the trailhead, and the lights of the house are visible through a stand of trees across the road that he speaks.

"Do you ever wonder about your father?"

"My mother never mentioned him," I say, because this is true. He came, and went. That was the phrase she used, and I assume it meant he was a guest at the hotel. I stopped asking for further information at a very young age, because I could see that something about the topic made my mother irritable. And as I grew older, I began to consider it unimportant.

"You're not curious?"

"I was. I'm not anymore."

"I hope this isn't a difficult topic, Henry. I'm sorry for bringing it up."

"It's not difficult. I just haven't thought about it for a long time," I say, recalling the list with his name on it beneath the seat of my car. "It's strange. People have been mentioning her lately. I ran into Wilbur at A.P.M. earlier this week, and I had a copy of *The Widow*, with me, you know, Georges Simenon. Wilbur said it was the last book he saw her reading before she died. Or disappeared. I don't know how he knew that. But there it is. He was drunk, or on his way to drink. Strange, right?"

"Maybe. I was always telling her to read him," says Mr. Castle, wistfully, and without suspicion or discomfort. Not that I suspected him of knowing much or anything to do with my mother's disappearance. But probing him with a small lie doesn't hurt. "She said he always described his male characters sweating, and she could only take so many 'moist armpits.' But it looks like she might have taken my suggestion after all."

"Did you often recommend books to her?"

"No. Your mother was an educated woman, Henry. She had her tastes," he says, stopping and turning to me as we reach the road from the bridge. "You know, I wanted to take you in. When she disappeared. I really did. But I never asked because I knew you would say no."

"Izzy told me, though he didn't know why you wanted me in your house."

"Your mother managed the Herrenhof for a long time, Henry. I watched you grow up," he says, as we cross the road toward the house. "I guess I felt like you might need something resembling a parent. Or a father."

"But you're not my father."

"Wouldn't that be unfortunate?"

"For you?"

"For you. No son wants to hold his dad's hand while he poops," he says, chuckling as we reach the driveway of the house. "Speaking of which, why does it say 'penis' on your hand?"

6.

I DECLINE JOINING MR. CASTLE for a post bowel movement beer on the deck, and use my date with Denise as a pretext for not even following him inside the house. After the moment we shared on the summit of Mt. Abandon, I think we need some time apart. But neither the date nor the subalpine feculence is the reason I'm fleeing across the yard toward my car, trying not to run, or look behind me. If I were a churchman, I'd thank whatever votive phantasm had provided me with a legitimate excuse to abandon the property for the evening. Saying 'I have a date' sounds normal, perhaps even cute coming from me, as opposed to 'Your wife is a bloodthirsty hellbitch, and I fear whatever villainy she plans on this dark night.' Yes, I'm afraid of seeing Jo, and dreading her detainments even more, the invitations to dessert, a drink, a game of chess, anything to pillory me within the walls of the house. What was once merely annoying, and even occasionally sweet, has adopted a malevolent aspect over the past week. I do my best to pilot the car out of the driveway at a moderate speed in case she's watching from a window.

The fear is only more acute for being incorporeal, without defined edges, or even a single, knife-like plane dividing it into alternate outcomes, between which I would likely find my place: A man (or lizard) with both feet (or all four) balanced on the blade.

This was the problem I tried and failed to discuss with Cornelius earlier today. And since I don't know what to fear, I don't know what to forefend.

But as the car crests the declivity toward town, I recall a photograph I saw once of a gallery of antiquities in a museum entirely destroyed by an earthquake, the mosaic floor littered with shattered statuary, amphorae turned to an ochre dust, a Romanesque bed tilted sickeningly against the cracked security glass housing it. And yet, amid the fallen busts, and disunited artifacts, the singular figure of Mercury stood on a pediment in the center of the room, untouched and serene, frolicsome and very much at home amid the finality of the loss surrounding it. Must I necessarily prevent anything? Do I have the power to do so? I certainly don't want it. Isn't it best to just allow things to happen as they will? The belief in fate is just a failure of reason, but so is earthquake prevention. Rates may vary, but people eventually destroy each other. If I take action, I would be fighting a natural process. Is that even my job? Once again, I'm halted by the problem of my title, and the duties associated with it. If I make it through whatever is coming, I'll order business cards. Henry Hoffmann: Ambiguous Servant to the Doomed. You Act. I Watch.

As the car rolls through a stop sign at the base of Castle Road, I receive a text message from Blivet written in caveman English:

'got dog id'

Is that a question or a status report? I have no idea what he means until I spend a moment shuffling the reference library of untruths I've built over the past few days, trying to recall something about a dog. Oh, right. This morning, at Kranion Pond, and the story of my mangled finger. Of course, I didn't consider

the possibility that he might actually find a dog, and I'm somewhat overcome with pity for the poor, innocent beast consigned
to the sheriff's company. I suppose Blivet wants me to come in
and identify the cur. I write '8PM' and send the message, figuring
since I have no fixed plan with Denise, a canine lineup might be
a good neutral activity for our first date.

But a first date is never actually a date. It's an unpaid training
session during which both parties determine whether they can
tolerate each other. From there, they either graduate to a first
date, or become awkward friends. Knowing this, I regret intimat-
ing to Mr. Castle that I was doing anything tonight other than
meeting a friend. Jo will ask him where I am, and he will tell
her because he has no reason to keep my secrets, and I suppose
our earlier conversation on Mt. Abandon indicated that his wife
and I are confidants (rather than fuck buddies). Though Jo and I
have never discussed whether the gate of our relationship should
remain closed, or be allowed to swing wild and wanton on its
hinge, I assume the fact of her being obligated by the law of both
god and man to sleep with someone other than me means I'm
free to see other people.

But, as I said, we haven't discussed it. Jo is a talker. I am
a listener. Given her strange, threatening behavior lately, I can
imagine the knowledge of my activities this evening related by
Mr. Castle, a man she seems to hate, sending Jo into the sort of
internal tailspin that will evacuate the possibility of peace in the
household as surely as her husband's medication did his last meal
atop Mt. Abandon.

I suppose I'm being selfish. The practical action is to turn the
car around. Or better: go to Blivet's office, deal with the dog,
and return for dessert and anal sex. But it's impossible to balance
the peevish, inexact desire for Denise with the concrete, multi-

form sociopathy of a married woman. And if I had friends, they would probably tell me to date women my own age. Unless they were pragmatic cowards, like Grover, who would probably say I should do whatever I can to remain in Jo's favor as the towers of her empire begin to wobble. Huld would probably tell me to remain vigilant, and act with patience when the time is right, both of which require me to remain close to Jo.

But here I am, angling the Audi into a vacant space outside Sacred Grounds, the fictional advice of my imagined social circle catalogued and forgotten. Perhaps I imagine heaven as a bed of irrational lust in which I'm planted, watered by the nectar of risk, and sunned by the amplitude of unethical patience. Or perhaps, I'm just curious. Either way, Denise is here, and I'll see her even if it kills someone.

Or I assume Denise is hereabouts. The only definite part of the plan we concocted while navigating the death's head pram through the forest was that we would meet at 7PM. No location, or phone number. How did that happen? I assumed I would try the coffee shop where she works, and my plan ended there. But I'm relieved to see her behind the counter when I enter the café, handing a gourd of mate to an overweight sophomore-looking female with a thin copy of *Fatale* edging from the pocket of her coat. Denise notices me, and removes her apron.

"Can you leave?" I ask as she comes around the counter to greet me.

"I was just filling in. Shall we?" she says, taking her coat from beside the door, and leading me out into the evening. A gentle, probing snowfall has begun, and the flakes caught and melting in her dark hair give it the appearance of a moist ceremonial cowl, an appearance she defeats by producing a tattered baseball cap from somewhere, and clamping it over her skull as we stand in the yellow halflight thrown by the café's front window. "I'm sorry. Did you want anything? It's on me, obviously."

"Thank you. I'm fine."

"I realized after I rode off this morning that I didn't have your phone number. And I didn't tell you where to meet me."

"I realized the same thing," I say with a kind of moronic glee. "I was going to…"

"So I asked my uncle," she says, interrupting me. "You said you were from here. I figured he might know how to get in touch with you."

"Wilbur. Right," I say slowly, trying to judge where this conversation might lead. Nowhere good. Perhaps I'll be home early after all. "I don't think he has my…new number."

"I'm just going to say it, because if I don't, it will bother me. What you did to him was shitty, and I don't approve of it."

"He didn't want you to see me, did he?"

"No, he didn't."

"Did he say why?"

"Other than what you did to get Le Champo?"

"Yes, other than that," I say, adding, "but I don't understand. Everything I did was perfectly legal, Denise. He just didn't like it. Did he say anything else?"

" 'When planting,' " she begins. " 'His whole aspect and all his gestures were so malevolently and uselessly sinister and secret, that he seemed rather in act of dropping poison into wells than potatoes into soil.' It's Melville. He said other than the farming part, it described you perfectly."

"I don't agree."

"Neither do I. That's why I'm here, telling you about it."

"I'm sorry he's unhappy."

"He was unhappy before he lost the theater. But that didn't

help. Now he has no reason to attenuate the drinking."

"I'm sorry he's having a hard time."

"The theater gave him a reason to be sober during daylight."

"I'm sorry that things turned out this way."

"Are you actually sorry?" she says, her thin face angled against the light from the café, and beautifully halved by the shadow cast from the bill of her baseball cap. I don't answer immediately, watching her sharp, earnest face, her calm mouth, large, verdant eyes, and wait instead because the portrait is somehow erotic, and compelling.

"No," I say. "I'm not."

"I didn't think so."

"Does that disappoint you?"

"Not at all, Henry. I was afraid you might start equivocating. I know Wilbur is a shitty business owner, and I know that he ran the theater into the ground. I know all of that. And so does he. But I don't like the idea of him being compelled by you or anyone else to abandon ship, even if it's sinking."

"I just told him the truth," I say, remembering his gray head nodding and trembling in the windowless closet beneath Le Champo that he used as an office, redolent of popcorn and a sewage pipe that had been leaking inside the wall for some months, but which Wilbur had neglected to fix because of the expense. He said he couldn't afford to close for repairs, perhaps because he had shown the first reel of *La Dolce Vita* endlessly for the past month to fifty empty seats, the second either having been damaged or lost, though this point was left perhaps deliberately unclear. A low watt bulb hung naked as a lynched reprobate above, throwing insubstantial light on the papers I slid across the desk, and which Wilbur ignored. I explained what I was told to explain by Huld, once, twice, and a third time as Wilbur gathered the papers into a neat stack between us, and explained that he just needed more time. I said yes, six months ago. I said if he worked with us, we could get between him and the bank. I gave him a day. He showed up at the A.P.M. office three days later, shitlist drunk, and surrendered the keys.

"You say that like you expect praise," says Denise.

"I try not to tell more lies than I can manage."

"How many can you manage?"

"Less than I think, I'm finding."

"I understand that," she says, beginning to walk without direction down the darkened oblong of Clamence Street, and I follow like a shark pursuing a ship in the hope that someone will be thrown overboard. "Honesty isn't compelling, but stupid people expect it. And since the world is mostly stupid people, you can accomplish a lot by deceiving them. The first time someone called me a hypocrite, I was in a freshman English class, and we were arguing about animal rights. I said something pretty impartial, like 'I don't think animals should be mistreated,' and this sniveling turd called me a hypocrite because I was wearing a leather jacket. So I lied and told him the jacket was actually made of vegan rubber or something, and added that anyone who lives by the sword will eventually have to fall on it to prove a point. And everyone laughed at him, even the professor, who said that hypocrisy between individuals of equal standing does not exist, and is only used to end arguments that the accusing party is incapable of completing otherwise. My point here is lie selectively, and well. People will like you more in the end."

"I didn't lie to Wilbur, because the truth was enough," I say. "But I would have told him whatever was necessary to get Le Champo. I think you know that."

"I also know what you were trying to say when you came into

the café with that huge man the other night," she says (meaning Huld), pausing in her directionless ambulation, and turning to face me.

"And what was that, Denise?"

"Say it now."

"No. Maybe later."

"Say it. Tell me what you wanted to say instead of putting twenty dollars in the tip jar."

"I can't."

"If you don't, I'll consider you one of them," she says as her hand touches my frill, adjusting it away from my face, and resettling the collar of my pea coat in a more typical position. I take a step to the side, as if to avoid this, but she moves with me in a kind of box step, until I surrender.

"I wanted to say," I begin. "That something about you reminds me of my mother. But I couldn't think of how to say that without sounding Oedipal."

"I know what that means," she says. "You don't have to explain it."

"I'm not sure I can," I say. "Wilber told you something?"

"He said that it wasn't your fault. But I still shouldn't see you."

"I appreciate you coming anyway," I say, regretting how limp and robotic this sounds. "What I mean is I think you're so interesting, Denise. I know this sounds creepy, but I want to colonize you."

"Let's not be too honest too fast," she says, though the strange complement seems to please her. "It would be less creepy if we went somewhere rather than walking down a dark street. What's interesting in Acheron, Henry? Aside from me?"

"There's actually an excellent opera playing at the movie theater," I say without thinking. Apparently, I'm so pleased that things are going well that I'll say anything. "A sort of Nazi rendition of Tosca that I choose myself..."

"Is that a joke?" she asks, authentically puzzled.

"Yes. Yes, that was a joke. Apropos of...you know. Actually, it's probably close to 8PM."

"What happens at 8PM?"

"I have to see a man about a dog."

"That's a fuck-off. Do you know that?"

"I didn't, but in this case it's true. Have you met sheriff Blivet?"

7.

THE ACHERON POLICE DEPARTMENT is barracked in a second floor wing of the eponymous town hall, and is normally a pleasure to visit. The hall itself was designed by the same architect responsible for Holmes Hall, a native of St. Johnsbury, VT, who used the Athenaeum in his hometown as model for the building's design. But being a place of civic business rather than a library or art gallery, the blueprint necessitated an augmentation or two (the addition of third story, for example). The outcome is a pleasantly looming edifice of red brick helmeted (or hatbanded perhaps) by a mansard roof, from which extends a periscope-like cupola housing a four-faced clock. The interior is an orderly warren of suited rooms, joined from one floor to the next via spiral staircases (and an elevator in compliance with the firecode), and thematically federated by ash and walnut woodwork, and large Venetian windows. But it is only after I've stood beneath the domed, gothic portico, and cupped my hand against the glass of the front door that I realize however grand it may be, Denise and I are in the wrong place.

"They're closed," I say. "Why are they closed?"

"It's only 8PM," says Denise, backing out from beneath the entrance in order to read the clock above it. My gaze settles on her performing this small, helpful action, and blithering affection swells some internality hidden by my pea coat. I'm suddenly interested in how she feels, rather than what she will do, a sensation of which my life is normally bereft. And rather than unsettled by it, I feel peculiar and fortunate. That is, until my eyes travel from her to what looks like a hurricane relief encampment in a vacant lot across the road; three house trailers arranged in an angular horseshoe, with several police vehicles docked nearby. Now it makes sense.

"The second floor is being renovated," I say, joining Denise on the sidewalk. "I forgot."

"Where are we going then?"

"Across the road," I say, gesturing toward the trailer park bivouac. The lights in the center trailer burn bright, meaning that the sheriff or one of his subalterns is at home. "Prepare to meet a slob."

There is no way to enter a house trailer without feeling impoverished, though tonight the sensation is obviated somewhat by Blivet's congruous occupancy of the place. As Denise and I stand amid a scattering of folding chairs meant to convey the impression of a waiting area, the sheriff lurches in greeting from behind a desk (at which he has just finished a meal that could sate a division of light infantry), his movement spilling a seventy-two ounce wax paper goblet of cola across the shredded remainder of a dozen hamburger wrappers, an equal number of fry cartons, and the latest issue of *Pig Hunter* magazine. No paperwork. That's my job.

"As promised," I say to Denise, though I'm looking at Blivet, whose intentionality is suddenly split by the canine lineup scheduled with me, and the fizzing puddle of rubbish on his desktop. He stands halfway between the sodden furniture, and us, shifting his considerable weight from one foot to the other, his body and brain paralyzed by this unwelcome division of priorities.

"It's like when you give a dog two slippers," whispers Denise (to me). "And it can't pick which to chew first."

"Give me a minute, Henry," says Blivet, the tire of his volition suddenly catching the soft earth of his mind as he casts about the room for something to absorb the soda flooding his workspace, and his eyes settle on the Vermont state flag pinned to the wall behind his desk. He tears the pendant from its mooring, balling the thing between his hands and pressing it at hazard into the puddle on the desktop which, rather than absorbing the soft drink, just washes the pabulum in a tide of brown retrograde effervescence onto the floor.

"Blivet," I say. "Leave that for now. Where is the dog?"

"Goddamn piece of non-absorbent plastic Chinese crap," he says, ignoring me. He drops the stained flag into the puddle on the floor, using one leg to stir it through the congealed and sticky mélange that remains of his meal. He's exerted himself, and the air of the office is briny with the odor of sweat, corn syrup, and food that can be ordered without leaving a car.

"Blivet. Where is the dog?" I repeat, and he pauses in furthering the squalor of his professional environment, the hoggish eyes that earlier fastened obliquely on the now defiled standard of the state paying him at this very moment to continue its debasement settle on me with a puerile species of indignity. As though Blivet and I are two children at the seashore, and for the entire afternoon, I have watched him patiently build sand castles without telling him until his labor has been washed into the ocean that his first mistake was laying its foundation in the tide path.

"Dog's in the jailhouse," he says, his reddened, bellicose face wet with either sweat or tears. I can't tell which, even as his sad eyes find Denise beside me. "Hello there, little lady. Anything I can help you with?"

"I'd like to see the jailhouse dog, Mr. Blivet."

"Sheriff Blivet," I correct, before he can.

"Sheriff Blivet," repeats Denise.

"Oh, that's alright, Henry. No need to be all formal," he says, laying the ruined flag over his desk like a tablecloth, and the ruined magazine over the backrest of a folding chair to dry. "Nice to see you with somebody instead of nobody. I'll take you over there right now."

"Over where?" I ask.

"Town hall."

"I see. You imprisoned the dog in an actual jail cell. I thought it was a figure of speech."

"Nope. I gave her some food and water, and the heat's on down there, so I don't want to hear nothing about inhumane conditions if you please," he says, pushing past us through the door, and out into the night.

"I dig the lawman," says Denise, watching his saturnine bulk wander across the lot.

With Blivet as our conductor, Denise and I recross the street, and navigate the red brick flank of the town hall until we reencounter the sheriff at the base of a set of stairs leading beneath the foundation. The jaundiced glow of a security lamp limns the small window of a door Blivet unlocks, and through which we allow him to lead us down to a cheerless block of cells. Each is as vacant and sterile as the next, until we reach the last, where Denise emits a shrill, affectionate noise as a brindled mongrel of medium-size approaches the bars, its tail swaying like the able arm of a metronome, its pink tongue coiling around her fingers as she reaches past the bars to cup the animal's jowls between her hands.

"Better not," warns Blivet, but it's far too late (as Denise and the dog appear to be holding a synod through the bars), and so his attention searches for something to either regiment or comment upon, passing over the non-option of me, and alighting instead on a sheet of newsprint within the cage. "Did her business on the papers. Good girl. This the dog, Henry?"

"Is this dog blond, Blivet?" I ask.

"Nope. Is any?"

"Not my question. Is this dog fierce?"

"I suppose not," he says, looking at the space above my head, rather than Denise, who is allowing the dog to lick her face through the bars.

"Then I don't think so. Is it even a female?"

"Oh, yeah. I checked out her...her particulars."

"What are you going to do with her?" Denise asks the sheriff, without looking at either of him or me.

"Well, that depends," says Blivet. "You sure this ain't the dog that got you, Henry?"

"I'm not going to answer that again."

"So in that case, I guess I'll call Animal Control over in Waterbury or I'll just drive her down there myself in the morning and see if they can't put an owner to her or find her a forever home or whatever it is they do, of course I might not have time tomorrow it being close to Halloween and got to see about some security measures up at the college and around Clamence, you know how those school kids get when they put on costumes, so maybe it'll have to be after the holiday, but..."

"Is that her food?" interrupts Denise, eyeing a milky puddle on the floor of the cell, upon which two soggy brown grams float like the coeval hatch covers of a scuttled steamship. "Was that an ice cream sandwich?"

"Sure is," says Blivet. "We had a box left over from the softball game with the fire department, good game if you recall, we had them nearly beat when…”

“That was in June,” I say.

“Yeah, but those things keep alright.”

“Dogs shouldn’t eat chocolate,” says Denise, removing her severe, patrician face from between the bars to frown at Blivet.

“Don’t worry, little lady,” he says. “You won’t find much of it in there.”

“Keys,” I say, holding out my hand, and the sheriff places the ring in it with a reflexive obedience not unlike the wagging, drooling quarry I’m about to set free. A twitch or tremor of delayed apprehension seems to scuttle with hairy-legs across the antipodal ponderance of his cheeks, and down the acclivity of his chins, coming to rest (I imagine) between the hairless tumuli of his manbreasts (for warmth, perhaps). I unlock the door, and the dog prances out, bounding between an immovable Blivet, who is still unraveling the mystery of how all of this could have happened, to me as I pass Denise the keys to my car, and returning then to her, who begins leading it up the hall, and toward the door through which we entered the jailhouse.

“I’ll meet you outside,” she says, before the double doors close behind her and the animal, and leaving me alone with Blivet.

“ ‘Surely, joy is the supreme condition of life,’ ” I say, returning his keys, which he accepts as if they are now tarnished, or unusable. “While people are incapable of that, dogs tend to embody it. I suppose that’s why we keep them around. To remind us of failure by way of revealed possibility.”

“What should I say if someone comes looking for that dog?” asks Blivet, ignoring me.

“Tell them a local couple are fostering it. Do not tell them you kept it in an empty building and fed it junk food. Call me if there are any problems."

"She's your girlfriend? Seems like a nice girl."

"Not relevant," I say, starting to walk away.

"Oh, I know it ain't my business, but I just figured you for a...a more quiet, alternative type of person, if you know what I mean."

"I'm not gay, Blivet."

"Of course not, that weren't what I meant," he says, following me up the hallway and through the double doors toward the stairwell. "I just couldn't see you wanting anyone around you, or maybe anyone wanting to be around you like that for too long, like I ain't the most patient fellow ever walked this earth, you can just ask Purvis about that, but you make me look like one those dolly llamas you're always hearing about and I guess I just figure you can't seem to stand anyone for too long so maybe that door swings both ways and that's why I never see you with a girl much longer than the week I figure it takes for you both to realize you're better off alone, and the thing is seeing you now with her I guess I thought the two of you looked sort like you made sense close up, but trust me, Henry, I know all about being a lone wolf, you get yourself kind of addicted to solitude..."

"The Dalai Lama?" I interrupt, pushing through the entrance, beyond which I can hear Denise coursing the dog on the back lawn.

"Is there one in particular that kinda leads the other llamas?"

"Yes. His soul is immortal."

"Must be quiet the alpha dog. Or llama, I guess."

"Goodnight, Blivet," I say, mounting the stairs, but he doesn't allow me to end the conversation.

"You get the chance to see to Dennis today?"

"Not yet. Tomorrow, I think."

"I'm not so comfortable letting something like this go, Henry."

"You're not. You're giving it to me."

"Well, not that I don't trust you, but I don't think that's good enough, because like I said earlier at the pond, I can't have perverts in my town..."

"What about a Purvis?" I say over my shoulder, as I reach the top of the stairs, and turn to face the sheriff remaining at their foot, whose ellipsoidal head sitting on its anti-neck is tilted upward toward me with a sort of turbid anguish in not so much the recollection of the misdeed as the morbidity of it entrusted to me for safekeeping. And as we stand watching each other like tribeless cannibals, he below in the defile of the stairs, and I above at their mouth, I understand it was a mistake to reveal what I know to this man who only a moment earlier knew nothing. I was impatient to join Denise and the dog, and I overplayed my hand, and embarrassed its utility, like shooting a songbird from the sky with a howitzer.

"That's over now," says Blivet, laconically for once, before withdrawing back through the door beneath the building, and leaving me alone, which may be the first time he has ever ended a conversation between us.

8.

DENISE IS SO BUSY MINISTERING TO THE DOG that she doesn't even ask where we're going until I've already passed the recreation field on the edge of town, the bleachers, backstop, and soccer goals softly focused in the pitch of night by a rime of inchoate snowfall.

"I have something I need to do," I say, watching the road through a sheet of flurries. "It's work related."

"I see," she says, pausing a moment. "No, I don't see. What exactly do you do?"

"I'm not sure. I'm currently lobbying for a title."

"How's that going?"

"I've been encouraged to bestow whatever it might be upon myself, and have business cards made."

Rather than responding, she returns to the dog, who sits on the back seat with the plenary and dignified bearing of a Romanesque household god at a lectisternium. She (the dog) is obviously the result of a large breed mated to a small one, with the long legs and sleek, shorthaired coat of a Boxer adducted to the breadloaf body, pointed ears, fox-like snout, and witlessly excited expression of a Welsh Corgi. It's a strange pedigree, but oddly congruent luggage when positioned between Denise and myself.

"I like this dog," I say, reaching behind me to pat its haunch.

A tongue laps my wrist. 'Lovers in a Dangerous Time' plays from the stereo.

"Isn't she dear?" says Denise. "But I think she has your problem."

"How so?"

"She needs a name."

"Something not silly."

"Yes, something not silly. For you both," says Denise. "When people think of another mammal as their property, they tend to get cute and name it something ironic and risky. That's why the founding fathers named their slaves after Greek tragedians, or why every dog in New Jersey is named 'Callie.' Simpleminded fucks. This dog will not be called Taco, or Bailey, or Shadow, or Precious."

"I'll leave it up to you. But how does that apply to my problem?"

"Well, you're an employee, which means that for a certain period of the day, you're someone's property."

"I hope that isn't true," I say, realizing that the reality of my driving to check on Izzy at 10PM in what is becoming a blizzard, after helping Mr. Castle take a shit on a mountaintop earlier this afternoon, only to return to a servant's cabin on his property to be raped by his wife late into the night, and rising early the next morning in order to retread the same irredeemable earth is evidence that would prove Denise at least semi-correct.

"If your time doesn't belong to you, it belongs to someone else," says Denise, sliding the blade of her point a bit deeper. "Work is necessary slavery."

"Not that I disagree, but if we could focus on the more immediate and earthbound problem of what to print on my business cards, I would be in your debt."

"Well, what do you do?" she says. "You claim to write poetry. You manipulate alcoholic cinephiles out of their property. You watch women you do not know with binoculars. You have a strange, corrupt relationship with that man ape of a sheriff. How about: Henry Hoffmann: Poetics. Stalking. Property Management. With a full stop after each?"

"I'm serious, Denise. This is starting to become a problem."

"You still haven't told me where we're going."

"The Sutpen House," I say, knowing this means nothing to her, but trying to think of a way that will sound professional to explain what she will see there. "I'm sure Wilbur told you that I work for Jeremiah Castle. He is a man of some importance around Acheron. You might know his brother, Cornelius, from the college. His son, Isidore, has started a kind of club, and Mr. Castle asked me to help with it. Find locations, stock them with props, and make up background stories for Isidore."

"What sort of club?"

"It's a bit dorky," I begin cautiously, but aware that there is nothing to do except tell it. "He and the sheriff's son, Purvis, they...they look for ghosts in old buildings. They call it the Acheron Paranormal Society. Mr. Castle asked me to look in on him tonight. So that's where we're going. It shouldn't take long."

"So...you're also a babysitter?"

"They call me a 'location scout,' and a 'research consultant' in the credits."

"Credits?"

"They're filming a pilot," I say, as if this somehow justifies anything I've said. "I don't suppose that gives you any ideas?"

"You're the eldest child," replies Denise, rotated in her seat and attending the canine whose yellow eyes meet mine in the rear view mirror with a species of ecstatic, ineradicable contentment I envy. "A son. That's what belongs on the business card."

"Wilbur told you more than I thought you knew," I say, empty and frustrated, yet becoming attached far too quickly to this serene, boyish woman sitting with her feet folded beneath her on the seat beside me, and unwilling to press whatever issue or revelation might subsume the evening if I were to expect something further from it. I think of the playful genealogy of my conversation with Mr. Castle earlier after we came down the mountain, which suddenly seems accidentally sadistic on his part, perhaps only because I expect the townsfolk of Acheron to know nothing more than I do, about me, or anything else. Why not cling to this? At the very least, it clarifies the question of title. My resume in seven words: Henry Hoffmann: Bastard. Tolerated pariah. Private lizard. As Denise said, honesty isn't compelling. But neither is lying to people you don't respect.

9.

Perhaps because of the long nights spent wandering the dilapidated halls of derelict buildings in the dark, with only the sea green glow of his camera's viewfinder as a guide and Purvis as company, Isidore has lately come to resemble a peripatetic, late-adolescent scarecrow. As I turn into the driveway of the Sutpen House, Denise gasps at the figment of him caught in the headlights, stooping to retrieve some characterless device from the rear of the A.P.M. van. In the winnowing snow, he seems part inclement illusion, part man, held to the locality less by the gelid drift climbing his ankle, and more by some unborn, yet wicked obligation to it. When he recognizes the car, his face brokers a smile that ameliorates nothing, adding instead a symptom of rapine to whatever task he's discharging as his eyes fix on me through the windshield, either pupil mounted on a syncline of lunatic fatigue.

"He looks...undead," says Denise, the hand that she is not using to scratch the dog in back seat flattening against the exterior of my thigh in a sort of gestural desperation.

"The opposite of irony is congruity," I reply, opening the door, and reluctantly leaving both the vehicle and her proximity, the anxious touch still warm against the place it fell on my leg.

"Dad said you might be coming," says Isidore, stuffing a bushel of wire into one of the pockets of his utility vest as I approach across the tundra separating us.

"And here I am. Everything okay?"

"Well, it's the last night of the shoot, so we're just trying to make sure we got everything we need so we don't have to come back out here, but since you asked…"

"Because it looks like you have everything under control."

"Oh…Well, sure. Yes, I suppose I do," says Isidore as the uncouth, Gordian knot of Purvis appears from the side yard, a shovel in his purchase leaving a jagged meander through the fresh snow as it drags behind him like a forgotten harrow.

"It's fwozen too much," he says, jamming the spade into a snow bank. "I can't get mowe than few inches down. She pwobably would have buwied them deepew. Hi Henwy."

"That's a problem," says Isidore. "I knew we should have started digging earlier."

"What are you excavating?" I ask, forgetting my story from earlier in the week. Amanda Sutpen? Was that it? Too late to check my notes. Denise and the dog step out of the car, capturing Isidore's eyes, though his attention remains (unfortunately) on me.

"The bodies," he says to me. "The dead babies. Don't you remember?"

"Of course. How could I forget? I just assumed you had them all up by now," I say, scratching between the dog's pointed ears as it passes me in torpedic pursuit of Purvis, who for some reason has attracted the animal's interest. "Isidore, Purvis, this is Denise and…a dog."

"Oh no. Pwease. Down boy," says Purvis, lurching (like his father did earlier in the house trailer) to avoid the dog as she plants her front paws against his columnar thighs, barks once, and begins scratching at his pant leg, as though the sheriff's son is a cupboard door rather than a man half-grown.

"I think what you're doing here is interesting," says Denise, taking Isidore's gloved hand in her own. "What made you want to become a paranormal investigator?"

"No one has ever asked me that," says Isidore, as if the four weeks he's spent attempting to wake the dead constitute a godhead, from which all proceeds with nothing coming before. His history entire, for which, as a man once said, there is no was. "I guess that's what makes it difficult question. P., why are we doing this?"

"Waising awaweness? No! Pwease! Bad dog!"

"Maybe. But I'm hoping it's more than that," says Isidore, either forgetting or refusing to release Denise's hand, though I can't tell which it is. I'm not jealous. I'm patient. "I mean, I want people to know what they see ain't everything there is. There's more here than we can figure out, and maybe we don't want to know about it. Maybe people are scared or maybe they don't care. I know it might seem like I'm just another Captain Arab chasing a whale, but I think part of being a scientist is forcing a horse to drink."

"But that wasn't my question," says Denise. "I asked what made you want to do this. Not why."

"Oh. Uhyut, Right. I see," says Isidore, finally releasing her hand, and looking at me as if I'm expected to either answer the question or remove Denise. "Well...I saw my mom. The day after she died. Just once. But that was enough. She came to my room when I was in bed. I thought I was asleep but I wasn't asleep. And she just came in through the door. She didn't float through the wall or nothing. And she didn't tell me everything would be all right, but I knew that somehow. It was like I wasn't there. She walked around the room a little bit, didn't even seem to notice me, and then she went out. I know how this sounds. I also know what I saw. It was my mom."

"I seen things too," says Purvis from somewhere beyond the vicinity of the conversation.

"Were you scared?" asks Denise of Isidore.

"Well, that's just the thing because I wasn't. I realized why should I be? Things don't become evil when they die. They're the way they are when they was alive. My mom is still my mom. So maybe I want to show people that there ain't always something to be afraid of. But that can go both ways. And a bad person is bad no matter how deep you bury them."

"You got snow tires on the van?" I ask, trying to remind everyone that I'm still working, and feeling somewhat exiled from the colloquy in any case. As Denise listens to Isidore and his war stories with a near anthropological interest, I remain on the margin with Purvis, who has established an armistice with the dog by hoisting the animal into his arms, and beneath his coat. The tips of her paws dangle just below the garment's meridian, and her head emerges from its collar alongside Purvis's like some tragicomic reimagining of Cerberus, while her tongue licks methodically at his patrilineal dewlap.

"We have whatever dad bought them with," says Isidore. "Four season radials or something."

"Be careful on your way back to the house then. It's the first snowfall. They probably won't salt the roads until tomorrow morning. And even if they do, Castle is always last."

"Sure will. You leaving, Henry?"

"I think so. I have to…get Denise home."

"You do?" she asks, more annoyed than surprised, as Isidore withdraws into the back the van to retrieve a black canvass reticule from which he produces an A.P.M. baseball cap and a sheaf of bumper stickers.

"Check out our website," he says, handing this assemblage to Denise. "It's printed on the stickers."

"I'll do that," she says, exchanging her tattered, colorless cap (which seems like a comfort item rather than a fashion statement) for the newer headpiece (which is neither). "Thanks for telling me your story, Isidore."

"Well, sure," he says. "It's good to know what to say when people ask you things like that."

"Hewe is youw dog, Henwy," says Purvis, opening his coat like a back alley watch dealer to reveal the mongrel at home within it, her eyes bright as the faces of two identical clocks as he sets her gently at my feet. "He's vewy fwiendly. Whewe did you get him?"

"Your father found her," I say, coaxing the animal toward the car.

"What's his name?" asks Purvis.

"Sheriff Blivet," I say, my patience exhausted. I tumble the dog into the back seat, and embay myself in the front to wait for Denise as she parses some inanity with Isidore amid the falling snow. The dog and I watch through the windshield, she whining from the back, and I grousing internally from the front.

"I understand," I say to it, the dog's muzzle touching my cheek as she leans between the seats in that peculiar canine habit of experiencing a voice by drawing closer to it. "Yes, I do. Look at her. How can she find all of this interesting? He isn't attractive, is he? You wouldn't know, of course. She's kind to you, and I suppose that's the most you can expect from us savages. Speaking of which, I'm sorry you had to stay beneath the fat one's coat. Though I'm sure it was warm and smelled of ham. But what are they talking about? Look at her. She is beautiful, isn't she? In kind of an ugly way, yes, but beauty at its extremity is an ugliness of sorts. Oh no, he's taken out his phone. Are they exchanging numbers? Now's he gesturing toward us. Or me, rather, I don't think you interest him. I wish she would remove that hat. It makes her look...impressionable. Is that the wrong word? I suppose you wouldn't know that either, because you're a dog. I am a lizard. Ah, here she comes."

Denise opens the door and sits down, greeting the dog but saying nothing to me while I back out of the driveway, the shape of Isidore and the Sutpen House falling into recumbent shadow as my headlights draw away, and angle down the access road toward town. It is only after we reach the main road, and are approaching the town center that she speaks.

"You're not really a poet are you?"

"Honesty isn't compelling."

"And lies are often a response to privation. Do you want to be a poet?"

"Maybe. There is still time for that, I suppose."

"Then what do you write in that notebook?"

"Notes."

"Because if you were a poet," she says, removing the A.P.M. cap (thank god!), and tossing it into the back seat. The interior of the car is vaporous with the scent of her wet hair, and the dog's moist coat caught in the heater. "I think you would find what they're doing very interesting. It's inspiringly ineloquent."

"I'm paid to pretend I'm interested. If they paid me to be inspired, I would appear inspired. And I thought you thought Isidore was pretty."

"That's why you excused us so quickly."

"I don't normally stay that long."

"Jealousy is a privilege, not a right."

"I'm not jealous. I'm at work."

"I see. Where are we going?"

"I don't know," I say, as we pass the recreation field, entering a dormant Acheron, the houses quiet in each dark street, and the few places of business remaining open (at 11PM on a weeknight) seem forever distant, the glow from their windows and doors like the remote running lights of a ship on a still, horizonless sea.

"You said you were going to take me home."

"That was a lie. I wanted to leave. But I will take you home, if you like," I say, turning the car onto Town Hill Road toward the campus, passing removed and sober homes built with their backs resting against the hillside leading to the college, including the abandoned house in which I occasionally watched my mother take her meals. But I don't say anything to Denise, whose mind is elsewhere.

"Isidore is nice," she says, as the guard waves my car past the gate to the student parking lot. "And he is well-intentioned, and passionate. But neither is attractive when underpinned by bull-shit. I'm embarrassed that you think I'm the sort of person who wants a nice man with absurd, inoffensive hobbies. Nice men expect oral sex when they pay for a meal. They put the pussy on a pedestal, and spend their entire career as men sawing away at the dado with their chivalry, not getting anywhere, and then don't understand why women prefer assholes like you."

"I drove you home," I say, angling the car into a spot beside the dormitories. "I could have made you walk. I'm not an as-shole. And I'm sorry for behaving as if I understood what you want, but I don't know you very well."

"Why are we stopped here?" she asks, peering through the windshield at the tenement-like silhouette of the dormitories.

"You said you were a student. This is where students live."

"I should have said something. I just assumed that whatever you were doing had a purpose."

"It normally does when I'm alone."

"Do you want to be alone?"

"I want to take you home so that I know where you live."

"I see," she says, leaning her body toward mine in what I mistake for an intimate prelude, though she is only trying to better reach the dog panting pacifically in the back seat like an oblivious chaperone. Even so, I surprise myself with my eagerness to meet or match her overture, unbuckling my safety belt, and laying a steady hand on the outside of her flank as it shifts toward me. But as her face turns away, I discover too late that I've misunderstood, and rather than removing my hand from her leg, I attempt to disguise my mistake by using it to leverage myself needlessly toward the stereo, which I engage as if it is a fire alarm, completing this pantomime of sexless groping by relaxing in my seat as the ghostly sound of my mother's voice saying my name fills the car. I forgot about that. Fortunately, the music is weirder than the ballet by which I commissioned it, and rather than asking why I would choose this particular moment to cop a feel, Denise examines me for some explanation of the racket I've heedlessly inflicted on her.

"The CD must be skipping," I say, because this seems plausible.

"What is this?"

"A...found sound recording...from Swaziland," I reply, choosing a location whose origin seems as distant and implacable as I wish to be from any responsibility for the recording.

"But...it's just static, Henry."

"You don't hear...anything?"

"It's white noise."

"A voice, for example? You don't hear any voices?"

"There's nothing to hear. Shall we go?"

"Yes. Certainly. Of course," I overassure, ejecting the disc, and returning the car to neutral silence. "Where are we going?"

"My uncle's camp out at the pond."

"Wilbur's camp? On Kranion Pond? You live there? I thought it was abandoned."

"It was."

So, there is no voice, or no voice without the expectation of a voice, which may exist as all things may exist between the umbra and antumbra of speculation and belief. But to an impartial, and emotionless mind, there is only noise. Am I so suggestible that I've allowed Isidore to influence me? Though my impulse is to fling the CD out the window, or better, deposit it in a storm drain where it could never be recaptured, I retain it anyway, changing the music to 'Shine On' by The House of Love, for the benefit of my guest. I need to hear the recording once more, if only to reestablish the frontier between the respective phantoms of Isidore's hobby (as Denise put it) and my private history. If there is really nothing there, I won't hear it.

We leave the parking lot, and at the booth, I have to stop my car to wake the guard, who is asleep with his bearded face resting on a copy of *Extraordinary Popular Delusions and the Madness of Crowds*. He raises the gate with a myopic diffidence, as if he is afraid for his job (a state with which I am beginning to identify), and soon we're descending Town Hill Road toward town. But as we once again pass the humorless lot containing the house in which I lived with my mother, I slow down, because now seems as good a time as any to show it to Denise. And perhaps in some way, I need to purposefully confirm this oomphalos through her, as I accidentally disconfirmed my mother's voice on the recording, by exposing this landmark, my anchor, to someone who doesn't assume it is there. Perhaps where I believe there is a childhood home, there is actually a post office, or an orphanage, or the ruins of a Norman citadel. I must check to be sure.

"That's the house where I grew up," I say brightly, trying to appear certain and not desperate as I point at what there is of it in the darkness beyond the side window. "I still own it."

"You groped me because you thought I was offering myself," says Denise, the house passing without comment or confirmation, though she sounds pleased with herself, rather than frightened by me, which provides a different sort of relief. "I made you think that, but you wouldn't have thought it if it wasn't already there."

"That was a test?"

"An interview, if you like. How does that make you feel?"

"Relieved, I suppose. I doubted my intuition."

"I admire your shame," she says, taking my hand from the steering wheel, cupping it between her own. "It was very sad. As if you couldn't imagine anything worse than being wrong. You improvised. You wanted to believe that grabbing my ass was necessary in order to turn on that awful music just as much as you wanted me to believe it."

"It wasn't music. It was a recording made by Isidore in that house, the place where we were tonight. I thought there was a possibility that it contained the spectral voice of my mother saying my name."

"Well, it isn't there. Her voice, or anything else. There's nothing there except noise," says Denise, glancing at my hand. "What happened to your hand?"

"An older woman chewed on my finger."

"That's interesting, but I meant why did you write 'penis' on it?"

"Your name," I say. "It was supposed to be your name. I didn't want to forget to meet you."

"Would you have forgotten?"

"No."

"So you were reminding yourself of something else, I think," she says, her attention emigrating from me to the dog asleep in back seat. "I imagine she's hungry. Is there anywhere to get kibble at this hour?"

Rather than responding, I stop the car in an alley between Grover's Market and another building, and ask Denise to hand me a circlet of keys and a flashlight from the glovebox. I'm reluctant to reach over her body again and get them myself, not because I don't want to be close to it (and her), but because I'm not certain what it would mean (to either of us). She opens the compartment, and hands me the flashlight and ring, and I shuffle through it until I find what I need, a large key with an internal cut, and a series of numbers taped to the black plastic bow.

"Are you stealing?" she asks, as I open the car door and step into the alley.

"Not exactly."

"Do you have keys for every building in town?"

"Most of them."

"Can I come with you?"

"Please stay here," I say, though I would like to have her company on this small, quietly illegal errand. Though I'm accustomed to working alone, it's refreshing to have a partner (perhaps 'accomplice' is a better word). And since a secret is only a secret if the information withheld is interesting to other people, I have nothing to hide from Denise, because she doesn't care. Is this why I like her? The palisade between my personal and professional life was breached long ago with little chance of repair. When a job becomes the vocational equivalent of an invasive species, people begin to refer to it as a career. I suppose my work for Mr. Castle may be this. Between helping him void himself in the woodland, seeing to Isidore's cryptozoology, and acting as a dildo for Jo, I'm left with very little time to myself. Aside from Grover, whose company I enjoy because of Releaf Tours (not because we schedule playdates), and maybe Denise (though this remains to be seen), I have no friends because I have no time for them.

Romance, as I understand it, is not an option. I haven't slept with anyone other than Jo since June, and even before this, my ancillary liaisons, mostly with young women at the college, were predicated on, or perhaps marked by, a deficiency of emotional progress. I became an expert at explaining why a relationship with me would go nowhere. This was less exhausting than becoming a better liar, which would be necessary if things went well. Because how would I answer the inevitable questions about what I did all day, or worse, all night? That I collect and abuse personal information from the townsfolk of Acheron? That I shelter sexual predators and passionate criminals in order to preserve the reputation of my employer? Or that I'm sleeping with my landlady like a character out of *The Postman Always Rings Twice*? Honesty isn't compelling, unless it comes easily. So I elected to remain alone, until I met Denise. Still, I'm glad she agrees to stay in the car. She doesn't judge the particularities of my life, but they may engulf her (as they did my mother, I suppose) if I don't make some effort to patch the levee formerly dividing my business and pleasure.

I've retained only the car's running lights, and the alley is dim, and soundless aside from my feet creaking in the fresh snow carpeting my path. Worrying about footprints is pointless, because who will catch me? Blivet? Not likely. Between a convoy of trash cans and an industrial dumpster, I use the key to open a side door communicating with a storage area, and type the numbers affixed to the head into a small panel to the immediate right of

176

the egress to disarm the security system. From here, it's a simple navigation with my flashlight between pallets of food, grocery equipment, and translucent sheets of plastic hanging in doorways until I reach the pet supplies aisle.

I have no idea what the dog likes to eat, so I do what seems logical, and choose something that sounds delicious. Thus I proceed with a bag of lamb, brown rice, and sweet potato kibble beneath my arm through the steerage-like murk of the shuttered market, stopping twice more for a bottle of low-sulfite, yeast free red table wine in aisle six, and at a dairy kiosk athwart the butchery for a wedge of caciatta al tartufo.

I take my time in these decisions, examining several cheeses and wine labels with the flashlight before making my selection, enjoying the rare privilege of solitude in public space. This is how I prefer to shop, and Grover is aware that I take certain liberties with his store. Unlike the other keys housed on the ring in my glovebox, the body of which required an equal measure of subterfuge and coercion to procure, the key and code to the market were voluntarily surrendered by its owner 'in case of emergency.' And a hungry dog, kept only hours before in the reckless care of Blivet, is as good an excuse as any to trespass on Grover's credulity. But as I told Denise, I'm not stealing. I'll stop by tomorrow and pay for everything.

I retrace my former path through the rear of the store somewhat clumsily, a wine bottle and thirty pounds of dog food hugged to my chest, and cheese stuffed the pocket of my pea coat. I manage to rearm the security system, and let myself out through the side door without disarranging this burden, and as Denise notices me coming up the alley, she reaches across the driver's seat and pops open the trunk. As I stow my purchases (or borrowings, presently), I'm flushed with the peculiar sense of wellbeing that appears only after a felonious success, a jubilant, adrenal balance between acts committed and comeuppance anticipated possible only when the former is the favorable inverse of the latter. I mean to share some of this with Denise, and perhaps tell her about the wine and cheese, or maybe keep them in reserve as a sort of Hail Mary, or possibly just continue the progress I've avoided for so long.

But when I open the car door, and settle into the driver's seat, the words and their correspondent emotions wither on my arid tongue as I see the beautifully strange and jagged contour of her face in the light from the glove compartment. It's tipped with an uncommon interest toward the pages of my notebook open in her lap.

Thursday

"I assume it's a journal. But if you want the truth, I've never asked, because I don't want to know, and I don't think he'd tell me."
— Grover Ratliff, owner of Grover's Market: Fine Food & Wine, press and logistics coordinator for Releaf Tours, LLC

"…a vibrant, and welcoming community, where everyone knows their neighbor, and won't hesitate to lend a hand…"
— Releaf Tours promotional brochure, authored by Oliver Himmel, copyright Acheron Ventures, LLC, 2011

1.

Denise and I reach the access road leading to the camps on the far shore of Kranion Pond. It is impassible due to the snow-fall, and probably won't be plowed at all. Most surrender these properties to the frost during winter, and the few who visit their summer homes over the season are wont to reach them by either snowshoe or cross country ski. And since I have no troika to portage Denise to her uncle's property on the other side of the unfrozen lake, we'll have to reach it on foot.

From the fishing access where I leave my car, Wilbur's cabin is about a half-mile walk in the lucid cold, and Denise has no jacket. I remove my pea coat, and furl it around her narrow shoulders like a riding cloak. She accepts it without altering her ardent hold on my notebook, but murmurs something resembling gratitude before setting off through the raw intention of the fresh snow, like some hierophant beginning a pilgrimage with the transliteral word of god folioed beneath her arm.

I don't know whether she expects me to follow, though the dog has no such perplexity. She bursts from the car as soon I open the door, tearing Jackal-like across the subarctic steppe between my uncertainty, and the place at the treeline where Denise has paused, half-swallowed in the endarkened throat of the access road. This is where I meet her, shivering with thirty pounds of dog food over my shoulder, and together we proceed beneath a sagging vault of tree limbs hung heavy with snow toward her uncle's camp. At the very least, I'd like to see the dog fed, and my coat returned.

As I glance over the shoulder not supporting the dog's repast, I feel partially exposed by the dim aspect of my car fading into the halflight of the early winter morning, not because someone might tamper with it. If that were to happen, I could find them, and make it right. What worries me is that Jo, or some other member of the household, might see it. The Castle house is only a few miles up the road, and in order to reach the pond, I had to pass it slowly to keep the car from spinning out of control and delivering Denise and myself into the dwelling's lap. She said nothing when I turned the headlights off as we crawled past the family's mailbox, her attention consumed by the notebook. But even the relative insentience of passing unseen before the gate of the house, flatly villainous against the cliffside as a mural in a baroque brothel, did nothing to mollify the sense of exposure I've preserved by leaving my car at the fishing access.

More unsettling is that when I checked my messages before abandoning the vehicle, there were none from Jo. Normally, I receive between three and five a day, and I expected that even if through some befuddlement or extraordinary solipsism, Jo had not learned of my plan to meet Denise from her husband, or the actuality of it from Isidore, she at least would have sent some venomous, jilted missive after finding the pool house in the pine grove empty. But I've received nothing, which can mean many things, all of them bad.

Yet here I am, enduring as we pass the silent, and frozen broadside of each shuttered summer home along the access road, their compound shape resembling not so much a ghost town as a spectral caravan immutably fixed along some icebound trade route. The dog is the only evidence of absurd, boundless life in the craven foreground. She pads between the houses and trees ahead, reestablishing her perimeter with each correspondent movement from us who (by way of this perdition-like artery) arrive intact on the flagstones before the front door of Wilbur's shack.

From without, it appears as ramshackle up close as it does at distance, like a clapboard bunker pitched inscrutably above the soil, with a pronounced, intoxicant incline toward the water. Within, it is a rather comfortable single room, with two large windows opening (though not in this weather) out onto the pond, and a woodstove ticking at the center. As we enter, Denise opens this, prods the glowing coals, opens the damper, and adds more kindling from a pile beside the door. I tear open the dog food, intending to pour some of it into a battered Dutch oven I find orphaned beside the woodpile.

"This isn't for soup, right?" I say, half kidding. But before I can remove the lid, Denise takes it from me, and returns it to the place beside the door.

"No. It's a chamber pot. I didn't realize I was having company."

"We're all adults here," I say, failing to appear as if I find this normal. "Most people don't have a pot to piss in."

"It would be different," she says. "But Wilbur set fire to the outhouse last summer. He was trying to scare a porcupine out of it. While drunk, I think. But you know about that."

"Do I?"

"It's in your book."

"That's why I have the book. I don't need to remember everything myself."

"So, you're a civic historian. Without you, it would be forgotten."

"Not necessarily. You remembered. Wilbur continues to drink. Stories return. But it amounts to the same thing, Denise."

"And what's that, Henry?"

"You making water in a cauldron."

"I shower each day at the campus," she says, setting an electric lantern on the windowsill with a resigned, irritable motion, as if arranging light in the room is a fixed tenet of explaining its occupation. "The facilities at the gym are nice. Since you're interested, I usually move my bowels there as well. I wash my clothes at Wilbur's house. I eat things I buy at Grover's Market. When I'm not doing any of these things, or in class or working, I read and write, or walk in the woods, or take the boat on the lake. I'm not dirty, or mentally ill. I live here because North American solitude doesn't exist, so I'm reinventing it. Maybe you can't understand that. I don't know where you live."

"In a private suite of rooms down the road. With a flush toilet. I would like you to visit."

"I can't understand why."

"Should I leave now?" I ask, the bag of kibble poised above the nothing meant to contain it. I'm unsure who her last remark was meant to disparage; her, or me, or both, so I repeat my question. "Should I leave, Denise?"

"Not yet," she says, setting a place for the dog on a sheet of newsprint beside the fire. Instead of a proper food bowl, she produces a hollow, jubilant-looking plastic skull from an unlit corner of the room, the sort of spooky bucket children use to trick or treat, and another in the shape of a grimacing orange Jack O'Lantern.

"More chamber pots," I say, discovering how stupid and unnecessary this sounds in the emptiness left behind as Denise steps outside to pack the pumpkin with snow to water the dog. Why must I keep mentioning this one shameful detail of her life (as I know it so far)? Perhaps because the rumor of serenity I noticed the first time I saw her paddling her canoe across the lake is no longer a rumor; she is authentically content here in this tumbledown shed. What I feel may be envy, or the fear that within this contentment, there is no place for me. So I disparage it, preemptively eroding the promise of an office I have yet to fulfill (and consequently reducing the chance of fulfilling it all). But if I'm turned out into the hollow night like a common recidivist, I will control the reason and intent. And thus, I will regain myself. I hope.

But as she retreats from the patient immobility of the room with the bereaved raiment of my pea coat across her shoulders, I understand that it is far too late to regain anything resembling my vanity, and I've only succeeded in casting an aspect of grief against what remains of our time together. And now, there is only duty to the ravenous animal whining at my side. As the dog climbs my leg, I fill the plastic skull to the brim with kibble, and then sit with my back against the wall below the windows, watching her eat.

"I'm sorry you were so hungry," I say. She ignores me, ferociously burying her muzzle in the undersized aperture, and tipping the vessel onto the newsprint in order to reach the grains on the bottom. "I'm also sorry that you don't have a name. Maybe Denise will pick something. She should do it. You like her. I like her, too. We have something in common, dog."

"Do you?" says Denise from the doorway which I did not hear open. She closes it, places the plastic pumpkin of melting snow beside the dog, and crosses the room to join me beneath the window, performing each motion with the privileged exactitude of a child athlete.

"I'm sorry," I say. "I don't care where you pee. I just don't want you to throw me out."

"I don't go in anything that can hold it," she says, gesturing at the dog's meal area or, more accurately, toward the skull and pumpkin from which the animal eats. "Wilbur was going to throw them away. I thought they were interesting. Now they're here. I don't know why he had them."

"I do. He took me trick or treating once."

"How old were you?"

"Young, but old enough to be uncomfortable. I could tell that my mother didn't want him to take me, but I didn't know why. There was a problem with the Halloween party at the hotel, and they called while she was putting on my makeup."

"What was your costume?"

"A basilisk. But everyone thought I was a dinosaur. It didn't matter. Wilbur tried to be fun. He wasn't drunk, but I think he was waiting to drink, which is much uglier."

"He rushed you?"

"No, I rushed us. He was sweating a lot, and his voice was too excited. His costume was embarrassing."

"He dressed up?"

"Like I said, he tried to be fun. I think he stopped somewhere to get a costume before he met my mother and me at the hotel, but it was Halloween night, so the selection was limited. I just remember him getting out of his car in this undersized..."

"What was it?" asks Denise from within the cowl of my coat. "You can't remember?"

"No, I can. I'm just still not sure what he was supposed to be. He was wearing this furry tunic that was several sizes too small, and a hairy mask that wouldn't fit over his head, so he just sort of wore it like a hat. He looked like a gerbil or some kind of rodent, but I can't imagine that 'vermin' is such a popular costume choice that he could have found it with limited notice."

"A werewolf maybe."

"Maybe. The point is I had to spend the evening with this man accompanying me to the homes of people we both knew. The hairy mask was really the worst part. It made his head look deformed, and had these ridiculous pointed ears similar to the dog over there, but not cute. Wait, no, I'm sorry, the tail was the worst part. I think he was too large around the middle to fasten it properly, so he just shoved it down the back of his pants. He looked like roadkill. And because the assemblage was made of cheap material, he sweated into it all night. And when he offered me one of those buckets to collect candy, it was so wet from his hands that I declined. I just couldn't imagine eating anything that had touched it."

"Was it the skull or the pumpkin?"

"Both. He wanted me to pick. He must have got them when he picked up the costume. I had a pillowcase that made sense in the context of my costume. And I was also old enough to be non-plussed by a strange adult buying my things."

"Wilbur is harmless."

"I know. But having to appear with him looking like a failed mascot in front of all the foolish townsfolk was mortifying, even for him, I think. Neither of us mentioned it afterward. I would have forgotten about it if these buckets hadn't returned to haunt me."

"Did your mother dress up?" asks Denise, tugging at a blanket spread beneath us. I raise myself a bit so she can straighten it properly, and realize that we're sitting on her bed, which seems promising. Though it isn't really a bed, more of a pallet or nest of soft things, mismatched pillows, several rugs, and two sleeping bags zipped together. Beneath these articles is what looks like an overstuffed body bag.

"On what am I sitting?" I ask, poking the thing with my index finger as Denise draws a sheet tight against its margin.

"It's stuffed with hay," she says brightly, watching me. "I piss in pots and sleep on straw. All the comfort of the middle ages. The year is in fact 1453, and Constantinople just fell to Mahomet II."

"I just meant…" I reply, scrambling for something that doesn't sound like an opinion. "I just meant…it's interesting. Did you make it?"

"One of the hippie girls at the college did. It was sort of a failure, as you can see. It's more of a bolster than a mattress. She was going to tear the thing open and start again, but I gave her twenty dollars for it because I was tired of sleeping on the floor."

"That's understandable," I say, returning to the haybag. "She was a cat. Just the ears attached to a sort of headband, and some very slight whiskers painted on either side of her nose. And a tail pinned to her skirt. She hated doing it, but she had to for the Halloween party at the hotel. Actually, she didn't have to do anything. She ran the place. But I think she didn't want to be the only person without a costume."

"No one wants that."

"Acheron is a small town. The people here don't notice anything important. But they see that kind of thing. Deliberate separateness. She was making her job easier."

"You should try that."

"You're the second person to suggest that this week. I understand what you both mean, but it's too late."

"Do they know what you know?"

"Some do. I try to only share what's important, when it's important," I say, standing, and stepping over the sated body of the dog sleeping before the ticking woodstove in pursuit of the wine. "Would you like a glass of something?"

"There are no glasses. Just bring it here, and we can share the bottle."

"Yes, but a corkscrew?"

Denise rises from the bed, and takes the wine bottle from my hand uncertain hands. Standing heron-like beside woodstove, she removes one shoe, and places the bottom of the bottle in the place formerly held by her foot. She crosses the room, and I follow with the apprehension of an acolyte preparing for induction into some intra-order mystery or rite, and watch with a certain worried glee as she bangs the heel of the shoe against the wall above the bed several times. The cork slides further from the bottle's mouth with each blow until it is removable. She hands it to me and removes her other shoe with one hand, while using the other to tap a cassette player on the floor. I hear the open bars of 'Total Recall' by The Sound.

"The lead singer was a schizophrenic," I say, nodding toward the music. "He killed himself."

"How do you know what's important?" she asks, ignoring me and reclining on the bed, her dark hair like a wave of dragon blood against the pale topsheet.

"I don't always know," I reply, sitting beside her bare feet with the back of my head resting against the cold window glass. "Tonight with Blivet I didn't know. I said more than was necessary. Now he knows too much. Or he knows exactly what he knew before. But he knows I know it. I was impatient. Being near you makes me impatient. Or, the possibility of being near you."

"What happens now?"

"Probably nothing," I say, withdrawing the cork from the bottle, and passing the wine. "He has no power over me. But our professional relationship will become harder. I'll need to watch him differently."

"How many people do you need to watch differently?"

"That depends on what I need from them."

"And you're not afraid one dark night someone will drop a brick on your head?"

"The people of Acheron are cowards, and most of them can't do anything to me without exposing whatever they're hiding. They're all guilty. Everyone has a something they wish to conceal, and whether or not I know what it is doesn't matter. They believe I know, and that's enough."

"Wilbur thinks you're revenging yourself on them. Because of what they think you did to your mother."

"How convenient for me," I say, accepting the bottle. "Of course, I couldn't enjoy watching simple people suffer. That would be monstrous. It's generous of him to provide me a motive and a chance of redemption. Once I've revenged myself upon Acheron, life will return to normal for the good villagers. What hogwash. I didn't create their despicability. I compiled it. Shame on me."

"I enjoyed reading it."

"What Wilbur doesn't know is that I've been watching and recording since before he took me trick or treating. I never knew why, and I didn't think I needed a reason. When I started working for Mr. Castle, it became more methodical, and orderly. But it didn't start because of what happened to my mother."

"Would she approve?" asks Denise, tugging the bottle from my hand with the same motion she used earlier on the sheet.

"I don't think so," I say. "Maybe she wouldn't care. My job isn't to please ghosts."

"Remind me what it is."

"We had that conversation."

"You're an adult child of workaholics. Your mother and Mr. Castle."

"I don't think he is my father. But I see what you mean. And even he was, it wouldn't matter. His enclave is mine, if I want it."

"You don't, of course."

"What would I do with it? My name wouldn't look right on a building. Hoffmann Hall. Abandon all hope, young scholars," I say, needlessly checking the time on my phone. "It's quite late. Or rather early. I should go."

"I assumed you would stay here," says Denise, dipping her feet into the doubled sleeping bag, and reaching for the lantern on the windowsill. "I don't think that sex with you is a possibility. But I can't send you back out there. Does your fancy car even have snow tires?"

"I usually get them after Halloween," I say, removing my shoes and folding my legs modestly beside her own as she darkens the light, leaving only the widowed glow of the woodstove. I'm maniacally relieved that I don't have to return to the house. Though I want her, I want this more, and as a sort of expression of gratitude toward my host, I do my best not to touch her at all. Instead, I balance my body like a plank on the margin of the narrow mattress to prevent it from rolling into natural depression in the middle. I'm determined not to make a pig of myself, even if I must spend the entire night this way. The discomfort is nugatory compared with another evening with Jo.

"Why are you all the way out there? Have you taken some vow, Henry?" asks Denise, reaching across my chest to grasp my shoulder, and roll the toppled pylon of my body toward her own. "I know I said no sex, but you can touch me. Unless my country manners repulse you."

"No, I just didn't want to seem like I didn't understand you."

"There is such a thing as listening too well. Please, come here. You can't possibly be comfortable. Have you ever done this before?"

"I don't know," I say, unsure what she means, even as she places my hand on her hip, and her mouth to my cheek.

"How unfortunate. I'm going to turn toward the wall and lean against you. You're going to support my body with your body so that we don't fall onto the floor."

"What do I do with my other arm?"

"It's your choice," she says, pressing her back into my chest. "There is no good answer."

I fold my top arm beneath my head as my nose and mouth touch the mantle of her hair. It smells not unpleasantly like lakewater and dog, with an unconfirmed, ligneous rumor of the cabin itself. The straw creaks as we settle against each other, and I try to keep my lips away from the avian contour of her neck, pillowing my cheek against it instead. Her pulse blinks against my eyelid like the opportune touch of an insect on still water.

"Dora, I think," whispers Denise through an interregnum of sleep. "For her. The dog."

And I simply nod into the shape between her jaw and shoulder, offering concord yet saying nothing. I remain dormant through most of the night, only waking once to stray sound of Denise using the chamber pot across the room. I hear it, like light rain falling on a breastplate, but see nothing, and fall back asleep before she returns to the bed.

2.

THE NEXT MORNING, Dora awakens me by installing herself six inches from where my face rests on the edge of the bed, breathing into my mouth. As I open my eyes, I hear her tail swishing the floor, her witless excitement apparent even before her tongue touches the space between my nose and upper lip (my philtrum). Beyond her, the dull wood of the cabin's interior is somewhat enriched by morning sunlight reflecting off the sheen of fresh snow I see beyond the windows as I sit up in bed. A note is stuck to the bottom pane with a substance I only realize is a chewed bit of candy corn after I've rolled it's abstruse constitution between my fingers. No matter. Her mouth touched my cheek last night. This is somewhat removed from that and, in theory, more hygienic. What does the note say?

Class & work. Stove is shut down. Return tonight, or pick me up at SG. Took notebook and jacket. Take Dora (dog).
-Denise

Rather laconic for a writer. The note reads like Blivet wrote it. I fold it twice and place it in my pocket, wondering whether I should worry about the welfare of the property with which Denise has absconded. I like the jacket, but do I need it? I don't know. At worst, I'll spend the day frill-less. On the other hand, the notebook is irreplaceable, but I've worked with it beneath my seat for so long, that I have no idea whether or not it is necessary. Nor do I know why Denise has taken it, yet I'm unbothered by her theft. She wouldn't let anything happen to it, and even if something did, what would that change?

As I swing my legs out of bed, the dog places her paws on either thigh, raising herself as if reluctant to reduce the distance between her muzzle and my face.

"I've been given instructions for you, Dora," I say, withdrawing Denise's note from pocket, and pretending to read it closely for animal's benefit. "Ah, here it is. It says that I'm to take you with me. Today is bring your dog to work day. But I suppose you're hungry."

Dora drops to the floor as I stand, and pads after me as I cross the room to fill her skull bucket with kibble. While she eats, I take the pumpkin outside, and pack it with fresh snow, standing for a moment in the yard before the cabin to judge how cold I'll be walking back to the car without my coat. The day is warmer than might be expected from the weather the night before, and the silence abiding the skinless lake at my back is interrupted only by the pacific impact of melting snow dropping from a tree branch onto the ground. Bare patches of wet dirt already scar the innate quiet of what would be a winter landscape if the day were not unusually vernal.

Dora passes me going out of the cabin as I walk inside to deliver her snow pumpkin, and I follow her down the edge of the lake, where she dips her muzzle in the water to drink.

"Smart dog," I say to her backside, as I empty the pumpkin and return to the cabin to gather my things. I do my best to make the bed, straightening the sheets, and smoothing the tandem sleeping bag. I notice the unimpeached cheese on the windowsill. Denise probably left it there after she discovered the wedge in my coat. I worry briefly that she might think I have a habit of storing food in my pockets like some itinerant ragpicker. Though if this were true, it would be far less repellent than keeping a diary of blackmail, or playing a spurious recording of my mother's ghost voice. Yet, after unearthing firm evidence of personal and professional abnormality, she allowed me to stay. I'm being fussy. The pocket cheese is likely a non-issue. She likes me at least half as much as I like her, which is fine for now.

The empty wine bottle sits on the floor by the woodstove, and I pick it up, intending to throw it away, but find no trash receptacle within what I hope will become a purlieu. I could not return to my small house in the pine grove beside the much larger house on the ridge, and remain content. But whatever I want, I must proceed as usual for the moment (though what is usual seems to change each day).

First, I need to see Dennis before Blivet leans on him. Though the words I exchanged with the sheriff last night were unwise, the warning may have been too subtle. It's possible I succeeded only in adding a family concern to the crisis of leadership defining our relation. There was already a target on my back, but mentioning Purvis' misstep with the underage girl didn't make it any smaller, and likely added a ring or two to the petticoat.

"Come, Dora," I say, gathering the little I brought to the cabin (subtracted from the pea coat), and closing the lockless door behind the dog as she follows me outside. We begin walking between the becalmed faces of the summer homes, all of which look empty rather than evacuated in daylight. I unwrap the cheese and gnaw it like piece of fruit, passing an odd morsel to Dora as we make our steady way back to the fishing access.

I'm quietly surprised that I remembered to drink the wine, but forgot the caciatta al tartufo. It would have made a nice complement. Although, in misremembering it, I've provided myself with accidental breakfast. Perhaps this is how god works; the fulcrum for interpreting symmetry in a vast, amoral, and more or less gentle universe. By way of some garbage left in a slough, I've found Denise, a beading of circumstances only problematic for it elevating Morton Downing, a drunk and a day laborer, to divine office. I suppose this is why the science of fate is not a science at all, but an emotional prefecture for cowards. I don't think I'm a coward, but I'm usually lucky, which is to say I often benefit from the particular draping of events along the overhung clothesline of mortality. And since nothing listens, I am not grateful. But after last night, this is the only morning I can recall waking up and wondering whether Fortune, who so blindly distributes and resumes her favors (as Gibbon said), will reduce or end my happy accidents, and return me to the body of those acting in her shadow rather than at her side.

3.

I knock three times on the door of Dennis's bungalow before trying the handle. It's 9AM on his day off, and there's no reason he wouldn't be at home, and even if he isn't, I'll wait. Also, his car is in the driveway. There's no hiding from me, or Blivet. I just hope I've arrived first.

The nob turns in my hand, but the door swings open voluntarily, because Dennis is standing on the other side of it. A bathrobe carelessly bands his middle, a cup of decaffeinated tea steams in his club-like fist, and his pink, depilated legs are planted in a puddle of moisture darkening the runner, as if he has wet himself.

"Sorry, Henry," he says. "I was in the shower. I only just heard the door."

"We need to have an unpleasant talk," I say. Beneath the wet recession of his hairline, two undisciplined eyes like bits of coal leavened into the head of a snowman travel the length of my arm until they fix dully on my hand still grasping the doorknob.

"If I had known you were going to see yourself in, I would have finished my shower."

"Now you know," I say, walking past him into the living room. Dora follows without waiting for an invitation, and jumps onto the couch beside me as I sit down.

"Henry, if we could..." says Dennis, gesturing at the dog, who has started digging at the cushion beneath her.

"Could we what?"

"I'm allergic."

"To what, Dennis?"

"Dogs. And cats. Things with fur."

"Suffer then."

"But, please, couldn't we just put him outside? I have a nice yard out back, with a fence and he would..."

"She," I say. "It is a lady dog, Dennis. And no. This won't take long."

"But the last time I allowed a dog in my house, I was sick for weeks, and I know how you are about attendance at A.P.M., so you're really doing us all a disservice because..."

"Don't threaten me, you graceless clod," I say. Dora pauses in her excavation of the cushion, turns three concentric circles, and lies down. Aside from her tail beating against the backrest of the couch as her eyes watch Dennis fixed wetly in the egress as if he just emerged from a shipwreck, she is still. "Has Blivet been here?"

"Not yet."

"What does that mean?"

"I don't know," he says, his eyes watching everything other than me above the rim of his mug as he sips primly from it. "What do you want, Henry?"

"I need everything that proves you're a pervert. Pictures. Cameras. Photo albums. All of it. And the belt Sharon gave you."

"The belt?" he says, somehow looking both indolent and bereaved. "I'd prefer to keep that. It was a wedding gift."

"Well, next time you're planning to lie around someone's flowerbed, don't wear anything that has your name printed on it. Don't get me wrong. I'm just as surprised as you to learn that Blivet is not only literate, but can read backward. But however remarkable, those are the facts. Why are you still standing there?"

"She's licking my couch," he says, looking with muted horror at Dora, who is tonguing a stain of some kind on the furniture's armrest.

"In the future, watch where you lay your gravy," I say, standing up. "Do you understand what I need?"

"Yes, Henry."

"Then go get it. I'd like to leave. Your house makes me uncomfortable."

I hear his wet feet slapping the wooden floor as he withdraws into some annex of this spider web he calls a home to bundle his archive, leaving me alone to wonder why he agreed to surrender it so easily. I expected some kind of argument, but Dennis seemed more upset about Dora than losing what, for better or worse, could be considered his life's work. Could it just be the stultifying dispassion that comes with using pharmaceutical medication? Perhaps for Dennis, the emotional impact of a plane crash is the same as a sparrow colliding with his dining room window. I've seen his scripts. There is no way he could take that many pills without his sense of tragedy flatlining. But there is never a single reason for anything, and even as I stand in the foyer, and accept the duffle bag from Dennis, I can't decide whether I'm doing the right thing.

"I don't want to see what's inside," I say. "But I'm going to assume that it's all here."

"Yes," says Dennis, the eerie complacence hanging about him like a sentient, mocking shroud. "Even my laptop. What will you do with it all?"

"That's no longer something you need to think about," I say, opening the door. "I wasn't here, and you didn't give this to me, because there was nothing to give."

"As you like it," says Dennis, joining his hands behind his back, and rocking backward on his heels like a butler waiting for a parade. He appears almost cheerful. I can't take much more of this.

"Why are you doing this?" I say, closing the door, and setting down the duffel bag.

"Doing what?"

"Giving up everything that makes you interesting without a fight. I expected more, Dennis. Even from you. Tell me why."

"Because you told me to," he says, unclasping his hands and spreading them to either side of his rotundity like a distended portrait of Jesus Christ. "I don't like you, Henry. But I trust you."

"You're lying."

"I wish I was," he says, turning at the sound of a kettle from the kitchen. "I always thought you pick the people you trust. But it's not that way."

"Faith is for stupid men," I say weakly, and to his back as it disappears up the hall, waddling toward the ecstatic whistle. I have no idea whether he heard me, and I don't care. His answer left me unsatisfied. And though I want to pursue him to the kitchen, patiently explain my dissatisfaction, and perhaps shatter one or two of his teacups against an opposing wall, I simply don't have time. Blivet might appear at any minute, and I'm standing in the foyer with a bag of what he would consider evidence.

"Let's go, gorgeous," I say to Dora, who snatches one of Dennis' running (or lumbering) shoes from beside the door before padding down the front walk after me. I cross the street to my car, and drop the bag in the trunk, relieved to be rid of its weight, which is probably great enough to consign the thing to watery grave beneath the surface of Kranion Pond. No stones needed, should I decide to get rid of it that way. But there is always a chance that some unemployed sportsman like Morton will snag it, and mistake the burden for treasure chest or something of similar fictive value, and draw it stubbornly from the water. I could burn it. But where? The incinerator beneath city hall is too close to Blivet's bivouac, and the woodstove in Wilbur's cabin is too small. I also can't imagine buoying the sort of lie necessary to explain to Denise why I'm using her home's only source of heat to cook pornographic photographs if she caught me. I could just drive to an isolated location, like the back yard of the Sutpen House, and douse the bag in accelerant, drop a match, and let it take care of itself. Or better, I could simply expand one of the holes dug by Purvis last night, and bury the entire thing. But this presents the same problem as sinking it. No matter. The point remains the same. Dennis' collection must be destroyed today.

I open the side door for Dora, and once she is comfortably installed in the passenger seat gnawing Dennis' sneaker, I start the car, and instantly hear a siren. The shoe falls onto the floor, as Dora sits upright (for a dog) in her seat at the unpleasant noise. The police cruiser must have pulled up after I went inside the house, because it was not parked out front when I arrived. I suppose I was too busy drafting the demise of the porn collection in my trunk to notice it on the way out. But there it is. Or here they are actually, Deputy Roland and his new partner in peacekeeping, a sort of bell-shaped human avalanche whose name I do not know. The nameless one rolls down the side window of the police car as it slips shark-like beside mine, his face impassive as the underside of a paving stone, and I do the same without expression.

"Turn the siren off, please," I say. "It's bothering my dog."

"Sure," says Roland, bobbing his ginger head and obliging me, but leaving on the lights. "Can you cut the engine, Henry?"

"Afraid not, Roland. I was about to leave, you see."

"Deputy Roland," says the man who we've been speaking across as though he's a dining room table.

"Your name?" I ask him.

"Deputy Downing," says Deputy Downing. He's the sort of man who can't look at anything without rotating his entire body like a paper target at shooting range, and he does this as he speaks to me across the distance between our car windows, his shoulders entirely eclipsing the tensed, freckled face of Roland in the driver's seat. "And you'll remember to call me that. Same with Deputy Roland."

"Downing. That's an interesting name," I say. "Any relation to the alcoholic?"

"He's my father," says Deputy Downing, apparently speaking from reflex, because he suddenly looks ashamed, as if he's been answering this question his entire life, and yet, can't believe what came out of his mouth. Though, like his father, this transitions quickly to anger, not with himself, for answering the question, but me, for asking it. It doesn't matter that the information we've just exchanged is accurate, and not particularly impolite. Wrath is beyond truth. "And I know you, Henry Hoffmann."

"You know what you're told," I say. "And that is all you know."

"The way I figure it," says Downing. "You probably stuck her up there with all them other ones. In that forest they got out back of the college. A lot of bodies up on Aornum Hill come Halloween. What's one more? And I figure that's why no one could find anything, because she was right there the entire time."

"Who was right there the entire time?" I ask.

"Your mom," says Downing, the wicked flatland of his face contorting into a smile of sorts. "See? I know all about you."

"You've inherited your father's gift for crapping where he eats, and then passing the plate," I say. "Do you see how that applies to your birth, Downing?"

"That's enough, both of you," says Roland from somewhere behind Downing. "Please, Henry. We're not here for that."

"Why are you here?" I ask him, though my eyes are on Downing. Beneath his view, I hold the running shoe that Dora dropped on the floor. He has a head like a turret, and the performance footwear would likely stun him at most. I wish I had something that would draw blood.

"We need you to turn the motor off, and step out of the car, Henry," says Roland, with a solemn, apologetic gravity. "I don't understand it myself. But we got a call…"

"Why are you telling him all that?" says Downing, rotating himself to address his partner, whose face reappears from behind the storm cloud of the other deputy's shoulders like a beleaguered ginger sun. "We need him out of that car. It doesn't matter why."

"That's fine, officers. I know who called," I say, as Dennis incautiously steps from the front door of his house across the street. He stands on the front steps as he did earlier in the entrance to his living room, wearing only a bathrobe with a cup of tea billowing in his fist, watching the scene of which he was doubtless a draftsmen. So this is what I missed. Pawn takes rook. So be it, sly fox. I wave, and he waves back, attracting the attention of the officers between us.

"Get back inside, retard!" shouts Downing.

"Back in the house, Dennis," affirms Roland.

"Just checking the mail," says Dennis, fishing in the mailbox attached to the house with his free hand, but retreating inside as Downing steps out of the car, though he isn't interested in Dennis. He's interested (the wrong word, perhaps) in me.

"Get out of the car," he says, laying a large, saurian hand on the window. Somewhere in the foreground, I hear Roland's door open, and his shoes touch the pavement. "Don't make me drag you through the window."

"You want what's in my trunk," I say. "Isn't that right?"

"We don't know what's in your trunk. That's why we need to search your car. But we can't do that with you sitting in it. I'm going to ask one more time, and…"

"You'll stand right there while I call Blivet," I say, removing my phone from the console. "And get your dinosaur hand off my car before I close it in the window."

"You want to call Blivet?" he says, momentarily withdrawing his bulk to address Roland, who is presumably stationed nearby. "He wants to call Blivet! Isn't that something?"

"He told you to come," I say, more to myself than either Deputy. I toss the half-dialed phone into the back seat, because it can do no further good. This is the sort of mess in which Mr. Castle pays me not to involve him. If I need his help, I'll go through Huld, though a call to him now would only immobilize the situation with the deputies even more. I don't want to spend the rest of the day locked in my car in front of Dennis's house, providing him with an impotent cinema of revenge, and Downing with an excuse to use any of the sadistic implements girding his middle, while the family lawyer drafts paperwork. Like all empowered fools, Blivet is a man of bottomless will. I could be here all night. And calling Jo is not an option, a priori.

"Gentlemen," I say, as I shift the Audi into drive, and roll it calmly out of the parking spot, around the parked cruiser, and in the direction of Clamence Street. Downing is still facing Roland, and it only seems to catch the former by surprise. In the rear view, the larger deputy begins doggedly chasing the car, his body like the nose cone of a misaligned shuttle losing speed at middle altitude. I engage the window, muting whatever warning he's bellowing at my retreating vehicle, and continue driving until his uniform bulk grows small (or of normal size, for him) in the mirror. As I turn left at the corner, he rejoins Roland, who hasn't moved from beside the cruiser. While his partner gave chase like a ponderous foxhound, the other deputy only watched, shaking his ginger head, and wringing his pale, freckled hands. I remember Roland from high school. He was consistently nice, and devoid of superlatives, the sort of boy child forever found in a state of middle achievement, and who, in recognizing his incapacity for anything truly remarkable, seeks instead to befriend those who will eventually establish the social margin in which he shall be a permanent citizen. In following, he's grown into a forgettable man, useful only as a vocational foil for people like Downing, who wield volume in place of credibility. If they weren't trying to clap me in irons, their need for one another would be almost sympathetic.

"That was fun, wasn't it?" I ask Dora, who is somewhat becalmed now that the car is moving again. She politely sits with her front paws between her haunches on the front seat, watching the road rather than the squalling cop car that has just turned the corner behind us. "I have no idea what to do next. Though I should probably drop you off someplace neutral. Unless you want to go back to jail."

She licks my chin as I lean between the seats to retrieve my phone from the back of the car. I don't have Denise's number, but since Isidore is fond of using it as a rendezvous, I do have the listing for Sacred Grounds. If she isn't there, they might know how to reach her or I'll leave my number, and hope she calls me back. But apparently my luck hasn't entirely deserted me this morning, because she answers the phone on the third ring.

"You're calling me at work," she says. "I don't like that."

"I'm sorry. I had no other way to reach you."

"Pull over now!" shouts the stentorian voice of Downing from a speaker atop the police car behind me.

"What was that?" asks Denise. "Are you at an auction?"

"I'll tell you later. Can you take Dora if I bring her to you?"

"I'm at work, but…"

"Henry! Pull the goddamn car to the side of the goddamn road right goddamn now!"

"Seriously, what is that?" she asks. "Are you in trouble? I hear sirens."

"What I need you to do," I say. "Is meet me outside the coffee shop in about ten minutes. I'm going to pull over and open the door, and you grab Dora. She's in the front seat."

"Yes," she says. "Fine, I think. But I don't understand why…"

"Please, Henry," cringes the sedate voice of good cop Roland from the loudspeaker. "We just want to sort this one out, but we can't do that unless you pull over."

"Look, Denise, I'm in a bit of a situation," I say, watching the cruiser draw within a foot of my bumper in the rear view with Roland's voice bleating from it. "I just want to make sure Dora doesn't go back to jail. Do you understand?"

"No. Why would she go back to jail? What did you do, Henry?"

"Come on, Henry. Pull over, so we can talk about this. Just talk, on my word."

"It doesn't matter what I did," I say. "And in point of fact, I didn't do anything. I was in the right place at the wrong time. You have my notebook?"

"Yes."

"And it's in a safe place?"

"I suppose. It's here with me."

"Good, so that leaves only the dog to worry about. Can you take her from me in ten...actually, closer to five minutes. I'm about to turn onto Clamence. Will you meet me?"

"Yes, Henry. I hope whatever you didn't do was worth it."

"It wasn't," I say. "Not this time."

As I turn onto Clamence Street, the midday pedestrian traffic bear witness to the peculiar matinee of my Audi purring past them at a polite speed with an Acheron Police Department patrol car following closely behind it as though I'm being martially escorted rather than pursued. The blaring siren seems to attract most of the attention from the passerby, while the voices of Roland and Downing broadcasting a program of alternating precatives and threats from the rooftop of their vehicle hold and sustain it. I crank up the music, 'Red Sails' by China Crisis, and wave to a few people stopped on the street to watch the parade, and they respond with a hesitant decorum, like theatergoers after the fourth wall has been torn down. Denise is among them, standing between parked cars in front of Sacred Grounds, with her arms crossed as if held by a straight jacket, and her brow forming a worried knot above a face that seems frozen by the choice of which question to ask first.

As my car draws abreast of Denise, I tap the accelerator to place some distance between myself and the other vehicle, and then stomp on the brakes. The Audi stops easily enough, but the police car behind it emits a querulous, mechanical bark as it lurches to an unexpected halt. I undo my safety belt, and quickly reach over Dora to open the passenger door, but Denise has already scooped the dog into her arms, and withdrawn to the street where she watches me with an unreadable expression as I watch Roland and Downing exit their vehicle through the back window. Downing cups a bloody hand over his nose and mouth, and Roland looks slightly more worried than earlier.

"I didn't want to leave her alone," I say to Denise as if this explains everything she has just seen.

"Whatever this is," says Denise, gesturing with her body toward the two cars, and their occupants. "Return from it. I think that's what I want."

She closes the passenger door before I can respond, which is fortunate, because Downing and Roland are in formation, skirting the flanks of my vehicle. And it's too early to know how to reply to her. She and Dora are reabsorbed into the breach between the parked cars, and I touch the gas pedal, and slip from between the officers, both of whom look defeated in the rear view as I pilot the Audi to the head of Clamence Street, and turn left onto the road leading out of town.

I'm not trying to outrun Roland and Downing. Where would I go? My tenuous dominion ends for the most part at the county line, while theirs (that of the law) is theoretically infinite. If I drive to the next county, I'd be outside Blivet's jurisdiction, but if he is serious about catching me, he'll probably involve the neighboring police department. Even with Huld's help, that would make this chain of nonsense far more difficult to unlink.

But if I remain in Acheron, I can't allow Roland and Downing to search my car. Or perhaps I can, as long as Dennis's prowling compendium isn't in my trunk. The Sutpen House isn't too far ahead, and the police vehicle hasn't reappeared behind me. If I hurry, I should have enough time to conceal the incriminating retrospective before Blivet's retinue catches up with me.

I depress the accelerator, and the engine makes a confirmative, obliging noise as the car barrels past the recreation field. How strange that I considered immolating or interring the duffel bag at the Sutpen House, yet, when I turned onto the road leading to it a moment earlier, aside from tormenting Downing and Roland with a staid automotive tour of the surrounding area, I had no destination or object in mind. I assumed I would lead them around the local autumn landscape until we ran out of gas, or they called for back up. But I did not know where I was going, or what I would do. Yet here I am, arriving at the mouth of the Mt. Abandon access road, with neither the police car, nor anyone who might alert it to my detour in sight. Though I thought she might have deserted me, it seems the confounding hand of Fortune remains upon my shoulder, and if I was the sort of person to closet my luck in an idol, or treat it as a supernatural agent, I might be thankful.

4.

Twenty minutes later, I leave the entrance to the access road, and travel a scant half mile in the direction of town before the police cruiser transporting Downing and Roland passes me heading in the opposite direction. Whichever of them is driving pulls an inelegant U-turn in the center of the road, speeds toward my bumper, stopping at a distance that seems inches from it, and reengaging both the siren, and rooftop loudspeaker.

"Henry, please pull over before this gets any more ridiculous."

"So, we're doing this again," I say, forgetting that Dora is no longer beside me, but safely stowed with Denise, and feeling an entwined sense of relief and loneliness at the recollection of her, standing with the dog in her arms, and requesting my return. It is perhaps the least original of all human emotions, but almost entirely original in the context of me, Henry Hoffmann, fugitive lizard, reptilian outlaw, poikilothermic campestral police force evader.

However, the dubious thrill of the pursuit has faded. I'm tired of driving, and only leading the feckless lawmen back to town so I can find a good place to park my car before I surrender. The lot in back of Town Hall is unmetered, and since I probably can't count on Blivet to take care of my tickets any longer, it's a logical choice. It's also within walking distance of the Sheriff's trailer park, and municipal facilities (the jail), so if Downing and

Roland actually manage to arrest me, I won't have to ride in the back of their patrol car like some shoplifting teenager being taxied to reform school.

Just because I can, I lead them once again down Clamence Street, slowing the car to a crawl in order to watch the confused expressions of the students outside the coffee shop and bookstore, and the regular townsfolk weaving between them. Amid the uniform puzzlement of each face, I notice one looking slightly more worried than the rest, and as the body attached to it slips through the stalled crowd on the sidewalk, and into the street, I recognize the sober, unremarkable deportment of Grover. I'm driving slowly enough for him to keep pace with the car by walking beside it, and he does this as I lower the window.

"Some people in the market said they saw you with a police escort," he says. "You seem like you need a favor."

"Sir! Step away from the vehicle," says Downing via the loudspeaker. Gordon ignores him.

"I think I have it figured out," I say. "But if you could give Huld a call in case he doesn't already know. I forgot."

"You didn't forget," says Grover. "Don't lie."

"Grover, please return to the sidewalk," says Roland from behind us.

"No, I didn't forget," I say. "But I wanted to see how this will go before he pulls me out of it."

"You can probably guess," says Grover, eyeing the other car.

"Indeed. But I don't pay Huld. He has no reason to tell me everything. Also…," I say, handing him my wallet. "Hold onto that for me, and take however much you charge for a bottle of sulfur free red wine, caciatta del tartuffo, and a bag of sweet potato, lamb, and rice kibble."

"Oh, you got a dog," says Grover, tucking my wallet into his pocket. "That's nice. I've always wanted a dog. Did you find everything you needed? Even after hours?"

"Quite. And thank you."

"It's nothing. Be careful around the large one. He's an imbecile," says Grover, turning back toward the street, but pausing in mid stride. "Do you need your I.D.?"

"They know who I am," I say, accelerating only enough to meet the speed limit, and holding it until I reach the nearly empty lot behind Town Hall. It's only midafternoon, but the sun is already beginning to hug the less than distant rib of Maybrick Peak to the east, which imbues the otherwise disparate realities of the elegant municipal building and the shanty town sheriff's department across the street with the dramatic tension of a sound stage. I park in a space directly opposite the basement door leading to the jail, pocket the keys, and step out the car as Roland and Downing station their own at a perpendicular angle to my bumper. They're trying to block me in, though there are no other vehicles to either side of the Audi, and if I wanted to escape, I could just drive the car over the lawn until I reached the main road.

"Stay right there!" shouts Downing, bursting from the vehicle with his hand on his sidearm. His nose is covered in a large bandage held in place by two overlong strips of medical tape encircling his head, and from a distance, it looks like he's wearing a jock strap over his face. I'm about twenty feet from him, standing beneath a tree planted at the edge of the parking area, and spinning the car key around one finger. "Don't you move, motherfucker!"

"He isn't moving," says Roland, skulking from the driver's side, his tired face reanimating as he notices his partner. "Jesus, settle down, Downing. And take your hand off your gun. He isn't armed."

"We don't know that!"

"Henry, do you have any weapons on you?" asks Roland.

"Only my jawline. Downing's mom uses it to cut sandwich bread."

"Not fucking funny!" shouts Downing, stomping toward me across the grass. "At least I didn't kill her, and sell her clothes to the church!"

"They were a donation, you hayshaker," I say, retreating several steps. "What happened to your face?

"What do you think?" he asks, still advancing. "It hit the fucking windshield when you brake-checked us on Clamence Street!"

"Well, I'm sure anyone raised by Morton is probably used to taking blows to the head."

"That's it!" says Downing, pausing to unbuckle his utility belt, and remove his badge, which he flings toward his partner. "Roland! I quit. You can arrest me after you call an ambulance for this shitbird."

Downing charges while Roland speed walks after him, holding a canister of pepper spray like a tube of lipstick, and impotently barking his partner's name like a dispossessed schoolmarm. Part of me thought that Downing's bellicosity came with his uniform, but it seems I was wrong. I can't remember the last time anyone has made good on a promise to hurt me with their hands. And since I don't know how to fight (and even if I did, would probably stand little chance against the large man rushing at me across the lawn), I run toward the corner of town hall, hoping that I can somehow disappear around it, through an open window, or unlocked door, or just vanish from the footrace entirely like a bit of idealistic sense data, unproven when unseen.

"That's right. Keep running, you show pony," says Downing from somewhere behind me, the finite decision to kill me apparently salving and refinishing his initial rage to sort of organic, unlettered sadism. "Because when I catch you, I'm going to break my dick off in your ear."

Still running, I look over my shoulder to check the distance between us, and collide with the gelatin levee of Blivet as I round the corner of the building. The sheriff is skirting the other side having likely walked from the direction of the encampment across the road, and I'm neither cushioned, nor punished by the impact, but rejected like a donated organ from the body of the chief lawmen. He is immobile as a Merovingian castle wall, and indifferent to the concussion of my chest meeting his gut, which draws the breath from my ribs like a bellows dipped nozzle first into surprised shape of my mouth. I take several crab-like steps backward before falling over, trying and failing to recapture my equilibrium, and toppling into a sitting position with my legs splayed like a dog in front of a fireplace, while the sheriff prevails, entirely unaffected. He doesn't acknowledge me, his attention falling instead on the larger of his two deputies, who hasn't yet noticed his boss lurking around the corner.

"Now, ain't that fortunate. Better not keep your asshole tight, ladyboy. That'll only make it worse when I open you up," he says to me, his limited perspective eschewing the sheriff standing on the flank of the building, but including me, who he has just seen disappear around the side of town hall, only to come toddling back seconds later to collapse in the path of his campaign. "I got my pussy finger ready for you."

"I don't want to hear that, Downing," says Blivet, stepping from his concealment around the corner. "What the hell kind of way is that to talk?"

"Chief? I...didn't see you...standing right there," says Downing, rotating his torso with the (now familiar) rigid, paper target motion to face Blivet. "The suspect...he was running!"

"He was running, because you were chasing him, and saying them vulgarities, to boot," says Blivet, eyeing the other man like a mustering officer. "Where's your badge? And your belt, for that matter? You going native on this man?"

"Uhyut, Chief," says Downing, looking shamefully at me on the ground. "Afraid I might have been."

"I got them right here, sheriff," says Roland, meaning the belt and badge, both of which he extends toward Downing with an amity that is as forgiving as it is without allegiance.

"Jesus, Roland, you ain't his dressmaker," says Blivet. "Give those to me. And tell the suspect to stand up."

"Stand up, please," says Roland to me, and I do, taking several shaky steps toward what feels like a neutral area of the lawn.

"We got a call," says Blivet, speaking to both deputies. "It was eight hours ago. Suspect transporting certain materials by car, to an unknown location. Now, your job was to search the car, seize the materials, and bring him in for questioning. So, what've the two of you been doing for eight hours?"

"Chasing this fucking..." begins Downing, gesturing at me, but changing his tone of voice at a look from Blivet. "Well, see he ran away, Chief, refused to get out of the car and was... uncooperative so we had to chase him, and there was a...like an accident, my nose got broke, as you can see, and then we lost him, but we..."

"Yeah, I heard about your chase," says Blivet. "Thirty five miles an hour with your flashers on, begging him to pull over through the bullhorn like a couple of little old ladies lighting prayer candles, and you did it twice, and in the middle of the goddamn day, but it sure must've really impressed them students up on the hill, like they don't already think we're a bunch of birthday clowns down here. Tell me about the accident, Roland."

"The suspect engaged his brakes and...I was unprepared, sheriff."

"You were unprepared?"

"That's correct, sir."

"Then how come Downing's wearing that diaper on his head?"

"He...hadn't properly engaged his safety belt," says Roland, staring with a Catholic intensity at his feet. "But I think he intended to."

"Roland, I'm going to give you some advice," say Blivet. "Part of being a man, not a policeman, just a man, is learning how to talk about it when someone fucks up, even when it isn't you that's done it, because it's easy to admit when you done it, but it's harder to tell someone else when they done it, so now, Downing here fucked up, and you both know that, but if you keep carrying around that cross much longer, I swear to god I'll nail you to it. You understand?"

"I think so, sheriff," says Roland.

"Good. Moving on," says Blivet, glaring at the parking lot, or my car, more accurately. "I'm gonna go ahead and guess that little pussy wagon in the parking lot ain't been searched. What do you say, Downing? Am I a winner?"

"Well, thing is, Chief, we couldn't get him out of the car long enough to search it, and-"

"Well, he's out of the car now," says Blivet, throwing the belt and badge at Downing, who fails to catch either. "How about you go ahead and ask him now?"

"Well, yessir. I sure will," says Downing, rotating himself once again to loom over me sitting in the grass. "Henry...Mr. Hoffmann. Give me your keys. Please."

Rather than answering, I stand up, and take several steps away from the company of the officers before producing the keys from my pocket, and lobbing them underhand at Downing. Either he isn't expecting this, or his eyesight isn't any good, because he twitches like a hornet stung him when the keys bounce off the khaki pout of his groin.

"Goddamnit, Henry! Ain't I been through it with you today?" he says, failing to recover himself as Roland stoops in the grass to find the car keys at his partner's feet. "Sheriff, that's assault, ain't it?"

"Downing, if I gotta keep mediatin' between you and the suspect, your badge and belt are coming home with me," says Blivet, as Roland returns to his feet hold the keys. "Now, let's go see what's in the car."

The three officers seem to forget me as they walk like a company of uniformed chimps toward the parking lot, with Blivet as the apparent alpha leading them, and the two betas dogging his mosey unable to conceal their glee, or perhaps relief, or perhaps both, at finally fulfilling their protracted duty. It's the ideal moment for escape. I could run, and disappear into the trees behind town hall, find my way back to the cabin on Kranion Pond, and beg asylum on behalf of Denise, while Huld straightens out this mess.

But if I ran, I would look afraid, and I'm not afraid. Blivet can't get me in any serious trouble with this sloppy setup. As I told Grover, I'm humoring it to see what happens. But while I watch the convoy of lawmen open the trunk of my car, and remove the duffle bag, my curiosity withers to a forthright boredom, as if the hands of clock in the cupola above were ticking off the minutes of my life in place of the hour of the day. Can I afford to humor these halfwit savages, allow them to rummage through my car in order to match the choreography of my violation, and detain me when I could be coursing Dora on the shore of Kranion Pond, or convincing Denise to allow me to stay with her. Perhaps as just a roommate or houseboy, anything would do, as long as it provided me with a tenuous quitclaim to the life she seems not reluctant, but indifferent, to share. If Blivet and his cavalcade of shiftless hill tribesmen hadn't made a pagan holiday of my time, I could do these things, and perhaps more. But they've done it, and for that, I will never forgive them.

"Found anything?" I say, dangerously forgetting myself as I approach the car. Aside from the crowns of their Stanton hats, the raised trunk blocks my view of the gentlemen invading it. But at the sound of my voice, a hand like the carcass of a skinless, overfed rodent seizes the top of the trunk, and slams it shut, while the other holds a ragged, duplicitous-looking Jack-in-the-box, the villainous head hung infirmly over the edge of the crate anchoring it, the tired spring of the overlong neck stretched past coil. And yet, the expression on the face of the box-bound devil remains of an essential, though malignant mirth, like the eddy of laughter following a man who has just lost his footing on a sheet of ice, and fallen to the ground. It is the expression of the moment before an injury, when the reality of suffering is unmet, and the fallen man even joins his laughter to that of the crowd.

"Where is what we're looking for?" asks Blivet, his unlearned hand throttling the toy as he raises it between us, while his rubicund mouth pronounces the words with a weariness so great that it seems to straddle two worlds. The question hangs in the air afterwards like an effluvium of profound and conclusive failure. The two deputies standing behind him each clutch a plaything, Roland with a wilted and mossy stuffed bear, and Downing with a doll that looks like it was recovered from an air raid, but rather than answer, they both look at me with something between malice and perplexity. "I'm asking you, Henry."

"Seems to me you found it, Blivet."

"We both know Dennis didn't give you no bag of creepy toys."

"Far as I know, you're right," I say. "The toys belong to me. And if you know what's good for you, you'll put them back where you got them before Huld gets here."

"What were you doing with a trunk full of spooky knick-knacks?" asks Downing, curious rather than accusing.

"Your mother asked me to take them up to the Aochegahara for the Halloween thing," I say. "We exchange favors like that."

"This isn't Huld's business," says Blivet, handing the Jack-in-the-box to Downing, who looks like he is about to detonate. "Boris does what he's told, same as you. And right now, ain't no one told him to come down here to get you out of this, so now, you tell me what you did with what Dennis was keeping for you, and maybe..."

"You're elbow deep in my property without a warrant," I interrupt. "It goes back in the car, Blivet. Or I call her parents. You know who I mean."

"I can't say why you're wrong," says Blivet, ignoring the Purvis-shaped gauntlet I've laid at his feet. "But I'm gonna to ask you to trust me, even though it won't do no good, because you got this all wrong, and if you don't cooperate, you're only gonna be wronger, and I imagine a fellow like you hates that more than..."

"Being wronger?" I ask, and the sheriff nods. "Maybe so, Blivet. But I hate whatever this is quite a bit more. I'm going to leave, with my car and my toys. The first man that touches me loses his sense of belonging."

"Put him in the cage," says Blivet, his voice sounding disappointed rather than vindicated. Downing steps toward me, but the sheriff shakes his head. "No, not you, Downing. You need to work on your toleration skills before you go escorting suspects like Henry. Roland, take him downstairs."

"Yessir," says eternally compliant Roland, taking my arm and walking me across the lawn as if I'm being courted rather than arrested. "Sorry, Henry."

"I'm sorry too," says Blivet, from behind us. "I wish we could have solved this like gentlemen, Henry, but sometimes that ain't a possibility, because I know it ain't been no church picnic with your mom and all, which is why I'm willing to give you the benefit of the doubt here, and assume that whatever you meant to do with them girls and those pictures, it wasn't no evil thing, just something that got broke in you after she wasn't around no more, and I guess it stayed that way, and maybe if folks had known early they could have helped you some, but I think we both know you ain't the most open person, always walkin' around not talking to no one with your collar up, and I can respect that, sure, a man's gotta keep some things to himself, which is why I'm going to give you another chance, like I said, to tell me where you put that stuff you stored over at Dennis's house, because I know you ain't no villain, Henry, and I always knowed it, there ain't much good to you, sure, but there ain't much bad either, so what I think is maybe you're just found some place betwixt all that, and that's why I know you wasn't gonna hurt them girls, I think you just wanted to see them, is all, and I'm sorry for you, Henry. I really am. So tell me where it is, and I'll make sure you get through this. You have my word."

"You got one thing right," I say over my shoulder, as Roland and I reach the steps leading down to the jail. "Mama didn't raise no rapist. Not much, but more than some folks can say."

Blivet turns his back to me rather than responding, but in the moment before his overfed, crimson face swings away, it appears decorously bereaved, as though the sheriff actually believes the compound of lies he's just shared. I misjudged his earlier weariness, took it as symptom of concomitant failure on the part of all those involved. The deputies for failing to apprehend me, the sheriff for failing to anticipate this difficulty, and me, for midwifing these failings, as anyone with even an imperfect understanding of my relationship with the Acheron Police Department could have foreseen.

But Blivet saw it, and knew it, because what I noticed in his face a moment ago was not a surrender to ineptitude, but a sort of battlefield grief that appears only when an opponent is vanquished to the furthest extreme of defeat while still retaining life, and only life, preserved on the edge of his enemy's sword. A genus of pity, but pity without charity, because charity is only possible after all is lost. Blivet has won. I don't know what (or how). But something has allowed him to triumph.

"I read somewhere if you put oranges in a towel, it don't leave no bruises," says Downing. "Is that true, chief?"

"You didn't read that," says Blivet. This is the last thing I hear before Roland leads me inside.

5.

ROLAND TO JAILS ME IN THE CELL formerly used for Dora. The lambent skin of his hand seems about to crack like weathered parchment as he twists a key in the inset lock, his moist blue eyes downcast as if he travels with a pit of bottomless longing at his feet. Even now, it would be so easy to overpower him, to reach through the bars, grasp his twig-like arm as he did mine when he escorted me inside, and buckle him against the cage, until he surrendered the key, or his life. But without Blivet, who would I call to cleanup? Violence is messy, but even the specious promise of it is sterile as a research tool. How much of my hold over the people of Acheron was couched in Blivet's 'reasonability'? I don't know the answer, but the sheriff's coup will certainly make it clear.

In any case, I don't want to hurt Roland, and I wonder if Blivet knew this when he assigned him to cage me. In the rare moment when his ginger head lifts from its dour fixity on his freckled neck, he appears not so much sorrowful, or ashamed, but needing an abeyance from one (or perhaps both) of these. Even if I were to attack him, he doesn't look like he would fight back. If the circumstances were dire, I might take advantage of this manifest frailty. Instead, I ask him what's wrong.

"I never want to be the guy putting someone in a cage," he says. "I feel like a zookeeper."

"Well, you can't please everyone, Roland. You picked your camp."

"Right, but I've known you since elementary school. I know we weren't friends or nothing, but I remember you. And I know you didn't do this."

"How?"

"Well, I figure it's like Blivet said, but he got it wrong. Or maybe it doesn't have nothing to do with your mom. Sorry to mention it again. But all I know is what I see, and what I hear. Mostly what I hear. And I ain't never heard of you being anything but polite to the women in this town. The men are a different story, of course. Just something I noticed. I don't know why a guy who seems to get along so well with the ladies would need to be taking pictures of them when they ain't know it. That just don't make sense."

"People say nice things about Dennis too," I say. "And they're his pictures."

"I suppose they do," says Roland. "But I think that's what folks do with someone who disappointed them without it being his fault. Say nice things about him. Hope he goes away. I know they do it with me."

"I think you're in the wrong line of work," I say, somewhat impressed with the deputy, and ashamed that only a moment ago, I considered harming him. "If you weren't here, I might doubt myself. You'd make an excellent priest, Roland."

"I think I've spent too much time around people to believe they was made on purpose. Being a cop means I don't have to worry where they're going. I usually know it."

"Do you like helping people?"

"Not overmuch. But I prefer it to telling them what to do," says Roland, pocketing the key, and checking his watch. "I better go. You hungry? Do you need anything? If you want a phone call, you can use mine."

I decline both the food and the phone call. I never liked ice cream sandwiches, and I don't know whom I would call. Denise can't do anything, and calling Mr. Castle would doubtless involve dealing with Jo. Grover is reliable. Huld is probably aware that Blivet is holding me illegally, and unless the sheriff actually knew what he was talking about, I should be released soon. But what if Blivet knows something I don't? This may be the first time I have pondered this contingency. What did he mean when he said Huld wouldn't come? If this hadn't been parceled with his other fictions, I might disregard it. But a bundle of lies is usually held together with a fixative of truth, and the foremost evidence that something about my arrangement with the local enforcement has changed is the cell in which I'm confined. Blivet wouldn't try something like this unless the Castle household was compromised. Though his plot was clumsy, he was far too easeful in executing it for this to be a passionate misstep on his part, revenge for my threatening his philandering dump truck of a son. Whatever I don't know is holding me here. Perhaps I should have accepted Roland's offer of a phone call.

In its accommodating sterility, the cell is positively Scandinavian. The toilet, basin, and bunk bolted to the wall appear forged of the same metalloid substance, the muted composite sheen of these fixtures like something out of a fascist hygiene magazine. Though the small, human touches are what truly make the room dreadfully impersonal. A handwritten sign attached to the opposing wall alerts the inmate that if they need anything, they are to ring a buzzer installed beside the notice. A wire leads from it like the shadow trail of determined arachnid along the wall, between the bars, and out through a window at the end of the hall. A bottle of unopened hand sanitizer sits neutrally on the rim of the basin. And the bunk where I sit is shrouded in a clean, smallpox-styled blanket, making it look less like the desk of a coroner, and more like what it is: a place to count minutes.

As the daylight from the window at the end of the hall fades to limitless night, I sit down on the autopsy table, and stand again, pacing the length of the bars, and repacing them, sitting once more, and returning to my feet. The hissing of the flat light fixtures above my head, and running the length of the hall is the only audibility, and were I lesser in some sense, prone to associating unbent silence with a kind of heraldic dread, I might ring the buzzer, if only to provoke the retreat of whatever malformed entity haunts the gatehouse of a human mind in seclusion. It isn't the quiet of the cellblock that continues to unseat me, but the restricted vigilance suggested by the bars, and correspondent unmattering of me, Henry Hoffmann, reformed lizard, contained by them. Incarceration is meant to prove that the world will continue the same, if not better, without the inmate, and thus, as the clock crowning the building tolls 8, 9, and 10PM, my relevance fades inversely proportionate to my vigilance. No one has come for me yet, and I'm beginning to doubt they will. Blivet was right. For the second time today, pawn takes rook.

Despite becoming something of an unperson, I'm interested rather than relieved when I hear the door at the far end of the hall clatter open, and deliberate, mammalian footsteps stomping toward me. Downing appears with a grease-stained bag before the bars, his wounded nose redressed in a sort of cozy resembling a sanitary napkin rather than an athletic cup, his badge replaced, but his belt still absent.

"Blivet still has your tool belt?" I say, trying to sound amicable. No matter which side he occupies, there's no sense in teasing man through a set of bars.

"No, but he said I should bring you food, so he took it again," says Downing, cautiously offering the bag. "No more remarks about my mom, Henry. You say what you want to make yourself feel like you're not in there. But you don't say nothing about her."

"I don't understand why it bothers you, Downing," I say, accepting the bag through the bars. "I don't know your family. Except your father, but I don't think you want to be anything like him."

"Well, that's it right there. If you just kept to yourself, and didn't talk about things that you don't know nothing about, I wouldn't be having to feed you."

"So you know too," I say, trying to meet his eyes without looking at the bandage. "And you're fine with allowing this to happen?"

"Why would I stick my neck out for you?" says Downing. "I'm thinking you probably look through plenty of key holes in this town. What does it matter if we don't get you at the right one? I'm a cop, so I know that sooner or later I get a call telling me something happened that I knew was gonna happen, and I can't do nothing about except cleanup because some shitbird like you was smart enough to be where I wasn't every time. That's just the law, I suppose, but I can't help but think what if it wasn't that way. If I could take a man in because of what I know instead of what he did, I could retire this weekend. That's why I won't speak for you."

" 'Silence is an objection,' Downing. You don't like me. But you know I'm not dangerous."

"I don't need none of your riddles. Everyone's dangerous. Eat that before I take it away from you."

He remains to watch me open the bag filled with a once fresh-like, now tepid meal that was no doubt commissioned through a speaking curbside menu. A withered patty like a nodule of dung flattened by a tractor sidles from between the platelets of an aeronautically perfect bun into a nest of fries stiff as bayonets. I neatly crease the top of the bag, and pass it back through the bars.

"No," I say. "I won't be eating that."

"Someone will," says Downing cryptically. He receives the bag, and stomps up the hall, and out of the jailhouse, leaving me alone once again.

Or nearly alone. As I return my attention to the immediate concern of my cell, I find my mother has returned. She sits on a folding chair outside the cage, dressed as she was during the last visit (business-like), with her tweed-sheathed legs crossed and the pommel of her chin cupped in her left hand, watching me with my face.

"Hi, mom," I say, approaching the bars like a pet during an adoption fair. "Have you come to let me out?"

"I don't think that would help," she says. Her high cheekbones are locked in undeviating cleavage, like the wall of an iceberg. "Because I don't think you want to be released, do you? I mean, maybe you do. But only because Blivet put you here, and you think that's wrong."

"Isn't it?"

"The sheriff is just following orders, albeit gladly, in this case. He isn't creative enough to hang Dennis on you. Can you guess who is?"

"Not Mr. Castle."

"Yes, not him. Try again."

"Not Jo. She doesn't have that sort of influence. Even with him."

"If would benefit you to learn to get along with her."

"I don't think that's fair, mom. I'm very accommodating."

"Anal sex is not an accommodation, Henry. But it's probably

the most responsible behavior you've demonstrated in the past few days."

"You sound like you think this," I gesture at the cell confining me, "is somehow my fault."

"Let's consider how you arrived here," says my mother, drawing her chair closer to the door of my cell. "You protected Dennis, not because you care anything for the company or Castle family name itself, but because you enjoyed the risk involved in sheltering a deviant. It wasn't boring. And you overplayed your hand with Blivet to prevent him from finding out what he already knew, so that you could spend more time with a girl that relieves herself in a soup kettle..."

"Dutch oven, mom"

"...And you did it at exactly the worst time. Not that you could know that, but I somehow doubt you would have done anything differently, if you had known how jealous your little vacation would make the wife of your employer. And here you are. This is what happens when you either lack or disregard intuition. I'm still deciding which is you."

"I'm great with people," I say, waving toward the window, in what I assume is the direction of town. "Even when they're difficult, I know how to handle them."

"That's not what 'great with people' means."

"Well, it won't matter," I say, withdrawing from the bars, and returning to my autopsy bunk. "When Mr. Castle realizes what happened, he'll send Huld down here to pull me out, and..."

"You like it here, don't you?"

"...Well, I like not knowing what happens next," I say, cautiously watching my mother. "I mean, I think I know, but I really don't. He may not come. But I'm excited by that, because it's different, and strange. I'm so tired of watching the same people misbehave. Or watching myself react to them. I don't hate my job, but I don't enjoy it. I'm indifferent, and unable to separate it from my other interests, if I have any, so it's the same as being indifferent to my own existence. So, yes, if Blivet weren't responsible for me, this would be refreshing."

"That's not how you're supposed to feel about being in jail," says my mother, a species of sadness thawing the taut muscle around her mouth, and entering her voice. "But you were always a weird kid."

"I suppose if I'm only here because Jo is angry with me, then technically, I'm still on the clock. So, I lose," and then, apropos of nothing, "I have a problem of basic emptiness, I think."

"Fortunately, you don't need to know how to make yourself happy to be good at your work."

"No one does," I say, but she isn't there to hear me, having disappeared in not so much the blink of an eye, but the unsteady wavering of it between the different modes of unremarkability composing the cellblock. I walk back to the bars, and thread myself through them, my eyes fixed on the folding chair where she sat. I reach for it without hope, both arms extending stiff and feckless from the cage, and claw the air between myself and the furniture with a determination I only realize I've misapplied until after I've to failed touch the chair's metalloid seat.

6.

THE FIRST THING I SEE when I open my eyes is the basement window, and nothing beyond that, meaning it is either night, or early
morning. The second is Downing, bent and trying to dislodge
my arm from where it has fallen between the bars so that he can
open the cell door. His problem is that my face and chest lean
against the grill, weighting my arms, which I looped through the
cage in order to prevent myself from falling asleep. I hoped that
this arrangement of limbs might steady my pointless vigilance,
and escort it through the inevitable fatigue of the interzone between catch and release. But I've fallen asleep at my post, and
rather than supporting my body, the bars have only positioned it
oddly. I kneel, with my chin tucked into my chest, one fallen arm
draped behind me, while the other extends out into the hallway
with the palm facing up as though frozen in mendicancy.

"I could just break this and solve a number of my problems
all at once," says Downing as he sees my eyes open, his mit-
ten-like hands attempting to stuff my appendage back into the
cell. "Never seen anyone sleep that way...

"What are you doing?" I ask, pulling my arm out of his hands,
and standing up.

"Letting you out," he says, sliding the door open, and standing aside. "Much as I don't like it, that's the word."

"Who called?"

"Don't know."

"Where are my car keys?"

"He has them."

"Who has them?"

Rather than answering, Downing walks away from me, past the cellblock, and opens the door at the end of the hall leading outside.

"You coming?" he asks, pausing in the entrance, his hand holding the door. I follow, passing through the other door to the outside, and up the stairs to the parking lot. Beside it, a man stands in the shadow beneath the tree where I stood earlier that day, waiting to be assaulted by Downing, who now raises a hand at the figure.

"All yours," he says before disappearing around the side of the building, in the direction of the trailers across the street. The man makes a discursive gesture at the retreating deputy, but doesn't remove himself from the cowl of shadow beneath the tree. He's far too small to be Huld, too large to be Mr. Castle, and not average enough to be Grover. And yet, I know him. Something about the stooped, malfeasant pillory of the shoulders, the wide splay of the feet, the hands neither at rest nor attention, but poised in a sort of proto-attack, each claw-like fist hung from either arm like the bucket of an earthmoving machine.

"Keys, Al?" I say, and he emerges from the belt of unlight with them extended from the crook of an index finger, neither delivering nor withholding them, but making me come to him. "Where's Huld?"

"Away."

"Did he send you?"

"No."

"Who did?"

He makes the same gesture he did at Downing, this time in the direction of the Castle homestead on the hill behind us, and turns toward the parking lot. I follow and get in my car, knowing that I should return to the house, but wondering whether it is too late to drop in on Denise. I'm less interested in having tonight explained to me by Mr. Castle, than I am in explaining it to her. But as I turn they key in the ignition I'm left with little choice of destination, because nothing happens. The interior lights flash, and fade, once, twice, and by the third time, Aloysius pulls up beside me in a battered Ford Ranger, and I roll down my window.

"I need a jump, Al."

"Nope," he says, not offering a ride, but it's apparent by his professional patience in waiting at the wheel as I gather my necessities, and lock the car, that if he left me there, it would be a problem.

"What did you do to my car?" I say as we turn off Clamence Street, heading toward Castle Road.

"Nothing that can't be fixed in the morning," he says tonelessly, pushing a Floyd Tillman cassette into the tape deck. "You could've maybe done it yourself if you knew how to take care of nice things."

"That doesn't mean whatever you think that means," I say, as "Drivin' Nails in My Coffin" begins playing from the stereo. "Why was I left in jail for six hours?"

"What makes you think you don't belong there?"

"I'm not answering that," I say, watching Al watch the road like a man approaching the mouth of Hades. "And why are you driving Mr. Castle' truck? He doesn't let anyone use it."

"She said I could take it to get you."

"Jo said. But it isn't hers."

"Ask her," he says, stopping the truck in the driveway of the house standing bright as a casino barge against ridge. "She's inside waiting for you."

"Tell her I'm too tired for whatever she wants," I say, stepping out the cab. "Or don't tell her anything. Thanks for the ride. In the morning, I'm coming for your job."

"You think so," says Al, perhaps saying more, but I slam the door before I can hear it, and cross the lawn toward the pine grove. Even if I could see Denise tonight, I'm far too exhausted to make the journey on foot. Perhaps I'll pack a bag before I go to bed, and present myself on her doorstep early tomorrow morning, plead for sanctuary, and hope that she grants it. If whatever happened this evening is part of some rupture in the established order of the town, I would rather not put myself at any greater risk by learning more. I am not curious, and even if I can't escape, I want to withdraw.

But Jo is waiting for me in the front room of the house, meaning that the evening herein will be bereft of both tranquility and emotional progress. She sits in a chair by the cold fireplace; a scarf swaddled around the lampshade isolating the light to a space no larger than her lap, on which a library copy of *Watership Down* is splayed like a pinioned albatross. If I had seen light through the window when approaching the pool house, I wouldn't have entered it. As I open the door, and stand on the threshold realizing I've been tricked, I have to battle the urge to flee, even if I don't know where I would go. A dash toward uncertainty seems better than a trot toward assured ruin.

But I'm held in place by the incautious triumph for which the civilian twilight of her eyes serves as a marquee. It is the visual companion of the victory earlier conveyed by Blivet during his justification of my apparent crimes. The expression of remorseless pity, not only for what has happened, but what will. And however incurious I claim to be, I know that if I leave, she will somehow return me, because for the better part of today, I have been directed, held, and directed once more to places that I did not chose. How could she, my queen, not have a hand in that? Somehow, she grew clever, or perhaps I made a hobby of under-estimating her. It's not just the raiment cast over the lamp, but the small suggestions urging me toward this parlay, the needless, overlong confinement followed by 'car trouble,' wherein Aloysius was available to act as a sort of Charon, and shuttle me to his singular destination, toward which I had been encouraged from the moment I heard the siren outside Dennis' house. In each articulation, I see her hands, the right shifting the pieces, the left beneath the table.

"He said you were inside," I say, meaning Aloysius. "He didn't say which inside. Why am I only here now, and where is Mr. Castle?"

"He's away."

"With Huld?"

"I don't think so. Sit down."

"He wouldn't have let it happen. So you did. Why?"

"I don't want anything bad to happen to you. Sit down."

"No, that's wrong. You don't care what happens to me, as long as you allow it to happen. Blivet doesn't do anything unless he knows he can get away with it, and he knew. Why?"

"People make mistakes. Sit down."

"No. I'm not staying," I say, knowing it isn't true. "And people don't make mistakes, they make excuses after they have done something on purpose. Did he tell you I was a pornographer?"

"No. I know you're not that. That's why I thought it was necessary for the police to do their work. I assumed you would cooperate, and they would find nothing, and that would be the end of it," she says, closing the book, and crossing her short legs. "But you didn't cooperate, and there were consequences. Where are you going?"

"You know that's not how it happened. And you have no idea what you've allowed. Blivet is only useful if he is kept at heel, and if he has the right to treat me like any other citizen of Acheron, I can't do that, which means I can't do my job, which means..."

"Which means what?" asks Jo, though she knows the answer.

"Consequences," I say. "You said there were consequences. You meant for me."

"There are consequences for everyone."

"There are now," I say, crossing the floor toward the bedroom, intending to at least pack a bag, though I won't take it anywhere. That has become clear.

"You won't find her there," says Jo, and I pause in the hallway, because I know exactly whom she means.

"What have you done with her?" I say, returning to the mouth of the living room.

"Nothing!" says Jo, smiling wickedly. "I just meant she's with her uncle tonight. She stays there sometimes when she has an early class. I believe the dog is with her there."

"I'll go anyway."

"I thought we might spend some time together."

"You thought wrong," I say, returning to the hallway but not even bothering to go further, because there is nowhere to go. "Where is Mr. Castle?"

"He had business in Burlington," she says, sounding suddenly irritated. "He's trying to secure some advertising for Releaf Tours with the free weeklies, and is also looking at sponsorship possibilities for First Night. He said he wanted to see 'foliage gateway' on something during New Year's. He's really happy with everything you've done for the business. It's turning into a real thing. He said he would like to see you do more of that in the future. He needs you, Henry."

Just as a virulent pathogen contains some hint of its antidote, so this fable unspun by Jo shelters a simple truth having nothing do with her husband's whereabouts, but the more global fact that neither of us will ever see him again. It isn't the overworked details of her explanation that entirely give it way, nor the possibly genuine impatience with which she pronounces it, as if all of this should be obvious, or even the fact that Grover already handled advertising in the surrounding area, because all of these are what is expected of someone who wants to appear as if they are not lying. Instead, it is Jo's apparent effort to do no more than conjure this duckblind of truth in order to placate me, and her authentic uncaring as to whether or not I believe it, as long as there is a veneer of credulity between us, not because I must not know the truth, but because it is not something she feels like discussing. The chair in which she sits might be a throne raised on a magnificent dais, and she a newly minted Byzantine tyrant occupying it with a hideous impatience for anything that might defer the satiety of her design, and yet still retaining the emollient mannerisms of the lesser nobility and courtiers from which she was drawn, whose own decorous habit of mating decorum to morally insolvent falsehood will eventually disinvest her of the purple. But for now, no one is ever executed beneath Jo's tutelage. They just leave in the night without telling anyone, and are never seen, or heard from again.

"When do you expect him back?" I say emptily. What I want to ask is where he is buried. But I can't, so I take her suggestion, and sit on the floor at her feet, because my legs are suddenly weak, and I'm not certain I will make it to the furniture. The answer doesn't matter, but I needed to say something that didn't sound like an accusation, and indicates that whatever is happening, I will comply.

"After Halloween," she says, the impatience fading. "Come here now."

And I do, scooting forward like a dog scratching its glands on the carpet, allowing her to twine her fingers in my hair and draw my cheek down upon her thigh as if it is a chopping block.

"What happened today was because you didn't listen," she says. "I need you with me, and not with her. Do you understand that?"

"She's just a friend," I say. It's technically true. "I'm not even attracted to her. She looks like a boy. I don't have many…any friends."

"I'm pregnant," says Jo, trumping me.

"You're lying," I reply automatically, and her fingers twist in my hair. "I'm sorry, Jo. You're pregnant, why not? I meant…is it…ours?"

"Why is that your first question?"

"I suppose I want to know if you need a father or a nanny."

"How many people am I fucking, Henry?"

"Well…" I begin, realizing there is no correct answer to her question. "I'm sorry. I'm just surprised. It isn't bad news. I'm… I'm very excited to be a…father?"

I raise my head cautiously from her leg to meet her eyes, and she nods, appearing disgusted that I would bother confirming the ghost child's paternity. I don't believe her, but she appears to believe herself, so I must behave as if mingling my genetics with those of a woman who will have me jailed if I do anything other than agree with her is an opportunity for celebration.

"I love you," she says. "Don't worry. Just listen. Everything will be fine. I love you."

I nod agreement against Jo's leg as her fingers trace the phrenology of my skull, recalling the unexpectant shape of Denise bending against me in the cabin, with the woodstove keening beyond the narrow mattress, and Dora snoring on the floor beside it. I would trade an epoch of miserable, indentured comfort with Jo to once more hear the sound of Denise urinating in a kettle. The reckless ingratitude of this proportion is so overwhelming and wrathful that I only prevent myself from sinking my teeth into Jo's leg by imagining that it belongs to Denise.

"Yes. I love you, too," I say aloud, though not to Jo, perhaps not to anyone. But whether or not they're true, I'm can only pronounce the words by pretending that Denise can hear them.

Friday

"What don't kill you probably will."
— Morton Downing, seasonal worker and amateur philosopher

"…hunting lessons available through our Releaf Extras! package…"
— Releaf Tours promotional brochure, authored by Oliver Himmel, copyright Acheron Ventures, LLC, 2011

1.

THE FOLLOWING MORNING, when Jo drags the top sheet from my naked body, and stomps from the pool house like a clubfooted boatswain to greet the muted dawn drawing over the ridge with my coverlet cowling her as she crosses the gelid lawn toward the main house, it occurs to me that the only way to restore the emigrant remnants of my former (as of last night) liberty is to kill her. Yes, end things before they begin. Or progress, I suppose. What are my other choices? If I disobey, I'll be returned to the jailhouse, which Jo is prepared to use as a kind of adult timeout. If I quit, I can't remain in Acheron. What would I do? Serve coffee? And if I flee the town, she'll find some way to bring me back. Attempting to frame me for Dennis' photojournalistic lurking was clumsy and needless. There is plenty of authentic leverage she could use to pressure me further, not the least of which is Denise (and Dora), as she mentioned last night. I don't know how Jo found out. She probably had Al follow me. But it doesn't matter. She knows enough to be jealous, which is troubling, though somewhat ironic. If she didn't love me, as she says, I'd be dead now. So if I'm to escape this indenture, and return to a semi-normal life, I must reunite Jo with her husband. But how to accomplish her debarment without implicating myself? This is the moil occupying me as the confident daylight anoints the disrobed mattress on which I shiver, with my knees drawn into my chest, and my head bent toward them like the inmate of corpse's womb.

I could lure her to the rear deck of the main house, and when all is clear, tip her from it. Were it not for Aloysius, this would be the perfect plan. I'm never certain where he is at any specific time, and the chance of him witnessing me toppling Jo down the mountainside is too great. And even if the actuality of the crime escaped his purview, he would probably lie, and tell Blivet he saw the entire thing just to be rid of me. And Blivet would believe it. Men of little consequence are always eager to share an enemy.

Of course, I could poison her, which would implicate Al, since he prepares the family meals. But it would involve conjuring some pretext for hanging around the kitchen while he cooks, which would appear suspicious even if he and I were friends. Perhaps I could swap his ingredients with something toxic, exchange saffron for hemlock, salt for ricin, pepper for Prussian blue. But there is always the risk of him tasting his pabulum before serving it, and thus dropping dead before feeding it to Jo. Perhaps I could invite myself to dinner, and deposit something in her drink while she isn't looking. But this entails the same problem as dumping her over the cliff: the vigilant eye of Aloysius.

It's more or less fortunate that he, like one of Isidore's unsettled spirits, is umbilically tied to the house. More, because it means I can shed his omniscience at the property line. Less, because disposing of Jo somewhere in greater Acheron means that my chance of being seen or caught rises exponentially. As I lay naked and shivering on the mattress, bereft of cover, yet bedewed with the torpid afterbirth of Jo's body, I retrieve a pen from the bedside table, and tear an intentionally blank page from the rear of the book she left behind.

Car accident→ Disable passenger belt in some way. Drive car into tree. Blame ice, or a deer.

Boat ride→ Hit her with oar. Sink body. Scuttle boat. Claim solitary excursion.

Hike up Mt. Abandon→ Push her off Mt. Abandon. "She slipped while taking a photograph," etc.

The possibilities on the list have some potential. But even as the thought of murdering Jo tests the rim of possibility, like a snakehead nosing the lip of a wicker basket in which it is imprisoned, I know that the one thing I must do is the only thing I will not do. It isn't a question of capability. When provided with the right set of circumstances, brutality will always unseat reason, even in the heart of an apostle. Nor is it concern for the unborn child she may or may not contain. Like everyone else, I've always wondered how it feels to kill someone, but fear punishment too acutely to find out (This is the human condition, as much as I care to define it). Ideally, I would like the benefit of an execution with the responsibility for it. But even when it is successful, murder is a logistical nightmare (I imagine). Disposing of Dennis' baggage presented a significant hurtle even before the police were involved. I can't imagine what I would have done with an actual body. In the gallows of my imagination, every hangman has his janitor, and I suppose I always assumed that if my work for Mr. Castle ever required that I dispatch some unlucky resident of Acheron, Blivet would act as my custodian. But it never came to that, so this theory was untested.

But it seems I was correct, in a way, because whatever Jo has done with her husband couldn't be accomplished on her own. And judging by Blivet's apparently seamless (and rapid) shift of allegiance to the Widow Castle, I find myself in the unwelcome position of knowing less than he about the family's private business. But surely I'm not the last to know. Even in his bottomless pragmatism, I can't imagine Huld standing by while Jo disposes of his foremost client. And what about Cornelius? Didn't I warn him that she was plotting something? Why didn't he listen? The Castle brothers were never exactly close, but both men kept to their respective hilltop cloister, which preserved their relationship like a mosquito trapped in a nugget of amber, forever frozen in ambivalence. Neither had any claim on what made the other important, and the town was far too small to fabricate one, so they left each other alone. I suppose I should speak with Cornelius today. He won't be able to solve anything, but at the very least, he might be able to hide me on the campus, should I need it. And he'll know I was right. Though so far, this fact has done me little good.

Though I'm certain I can't do it, I'm reluctant to abandon the possibility of retiring Jo. Perhaps I just haven't been pushed far enough. Capability is best measured in retrospect, isn't it? If she seriously threatens Denise, I can't say what I might do. Rather than destroying the list of ways to rid myself of Jo, and fold it in half and place it on the bedside table just as Aloysius appears in the doorway of the bedroom, neither stepping into it like a man politely revealing himself, nor edging his predatory face around the jam as I would expect. But in the space of a glance, my own, from the empty doorway, to the paper in my hand, to the bedside table, to the doorway once again, he is suddenly there, as though belched from some servant's barrack of perdition into my home, and framed now in the doorway as stolid, unmoving, and self-evident as a totem pole.

"I didn't hear you knock," I say, displaying, rather than covering myself, since Jo took the means to conceal it with her. I prop two pillows beneath my head, and roll onto my back, my legs spread, and my hands folded across my abdomen.

"Door was open," he replies, apparently undisturbed by male nudity, which makes me wish I had covered it. He extends a bit of folded paper without stepping into the room. "This is for you."

"What is that?"

"Don't know."

"Yes, you do."

"Don't care."

"I see. Set it on the bed."

He doesn't move. The folded paper in his claw remains at an insolent, unreachable angle.

"I'm to be here when you read it," he says.

"Fine. Set it on the bed."

"I don't intend to come in a bedroom where a man is baring himself."

"That's why people knock, Al. Consider this a lesson."

"Take this," he says, raising his delivery in a sort of gestural compromise. "Take this so I can leave."

"Fine," I say. I'm already tired of whatever this is becoming, and apparently, so is Al. "I can hear you begging, even though you don't think it's that. It sickens me."

As I step out of bed, I place my foot on what, to Al, must look like the dismembered proboscis of some seagoing invertebrate from his embrasure across the room, but is in fact a cord of synthetic polymers of descending girth designed for insertion into the cavity which, for Jo, has become a sort of wayside adjunct to our sharing evenings. Last night, when she said, "I thought we'd spend some time together," she knew exactly what she meant, and I pretended I did, fearing imprisonment for anything aside from compliance. And so, we existed.

The beads remain slick with whatever unction Jo applied to ease their purpose, causing them to slide from beneath my foot as though I had stepped from the bed onto a patch of nodular ice. My ankle buckles, collapsing upon itself like an abutment swallowed by an earthquake, and I fall sideways into the nightstand, toppling the lamp onto the floor, knocking Jo's book along with it, and sending the list of homicidal possibilities drifting across the room to settle ineluctably between Al's shoes. He's watched this pratfall without altering his posture, or the angle at which he offers the missive, and seems not to notice the stray bit of paper kicked up by the concussion of my naked body with the bedside table.

"Whenever you're ready," he says, his eyes falling with a kind pro forma disgust on the agent of my collapse, coiled between us on the floor like a recently fed snake. "I don't want to see no more of how you live if I can help it."

"What you don't know fills libraries," I say weakly, my own gaze finding Jo's lent copy of *Watership Down* where it fell open on the floor, the words on the page seeming far too appropriate: "All the world will be your enemy, Prince of a Thousand enemies." I stand and limp over to Al, snatching the paper from his hand, and kicking the sex toy past him into the hall. "I've taken it. Now go."

"I'm supposed to be here. In case you have questions."

"You can't answer my questions," I say, glancing at his feet. The paper, my short list of Jo disposals, is gone from between them. "Where is it?"

"Where's what?"

"Don't mess with my head, Al. I'm going to be a father, which means you better start acting like a governess."

"I saw what it was," he says, a smile like a syphilitic crevasse breaking the terraform veldt of his face. "You don't believe her. Otherwise you wouldn't have written it."

"I'm planning a book. A mystery. A mystery novel, Al. What you found is part of an outline. Return it."

"Seems awful close to what is for just a story."

"Well, since I can't win with you or her or Blivet, I thought I would write not what I know, but what I wish I knew. The ending I hope for but don't expect. Return it."

"You can't kill her. You ain't ever even followed a gut trail. You don't know killing."

"Everyone has to learn sometime," I say, realizing this is perhaps too close to the truth. "Return it, and the character based on you will live."

"You'd kill her and your child just to see that other who you haven't even done it to yet. How I know is that if it was the other way and you had done it to her, she'd not be her, but another her you was trying to do it to."

"Was that English?" I ask.

"I think you understood it all right, but mayhap not. That's how men like you are stupid. If she is the one here, or if she is the one at that cabin by the pond, she is always her. What the thing is that's different is how much you think you're getting away with."

"We're having two different conversations," I say. "And one of them makes no sense. What the character does in the story is what I wish I could do to Jo, and it, and you. But I can't, because I'm afraid. That's my secret. Now you know. Don't return it. Show it to her. My answer will be the same."

"I don't want to be a person in that story."

"Too late, Al," I say, opening the paper, and frowning at it. "This is a shopping list."

"Could be."

"Buying groceries is your job."

"Cooking them is my job."

"Did you write this?"

"I added what I need."

"And here, it says 'Isidore, 4PM.' What does that mean?"

"You said you wouldn't have any questions."

"If you want you're groceries, you'll tell me."

"Don't know. He said he wanted your help."

"That's nothing new. He always wants my help."

"Well, now you have the time to give it."

"And I suppose here, 'Costume, 5PM,' means I'm picking up her holiday wardrobe?"

"And yours too," says Al, shifting from the frame, almost seeming to detach from it like a portrait given life. "Now, unless you're going to cover yourself, I think that's about all the questions I feel like answering. If you have any more, call me."

"Call you."

"Uhyut. On the phone."

"This isn't what it is supposed to be, Al. You know that. I don't do grocery shopping. That isn't my function. I supervise Isidore. I'm not his assistant. And I don't wear costumes."

"Don't worry about that. I helped choose it," says Al, his tone becoming both menacing and jocular. "You'll look real pretty."

"I'm being kept. That's what it is. I might as well be back in the jail."

"It isn't that way."

"But it is, and you know it is. She doesn't want me to do what I did, because that involved influence, and knowing certain things, and having people like you answer to me. But she can't keep me locked up, so she keeps me busy running your errands, because if she didn't, who knows? I might see Denise, or not be here late at night, or discover what she did to Mr. Castle!"

"Now, you're just being paranoid, Henry," he interrupts. "Jo says Acheron is only so big, and having you tormenting the townsfolk is bad for business. She says a smart, educated, organized person like you could be put to better use than all that. She's got plans, Henry. You'll see. Jo says she wants to do better with what we already have before anything gets any bigger. And she also says you been worrying about having no clear responsibilities. But considering this new direction here, it was a pretty easy fix. Your cards…"

"My…cards? Like, business cards?"

"That's right," says Al, smiling again. "The printer said Monday, but you might want to check in today, just in case. The place is right there between Grover's and the costume shop, so it's on your way. If it's Sunday, they might send it over special messenger. Good service."

"I'll get the police," I say, without meaning it, even as the words leave my mouth. "Not Blivet. Someone from outside. You can't stop me."

"We don't have to," says Al, looking at me with what might be a sort of pity as I sit heavily on the bed, naked, spent, defeated. "You know what you won't do better than us, because you know what you could lose better than us too. So maybe give that some thought. She wouldn't want that. The one out at the cabin I mean. For you maybe, but for herself for certain."

"Don't say that."

"I didn't say it. You heard it that way."

"I don't know what that means, Al."

"What it means is the stories you write down are never the ones that actually happen, because who wants to read something they already know about? Don't get the two confused."

And here, he leans into the room without entering it, removes the paper that fell between his boots from the breast pocket of his shirt, and casts it toward the bed (as I asked him to do earlier with the shopping list). It drifts on an unremarkable current before touching down beside my bare flank, and I understand I have been warned. This done, Aloysius escapes the frame entirely, his boots treading with a martinet's confidence down the hallway, toward the door, and out into the yard.

But at the sound of the door slamming, I rise rigid and mechanistically from the bed as if induced rather than awoken from coma, and run after him, stopping only as I pass through the kitchen to enshroud my pelvis in an overlarge dishtowel, before calling his name out of the door beyond which he stops, midway to the main house. I watch him retrace his steps, listening to the ascendant creak of his boots in the snow as they approach, the sound like the hoof-fall of an unhurried Scythian warlord atop his steed, until he stops at the foot of the front steps. I see what I must look like in the arrangement of his features as he looks up at me from the lawn, his face a mirror of what is most pathetic about me even as I stand above him, clutching the overlarge, yet still too small, towel to around my waist like a pendant of surrender.

And what I mean to ask is how I'm supposed to get from where I am now, to the places I am supposed to be (according to Jo's list) without my car. But this question is subducted beneath a more urgent one originating with the face watching me say nothing from the yard, the dark forelock combed to the side, or perhaps trimmed, and the line of the mouth wintering the same removed disgust from earlier when he found me naked in the bedroom, and the undersized frame from which the arms sprout as though frozen in the act of digging a trench. But more than these vague, overfamiliar attributes, it is his blue eyes that I notice now in the nascent light of the morning as resembling in color neither the sky above our heads, nor the icebound terrain beneath our feet, but those of the women in whose palm we both sit, waiting to be crushed (in my case), or stroked (in his).

I don't know how I didn't see it before, but I suppose that Aloysius was, by the nature of his former profession, unseen, a specter distributing chairs, laying plates, or taking coats, and making himself scarce during the interim. But is it possible that I have never actually looked Aloysius in the face? Or perhaps I did not know what to look for, until this moment, when being invisible is no longer part of his duty.

"Did you just ask me back here to expose yourself, or should I guess what you want?"

And when he speaks, the resemblance is further pronounced. Some unaffected, genealogic timbre, or heritable intonation, the sort of imperfect similarity that is in fact perfect, the shibboleth of consanguinity. I may never have noticed it had I not first seen his eyes, and her in them, seeing me from him as if Aloysius were himself a watchtower set above the cornerstone of her compound (from which there is no escape).

"I know what you're going to say isn't important enough for me to wait on it," says Al, turning around, and seeming to recede rather than walk, like a man conveyed by the landscape itself rather than his own isolated power, and past him, beside the house, I notice the hood of my Audi next to the Ranger which Mr. Castle would never allow anyone to drive if he were still of this coil. I have no questions. But still, I call Al's name from the steps again, because I want to see it once more, or know it once more, confirm that whatever I assumed about him was entirely wrong and that whether it was my lie or his, I lived it fully until this moment.

"Al! Hold on!" I yell, intending to ask him about the car that I know is there. But when he turns, curious and irritated, I see her even more than before, not just watching, but condemning. And whereas a better man might be too stupid to be afraid, and might pronounce this sighting, decry it to him (Al) as being not only seen, but understood, I am not the one to do it. Instead, the fear of knowing what I couldn't have predicted, and what I will not foresee, or what is unstoppable because it moves with the masterless ordination of time itself, shakes me from my tenuous equilibrium in the doorway. I bend at the waist as if struck, the towel dropping from my pelvis and drifting onto the lawn like a token of failed knighthood as my copper green eyes meet hers, or his, blue as veined blood. The last thing I see before I close my watery eyes and vomit onto my own foot, is Al's swarthy fore-lock draw close to his skull, and become blond, as if it had been stuffed under a wig. I realize I've vomited again when it splashes against the same foot, and Al speaks.

"Is there some reason you wanted me to see that?"

"My car…" I murmur with my head between my knees, afraid to raise it and open my eyes. But I do, because I need to know that everything has returned to less abnormal. "It's here."

"I told you last night it was an easy fix," he says over his shoulder as he walks back toward the house. His forelock has returned to its normal shade and cut. "You'd know that if you knew how to care about nice things."

"You said that too."

"What it means is that a man shouldn't have what he can't rightfully see to, and if he does find himself in that position anyway, he should reflect that luck ends the same as everything else, and when his does, because it will…"

"Don't worry, Al," I say, using the doorframe to raise myself, and scraping the vomit from my foot on the edge of the top step. "I'll continue fucking your sister for as long as you're willing to hate me for it."

"That isn't why," he says, the implication of what I've said having apparently no effect on his response. "You stole from me, and I want her happy. So you keep her that way, and I'll forgive you for that when I feel ready or maybe not. But what I can say for sure is I'll learn to live with it because family don't forgive grudges, but it makes room for them. I don't need to love you if she does, and I'm glad of that because even without you thieving from me I ain't sure I could."

"We're not family," I say, though I'm no longer sure that it is true.

"I wouldn't expect someone like you to know the difference," says Al. "Clean yourself up, Henry. Go to work."

I retrieve the dishtowel from the grass, and use it to wipe the rest of the puke from my foot, before casting it back into the yard and going inside. There is a text from Denise asking if I can meet her at her uncle's house, and take Dora for the day. Before responding, I check the list delivered by Al, to make sure I have nothing that will conflict.

2.

I haven't visited Wilbur's house since I was very young, and as I park my car at the curb, the structure evinces not so much a cry for help, but howl of ungodly debasement far beyond the point at which assistance would make a difference. When a bachelor lives alone for long enough, his dwelling becomes an extension of solitude, and thus, a sort of curbside noticeboard reporting the occupant's inner condition to the broad world without -- as if the house itself seeks to claim a share of the responsibility left by the absence of a spouse, and, in the lack of language (since architecture cannot speak), begins to shadow its owner, absorbing his success, or enduring his failure. Thus, a man's home is both his monument and mausoleum, weaving a rubric of either wellbeing or malignancy for the observant pedestrian. I wonder if perhaps Wilbur moved. Aside from a wisp of smoke from the crooked chimney, his property looks abandoned.

"If you want to know if someone is depressed," my mother once told me, "look at their front yard. If they have political signs, holiday decorations, a car on blocks, a speedboat, an above-ground pool, or a lot of sun-bleached children's toys, you can bet the owner is in a dark place." Except for a colorless rowboat laid belly-up beside the garage like a capsized turtle, Wilbur's yard has none of these items. Or what I can see of the yard.

A shaggy hedge girds the lawn like the untrimmed beard of a man lost at sea, and the lawn would doubtless be overgrown, were it not entrapped beneath several inches of snow.

I tramp up the unshoveled walk to the door, and tap on it with my knuckles, since the lower jaw of the doorknocker seems to have gone missing. Displaced flakes of the same paint once used to caparison the rowboat (an indeterminate, neglectful hue) rain from the panel, peppering the area around my feet as if simply touching the house quickens its decay. It's a shame. The property could be attractive if someone other than Wilbur owned it. The house is an elderly New England cape set on a half-acre lot that backs up onto the woods at the base of Maybrick Peak. It would make a desirable addition to A.P.M.'s listings, and for a moment, I regret not divesting Wilbur of it during the (one-sided) negotiation over Le Champo.

But that was when Mr. Castle was around to protect me from his wife, and I was free to turn up my collar, call myself a lizard, and take what I wanted. Apparently, that's no longer how it works. Jo says she wants to improve what we have, which is like saying she wants to do more with less. And if today's list of duties is in any way portentous, I probably won't see much of A.P.M. in the future.

I hear barking from the other side of the door, and as Denise opens it, Dora charges out, and I squat on the walk to greet her, touching her ears, and head, but this feels insubstantial after our time apart. I sit down on the front step, allowing the dog to lean against me, and place one arm around her, and then the other, with my head rotated toward Denise, who is watching me hug the dog from the doorway.

"I've missed you," I say to her, leaning my face on Dora's back. "I realize that's unusual. And I'm sorry about yesterday."

"She missed you, I think," says Denise, impartially. "It was fine. Wilbur took her while I was at work."

"Wilbur can...care for an animal?"

"Wilbur is one of those people that loves dogs but doesn't think he should own one," says Denise. "He's right, of course. Would you like to come inside?"

"I thought you had to work."

"I do," she says, moving out of the doorway to admit me as I stand up. "But not for a few hours. I asked you to come get Dora now because I was hoping you might explain yesterday. I don't want to be curious about it. But I am."

"It might be more than you want to know, Denise."

"Tell it anyway," she says, closing the door behind me, and leading me through a hallway lined with perilous stacks of VHS cassettes, and thinner columns of DVDs. I don't remember much of the house from the time when I visited it with my mother. We were never here for long, and I wasn't told the purpose of our visits. But I do recall Wilbur's movie collection being a bit more polite, the body of his library contained in a massive brace of bookshelves in the living room, which, as Denise and I enter it now, remain intact, though overstuffed. Framed posters hang crookedly around the room, all obscured by isolated, leaning towers of media except that above the mantle, a striking, morbid oil portrait of a Yanomamo warrior from 'Cannibal Holocaust,' in which the subject gnaws a length of what is presumably intestine.

"Strange choice," I say, gesturing at the poster above the fireplace, the popping flame beneath it providing the only light in the otherwise cave-like living room.

"I haven't seen it," says Denise, sitting on a couch to the side of the fireplace.

"It's probably the best of the Italian cannibal film boom of the 1970's and 80's," I say, crossing the floor to join her. "The director, Ruggero Deodato, had to produce the actors in a court in Rome to prove he hadn't murdered them to make it."

"I won't see it," confirms Denise as I sit beside her in what feels like the same place I once waited for my mother. It is possible the couch has not moved since that time? I remember Wilbur asked me if there was anything I would like to watch, and when I said I didn't know, he put on something by Ralph Bakshi, and disappeared. This established the template for return visits. I would watch the same film on the same couch for the same length of time. I don't want to believe my mother was sleeping with him, and I can't imagine Wilbur provoking the sort of passion that would compel her to bring me along, rather than wait. But what else could they have been doing?

"There was a television," I say, forgetting why I was invited inside, and gesturing toward the space in the room I recall the appliance filling.

"He got rid of it," says Denise, curling her knees beneath her, and jabbing at the hearth with a poker. "He says he doesn't have the energy to watch them anymore. Films, I mean."

"And yet, they're everywhere."

"Function is the enemy of the collector," says Denise. "I'm sorry it's so dark. I tried opening curtains but the cassettes were in the way…"

We're both quiet, and staring at the windows across the room, through which gray, wintery light is divided by the skewed slats of a venetian blind. Dora pads into the living room, chewing something, and lies down in front of the fire.

"We're both stalling," says Denise. "Maybe I don't want to know. And maybe you don't want to tell me."

"It's not that, Denise. I don't know where to begin, and even if I did, I'm not sure what any of it means."

256

"Are you in trouble, Henry?"

"I think I've been in trouble for some time," I say, her question making me feel more comfortable in the room for some reason. "And I'm worried that if I tell you everything, you won't like me anymore. I know when I say that, I sound like a child. I don't regret anything I've done. But right now, I wish I didn't have a past."

"Regret is a form of emotional weakness," she says, resuming her torment of the hearth.

"Must you always speak that way?" I say, feeling impatient, though for what, I can't say.

"What way?"

"In aphorisms. I'm trying to..."

"Are you going to tell it?" she says, dropping the poker with a clatter, and turning to me. "I don't like people who make me wait. Dora is half yours, which means that I am tethered to you. Whatever you say, I will like you enough to see her. Now, no more preamble. Speak, lizard."

"How did you..."

"It's written in the margins in your notebook. Frequently, and with illustrations."

I don't respond. I know I have a choice. I could say nothing, and leave. Exit this creepy house, return to my car, and go about my errands, essentially fulfilling the role written for me the night before, and delivered this morning by Aloysius. I can imagine my life without the possibility of seeing Denise (and Dora). How easy it would be to comply and spend the rest of my days running trivial errands for Al, and watching Jo grow old in the pool house. I don't fear being alone. I fear being unable to be anything but alone.

So, I begin to speak, starting with Jo exposing herself to me in the kitchen of the Castle house after it was first built (because this seems as good a place as any), and moving forward from there, allowing the ineradicable, entwined history of my personal and professional life to unfold before Denise, who does not remove her gaze from my face for the duration of the telling, appearing to listen with her expression like a dancer speaking with his or her body. I talk, and she watches, as Dora snores between us on the floor.

Telling it takes all of an hour, less time then I would have expected for what amounts to a quarter summary of my entire life. But my biography occupies so little space in the retelling, that as I finish explaining this morning's conversation with Al, I feel as if I've left something untold, and that I should go on, even if nothing remains.

I don't. Instead, I sit quietly on Wilbur's couch bereft of secrets, an unfamiliar and entirely unwelcome feeling. Truth pillories the honest man as often as it liberates him. Too late now. I'm afraid to look at Denise, but I need some way to indicate that I've finished speaking. The silence raised in the wake of my full stop is so paralytic, that when Denise speaks first, I'm about to pronounce 'The End' aloud. But her voice turns the words on my tongue to sand, which I neither swallow nor spit, holding it instead like a wadded portion of dip lodged in my cheek.

"So...you were demoted," she says, her incautious eyes finding mine, peering around the corner of my own body. "And you're going to be a father."

"Please don't be afraid of me," I say. I try punctuating this with a smile, but notice my reflection in the glass joining of a frame edging from behind a menhir of videocassettes at her back, and see that rather than a cheerful young man, I resemble a snake trying to disengage its jawbone to swallow something whole.

"I need a picture," says Denise, standing and crossing the

room to rummage a bag in the far corner. She returns holding my notebook, and sits far closer to me than I would have expected, the cover falling open across our legs, which sit beneath it like parallel sets of track. "You don't care if I draw in this?"

"No," I say, watching the still familiar (now useless) names, dates, and infractions pass in a flurry of pages as Denise shuffles them, seeking a blank one. "I don't think I'll ever need it again."

"So, Mr. C.," she says, writing this in the center of a vacant page. "He marries...

"Lenore."

"Jo's sister. Younger or older?"

"Older," I say, watching her add two branches to 'Mr. C.' "Lenore is Isidore's mother. She died in a car accident two years ago."

"And he marries Jo."

"Yes. No children."

"And you think Jo and...the name of the creepy butler, once more?"

"Al. Aloysius."

"You think they're related?" she says, adding Isidore to a branch depending from the names of his parents, and creating a separate stem for Al. "But how?"

"Siblings. They have to be brother and sister. They may even be twins."

"And you're fucking her," she says, adding my name to the page beside Jo, and circling them both.

"Not willingly. If I don't do it..."

"She'll send you to jail with Blivet. I know. You told me," says Denise, looking at the sinister family tree between us, tapping the page with her pen. "Your mother belongs here, I think. What was her name?"

"Winifred. Winnie. She hated it. Her name, I mean."

"And she disappeared after Lenore died."

"Yes. The following October. My final year in college."

"On Halloween."

"Yes."

"So tomorrow is the second anniversary of her disappearance."

"I...suppose it is."

"And you haven't seen Mr. Castle since..."

"The night at your cabin. Wilbur's cabin. The cabin."

Denise stares at the chart, my mother's name orbiting the others untethered, while I pretend to stare it, unsure what I'm meant to divine. A log pops in the hearth, and Dora stirs beside it, but doesn't wake up.

"It has to be Jo," says Denise suddenly, setting the notebook at her feet, and standing up. "Whatever happened to your mother also happened to Mr. Castle, and she did it, or had someone do it."

"I want it all to be a coincidence, Denise."

"Even if it is, something about Halloween in Acheron makes disposing of a body very convenient."

"It's possible that he's out of town, and she's just playing, keeping house in her own way until her husband returns," I say, speaking my wishes aloud, allowing the falsehoods to sooth me.

"You don't honestly think that, do you?" asks Denise.

"No. Not at all," I say, her statement evicting all hope from my own. "But I wish I could escape the finality of it all. I told Cornelius this would happen, but even when I said it, I thought I was wrong, or I didn't want to be right, and he didn't believe it either, so I let it go. But I could have done more. And I didn't."

"You feel guilty," she says, sounding almost bored, which causes me to pause for a moment before responding.

"No. I'm not really familiar with guilt," I say. "Mr. Castle was kind as long his expectations were met, which makes him a normal employer, and therefore, impossible to admire. Or love. I don't miss him. I miss the balance he provided. People are horrid when they have nothing to conceal."

"Will something bad happen to you because you saw me today?" asks Denise, without discernable emotion. She reaches down for the notebook on the floor.

"Well, Jo says she loves me, and is having our baby. So I'm confident she won't kill me."

"But she knows about me."

"Yes, and I'm sorry for putting you at risk by coming here, but you're the only person in town who doesn't think I killed my mother, and that's…valuable. Even the people that like me think I did it. But yes, Jo is aware of you and Dora. I don't know if I was followed, or what they might do if they found out I was here, but it might best for you to avoid the cabin until I…"

"Until you what, Henry?"

I try to think of an answer that will satisfy us both, but I have none.

"…I don't know, Denise. It may best if…"

"Tell me."

"I could live this way. I could stay with her, and live there with them, and perform errands until I…until they retire me, I suppose. It would be peaceful, and easy. Perhaps after a while I'll regain some of autonomy, and then I could see you again. If Jo is in fact pregnant, she'll probably be very occupied with the child, and I could sneak out to the cabin, your cabin, or Wilbur's cabin. It should be safe for you to go back there by then, and maybe the would allow me to have Dora on weekends, I could…"

"You're willing to live that way?" says Denise, clutching the book to her chest, and looking revolted. "And you think I will wait for you to live like that. Or hope maybe that when she's finished fucking you, she'll forget about both of us long enough for you to come pick up the dog? This is the best you can imagine?"

"Accept. Not imagine."

"I won't be here forever. And neither will you, unless you allow it. You're being deliberately uncreative. This is why Cornelius didn't listen to you, and why you didn't do more when he didn't listen to you. Because even when you know what you need to do, you're a coward."

"But I don't. If I run, you won't be safe..."

"Stop saying that. It isn't true, but I think you want it to be so that you won't have to leave. Why do you want to stay?"

"Please let me finish. Even if you are safe, they could dredge up the Dennis thing, or something else. Mr. Castle took most of it with him, but there is plenty they could discover by canvassing the townsfolk."

"They shouldn't find this," says Denise, nodding her chin at the notebook cradled in her arms.

"No. That would be bad," I say, and she nods once more, before turning around and dropping it in the fireplace.

"Now they won't," she says, resuming her place on the couch. I'm determined not to react. We watch the flames grasp the book like claws drawing it deeper into the hungry embers, the covers wither, the paper between them catches, and within seconds my unofficial guide to Acheron's private life is entirely consumed.

"Telling the authorities presents a similar problem," I continue, as if nothing has happened. "I can't expose Jo without exposing myself to whatever she might tell them. And if I do that, she will tell them a lot. I don't think I'm a criminal, but it's possible that a jury might."

"So you're afraid of having to go to court and risk jail because of a woman who will send you there anyway if you don't fuck her?"

"I'm more afraid of discomfort than death."

Denise looks at me for a moment as if trying to guess whether or not I'm serious (I am).

"Martyrdom is a selfish act anyway," she says. "And no one knows what she is. They won't thank you for surrendering yourself to ensnare her."

"I'm beyond their absolution anyway. To them, I will always be the lonely bastard who orphaned himself."

"So you have to kill her," says Denise. She's joking, though I don't realize it. "That's the only choice left."

"Yes, I know. I was actually making a list of ways it could be done, before Al came to my house this morning," I say, speaking frankly, still unaware that Denise was kidding. "But I realized after he left that I'd have to kill them both. I couldn't have Al running loose afterward. So that would be a minimum of two murders to regain my liberty. Three, if you count the baby."

"You made...a list?" she says, grimly fascinated.

"Well, yes. I'm in the habit of writing things down, as you know, but list making helps me approach a problem with multiple solutions, and choose one. In this case, my ideas were sound, but writing them down drew attention to other problems. For instance, it occurred to me that I can't kill her on my own. But I could if I had help. And Al found my list, and knew what it was, which means I...or we, if you're willing, need to kill him too."

I pause, because I feel like I'm talking a lot, and sound perhaps too eager to dispatch them both. And when I turn to Denise, watching her across the waste of silence that has gathered between us on disparate sides of the couch, I realize based on her expression that what I mistook for eagerness to spitball this topic (murder) was actually a joke. She doesn't look frightened exactly. Instead, her mouth forms a bemused pinpoint in the center of her thin face, while her eyes appear overfocused in an effort to remove me from the room by unimpeachable force of will.

"Please don't be afraid of me," I repeat, not even trying to smile.

"For you," she says. "That's how I'm afraid."

"Well, that's better, I think, than the other. Fearing me, I mean. I don't want to hurt anyone, but sometimes they make it so unavoidable."

"Have you ever killed anyone, Henry?"

"Do I need to tell you that I wouldn't ever hurt you?"

"That's not why I'm asking. If we're going to do this, prior experience would be helpful."

"No, I haven't. I'm sorry," I say, apologizing for my categorical ignorance of bloodshed, but stupidly happy that she has agreed to help me learn something of it. "That's what Al said when he saw the list. That I don't know killing. But how hard could it be?"

"I don't think it's the killing that's difficult. It's the not getting caught. And the living afterwards."

"Well, making certain they're dead seems obvious."

"That's not what I mean," she says. "It's about you living afterwards, with the success of that killing on you. Would you rather live with remorse, or Jo?"

"But I don't like them," I say, simply. "Why would I care that they're gone? Her, and Al, and that ghost child of hers. And isn't remorse just a different form of regret, which is weakness, according to you? I'm not weak. Or, I won't be weak."

"Some would say that our capacity for reason over animal instinct is why we're human. And by using your reason to choose instinct in order to solve a problem makes you subhuman, and condemnable…That's why we kill people who kill people. Because by taking life, they no longer deserve it. This isn't about me, Henry."

264

"But we kill everything. That's what humans do. When something is in our way, or by accident, or because we just feel like it. That's our purpose. To bathe our hands in the blood of all creation. Our 'reason' just means that we can invent new ways to be more horrible while calling it something else, like 'initiative,' or 'ambition,' or 'progress.' But we can't escape the killing because we are the killing. All I want is to get rid of two people who, by your standard, are subhuman anyway..."

"Not my standard. A standard."

"Well...Yes, I see. But I'm being threatened. I can't think of another species that won't kill to save itself. Can you?"

"We can't kill them together," she says, as if she hasn't heard me. She crosses the room to tug mindlessly on the string of a blind barricading the window. "But we should take them soon, one after the other, I mean. Before the second knows the first is missing."

"I suppose this is why people have accomplices. I've always wondered."

"So, it's less about how, and more about when."

"The how is still important. I can't imagine sticking Jo with a knife. But I could easily push her off something, or hit her with a club. However, I think I could easily stab Aloysius. I suppose I'm limited. Is that inconvenient? Or unusual?"

"You said she's having you pick up costumes," says Denise, ignoring me again. "Is that for the ball at the hotel?"

"I suppose. No one will come up the mountainside to trick or treat at the house."

"Then that's when it should happen. After the Halloween party. When the townsfolk are altered, and displaced. Will Al be there?"

"I don't know. He would normally stay at the house, but I

don't know what normal is now. He may come."

"As soon as you find out, let me know. Either way, I will meet you at the house after the thing at the hotel."

"If it doesn't affect where you meet me, why do you need to know?"

"Because if he stays at the house while you and Jo are at the hotel," she says calmly, once again fiddling with the pull of the blind, "they won't be together."

"I understand," I say, hoping that I do. The shade gives with a report like a musket, and the room is immediately drowned in neutral gray light from the window. Dora raises her head at the commotion, but settles her snout between her paws, watching me, when nothing else follows it.

3.

It doesn't occur to me that bringing Dora grocery shopping might be a problem until I'm approached by the produce manager at Grover's Market, a lean, officious beansprout who looks like an unhappy student. I don't notice him right away, even when the leash tugs my right wrist as the dog sees him coming. He says something that I don't hear, and even if I did, I can't turn around to listen. My torso is anchored by a shopping basket, overfull of Al's comestibles, and slung across my forearm, while the corresponding hand raises an eggplant as if it is a lantern from a mound of them arranged in the cold case. In the other hand, I hold Al's list at eye level, trying to decipher his handwriting. It's a rare circumstance when literacy is more of a handicap than a benefit. No matter. The threatening cuneiform on the page could say 'eggplant,' or 'escargot,' or 'enchiladas,' but whatever he cooks, I will not eat. Or perhaps I will. Denise said everything should remain normal until it isn't (meaning tomorrow evening). So I'll partake of the meal, if necessary. But none of them, Al, Jo, or even Denise, can force me to enjoy it.

I stow the eggplant in the basket hanging from my arm, and turn around just as the produce manager, whose nameplate reads 'Oliver Himmel' (so 'Oliver' then), is preparing to tap me on the shoulder. But as I lurch to face him with my dog and groceries, his finger misses this mark, tapping my sternum instead, as if my chest is a sheet of glass, and Oliver is trying to signal a friend or coworker on the other side of it. His finger makes an ugly, ossific noise against my breastbone, which startles us both, and for a moment, the only sound in the barren aisle is the hum of the vegetable housing behind me, and scuffling of Dora's paws on the tile as she struggles to make herself relevant in this new circumstance.

"Yes...Oliver?" I say, staring first at his chest (and the nametag) and then at the bewildered face hovering six inches above my own. "Is that how we ask for things?"

"You...I'm sorry...I meant to...," he says, collecting what there is of him to collect, straightening his apron, and trying to look both authoritative and apologetic. "On behalf of Grover's Market, I apologize. I meant to touch your shoulder, because..."

"You can't touch my shoulder," I say, deciding to antagonize him. It's only noon, and already the day stretches before me like the waterless plane of a desert I am compelled to cross, one unrecoverable dune after another. And I still have to pick up the costumes and meet Isidore, both of which are beneath my dignity. But more than this, I have not adjusted to the reality that my time is now planned for me, and this makes me intemperate and aggressive. Thus, Oliver shall suffer. I know it's cheap, but it will make me feel better.

"Well, you were ignoring me," he says, unbalked. "And dogs are not allowed in the store."

"I only see a dog."

"Right. They're not allowed."

"I heard you. But there is just one."

"I understand, Mr....?"

"Mr. none of your business, Oliver."

"Please, sir. You're not listening," he says, his placid head flushing with a dull, angry heat above me like the bulb crowning a lighthouse. "Please take your dog, and leave the store. If you wish to complete your shopping, I will watch your purchases while you remove…"

"But you indicated that the problem was related to a plurality of animals in the store."

"I did not, sir"

"Indeed you did, Oliver. You said, 'dogs are not allowed in the store,' which led me to believe that unless I travel with a pack of them, I'm free to complete my shopping in the company one pet, a single beast, a solitary animal companion. Or this dog here, for example."

I gesture at Dora, rocking between us on her haunches.

"I see," says Oliver, struggling to produce the grammar of the rule. "I misspoke. No dogs…I mean, all dog…any dogs is…a dog is not allowed-"

"A dog, certainly. But what about this dog?" I say, gesturing once more at Dora.

"Any dog!" corrects Oliver. "Any dog, and all dogs, anything with four legs and fur is not, and are not, allowed in the store. Now, please leave, and return without him-"

"Her."

"Without her! I will see to your purchases…"

"You'll see to them, will you? May I ask, Oliver, from where you derive the authority to eject a customer from the store?"

"I'm the produce manager," he says, gesturing at the nametag, which doesn't indicate this.

"Does that also make you the grocery police?"

"No. Yes. I don't know. That's not relevant. Please take the dog out of the store. I will…"

"See to my purchases, yes, I know. But if you only manage the produce, then rather than leaving, I could just move to the dairy section, or the butchery, beyond the fruits and vegetables in other words, since this is where your domain ends. Perhaps a different manager will be more hospitable."

"No!" he shouts, catching the attention of several other customers, who stare for a safe amount of time before returning to their shopping. "No! They will tell you the same thing I'm telling you! Why are you this way?"

"I'm no way, Oliver. I'm just trying to understand a policy that cannot be understood from talking to you, apparently."

"No!" he shouts again, taking several rapid and unsteady steps away from me, and placing a hand on the salad bar to regain his balance. "No! It isn't true! You're doing this for some other reason! I don't know what you're so angry about, and I don't care! Just please stop taking it out on me! Please!"

"So, can the dog stay or not?" I ask, as tears ebb from his dull eyes, tracing a singular trajectory of anguish down either cheek, just as a familiar voice speaks from behind me.

"Can I help with whatever is going on here?"

"I told him no dogs! I told him, Mr. Ratliff!" says Oliver, as Grover moves between us, touching the top of Dora's head, and listening to his stricken employee with what appears to be genuine concern. "But all he does is stand there, asking questions, and I just can't listen to it! He asked me if I was the grocery cops!"

"Grocery police," I correct.

"Like that!" says Oliver, pointing with the same finger he used to doorknock me. "Just like that! Do you see what he does?"

"It's fine," says Grover. "Lower your voice, Oliver. And take a break. Or better, go home. You're not in trouble. I think you need some time not here. See you tomorrow, please."

Oliver edges around the salad bar, his eyes fastened on me

until he disappears behind a translucent plastic curtain hung in a doorway at the rear of the section.

"Cornelius hiked tuition," says Grover, turning back to me. "So, he, Oliver I mean, has been pulling double shifts, and continuing his studies without sleeping or eating, as far as I can tell."

"What does he study?"

"Military history, I think."

"I'd expect him to have a greater tolerance for conflict."

"Some people wage uncommon war," he says obliquely, his mild gaze traveling to the basket hung from my arm. "Normally you do your shopping after the store is closed. Is something wrong?"

"This is for Al."

"Then something must be wrong."

"I think you know more than nothing about it."

"I don't know if I do," says Grover, unruffled. "My office? I'd be surprised if you didn't need to talk."

"Thank you," I say, and he nods, and starts to walk up the aisle toward the front of the store, but I don't move, and after a moment, he notices that I haven't followed.

"I can't assure you that you can trust me until I know more," he says, and continues walking toward his office. "It's your choice, Henry."

This may be true, but it doesn't feel like my choice, even as I beckon Dora and hobble with my basket to the head of the aisle, past the phalanx of registers, ignoring the fawning chatter from the clerks at the sight of the dog padding behind me, and through a door which Grover has been good enough to leave open. The interior is further disordered from my last visit, and with stacks of fliers, and boxes of Releaf Tours promotional material reaching nearly to the ceiling. Grover has cleared a pair of chairs before his desk, behind which he taps gently on a computer, his expression behind his steel-rimmed spectacles a portrait of the sort of concord only achieved by merciless pragmatism. Pride does not allow me to envy him.

I close the door behind me, and take one chair, and Dora hoists herself onto the other, as if she is a constituent of some kind. We both wait patiently for Grover to discontinue his tapping on the keyboard, and acknowledge us.

"Cute dog," he says, closing the lid of the computer, and watching Dora with an earnest tenderness. "She's welcome in the store anytime."

"Why don't you have a dog?" I ask in order to turn his attention to me.

"It isn't necessary," he says, without looking away from Dora, or altering his affection expression.

"I see," I say, and pause. "No, I don't. What does that mean?"

"I think some folks are blessed with understanding people, some not," says Grover. "I understand people, so I own a store. People come here to buy things they need, or that make them happy. I enjoy helping them do that."

"You're extroverted. This is the right place for you."

"I didn't say I like them. It's different. If you understand people, you're consigned to work with them. In fact, understanding them probably precludes liking them. But unless I want to live without doing the best I can for myself, that's my role. I think that's your problem."

"Among others."

"It's all the same problem. Or, it has a common source. You don't understand anyone, Henry. But you think you do, and worse, you think they don't know you think that. But they do. And it makes them feel like furniture."

"You can sit on furniture," I say, beginning to wonder why I'm here.

"My point is that you're misapplied," says Grover. "Mr. Castle should have hired you to tend his garden, not manage the townsfolk. Anyone could have seen how that would go, and maybe that's what he wanted. But it's sad and inefficient, because you understand other things very well. You care for this animal, because you understand her deeply, and without effort. When I look at your dog, I see intelligence. Just not the sort I know how to make happy. That's why it isn't necessary for me to own one. It isn't part of my role. But it's part of yours."

"I don't believe in fate, Grover."

"It isn't fate, Henry. It's working with what you have."

"Funny. Jo said that's what we're doing now. Actually, Al said that was what she said."

"Yes, he was in here this morning. That's what I meant to tell you. He seems to have appropriated your position with the tour company. He wanted to look at the account statements, and booking records. You're buying his groceries, so I'm sure you knew it was coming."

"I'm no longer surprised by misfortune."

"Well, apropos of what I was just saying, maybe it isn't unfortunate. The worst that can happen is you find something better to do with your time."

"That isn't the worst," I say, standing up. Dora remains in her chair. "I wish it was."

"Whatever you think you're going to do, know that even if they don't see it coming, it will turn out poorly for you," says Grover, reopening his computer. "You're broadcasting vengeance. Do you even remember how to appear normal?"

"Yes, and I am not."

"Exhibit A: Oliver."

"That was...an experiment," I say, even though I know how

hollow it must sound. "No, that's wrong. It was what you said. Or, it was part of it. You don't know everything, but even if you did, I think what you're saying wouldn't change much. So, I'm going to apologize in advance for not taking your advice."

"If I can help you without putting myself in harm's way," says Grover, once again beginning to type, "please, let me know."

4.

AROUND 4PM, I PASS MR. BASH on the stairs leading to the office of Acheron Property Management, where I'm supposed to meet Isidore. He doesn't recognize me immediately, but when he does, his eyes narrow and set as if expecting a challenge, while my own settle on his exposed tonsure, or the place where a hat should be, as per our agreement (in writing).

"Hello, Mr. Lizard," he intones. "Hot on the trail of a banshee?"

"No hat then, Norman?"

"Mr. Bash! And he said I didn't have to wear it."

"Who said?"

"A man who stopped in this morning."

"Do you always listen to strangers, Norman?"

"Mr. Bash!" says Mr. Bash. "And I'm sure you know who I mean."

"I'm sure I do," I say. Al had a busy morning. "He's new, and unaware of our agreement which, I should remind you, is now attached as a rider to your contract. There is nothing any of us can do about that, except hope that you hold up your end, Norman."

"Stop using my name that way!"

"What way, Norman?"

"Like that!"

"I don't understand, Norman."

He descends roughly past me, as if he can't stand another moment alone with me in the stairwell. But pauses on a lower step, and turns around.

"I'll put it this way: fuck your hat. Do you understand that? It's clear to everyone except you that you no longer have any power here," he says, more smug than angry. "Time to grow up, Mr. Hoffmann. Good luck chasing goblins."

This said, he turns back around and takes one step toward the exit before tripping over Dora, who is hunched on the step beneath him, and thumping to the bottom of the stairs like a duffel bag stuffed with overripe fruit. I've turned away as well, so I don't actually see him fall, but I hear it. A series of arrhythmic reports following the initial collision between his body and the steps, and the scattered, hapless sound of his limbs failing to find steadiment, punctuated by the finality of a window shattering as he rolls onto the landing, and then stillness. Mr. Bash rests in a cradle of broken glass at the bottom of the stairs. His fall was quite literally broken by the front door, which, rather than admitting Mr. Bash into the street, exploded upon him as if someone tossed a brick through it.

He looks dead from where I'm standing, but the fetal heap on the landing emits a sort of querulous pant, which lures Dora from the step where she ambushed the efficiency expert, to his side. Mr. Bash lives. Her muzzle dislodges the skeletal frame of his now empty spectacles as she begins licking his face, her tongue probing the corner of his mouth as he speaks.

"Henry...Are you there?"

"Yes, Norman."

"I'm...very hurt."

"Me too."

"I...I'm sorry...for what I said, a moment ago," says Mr. Bash, trying to brush Dora away from his face. I call her and she pads up the stairs, and lies beside me on the upper tread. Her tail sweeps nervously across the floor, her muzzle planted between her paws as she watches Mr. Bash try to rise from the floor of the landing. He fails grandly, resettling his body at the foot the steps with a granular popping of broken glass, his right hand leaving a thin service road of blood on the wall above him as it founders for a hold. "I don't think anything is broken. But I'm bleeding, and my leg..."

"Tell me about your pain, Norman."

"Please, I'll do anything Mr. Hoff...Henry. It's Henry, isn't it? I'll wear that hat, Henry. Call someone, or get help, or just give me your phone, and I'll wear it every day. I promise."

"I've grown up since we last spoke, Norman. I no longer care about all that."

"Please, Henry. Be a human being. I know how angry you are. I knew when we first met. I don't know why, but I know it isn't all about me. You have to see that. I'm know we're both in trouble, but I'll ask first. Help me. Please."

"Why do you think I'm in trouble, Norman?"

"He said it earlier."

"Who said it?" I ask, but I don't wait for the answer because I know whom Mr. Bash means. Apparently, I've gotten into some 'trouble,' and it is this vagary that is being fed to the townsfolk to explain my diminished presence among them. They wouldn't spoil my already poor reputation, because Jo wants me around for private reasons. But they'll certainly cast aspersions on it to dissolve the remnant of my former dominion. Perhaps Al fed Grover the same story earlier today. It may have prompted that motivational speech in his office. Yes, I am in trouble, but not the 'trouble.' They are not the same, but I can't prevent anyone from believing what they want. I never could, which is why the idea that I, a troubled orphan with a checkered past, have disappointed the expectation of my powerful employers in some unrevealed yet entirely credible fashion is likely a welcome and unshocking bit of gossip for the Acheron rumor mill. They always knew I was an erratic, if not outright bad seed. And now, I'm just as guilty as the rest of them. Thanks, Al.

Before he can respond, I leave the efficiency expert at the bottom of the stairs and pass through the vestibule into the A.P.M. office. The interchangeable receptionists pronounce an interchangeable greeting as I pause at their station.

"Someone broke the window on the front door," I say. "Call the guy who fixes that sort of thing. Is Isidore here?"

"Yes, he's in the meeting room," says one of them, looking concerned.

"How did the window break?" asks the other, mirroring this concern.

"Go and see maybe," I say, leaving them, only to catch the owlish eye of Dennis watching me over the rim of his mug as I pass athwart the desks.

"I heard you were in trouble," he says, rotating in his chair to face me in the aisle. On the computer behind him, I see the white and red insignia of a dating website. "I hope it's nothing serious?"

"Shopping for a Moldovan bride?" I say, nodding at the monitor. He smiles, but doesn't turn around.

"A man gets lonely. Is it medical?"

"You think you're lonely now?"

"Compared with who? You?" he says, sipping from the mug. The thread of a teabag catches the corner of his ichthyoid lips as they smack together with myopic triumph, and he burps like a bullfrog, blowing it into my face before I can turn away. The composite odor of his insides is split between fruity, over-sweetened tea, and some sort of meat sandwich sitting half eaten on his desk. "Whoa! What a stinker! Excuse me."

"Why is everyone daring me to kill them today?" I ask, trying not to flinch at his extrusion.

"Maybe it's the other way. Sometimes I only notice things like that after they get me in trouble."

"Someone has to be hated so the simple people, like you, Dennis, don't get confused."

"Well, thanks, Henry," he says, his smile swallowed by the mug as he raises it to his mouth. "We're all real appreciative. I'm sure your key to the city is in the mail."

"If I'm already in trouble," I say, no longer looking at him, but the window behind his desk. "Why am I allowing a slob like you to berate me?"

"So you don't get yourself in a worse fix, I imagine."

"But she loves me. There is always that. And because she loves me, I am free, in a sense, because even if I'm stripped of my duties, and most of my privileges, she will still love me, because that's how a person like that understands love. It's a decision you make, and once made, there is no remaking it."

"No one loves you," says Dennis, returning the mug to lips in a motion that has become excruciating for its smug predictability, as if he were sipping from a goblet of my personal sorrow, and relishing every drop.

"But you're wrong. And because you're wrong, I am at liberty to do…well, this for example," I say, reaching out, and goosing the bottom of the mug as Dennis tips it against his chin. The porcelain lip hits his teeth, and he chokes and sputters as a tepid breaker of decaffeinated tea washes down his windpipe, and onto the collar of his shirt. "Do you understand now, Dennis? Someone loves me, so I am protected, perhaps more than I ever have been. I don't know why I didn't realize it before. But you helped show me that I have to take even less shit from simpleminded fucks like you than I did when he was alive. Yes, you've done all that, so thank you, Dennis. Thank you so much."

"I think my tooth is chipped," he says, coughing, and probing the interior of his mouth with a stubby finger. A filament of blood trickles down it, dripping from his wrist onto the sandwich at his elbow. "My lip is cut."

"Liberty and love always have a price."

"Does this look like it needs stiches?" he asks, folding his upper lip over itself like a tortilla to expose a minor wound, and inclining his idiot head toward me. "I taste a lot of blood."

"Bleed then, I suppose"

"In fact, all I taste is blood. I'm calling an ambulance," he says, picking up the phone just as an EMT enters the lobby from the stairwell with one of the secretaries, both of them looking like they've just seen a collection of war photography.

"And they've arrived," I say, gesturing toward the technician in the vestibule. "Tell them you tried to swallow your own head."

"But how did they...I didn't even finish dialing...Doesn't matter. I'm injured," he says absently, setting the phone back in its cradle, and heaving himself from the chair toward the reception area. "I'll say I bit it. For now."

"Say what you like, deceiver," I say to no one, Dennis having passed beyond the glass. "I'm taking this."

His half eaten sandwich is cold in my hand, and I don't remember removing it from the desktop. But here it is, suddenly in my possession, the beige meat and dry orange cheese edging from between bread dappled with his blood. I'm not hungry but I want to derive some plunder from this exchange, if only to remind myself that I am loved, and safe, even if it is isn't the sort of safety I would choose. For now, the sandwich will act as a placeholder until I find something more suitable. Denise said everything should appear normal, but I'm weary of running errands, and being treated like an erratic ward of the townsfolk. It's ostensibly the first day of my new job. What's more common (or 'normal') than a few mistakes? And considering this will all be settled tomorrow night, a little recklessness is in order. Thus, Dennis and the Mug of Sorrows. At worst, my misbehavior will provide Jo with the opportunity to chastise and forgive me, or otherwise exercise the power differential she conflates with affection. And since inflicting her particular tenderness seems to strengthen it, I can't lose. Denise knows enough to protect herself until tomorrow, and Jo wouldn't play that card unless she needed it. No, my penance will likely be a long discussion of responsibility, or a shorter one relating to leverage, followed by acts against nature, and an expanded to-do list delivered by Al at the break of dawn. Nothing extraordinary, and certainly nothing I can't handle. "Always give a person what they want if it doesn't cost you anything. Just make sure you remember it for later." Thanks, Mom.

I leave Dora with the secretaries, who watch me as if they're afraid I'll fling one of them out a window. I suppose it's a superficially reasonable fear. Both of the people I last had contact with left with the EMTs, but the dog obviates whatever tension remains between the reception staff and myself. As I leave them, and pass through a door beyond the desks in the main office, Dora is seated on a stray desk chair between the two identical young women, eating the combined remainder of their lunch out of a plastic take-away container on the desktop.

The meeting room is at the end of a labyrinthine hallway, and neither Isidore nor Purvis notice when I enter it. Their combined attention is pitted against whatever is taking place on one of three laptop screens open on the large table before them, and they're both wearing headphones. A picture window set in the wall behind them catches the steady glow of each terminal, casting it back into the room like the gaze of Polyphemus upon his pillaged flock. It looks as if they've been embedded in here for days. Their workstation is littered with food rubbish and soda cans, and the entire room smells of body odor and French fries. In the light of the computer screen, Isidore's witlessly cheerful features are drawn against the bones of his face as if someone tightened a winch on the back of his head, and Purvis looks like he's been crying.

I set the sandwich on the table, and cross the room to stand beside the window. Clamence Street is warmly lit beyond the glass, its perpendicularity measured in the regular beacon of streetlamps, and less regular wash of light thrown from shop windows. Pedestrians move amid the beds of snow-dampened leaves, stepping in and out of doorways, and crossing the street. The trees buttressing the thoroughfare on either side are nearly bare, and as I begin wondering when to shutter Releaf Tours for the season, momentarily forgetting my position in all this beautiful order. I glance over my shoulder, searching for the sandwich, just to remind myself that this, and everything like it, is no longer my responsibility.

"I think whatever it was is gone," says Isidore, removing his headphones, and despoiling Purvis of his. "I mean, this is just a fucking disaster, right here. Not just in footage, P. I know you understand that part of it. But time, too. We're wasting field hours doing this when we could be out there, you know, making progress."

"Sowwy, Isidowe," says Purvis, noticing me by the window. "Hewwo, Henwy."

"Henry?" says Isidore, turning jaggedly in his chair, his shopworn gaze searching the room until it finds me. "How long you been standing there?"

"In field hours, Isidore?"

"Well, the thing is, I thought you would have been here by now."

"I am here by now."

"You're what?" he says, popping the top of a soda can without removing his eyes from mine. "Al said you were going to put in work with us today, and call me a fool, but I believed him. Said you wanted more time with A.P.S."

"I'm here by now, Isidore," I say, gesturing at myself. "As you can see. And Al doesn't speak for me. He's just cooks your dinner."

"That's true," says Isidore, jerking his head back to drink from the can like a seagull swallowing a fish. "But I feel like I been seeing a lot more of him recently, like the past few days, just around the house, you know? Not doing much, which is unusual. Just kinda walking around like he lives there."

"He does live there," I say.

"You know what I mean," replies Isidore. "Purvis'll tell you. Tell him, P."

"Well, I seen him walking awound the living woom in his un-dewweaw and I was thinking maybe he was just asleep, so I says 'Hey, Al!' weal loud, and he just wooked at me fow like a second and then said 'Yes?' like I was wong to find him that way, so I says 'I want a soda, pwease' just because I figuwed I should say something that wasn't a question about why he wasn't dwessed pwoper, and he says 'Soda's in the kitchen, pwease,' but he actu-ally said pwease the way I say pwease like he was making fun of my pwoblem, and I…"

"You get the idea," says Isidore, to me. "That's part of why we have our base of operations down here. Too goddamn weird up at the house. I guess maybe he's acting up with Dad away, but…"

"Dad away?" I ask.

"Where you been, Henry? Yes, Dad's in Burlington for a few days, working on advertising for the leaves or something, and he may shoot up to Montreal afterward for some reason that I can't remember."

"Montreal? That's what she told you?"

"Something like that, Henry, but I was too busy-"

"Your dad hasn't been off the mountain since commence-ment," I say. "You don't think it's strange that he's just gone now? Did he even say goodbye to you?"

"You make him sound like a shut-in," says Isidore, smiling to himself, as if he knows (or knew) his father far better than I do (or did). "And no, he didn't, but I was out of phone range and Jo said he couldn't wait."

"Seems weasonable," says Purvis.

"Nobody asked you whether it was or not!" shouts Isidore, upsetting a detail of soda cans as he slaps the meeting table, his hand rising and falling against the indifferent Formica surface so fast that his shoulders barely move. Purvis starts as if the hand struck his cheek rather than the tabletop, but says nothing. His shapeless shoulders draw close to his ears, and he seems to with-draw into his adipose like a tortoise beneath its carapace. If I were asked an hour earlier whether or not I thought it was pos-sible for Purvis to become smaller, I would have said no. But de-spite the difference in size between him and Isidore, the sheriff's son suddenly looks puerile and prop-like beside the heir apparent of Acheron. I don't know how this was done, but I've seen it before, though I can't recall where, or when. It'll come to me.

"Sorry, Henry," says Isidore, lifting his hand from the tabletop as if he expects to find a dead housefly beneath it. Whatever inner turmoil spurred his outburst has faded to embarrassment, and he peers at me through the room's man cave aspect, hoping for either censure or applause. "I should explain myself. I don't want you to think I'm being cruel. It's just that me and P. have been having what you might call 'communication problems.' See, P. here doesn't know the difference between play and record, so last night when we were importing the audio footage, he kept recording over it whenever I told him 'hit play.' And there I am, wondering why I'm hearing nothing at all, not even my own voice during the E.V.P. sessions while P. is fucking erasing our footage."

"Sowwy, Isidowe."

" 'Sowwy' don't get much beyond me feeling bad that I'm sharing this with Henry here, so maybe save your 'sowwies' for something that we can't write off as complete and total loss. Now, where was I?"

Isidore stares into the room as if expecting it to answer, the space once more growing pregnant with a sense of rectitude so palpable it could be chewed and spat into a cuspidor. Someone farts, an unhurried squeal like the disused hinge of a cellar door, but none of us find levity in it.

"A little piece of Acheron air," I say, not to fill the feculent silence, but to prevent myself from telling Isidore that watching him brood, shout, and batter the furniture reminds me of working with his father. That's where I've seen it before. The solipsistic wrath of a man who, by virtue of his position, has come to view the people surrounding him as either assets or impediments to his design, nothing more. Stature never mattered much to Mr. Castle. A person was either a door or a wall.

"Oh. Right. Okay," says Isidore, having made his peace with the room. "Like I was saying, erased a good chunk of the audio, and

maybe because that wasn't enough, like because he hadn't completely sunk this fucking thing already, P. here, my good friend Purvis,
or P. Tard, as I like to say now, left a couple of our digital recorders
running all night up at the house. But the best part is that the next
morning, when I tell him to go get the equipment together so we can
wrap up the shoot, he comes back telling me that some of the audio
equipment was left running. So I ask 'What audio equipment?' and
P. says not to worry about it because he turned it off."

Isidore is either finishing speaking, or too angry to continue.
In the chair behind him, Purvis' head bobs on his neck as if he is
winding up for another apology, but he thinks better of it.

"What are you trying to tell me?" I ask.

"Well, Henry, because P. here turned off them recorders he
left on all night, we don't know which is which. Some might have
stuff we need, some might not, and there's no way for me to tell
where it is on the recording, because Purvis don't know the difference between play and record, as I said. So something might
still be there, but we don't know where it is."

"So, you're sitting here, listening to a recording of silence?"

"Well, occasionally we get a piece of something that might be
usable, a bump or a knock. But yes, mostly silence. We're trying to
split it up since we still have about a hundred hours that we need to get
through. That's where you come in. We got a terminal here set up for
you, so maybe grab a soda and some…I was going to say something
to eat, but I think we're basically out of food. So, maybe we'll take a
half hour dinner break in like three hours. Sound good?"

"I brought a sandwich," I say, searching the barren tabletop
for it. "It was here somewhere."

"Oh. Fine. Great. We can scrap the dinner break then," says
Isidore, holding a pair of headphones in my direction. "Pull up a
chair. Let's get you started."

286

The last time I did this with him, I ended up driving around town with a spurious recording of my mother's voice speaking my name on the car stereo. The memory embarrasses me, not because Denise caught me, and debunked it, but because I briefly allowed Isidore to influence me. I didn't want to believe my mother was speaking to me from beyond the grave, but I knew Isidore wanted me to believe it, and so I was reduced by his enthusiasm to a gullible clown, just as Purvis was shrunk to a boy-shaped mountain by his anger. He is every inch his father's son. Though I didn't see it then, I see it now. The only difference is that Isidore hasn't learned how to invest his energy. No matter. I've nearly sunk beneath his familial gravity too often. It won't happen again, and after tomorrow, none of this will matter, which means that it doesn't matter now.

"No, thanks," I say, walking from the window to the door. "I won't be helping you listen to bumps in the night. None of this is important, or real."

"You don't understand," says Isidore. "I clearly heard a voice say 'mexican fingerpaint' right next to my ear! Shit like that only happens once in a fucking lifetime, Henry! It was a career-maker, and it's probably lost, but there's a chance…"

"Ghosts don't exist, Isidore," I say, something he has likely heard before. But not from me. "And if you allow yourself to be subsumed beneath the dead, you will have little time for the living."

"What does that mean?" he asks, the headphones still dangling from his hand in the fetid air between us.

"It means get a girlfriend. You're rich, and everyone knows that. You have your pick, of a certain type, but your pick nonetheless. Does the phrase 'late fucker' mean anything to you?"

"Yes," he whispers, the headphones falling to the tabletop with a clatter as he leans back in his chair to glare at his feet beneath the table. "I know what it means."

"Then I've probably already said enough. I'll continue to find you playhouses if you like. I'll even fill them with props and make up crazy stories about them. But don't ever ask me to sit in an armpit listening to nothing. My time is worth more than that. So is yours. Get a girlfriend."

I've overmade whatever point there is to make, so there is nothing to do except leave. Even saying goodbye seems unwise, and as I step through the door, I feel as if I've escaped a catastrophe. But the feeling only remains for ten steps down the hallway, at which point I realize I've forgotten something, and I return to the meeting room.

"Where's my sandwich?" I say from the doorway. Isidore and Purvis appear not to have moved or spoken. "I brought half a meat sandwich with me. It had blood on it."

"I think I ate it," says Purvis, looking as if he wants to leave with me. "Sowwy, Henwy. I was just so hungwy."

"It's fine, Purvis. I don't need it anymore."

When I return to the reception desk, one of the secretaries is combing Dora's coat with her hairbrush, while the other feeds the dog carrot sticks from an apparent cache of them in her purse. Dora remains as she was when I left, her haunches settled on the desk chair as if it is a sort of rolling pediment meant to display her before a sacrifice, as the secretaries perform their feeding and grooming rites like a brace of vestals.

"My dog loves carrots!" says one of them brightly when I emerge from the lightless rear of the now empty office. She's apparently forgotten that she thinks I'm dangerous. "If you ever need a sitter, call me!"

"Thank you. I may," I say, gesturing to Dora, who steps from her platform, and follows me through the exit and down the stairs. The glass has been swept from the landing, and the entire stairwell smells of bleach, probably sprinkled by one of Dora's handmaidens. We step through the empty frame and out into the night, where tufts of snow drift on the suggestion of wind arriving from the direction of Mt. Abandon.

"Nice night," I say to Dora, just as the sound of a window shattering above our heads displaces the almost rigorous tranquility of Clamence Street. For a moment, I wonder if I'm not somehow reliving the moment earlier when Mr. Bash collided with the office door. But as splinters of glass rain from the darkness above me, well beyond the nucleus of the streetlamp, I understand that this is something new, and (I hope) unrelated. Something lands with a thump and a clatter on the sidewalk ten feet ahead, and the dog races toward it. I follow with more caution, ice and glass popping beneath my shoes. When I reach Dora, she is sniffing the mangled casing of a laptop resting in a scant inch of snow. The screen is shattered, and the battery, displaced by impact with the pavement, is lying at some remove in the eastbound lane of Clamence Street. The area is peppered with keys from the board like men's teeth after a street fight. I close the hood with the toe of my shoe, and rotate the machine so that I can read what is stenciled on it, though I already know what I will see: PROPERTY OF ACHERON PARANORMAL SOCIETY (A.P.S.), followed by instructions for its safe return.

I don't look in the direction from which the computer arrived, because I know what I will see there, as well: the near empty frame of the window in the A.P.M. meeting room, with just enough scythes of glass remaining in it to make the portal appear to snarl. And perhaps, if I were to allow my eyes to adjust to the darkness belting the second story of the building, I might see the tall, unhappy figment of Isidore standing where I was earlier, looking down on his work without judgment, or regret, but with a sort of dreadful acknowledgment rarely seen outside a courtroom.

"I've done many bad things," my mother once said to me. "All of them were glorious." Until now, I never understood what she meant.

5.

WHEN I PULL INTO THE DRIVEWAY of the Castle House forty minutes later, the windows are mostly dark, which means Jo is probably somewhere else, but I don't feel relieved. It's too late for that. The memory of relief remains instead, a dim recollection of finding the house empty after a long day of wrangling townspeople, and having the place to myself, of wandering the silent rooms with my feet swaddled in fur-lined slippers, opening drawers, reading mail, and helping myself to whatever food, drink, and entertainment I wanted while the owners were away. To have a sense of comfort is to have it forever, and what is impossible now was recently possible, and therefore may be possible again. I don't want the house, or the money, or even the responsibility that allowed me access to both. I want the illusion of trust and the suggestion of liberty that meant no matter how many times I manipulated an old drunk out of his property, or concealed the activities of a pervert, or slept with a married woman, none of it mattered because no one was watching. Of course, people saw me, but my reputation around Acheron had prefigured me as a sort of a blind spot in the town's eye. They may not have liked me, but they trusted in my unpleasantness, and allowed me to do what they expected. If I can just get through tonight and tomorrow, perhaps I can once more find a visibly invisible position above and beneath the notice of the people around me.

But this small hope is smothered in its cradle when I step out of my car and realize I've parked it between Blivet's cruiser, and Huld's Escalade. I don't know why they've come, but their purpose is surely conjoined. It's unlikely they would have arrived at the same time for different reasons. I tug Huld's car door, but it's locked, and even if it opened, I'm not certain what I would hope to find. Maybe something that might explain what Jo has done with her husband, though I'm not so much interested in his whereabouts as surviving his wife (at least until tomorrow).

And no matter what I might find in the car, Huld is beyond my reach, as always. I don't exactly feel betrayed, but I am disappointed. He was the most rigorously ethical of those employed by Mr. Castle, and I always assumed if I got into trouble, Huld would help me. But after the first few hours spent in jail, I knew that even before Mr. Castle disappeared, I had been alone, because Boris Huld (then as now) remains on the side of the people who pay him. Nothing left in the vehicle will change or challenge that. Still, I try all four doors, and mess with the latch on the trunk before giving up.

I don't try to break into Blivet's car, because there is never anything important to learn from him. The man is a born obstacle, nothing more. But as I remove Al's groceries from my car, I withdraw a large potato from the bottom of the bag, and hammer this into the cruiser's exhaust pipe with the toe of my shoe. "It's the small gestures that make life worth living. Lose them, and you're essentially circling the drain." Either Denise or my mother said that (I'm having more and more trouble disentangling their quotations), and with this is in mind, leaving Huld's vehicle unmolested feels morally asymmetric. I place the grocery bag in the open trunk of my car, while I try to cram the remainder of the potatoes into his tailpipe, but they're too small and soft to properly clog it. The eggplant does a better though imperfect job of encumbering the vehicle, and as I reach into the bag for something to bulwark it, I realize that what might look like minor revenge from the outside is actually just the desperate fear of the inevitable cloaking itself in a temporary sense of purpose and vindication. In other words, I'm stalling because I'm afraid of what is waiting inside the house. "Even when you know what needs to be done, you're a coward." Denise' words confirmed by me hunched in the snow, jamming organic produce into the butthole of an SUV, when I should be finding out why it is here.

"I'm sorry," I say aloud, and at the sound of my voice, Dora appears beside me, sniffing at the vegetable matter extruding from the tailpipe. I stand, removing the somewhat lighter bag of groceries from the trunk of my car, and together we walk toward the house.

When I open the front door, the foyer, and hallway beyond it, is so dark that it's like looking into the mouth of a whale. But Dora pads inside without hesitating, and I can't allow her to prove Denise even more correct by not following. The odd sense of relief sutured to the house's vacancy returns, only to be dispelled by an achromatic light cast into the hallway by the television in the living room. I hear no sound, and it's possible someone forgot to turn the appliance off. Unless the dumb sheriff, hypocrite lawyer, and villainous chef are all sitting together in the dark, watching the evening news on mute. But unless I want to carry the groceries back outside, and around the side of the house to the terrace door, there is no way to avoid whatever is going on in the living room because I have to pass it to reach the kitchen.

"Let's see who's here," I say without moving, once more allowing Dora to conduct my path down the hall, and through the entrance to the den. Blivet and Huld are not there, and I nearly mistake the room for empty until Dora walks up to one of the immersive armchairs at the far side of the room, and a thin arm appears over the armrest as if emerging from a sarcophagus, and scratches her between the ears.

"Hello there," says Al's voice from somewhere inside the chair. "You must be Dora."

As my eyes adjust to the gloom, I see two bare, similarly thin legs extending from the seat to an ottoman before it, and the cap of his tonsure rising above the armrest until what looks like Jo's face appears in the impoverished light from the television. A pair of headphones is clamped to Al's skull like a contoured vice, the cord trailing along the floor until it reaches a terminal beneath the television, which is paused on a grainy green still of the bassinet in the nursery of the Sutpen House.

"You shouldn't have said that to him," says Al when he notices me watching the screen. "Purvis said he was inconsolable for a moment until he threw the computer through the window down there at the office, and now we have to eat that cost, and because of you the only way I could get him to calm down was to agree to do the job I told you to do, which is why I'm sitting here, watching this nonsense when I could be figuring out how to make you understand that if anything like this happens again, you don't have a car, and you get Downing's kid for company when you're out working for Jo. Do you understand what I've just said?"

"I've heard honesty strengthens families."

"You heard wrong. Everyone saying what they know is wrong is what makes a family strong because that's how love begins for most people, unless they're like you and they don't feel love..."

"You're wrong. I do feel love."

"That's what Dennis said you said to him tonight but I wouldn't mistake that for progress because I know who you meant, even if he didn't, and I want you to know that if you think that one out at the lake can protect you, or will protect you more like, even though you haven't even done it to her yet..."

"You always mention sex. Why?"

"Because it's one way to tell when people are serious about what they want, even for a little while and it's one of the few things people can't lie about when it happens. It's done when you do it, and people usually think it means something other than what it does mean, and so forth. My point here is that you don't start acting up with that in mind, because it won't save you."

"From who? You?" I say, watching the exactitude with which he attends to Dora, his hand patiently scratching her beneath the chin while his eyes project killing toward me from across the room.

"Not me. Jo. I'm giving you advice. She'll love you as long as you allow her to believe it, and if you keep seeing her whose dog this is, then she's going to have a hard time remembering to love you as anyone would, and Jo don't have hard times like most women. Give her the dog back."

"She's my dog too."

"In part, maybe, but I'd suggest you give her your share when you give the dog back which better be tomorrow morning, because if the dog is still here by noon, I'll take it back myself, and I'm pretty sure she don't want to meet me under those circumstances."

"Try her," I say, uncertain why I'm even challenging Al. In twenty-four hours, he will be irrelevant. "She knows. She's ready."

"I guarantee that doesn't mean what the both of you think it does," says Al, raising his flimsy torso above the armrest in order to get a better look at the bag in my arms. "Those what I asked for?"

"Yes. Don't get up. I'm afraid you're naked."

"I ain't. I'm comfortable. You get everything?"

"Let's see," I say, overturning the bag like I'm spinning a rifle, and dumping the groceries on the carpet at my feet. This has no apparent effect on Al, who seems to sift and catalogue the mound of purchases with his eyes, before raising them to me.

"Where's the eggplant?"

"In Huld's tailpipe. Probably still good if you hurry."

"That's the other thing," he says, turning away from me, and sinking back into the voluminous furniture from which he emerged until all I can see of him are the skinny, boyish legs resting on the ottoman. "When I said I need to figure out how to show you about consequences, that was a lie because I already settled it this morning at the grocery store, so even if you hadn't said what you did to Izzy, or any of that other stuff at the office, they would still be here to let you know you shouldn't."

"Where are they?"

"Waiting where you live. Which is here, in case you need a reminder."

"Can you at least try to act like a servant, Al?" I say, patting my thigh to draw Dora away from him. "Make me dinner or something."

"Folks can't be what you want them to be just like you can't be what you want to be," he says, from the entombment of the chair. "You didn't eat my food for so long I stopped laying a plate. Even after you stole from me I did it because I'm good at it, and that's the shame. But you never sat at my table, because I think you knew that it was easier to eat something not as good then to look at me like an exceptional person, because that's what I am, when I do this. What do you do that makes you exceptional?"

"Your initial draft of the website was exceptional," I say, ignoring his question. "Pic from Quebec. I'm impressed you even got calls for it. There was nothing to steal. I helped a good idea not fail, and you know that Mr. Castle would have tapped you for it if I didn't. You should be glad it was me."

"He wouldn't have done anything," says Al, quietly. "Jo would have seen to that. You're just greedy. No, that's wrong. You ain't greedy. You're unexceptional, and it makes you a problem. If you were more than average, people might want to be around you."

"All that wisdom," I say, turning to leave the room. "Put it in your food maybe."

"All that anger about your mom," says Al. "Put in your storybook maybe."

I don't understand what he means at first, but the recollection of the morning comes floating back like a orotund plague bird coasting on a volcanic updraft across my field of vision, and I suddenly can't tell if I hate Al for embarrassing me, or myself for being embarrassed, or the both of us. In the reckless spirit the evening, I search the foreground for a door to slam or an item to throw, but there is only the yawning arch of the den's entrance, and Dora at my feet.

"Let's go," I say, but the dog has already gone ahead.

Denise phones as I'm crossing the yard toward the pine grove, using the steady light emanating from the front room of the pool house not as a guide, but a sandwich-like reminder of immunity. Whatever is waiting for me there can do no harm and I will meet it with the ambivalence of a lizard watching a storm at sea from a neutral branch safely ashore.

"Wilbur says the twins are twins," says Denise. "You were right. Though why it took you so long to see it, or why no one else did, I can't explain. Also, did you know Lenore was adopted?"

"No. And Al usually had his head behind a curtain or in a pot of soup. They were rarely in the same room together," I say, halting midway to the pool house. "Wait, how does he know that? And why did you ask him?"

"I didn't. He saw the family tree I drew. I left it in the living room."

"I thought you burnt it."

"No. I kept that. And he found it."

"But how does he know? And why hasn't he said anything?"

"He wouldn't tell me."

"What does that mean?"

"It means he kept saying the fire needed more wood whenever I asked a direct question, and then he'd go out to the woodshed, because he keeps his liquor there when I stay with him. It was bad, Henry. I thought he was going to have a stroke from carrying in all those logs. He would have burnt the house down if he hadn't passed out in the mudroom."

"Where is he now?"

"…In the mudroom. Rolled up in a rug. I went out to get wood before I called you and it looked like the only reason he stopped drinking tonight was because he ran out things to drink."

"I see," I say, beginning to walk once more toward the window glowing through the whiskered branches of the pine. "I'd like to speak with him. Any chance of waking him up?"

"Not unless you call a paramedic. And he won't tell you anything. He doesn't like you."

"I have to bring Dora over before noon. Will he be there?"

"If he doesn't know you're coming."

"Did you tell him about tomorrow night?"

"I didn't think it was important."

"Fine. I'll see you in the morning."

"Henry…" she says, just as I'm about the hang up. I pause, my feet rooted to the flagstones outside my house, waiting for her to speak. "How's Dora?"

"We've had a big day. She enjoyed all of it, I think."

"I'm glad you're part of her life."

"I want to be part of her life, Denise."

She hangs up without saying anything further, because there is nothing to add.

Inside the house, Blivet has somehow wedged himself into the living room's solitary armchair while Huld occupies most of the couch beneath the window, leaving no place for me to sit. Their compound shape suffocates the already small room into which they both face, like two grown men stuffed into a dollhouse. Neither greets me, but they appear relieved. They've apparently been waiting a while, because Blivet is twenty pages deep in Jo's forgotten copy of *Watership Down*.

"Ever read this here, Henry?" he asks me, raising the cover as I try to make myself comfortable in the overstuffed room. "It's about rabbits talking to each other. Makes no friggin' sense, but I like it, because..."

"Two fat men in my house," I say, looking at neither as I sit cross-legged on the floor in order to face them both. "It must be cookie time."

"That isn't nice," says Huld, his shoulders nearly obscuring the window behind him as he leans forward, the couch wheezing beneath him. "I know it's late, but the household wanted this matter settled tonight."

"Where have you been?" I ask him. "Actually, where did you go when I needed you?"

"I don't understand."

"How does a man the size of a mountain disappear?"

"I think I know what you think you mean," he says. "I was aware that the sheriff here was holding you. But I'm not a public defender, and as I saw it, there were reasonable grounds to…"

"You allowed her to do it. You know what I mean, Huld."

"I don't think I do, Henry. But I can tell you this: ethics are a result of luxury," he says, folding one of his moist hands around Dora's head as she sniffs his pantleg. "So it follows that I'm only able to exercise them when luxury allows. Whatever you thought I could do, or would do, was never an option for me."

"Coward."

"Occasionally, perhaps."

"I'd like to be included in this here discussion," says Blivet, thumbing back the brim of his Stanton, which somehow allows him to notice Dora. "Why hello there, dogface. I remember you. Don't you look happy. Shake?"

He opens the mitten of his hand beneath Dora's muzzle. She sniffs at it, and than raises her head quizzically, probably wondering why it smells of food but contains none.

"You need to train her better than that, Henry," he says.

"I could say the same for your boy, Blivet."

I don't realize the sheriff has hit me in the face, or even moved from his seat, until my vision returns, and I see him shoehorning his bulk back into the armchair. My mouth is wet, and pulsing with an expansive pain, and the room itself is sideways because my left cheek is pressed into the cool wooden floor.

"No more, sheriff" says Huld to Blivet, his tone no longer solicitous. "I can make a problem for you. That's within my power, and you know that. It doesn't happen again. Understand?"

The sheriff shrugs, watching me recover. My tongue touches the place from which the pain seems to emanate, and I find a manful tear in my upper lip, and one of my front teeth missing. I sit up, a shotglass of blood tipping from my mouth onto the floor as I search it for my tooth.

"Do you have any milk?" asks Huld (of me), but I just stare at him. "Nevermind, I'll see for myself."

The couch yowls with relief as he gets up and walks out of the living room toward the kitchen. I'm left alone with Blivet, who appears remorseless and becalmed as he watches me scour the room for my fugitive dentition. I pat the radius of floor around me like a blind beggar whose coinage has been shaken from his cup, but find nothing, and feel humiliated.

"Looking for this here?" asks the sheriff. I glance up from my search to see its object, my maxillary central incisor, pinched between his thumb and forefinger like an unhoused specimen.

"Give it to me, please."

"Naw," he says, shaking his head, and tucking the tooth into the front pocket of his uniform. "I'm gonna make me a good luck necklace."

I drop my pointless gaze back to the floor for a moment before returning it to the sheriff.

"I'll kill you too, I think."

"Well, that would require you being not what you are which is a man of mostly talk and not much else," says Blivet thoughtfully. "Being a thinking sort you can probably use your imagination and surmise how long you've been asking for a pop and how long I've been waiting to oblige."

"Give me my tooth."

"Naw. Remember next time we talk that I got piece of you close to my heart."

I hear the kettle drum steps of Huld behind me, and he enters the room with a beige glass of soymilk in one hand, and a dish-towel packed with ice in the other.

"Put this on your face," he says, handing me the towel. "And if you're able to find your tooth, I read somewhere that it's best to put it in milk. I don't know why."

He offers the glass, and I take it.

"This isn't milk," I say, as if the distinction is important.

"I know," says Huld, returning to the couch. "But it was all that was in there. I can't stomach it myself."

"It isn't mine. She left it."

"Who did?" asks Blivet, trying once again to join in the conversation. I can't think of an answer because I no longer know what he knows. But the speed at which the glass leaves my hand and shatters against the wall beside the sheriff's head, dappling his Stanton with soymilk, jettisons the need of any sort of formal response, and surprises everyone in the room, including me. I don't remember choosing to throw it. Rather, it was as if my body was compelled by a simple, reflexive atavism, something held over from an Australopithecan nightfall, to launch whatever was closest to me toward the sound of his voice. And yes, the missile fell shy of its mark, but made its point anyway.

"I'm afraid I can't let that pass as easy as your last remark, Henry," says Blivet, exposing the flushed globe of his skull as he rises once more from the chair, shaking his hat dry, and fiddling with some weaponry at his belt.

"Put that away," says Huld to Blivet, who pauses. "Now. If it comes out, you're finished. Do you hear me, you stupid man? All done. No more."

"Boy thought I was a clown until a moment ago," says Blivet, halfway risen, "but I can't help but feel he still thinks I'm part of his rodeo, lawyer, and the reason why I'm standing up now is because I was hoping to impart by way of this here correcting tool I been issued some sort of unknowing of what he thinks he knows about me, so if you'll just give me a few minutes, I'll…"

"Sit down. Shut up," says Huld, sharply. Blivet hesitates, but obeys. The lawyer inclines his bulk toward me. "Henry, no more of that please. We've already been here for much longer than is necessary, and I'm sure you can appreciate the economy of individual time. Now…"

"He has my tooth," I interrupt, a bit of gore dropping from my mouth onto the collar of my shirt.

"Who does?" asks Huld, looking horrified.

"He said he was going to use for jewelry."

"What?"

"Doesn't matter. I'm killing him tomorrow," I say, rather than answering. "You too, maybe."

"Look here, lawyer," says Blivet. "That there sounds like a threat, if you ask me, and part of my duty to this burg is taking things of that nature serious, just in case they turn out to be genuine, so if you don't mind, I'll just…"

"Return his tooth, sheriff. Now, you ghoul!" says Huld, without averting his weary gaze from my face. I hear a rustle of flesh and fabric, and something bounces off my cheek, and lands in my lap. Without looking down, I pick it up and put it in my pocket. "Can we move forward, please?"

I don't say anything. The only sound is the tick of Dora's nails on the floor of the hallway. Huld clears his throat.

"Now, what we came to discuss…"

"We know about the trees, Henry," interrupts Blivet. "Mr. Olaf said he didn't know you was doing it for the leaf peeper folks, but if he did, he never would have allowed you to use his equipment, and Morton just about shat himself when I explain what would happen if he didn't tell me why I had to take his fishing license a few days ago, and first he said you threatened him with losing his boat or his car, and then he told me you bribed him with beer, and when I asked him which it was, he said both, which I still don't understand, so maybe you could explain that, and while you're at it…"

I've removed one of my shoes while the sheriff is speaking, a business-like desert boot that catches him on the side of his mouth in mid-speech, cutting his summary short. Huld snorts rather than saying anything, and Blivet absorbs the impact with the stolidity of an outdoor statue, his hand playing at his belt with whatever implement of torture he has chosen for me, but he remains seated. A viperous tail of blood depends from the corner of his slack mouth.

"As I was saying," says Huld, still chuckling over the shoe. "The stunt with the trees was reckless. If you were caught, it could have sunk what is essentially a fledgling venture, not yet sturdy enough to absorb a legal or press-related shock of this kind. And people that don't have a vested interest in protecting not you, but the business, still can catch you, and that's mostly your fault, Henry, because you made shockingly little effort to cover your tracks. You engaged the off-hours services of Mr. Olaf and his staff, involved half the town's recidivists, and fed them all beer, and charged the expenses to the company accounts, which, had it not been for other recent trouble regarding your personal and professional life, you would oversee, with none the wiser. In short, this is a problem."

"Trouble?" I ask, staring at the floor.

"Well, you still ain't revealed where you stashed your porno collection," says Blivet. "Plus, I got it on good authority that you threatened Tyler Moskovitz with a knife for being late to work, not to mention you assaulting Dennis tonight at the real estate office, or pushing Mr. Bash down the stairs, or provoking Isidore to the point where he couldn't do nothing but smash a window because sometime a man just has to let it all out when there ain't no other means to freeing him of his demons, and…"

"I didn't push Norman," I say. "He tripped over my dog."

"Ain't your dog," says Blivet. "And does that mean you're admitting to all the rest of what I just mentioned? Sounds like a confession to me, lawyer."

"It's nothing of the kind," says Huld.

"Try to take my dog, Blivet," I murmur, unlacing my remaining shoe. "See what happens."

"Enough, both of you," says Huld. "This is a mission of mercy, Henry. The reason I'm here is to inform you that as a result of your erratic, threatening, and possibly criminal behavior both on your own and on the company's time, your duties will be assumed until further notice by Aloysius, and you will regard the remaining period of your employment with Releaf Tours, and Acheron Property Management, et al as probationary. Your are to do as you are told, nothing further, and remain on your best behavior, at all times."

"Consider this my notice," I say, watching Blivet flinch as I pretend to throw my remaining shoe at him. "I'll be gone in the morning."

"That is of course an option, Henry," says Huld. "But if you choose to do that, we will be forced to prosecute you in order to cover ourselves, and uphold the integrity of the family name and business. Should any of this appear later with us having taken no disciplinary action against you, and instead, allowing you to wander free, possibly perpetrating further misdeeds -- that would be imprudent. If you remain, we can claim that we took action internally, and, to some extent, protect you from yourself. If you leave, we will have to make sure we protect everyone, including ourselves, from you. But as I said, it's your choice."

"It doesn't matter," I say. "She loves me. You can ruin what's left of me in this town. But she has something important with me that is beyond your reach."

"Don't nobody love you," says Blivet.

"I don't know what that means," says Huld, rising from the couch. "But I should say that apropos of recent developments, we have a very strong case. Al has evidence that the tour company was only suggested by you because you had already taken guide fees from prospective clients without the means or organization to house, feed, or transport them, which is essentially a Ponzi scheme, Henry, and not a very good one, at that. He said you had a website with a picture of Canada before the domain was refurbished."

"I quit," I say. "Ready your case, lawyer. See you in court."

Huld sighs like a bellows, the acrid waft of his breath reaching me on the floor as he stands, towering above me, and gesturing to Blivet.

"I think you're being foolish," he says. "I'll ask again in the morning. Come, sheriff."

"Why did you bring him here?" I say to the lawyer. "What is his purpose in this meeting? Intimidation?"

"Cause you're in a heap of trouble," says Blivet, standing up just as my remaining shoe catches him in the groin, the impact and pain forcing back into his seat. He sets his jaw with a sound like the creek of nautical rigging. His eyes smolder beneath the brim of his hat as he cups a paw over his groin. "You ain't such a quick study for a college boy, but you got an arm. I'll say that much for you."

"Thanks," I say. "Leave now."

"Chief Blivet is here as a representative of the local law enforcement," says Huld, watching his envoy rising gingerly from the chair, shielding his face and crotch from further ordnance as crosses the room to stand beside the lawyer. "It's important that you know how serious this is, Henry."

"You brought Blivet to let me know you're serious?"

"Apparently so," says Huld, turning toward the door. He sounds tired, and calmly disappointed. "I'll call you tomorrow."

"I quit. Consider this my notice. Don't call me."

"You're in shock maybe, from the tooth. Tell me again tomorrow," he says, taking one heavy step toward the entrance to the living room just as Dora appears from the direction of the bedroom with the rubberized string of anal beads clamped in her jaws. She pauses before the sheriff and the lawyer, her eyes shifting between them as she tries to determine which is more likely to play with her. The dog wisely settles on Blivet, laying the toy at his feet and splaying her paws to either side of it as her tail strokes the maniac air of the room.

"I ain't in much of a mood to play with you, dogface. Sorry," says the sheriff, turning away from Dora, who barks once, and to Huld's and my own surprise, Blivet pauses, and then stoops to retrieve the item from the floor. "Well, maybe just one throw since your owner over there probably won't be in any mood to play with you too much tonight. What the hell kinda toy is this anyway, Henry? I ain't seen nothing like it before."

"Blivet-" cautions Huld, too late, as the sheriff has already sent the polymer chain bumping down the hall. I've closed my eyes in order to better nurse the web of pain that has begun to radiate across my entire face, but I hear the thing land in the hallway as Dora skitters after it. Huld whispers something, presumably to Blivet, though I can't make it out.

"No. That ain't right at all," says the sheriff, a note of horror in his voice, followed by a muffled, yet insistent intonation from Huld. "Now why would anyone do a thing like that?"

"You should wash your hands, sheriff," says Huld, a bit louder. I hear him lumber to the door, and the door open. "Goodnight, Henry. Until tomorrow."

The door closes, and I open my eyes. Blivet is standing in between the hallway the living room like a man astride a chasm, and looking at his hand as if he wants to remove it.

"I guess it figures you would have the kinda weirdo alternative lifestyle that means you gotta keep a butt rope on the premises at all times," he says when he notices me watching him from the floor. He drops the contaminated hand to his side without allowing it to touch his body. "But frankly, I'm disgusted by it. I should take your other tooth for my trouble."

"It's a long road to hell, Blivet," I say, grabbing my shoe from the place where it fell after colliding with the sheriff's crotch, and poising it beside my ear, ready to cast it heel-first in his direction. "But I'm happy to walk it with you."

"Don't think I don't know that you and me are overdue," he says, his eyes fastened to the footwear. "But I wouldn't want to rush it with you, Henry. I took my full ration of shit from you for more than a year, and you've only had yours for a few days. Nothing teaches a man patience like knowing he don't have to wait to win. But don't mistake me here, I won't forget you and I'm guessing that the tooth means I'm on your mind. But like I said, you're acting this way after just a few days, and I got a little bet with myself that you won't make it more than a week. If I'm wrong, like I said, I can wait. If it's the other way, then you know where I'll be when you tender your resignation, so to speak."

"I'm stronger than you," I say, dropping the shoe, and pulling my knees into my chest in a postural antonym of strength. "Because she loves me more than you don't."

"No one loves you, and saying it don't make it any truer,"

says Blivet, walking toward the kitchen. "If you'll excuse me, I'm going to go wash up."

I hear water running for a moment, and a confused noise, following by the cessation of water running, and footsteps returning to the hallway. I've closed my eyes again, pressing my cheek into my kneecap as I dream of Denise, her weight, her breath, the sound of her urine falling into an empty pot. Anything to escape the present.

"No soap," says Blivet. "I should have figured you would be fine living in your own filth. Like I said, it disgusts me. You quit tomorrow, expect a visit from me after supper."

The door opens, and closes, and when I open my eyes, I'm alone. Or nearly alone. Dora is sitting on her haunches, watching me patiently from entrance to the hallway with the anal beads between her paws.

SATURDAY

"I've arranged everything carefully / for to be glad / when it burns"
— Excerpt from 'Our Last Autumn,' a poem by Elmer T. Olaf, local poet and owner of Olaf Contracting, from his collection *The Ancient Immovable* (self-published, 1995)

"It's called the Herrenhoffmann. Four to five shots of anything in one glass, with ice. It was her favorite, but Winnie wouldn't let us put it on the menu, even as a joke."
— Brian Holzer, bartender at the Herrenhof Inn, and MFA candidate at Acheron College

1.

The next morning, Denise looks aghast when I arrive at Wilbur's door with Dora, my lip swollen and split over the incomplete smile I try to conjure through an afterbirth of pain gibbeting my face like a muzzle. Today is Halloween, and her fingers brush my face as if trying to determine that the damaged rictus isn't part of a costume. I try to apologize (for what, I can't say), and she just shakes her head, and tugs me inside without asking what happened, guiding me into the living room, where her uncle kneels before the fireplace, gorging it with tinder like an inquisitor preparing to burn a witch. He's so occupied with the fire that he doesn't notice as Denise seats me on the couch, and leaves the room, returning a minute later with a cup of coffee for each of us. She sits beside me, and we sip in silence, until Wilbur competes his business with the hearth, and stands up to find us watching him.

"Jesus backhaired Christ!" he says, collapsing backward into an armchair across from the couch, and releasing a mushroom cloud of dust to the rafters. "Denise didn't tell me you were coming. Thanks for announcing yourself."

"You seemed busy," I say, as Dora enters the room. "I had to drop her off. I won't stay for long."

"What happened to your face?" he asks, his unkempt gray

hair, like a pigeon frozen in avian anguish crowning his skull, waves in a backdraft from the fire.

"Blivet."

"You look like a hillbilly," he says to me, raising Dora from the floor, onto his lap. Though she is far too long-legged for this, she accepts it, settling across Wilbur's knees like throw rug. When I don't respond to the all too accurate comment about my face, he looks somewhat ashamed. "Blivet's an animal."

"Animals have nobility," says Denise. "He's something else. A servant."

"He's a dangerous buffoon, then," says Wilbur, turning to me. "I thought it was your duty to keep him at heel. Wasn't that part of your...business with those people?"

"It's different now," I say. "Mr. Castle is gone."

"Gone...gone where?"

I shrug, but don't answer.

"Well, I doubt that will make much of a difference," says Wilbur. "He didn't even come off the mountain after commencement. Or, after his marriage to his...that woman. Why are you here, Henry?"

"I was hoping we could talk about what you know."

"I don't know anything."

"You know that Jo and Al are twins. And that Lenore was adopted. That's more than I know."

"Well, sometimes, when I have...something to drink, I tell stories," he says, his reproachful gaze finding Denise beside me. "They're not the sort of stories we usually share, in this house... and they don't mean anything. They're not true. I'm a liar. And a drunk. I make things up. I blame them on ghosts."

"You know that isn't true, Wilbur," says Denise. "I mean, the lying. The other thing..."

"I don't understand why you're helping him," he says to her

while pointing at me. "He's spent too long alone to be any good to anyone, and whatever trouble he's involving you in with those... those...those savages up the hill isn't going to make it any better. You can't save him, Denise!"

"I don't want to save him, Wilbur. I want to preserve him. Do you understand the difference?"

"No, I don't. I want you to listen very carefully to what you're saying, and try to see it from my perspective. Those people, his people, are dangerous, and it only follows that by virtue of his close association with them, he is dangerous as well, and thus, you, Denise, are in danger."

"Can I be involved in this conversation, please?" I ask, feeling like Blivet the night before.

"If your mother was here, Henry, she would agree with me," says Wilbur. "But if she were still here, she wouldn't have allowed it all to happen like this."

"You can't know that," I say. He rolls his eyes, combing Dora's coat with his fingers as if he's trying to scratch his way out of a tomb.

"Do you know how long I've waited to speak with you about her?" he says. "After she...disappeared...I just assumed that you might approach me, and that we would figure out how we felt about it together. Isn't that foolish? I don't know if you realize how much I missed her after she was no longer here, Henry, but I still miss her, and I still imagine us having a conversation about it, but not now. I imagine this when you were still at the college, and I still had my theater. I tried because I wanted to know that it wasn't a complete loss, and that you still were in some way her son. But I failed, and then they got you. I knew I failed, because the only time we ever spoke at length after that was when you came to take my theater away from me."

"I'm sorry," I say, the phrase becoming a sort of reflex whenever I'm around Denise. Her hand closes around my finger as she watches her uncle struggle with some internality across the room.

"You keep your apology, and I'll keep my niece," says Wilbur. "I had to stop watching films because I hated seeing them end. This is like that, Henry. Do you understand?"

"You can't negotiate on my behalf," Denise says to her uncle. "I'm family, not property, Wilbur. Can you care for something without smothering it?"

"Isn't that better than destroying it entirely?" he says, looking at me again.

"What I know," I begin, trying to orient the conversation on a common axis, "is that if you don't tell us what you're pretending you don't know, some people will die. Probably not you, and probably not Denise, but me possibly, and I can't imagine my mother allowing that to happen. I've lived here my entire life, but everything has suddenly become unfamiliar, and I don't know that what you know can help. But I think that you've been sitting with it for some time, and I'd bet you're tired of that. So, you have the opportunity here to possibly help me, Wilbur, but also the opportunity to help yourself."

"This is a negotiation," says Wilbur, echoing Denise, but watching me. "This is what you did for them? Isn't it? Tried to wheedle what you need out of people by convincing them they were doing themselves a good turn. And when this didn't work you did what? Brought the tools out? Inserted your pear of anguish, as it were? Tell me, you swindler!"

"Actually, I mostly watched," I say, to him, feeling somewhat hopeless about leaving here with what I need. "And then I told them what I saw. Guilt is universal, Wilbur. And I don't like most people enough to put my hands on them...in the way you suggested."

" 'Like'?" says Wilbur (It isn't a question). He turns to Denise.

"I hope you're hearing this!"

She watches him, but doesn't saying anything. He removes Dora to the floor, and stands glaring at the fire, which is roaring and snapping as if it has begun to consume the house itself.

"This needs more wood," he says.

"No it doesn't," says Denise, but he's already left the room. The door to the backyard smacks the side of the house. Denise releases my finger, and leaves the room, returning a moment later with a glass of water that she pours over the flames, tempering through not extinguishing them. "It will slow his progress. The upshot is that he may be more inclined to speak when he returns. Try a direct question."

The rear door clatters again, and Wilbur reenters the room with a faggot beneath his arm and a peculiar jauntiness in his step. I don't need to smell the alcohol to know he has partaken of it as he squats before the fire with a two drink deliberateness, and begins gorging it with his burden.

"How do you know Lenore was adopted?" I say, loudly, but without particular direction, pronouncing the question as if it is not a question but a postulate of accepted and rehearsed fact.

"She's my daughter," says Wilbur, recapitulating my tone, but pausing in his work at the hearthside, as if the words left his mouth without passing the politburo of either his heart or mind. He resumes feeding the flames, a bit frantically, and I exchange a look with Denise to see if this answer seems like progress. She inclines her heard toward Wilbur without breaking eye contact with me, meaning I should continue.

"So...you're her actual father? Or you adopted her?" I ask, only realizing I've blown whatever chance I had as Denise mouths 'What the fuck?', and Wilbur stomps from the room without answering, presumably to get more wood.

"Is that distinction even important?" she asks, pouring more water on the fire. "You couldn't have moved this conversation forward a little? That was the best you could do?"

"I don't know if it's important. Do you?"

She doesn't say anything, but the back door yelps, and as Wilbur reappears with a log in either hand she gently relieves him of these, setting them before the fire, and leading him to the armchair.

"Wilbur," she says, leaning close to him with hand on his shoulder. "It's like Henry said. If you don't tell us, something bad might happen."

"Bad things always happen," he says.

"Worse things then," says Denise, pulling a chair in for herself, and taking one of his hands in both of her own. "They may not affect you, but they could affect me. Do you understand?"

"You're just like him now," say Wilbur, speaking to her, but looking at me across the room. "You will say what he wants you to say to get what he wants you to want, and here I am, loving you because you're my niece but being treated like a barrier because of love. Do you know what love is?"

"I think that depends on context," I say, somewhat joylessly, though I'm not certain the question was meant for me.

"Love," continues Wilbur, "is the wind shaking snow from a branch onto those walking beneath it. She is my daughter, and I'm her father, and I know this because her mother was my first love, and I was her first love, and when you're together in that way, it leaves little doubt. I refuse to believe it is any other way. Are you both happy now?"

"Not entirely," I say, but Denise raises a hand to silence me.

"You were young?" prompts Denise.

"Too young they said. We were only fifteen," says Wilbur, the words coming now in a faltering tumble like a division of

318

clowns escaping a confessional. "Actually, I was fourteen when she first took me out on the lake. But when I think of it now, I'm certain it could have worked. I would have raised the baby myself, not now of course, but then. It didn't matter. Her parents took her away when it become known, and I heard no more about it until much later, which isn't to say that I didn't try. I tried as best I could but no one knew I had any right to know, because she didn't tell them it was me, and how could I admit what I had done when no one asked? Even after they took her to Randolph, and put her in St. Dyer's, she said nothing, just worked in the laundry, ate her bread and water, and gave away her child, our child, when it was time. And I only found out when I went to see her for the first time years later. I was so stupid that I expected to find Lenore there, with her. I even brought a gift, a plush rabbit or something. But it was only her, pregnant again..."

"With Jo and Al?" I interrupt, forgetting myself. Denise looks as if she wants to frame my face with a guillotine, and Wilbur seems to have only just remembered that I'm in the room with them. "So they're not your children. Jo and Al, I mean. I'm sorry. Please, continue."

"It's strange," he says, watching me with an unreadable intent. "Winifred was the only person who knew. And now you know it, Henry. Your mother saw me at Lenore's wedding, and asked why I looked like I was watching a building collapse, her exact words, and I told her, because if I didn't, I would have told Lenore. And I couldn't do that."

"Why not?" I ask, trying not look at Denise, even though this seems like the right question.

"I said I wouldn't tell Lenore who I was. That's what I promised her mother, but I figured she would change her mind after we spent more time together. But she died before I could change her mind. So I compromised. I told Winifred."

"Who was her mother?" asks Denise.

"And how did she die?" I ask, knowing the question is irrelevant, but Wilbur seems to be unraveling, and it might be my only chance. He looks at Denise, than at me, his features suddenly gathering in a Gordian knot of fatigue, inebriation, and apparent recollection, as though he channeled the revealed truth of the past minutes rather than spoke it aloud.

"She drowned," he says, his eyes veering toward the inferno beneath his mantle as he stands. "And Lenore had to take care of the twins. It wasn't fair, but that's what she did. If I had known, I might have tried to help. That needs more wood. But I was told to stay away long before that, so I only found out later, when Lenore came here, and then Jo, and by then it was too late. Yes, that fire's going out. And that's all I know, or it's all I'm willing to share with you, Henry. Your mother knew more, but I won't dishonor the memory of two wonderful women by allowing you to sift their secrets like you do with everyone else. No, I won't do it. Do those flames look low to you, Denise?"

"Who was her mother?" repeats Denise.

"She was the most patient woman I've ever met," muses Wilbur, rising from his chair. "And the most selfish. A wonderful, uneducated creature, impure from birth, who treated me to the best boat ride of my life. And that's all I care to share. The fire is going out."

"No, Wilbur. Don't finish it like that," says Denise to her uncle's back as he retreats from the room. Her dark eyes travel the floor between us, reaching me as the reliable snap of the backdoor widows the inquiry entirely. "It could have been worse. He said more to you than he did with me. I wish you were better at guessing what people want, but I'm not blaming you for his secrets."

"I'm not certain they change anything."

"They could maybe. But we don't have time to know that."

"Telling Jo or Al that we know their dead sister was adopted because an old ruined drunk told us isn't enough to defeat what she calls love and he calls family."

"I know," she says, crossing the room to sit beside me, and wrapping her hand around my finger once again. "I'll meet you at the house after the thing at the hotel."

"Are you sure that's how it should happen?"

"I can't see it another way. Us and them together would be unmanageable."

"Denise," I begin, taking her hand as Wilbur did a moment earlier. "I don't really want to know what Wilbur left out, and I don't want to go back to the house. I want to leave. With you, and Dora. Right now."

"This was your idea," she says. "Dispatching them."

"Yes. But I can't imagine myself doing it anymore."

"You never could, Henry."

"That's true. But I think whatever it was that made me think I could imagine it is gone now."

"Why?"

"I don't know. I'm not angry with them. I was, but I realized last night that they're just obstructions. Furniture blocking a door. That should make it easier, but it doesn't. In fact, Blivet is the only person I want to harm, and only because of my tooth. And that's not the right reason to kill him, or maybe it is. But he's just a man-shaped hole in the world. I could walk through him. I'm not sure I could walk through Jo or Al, because, as I said, they're blocking the door. But I could use a window couldn't I?

There is always a window, and if it doesn't open, I'll smash it to pieces, I'll..."

"You're not making sense. I don't want to leave. I'm not done here," she says, releasing my hand, and standing up. "And neither are you. I'm going to meet you at the house because I want you with me, without them. Do you understand? I'll do this for you. What I won't do is nothing, even if you think that's what you want."

"Can you at least wait until I arrive with Jo?"

"I'd prefer not to have them alive in the same room, Henry. I said that. But if you give me a good reason between now and then to do it, I'll wait," she says, glancing at Dora snoozing before the dwindling fire, and then toward the door through which her uncle exited. "We should check on him. It's been a moment."

I mutely trail her from the room and down the hall to the kitchen, where the rear door is left open to the yard. Denise removes my pea coat from a chair beside the stove, tugging the overlarge garment around her as she steps outside, and closes the door after me. Wilbur's peregrinations have worn a distinct path in the snow. He's traveled to the woodshed so frequently in the past twenty-four hours that patches of frozen grass crunch beneath our shoes as they fall in his footprints. His shed is the graceless twin of his camp on Kranion Pond, and as Denise jerks the door open, I worry the entire structure will collapse on us like a card table. But there is only the murderous creak of disuse, and the work-like odor of cold wood as we step inside.

"I didn't expect to find him," says Denise, because Wilbur is not here. But an empty bottle stacked neatly among the logs seems to indicate that he hasn't gone far. She extracts a leaf of paper rolled inside the neck, and unfurls it, her eyes moving like a platen across the page three times before crumpling it in the pocket of my coat.

"He's 'gone for a walk in the woods,' " she says, walking out of the shed, and refastening the door.

"Should we go after him?" I ask, gesturing at a less defined set of footprints leading out of the yard, into the forest.

"Would you?"

I don't answer, but reach for her hand, hidden somewhere in the dark volume of my coat, but succeed only in snagging the sleeve.

"Please don't grab."

"Do you love me somewhat?" I ask, knowing that I've chosen the wrong moment, but aware that there is a chance each moment beyond this may be even worse, or more incorrect. I don't even want an answer, but I want her to know that somewhere in the goblin's nest of my mind, the question exists.

" 'Somewhat'?" she asks, just as a clump of snow descends like a bunched curtain from the upper reach of an elm tree over-hanging the shed, riming my shoulders and neck. She tugs her hand from my grip to dust some of the frost from my hair, as I stand like a mannequin to prevent the ice water trickling down my back from flowing into my pants.

"I have to go now," I say.

"Sit by the fire first."

"I said I would have dinner with them, and I have to buy the ingredients for the dinner, and they want to eat early because of the Halloween party at the hotel, so I need to leave if..." I say, trailing off as she crosses the yard, and falling silent when she reaches the house.

2.

I STUMBLE THROUGH MY SHOPPING at Grover's Market, toppling items from the shelves into the cart, praying godlessly that I won't appear unusual when I deliver them to Al. But even during a task as mundane as food shopping, abnormality clings to me like the pea coat once did. I don't know why Denise took it, and even less why I haven't asked her to return it.

Through a haze of anxiety, a familiar environment like the grocery store becomes a rancorous wasteland, populated by one remorseless mirage after another. If Oliver, or worse, the eponymous owner, were to cross my path, I wouldn't recognize them. I only make it through the aisles by allowing Dora to act as a sort of service animal, and lead me through them to the checkout line, and out into the twilit parking lot.

"Good girl," I say, patting my compass with a sweaty hand as I stow the groceries in the trunk with the other. "No matter what happens tonight, I'm sure you'll be fine. Not that you were worried. She loves you more than me I think, but I'm not jealous. It's harder to love something that doesn't have fur."

We reach the house on the ridge twenty minutes later, and though it's unlikely that trick or treaters would make their way up the mountain road in search of either, a Jack O'Lantern the size of a washtub leers from the front steps as I approach them with the bags of groceries. I set them beside the pumpkin in order to open the door, but the portal swings wide before I even touch the handle. And there on the welcome mat in what I mistake for a mushroom costume at first, because of the swelling, oval hood surrounding his head, is Al, dressed as a King Cobra.

"Fitting," I say, handing him the bags. He peers into each, as they cross the threshold, but mulishly bars my way when I attempt to follow them.

"She wants to see you at your place," he says, removing a set of celluloid fangs from his mouth as he speaks. "Gotta make sure it fits."

"What fits?"

"You'll see. Is it all here?" he says, waving a hand at the bags beside the coiled tail of his costume. "It's the first family dinner. Isidore is coming up. I want it to be right."

"I don't know. I don't remember buying those groceries."

"How's that? And why's that dog here? I said to leave it."

"What's with the costume?" I ask, ignoring his question. "Are you coming to the thing at the hotel now?"

"She meant to have you there with her alone, as I understood it. And I'm not for going out in this, though I'd like too. Jo said maybe, so this is me prepared. People don't understand snakes well enough to not be afraid of them."

"You look like a badminton racket. With a tail."

"I'd appreciate a minimum of what you think makes you special tonight, if possible. I've heard enough of it, and it don't buy you any privileges beyond what you're overallowed, in my opinion, and it just makes her sad to have you making smartmouth when all she wants is to be treated like any girl who made the mistake of caring for someone who don't have the skill to reckon his own luck against his own unluck. If it wouldn't make her sad, I'd drive you back to jail myself."

"I didn't understand any of that."

"It's the first family dinner," he repeats, reinserting his fangs. "Keep your mouth quiet, and try not to wipe it on the table-cloth."

The door slams, and the candle burning in the pumpkin's interior flickers and jumps, making the ornament appear to laugh. If I could lift the thing, I'd toss it through the living room window, but for the next few hours remaining recklessly normal is still the priority.

I leave the forecourt of the main house and cross the lawn toward the pine grove, and as I approach my bungalow, I see a smaller, more melancholic pumpkin lit and gutted on the top step. It's expression looks incomplete at a distance, but as I draw closer to the house, I realize the gourd is winking. Al's work. Jo meets me at the door, drawing me inside with one hand, and peeling my top lip away from my teeth with other.

"We'll have that fixed in a week. I promise," she says, tilting a reading lamp toward my mouth as she examines the hole left by Blivet. "I can't have you walking around looking like a person who doesn't have people who care about him."

"If you care about me, let me punish Blivet."

"Soon, you may," she says, releasing her hold on my face, and returning the lamp to its place. "But I need him agreeable through probably Christmas. After that, do what you must to make it right, though please leave the boy out."

"Boy," I say. "You mean Purvis?"

"He's an awfully good friend to Isidore, and after that...what you said to him at the office, he needs a good friend."

"A believer, you mean. Someone who will agree with him."

"Is there a difference?" she asks, her blond head tipping to one side in complete earnest.

"I don't know," I say, glancing around the room for some hint of why I'm here. Dora appears around the side of my leg, and sniffs Jo's shoe.

"Oh! I didn't know we had a visitor!" she says, squatting before the dog who collapses against her compact torso in a sort of canine embrace. "We didn't expect you!"

"I hope you don't mind. I know Al said…"

"Dogs and animals are always neutral," says Jo, standing up and threading her small, powerful hand through mine. "I want to show you something."

She leads me to the bedroom, and tells me to close my eyes, and I do it, grateful to be consigned to the dark insularity of my own skull for a moment as she clatters hangers in the en suite. I fumble blindly with the radio beside the bed, until Breathless' 'Here By Chance' begins lisping from it, and lay back on the bed to await her. Jo's easy kindness toward Dora surprised me. I would have expected anything else, and I know that because of it, this small normality, I can't kill her. Perhaps I never could, as Denise said. I don't feel guilty for considering it, but I feel stupid for allowing Al to know that I had. Not because I fear punishment, but because I don't want this knowledge to spoil what I see when she emerges from the bathroom, her feet softly falling on the carpet, and tells me to open my eyes.

She wears what (at first glance) appears to be a hirsute pair of coveralls, but as she inclines her glad head, I notice the long ears appended to it, but more than this, the affectionate tranquility bungling her quite beautiful face from within the furry hood. When I told Dennis, and Blivet, and Huld that 'she loved me' I thought I knew what I meant. But I'm no longer sure. It's strange that I would have to see this woman dressed in a rabbit suit in order to understand that she isn't entirely my enemy, and that, in truth, I find her attractive, and despite her potential to make life very uncomfortable, I'm at ease around her.

"It's because of the book," she says, her blue eyes shying away from mine. "I know it's silly, but I wanted to dress up like a rabbit. What do you think?"

"You look beautiful," I say, because it's true. She does. "What are you wearing underneath that?"

Rather than answering, she reaches beneath her chin, and draws a zipper down, between her breasts, creating a rift of skin amid the fur, at the bottom of which the swarthier crest of her pubic hair is apparent.

"Yes," I say, though to what, I don't know.

We arrive late for 'the first family dinner,' and while Al appears unmoved by my costume, Isidore, perhaps nursing some residual wound from our conversation the night before, is offended by it. The meal is laid on the overlarge table in the solarium, and Lowlife's 'From Side to Side' plays from the direction of the kitchen when Jo and I enter from the deck door, passing a company of carved and glowing Jack O'Lanterns planted on the railing over the cliff. When the household orphan notices us, he rises from the table as though he means to leave.

"I can't eat with you dressed like a troll, Henry," says Isidore, his wan face contorting beneath the crooked brim of an A.P.M. baseball cap. "I mean, how can you say you don't believe in nothing when you're willing to show up for people dressed like that?"

"I don't understand the correlation," I say, sitting at the table, and combing one of my long ears aside to prevent it from dipping in my water glass.

"We're rabbits," says Jo, sitting across from me. "Not trolls."

"Well that's even worse," says Isidore, pulling his chair out from the table but not sitting in it. "You dress up to honor a tradition, and then you just buck that tradition by not even dressing like you're supposed to. Halloween's a festival of the dead, and tonight is the night when the dead walk, Henry! That's what it's about, and if you're not gonna be a ghost, or a skeleton, or a witch maybe, then you might as well stay home! But supernatural creatures, like trolls and unicorns and rabbits are not acceptable!"

"A rabbit isn't a supernatural creature," says Jo. "And you don't have to believe in something to dress like it. Why am I explaining this?"

"Beats the hell out of me," says Isidore inconclusively. We sit in silence for a moment, watching Isidore even though he isn't doing anything. No one knows what to say. Al appears with a steaming tray between his hands, his befanged mouth hidden within the heart-shaped cowl surrounding his head, and the tail of the costume making a soft noise as it drags along the floor behind him.

"What do you think of Al's costume?" I ask, and Isidore rolls his eyes.

"I don't even know what he's supposed to be."

"A King Cobra," says Al, plunking his burden on the tabletop, and straightening his fangs. "My glands contain enough venom to kill a hundred people, but I'm actually quite shy."

"Well…I guess that's fine," says Isidore, surrendering to either hunger or something else as he sits down on the chair. "I mean, no. What am I saying? It isn't fine…Unless that fellow that you're dressed up like, King…What was it?"

"Cobra," says Al.

"Right, unless he's dead, then you could make an argument that you're honoring his soul by dressing like him, but you need to know that if your gonna dress like a particular person on this night, you're opening yourself up to a world of trouble if they see you that way. The idea of a costume is to conceal yourself so all them lost souls don't see you! Demonic possession ain't a joke, and I'm gonna guess that anyone who can kill that many people at once probably ain't so nice a person. So be careful, but if you end up with King Cobra's spirit inside you, don't call me, Al, because I don't know how to fix it!"

"That doesn't sound at all scientific, Isidore," says Jo. "I think you're looking for something to be angry about. Maybe because of what happened at the real estate office last night?"

"That ain't why!" he says, standing up again. "This is a busy night for me, and I only came by to be polite anyway, because P. and I have serious business-"

"Why don't we talk about it?" says Jo. "This is a family dinner, so let's behave like a family."

"He ain't family!" says Isidore, pointing at me. "And neither is Al. Sorry, Al, but you're just not, and to be frank, I'm finding it real hard to focus on my work with you hanging around the house in your underwear like you own it! Because you don't! This here is my house, and when dad gets back from Canada, he is going to hear about you!"

It's impossible to read Al's expression beneath the shade of his hood, but his blue eyes actually look merry (of all things) as he retreats toward the kitchen.

"Can't you control him better?" says Isidore to Jo, watching him go. "I mean, I never understood why we have a cook in the first place...This ain't like the middle ages or something..."

"Henry," says Jo. "Why don't you apologize for whatever you said last night so we can move this meal forward."

"Sorry for what I said last night, Isidore," I say, slopping some wine into my water glass, and not feeling as though I'm surrendering much one way or the other. "I didn't mean a word of it. Tomorrow, I'll..."

"You're lying," he says quietly. "I always knew you were a liar, but I just never saw it as having much of an effect on me until it did, but worse, I know you ain't through lying because I know you heard something that night with P. and me in the living room. I saw your face change, and I know you had P. loop it for you in the morning. I know all that, so now I gotta ask why you keep saying you don't believe when you do?"

"What's he talking about?" Jo asks me, her face appearing concerned from the furry hood.

"Nothing," I say, guzzling my wine, and refilling my glass. "Sit down, Isidore. Let's talk about all the things that are going well with your investigation."

"Fuck yourself, Henry," says Isidore, kicking over his chair, and stomping toward the hall. "I don't want you to be a part of any of this, but just so you know, when I find what I'm looking for, I'm going to sit you down, and make you see it like you did that night in the living room, and then you can tell me that you're sorry for what you said."

The darkness at the head of the hallway envelopes Isidore as he exits the solarium. The front door opens and slams, and an engine murmurs from the driveway as Al appears with another covered dish, which he settles amid the others, before joining the table.

"You need to fix whatever that was soon," says Jo, to me.

"Not sure there's any fixing that," says Al, removing the lid from one of his trays. "What we have here is what I'm calling Halloween Surprise. Help yourselves."

"You always did have a flair for names," I say into my wine.

"Ain't funny," says Al, adjusting his hood, and setting them on Isidore's empty plate. "Remember this is what makes me exceptional. I take it you're still searching out what it is that makes you worth a person's time?"

"Said the snake to the rabbit," I say lamely. Jo tugs the ear of my costume.

"Can you please make an effort to get along with the people who are important to get along with?" she asks. "It seems like everything said at this table tonight has to do with an unfortunate conversation you had with them. I'll give you Blivet for Christmas, but I need you to treat Al…"

"Like he's your brother."

"That's right," she says, either unsurprised or uncaring that I know this. "He said you saw it. So now you know. Isidore doesn't. Can we keep it that between us?"

"Surely. But when are you going to tell him about Mr. Castle?" I ask both of them. Jo shrugs.

"When someone finds out where he did it we won't have to," says Al, winking at me like the pumpkin he left on my front steps. Rather than asking what that means, I pour more wine, and try to remain normal. Forks and knives clatter against plates as two bunnies and a mass murdering reptile begin to eat. I feel strangely tender.

"I'll lower the lights, so we can see them better" says Al, meaning the pumpkins carved and stationed on the railing of the rear deck, all of which have been turned inward, toward the glass walls of the solarium.

3.

THE HERRENHOF INN is a three story Victorian mansion that served as a stagecoach stop during Acheron's foundational years, and then spent the better part of the following century decaying in the shadow of Mt. Abandon. The house was too large to be anything other than a hotel, and since it was listed as historical landmark of some kind, the state perseveration board wouldn't allow it to be converted to condominiums. Thus it moldered on the shoulder of Loomis Street, a somnolent husk with an overgrown brass placard buttoned to its flank explaining why it couldn't be anything else. It was only after Mr. Castle acquired the property, and appointed my mother to oversee its renovation and subsequent management that the townsfolk seemed to remember it was there at all.

I often thought of the hotel as her first child, or an older sibling, since she had watched it grow and become successful (according to her specifications) long before I was born. And whenever I came with her to work, and watched her walk through the oak-paneled halls, or arrange tables in the dining room, or count bottles behind the bar, I was aware of her immutability within the hotel, as though the mansion had been built entirely for her to look correct in it. It was her monument, and her sarcophagus, though the latter didn't occur to me until much later, after she disappeared.

But even now, as Jo and I pass up and down the street before the Herrenhof Inn looking for a parking spot, I begin counting all the things of which my mother would disapprove. Too many pumpkins carved on the second story balcony. Three to four above the main entrance are enough to make the point. The black and orange twines of crepe dipping between the doric columns supporting the front porch belong in a high-school gymnasium. This is a party for adults. And why is the front walk braced by rows of sand-filled paper bags with candles in them? Did we run out of pumpkins? Though she perhaps hated attending it, the Halloween Ball was her idea, as was everything at the hotel. She wanted it to be a place where both tourists and townspeople could come for a room or a meal (respectively) without being repelled by pretension, or smothered in kitsch. Though I don't understand the theorem she used to strike this balance, I've inherited her ability to spot deviations from it. And as Jo and I approach the front walk in our tandem rabbit suits, I'm overcome by the sort of privileged violation I haven't felt since I boxed my mother's things, and gave them to the church. But instead of digging through her drawers, entering the hotel feels like stepping inside her thoughts. In truth, I haven't been back here since she vanished.

"The decorations are atrocious," I say, taking Jo's arm as we mount the stairs, though I don't realize I've done this until she pulls away gently as we reach the door.

"Be careful," she says. "They don't know what we do."

As we step inside, I see that the careless ornamentation outside matches that within, making the main ballroom look like the semi-formal reception for a pagan boarding school. A horseshoe of tables gives way to a parquet square illuminated by a large, rotating lantern hung from the ceiling, its patterned shade casting the aspect of ghouls, goblins, and demons across the dance floor, and several more Jack O'Lanterns, all of which appear to have been carved in a hurry. Beyond this, a string band appareled as a murder of crows plunks through a dirge-like rendition of 'Down in the Willow Garden,' while pairings of costumed townsfolk waltz shadowless in the foreground.

Down in the willow garden where me and my love did meet
There we sat a-courting my love fell off to sleep
I had a bottle of burgundy wine, which my true love did not know
And there I poisoned that dear little girl down by the banks below

The side of the room opposite the musicians is anchored by the bar and refreshment table, and this is where I stand, overloading a plate with enough food to pad my stomach for the alcohol I plan to consume. I'm not nervous for any of the reasons I expected when Denise and I spoke about the plan for this evening. Instead of relief at the prospect of regaining my liberty from Jo, I feel only the doddering irrevocability of a man who has accidentally emptied a basket of snakes into a yoga studio, and can neither alert the students to this inclemency, nor herd the reptiles from the classroom without revealing his (my, really) culpability, and opening himself (myself, in fact) to their combined wrath.

"Four to five shots of anything in one glass," I say to the bartender, costumeless aside from a pair of plastic insect antennae wobbling from his skull. A plastic nametag pinned to his shirt reads 'Brian.' "And I could have used more effort on the costume, Brian."

"I'm here to serve drinks, not to make you feel less silly about wearing that," he says Brian, plunking a bedewed tumbler on the bartop. "What are you anyway? A furry or something?"

"A what? No, I'm a rabbit," I mutter, reaching for the billfold I left in my clothing at the pool house, after allowing Jo to convince me that the costume fit best with nothing underneath it. "Lepidoptera. I'm sorry…How much, please?"

"Free if you go away," says Brian, turning his back on me.

"I will tip you," I assure him, crossing with my drink and my plate to the empty tables opposite the dance floor, and skulking among the personal items left on the chairs until I find a purse. It's only after I've extracted the wallet from it, and removed the cash from this that I notice the driver's license with Cordelia Swan printed on it. I promised to call her, didn't I? A dinner date in exchange for the list of patrons that proved nothing other than proof my mother and Mr. Castle exchanged books. But she did me a favor, and here I am, returning it by robbing her. Rather than taking all the cash, I leave twenty dollars, and resolve that if I make it through the evening with something like a tertiary chance at a human life, I'll call her and either return the money, or buy her dinner.

"I saw where you got that," says Brian the barkeep when I set the bills beside my empty glass on the bar. "I don't need it that bad."

"It's alright. I know her. A refill, and we'll forget all about it," I say, but he leaves both the money and glass where I placed them and turns his back on me again. "I see. No problem. I'll get it."

I don't wait to see if he notices me lean over the bar and blindly grab a bottle of what turns out to be Slivovitz, and retreat with it and my snack plate behind a set of drapes to picnic on the privacy of the window ledge. I'm cracking up a little. I know that. But as long as I'm aware of it, there shouldn't be a problem. At the far side of the ballroom, the band continues sawing away.

I drew my saber through her which was a bloody knife
I threw her in the river which was an awful sight
My father often told me that money would set me free
If I would murder that dear little girl whose name was Rose Connelly

I stuff a cookie in my mouth, and peek my head outside the curtain to see if I'm missing anything important. Jo is across the dance floor, speaking with a group people I can't identify because of their guising, but I'm almost certain one of them, dressed in what looks like a rooster costume, is Cornelius. Oblivious charlatan. The feckless afternoon I visited him in his office at the college feels like it took place an ice age ago. I never expected him to help with Jo. I only told him I was worried to offload whatever responsibility might drop on my head during the reckoning that, as yet, hasn't appeared. No one seems to care that Mr. Castle is missing, including me.

The doe rabbit and useless rooster each tilt their heads backward into the space behind them, staring up at the ceiling. I can't see what they're looking at, and I almost emerge from behind the curtain to find out. But I realize they're laughing when the light from the rotating lantern passes across Jo's mirthful face, and I pause, and withdraw back into the drapes. Yes, she remains lovely, how unfortunate that I didn't notice until now. No, that's wrong. I always knew she was very attractive. But since she was my boss's wife, it didn't matter. I was lucky he didn't marry someone his own age with similar needs. I suppose what I'm noticing now as I watch her from my emplacement behind the curtain is what I meant to remind myself of with the sandwich: I have no need to recapture my freedom from this woman, because she is an expression of it. Sometimes you have to imagine killing something in order to appreciate it.

Now he sits by his old cabin door a wiping his tear-brimmed eyes
Mourning for his only son out on the scaffold high
My race is run beneath the sun the devil is waiting for me
For I did murder that dear little girl whose name was Rose Connelly

"I don't like this song," I say to no one. Jo moves to the dance floor with a gaunt man in a ladybug suit whom I recognize as Grover. In watching her interact with other men at the ball, I begin to understand how we might work as a couple, the baron and baroness of the valley, ruling in the place of the enfeebled heir apparent. I don't trust her pregnancy, but her love seems real enough. Granted, my experience with this sort of thing is limited, yet it (her love) must be worth preserving, especially when measured against my dubious intimacy with Denise. Wilbur seemed worried that proximity with me might derange his niece, and perhaps he was right. Mea culpa, I suppose, but I never expected her to agree to help me, or forbid me from no longer wanting her help. Both women seem to need me for something, but the difference between them is that I understand what Jo wants, while Denise remains oblique in everything other than her desire to extricate me from the remains of the Castle household. I'm fairly confident that I can convince her to leave Jo alone, at least for a little while. But unless I concoct some lie, or discover some evidence to forbear her, it may be too late for Al. And if he isn't there when we return to the house, I'm not at all confident I can handle what happens next. I suppose the worst outcome would be that I disappoint everyone and end up with nothing. But then, I'm a novitiate in understanding love. This may be how it works.

I'm roused from these considerations by a tapping from the window on which I'm resting with my back, and I revolve in my seat to find Isidore scowling at me through the glass, and pointing toward the full moon sitting like a cataract above the lawn. I don't realize he wants me to open the window, so I nod, and point to the moon as well. He's trying to say something, accompanying whatever it is with strange skyward jabs of his index finger, but the music is too loud for me to hear it. I shrug and point to my ears, and he leans close to the window.

"Please, open this fucking thing!" he howls from the other side of the glass. I make a gesture of apprehension, unlatching the interior pane, and drawing the window up. "Is there some reason you're sitting behind a curtain eating cookies by yourself, Henry?"

"Evening, Isidore," I say, knocking the bottle of Slivovitz from the sill with my elbow as I turn to face him. "I was counting my sins. I used to have a book for that sort of thing, but it was lost in a fire."

"Are you drunk or something?"

"It was almost possible," I reply, watching the bottle of Slivovitz empty itself in the flowerbed. "Did you want something in particular from me, Isidore?"

"Well, it isn't about what I want, but if you mean did I come here to see you, yes, that's why I'm here. I was going to come in to find you, but I saw you sitting in the window from the street, so I figure this was easier. Anyway, I'd appreciate a moment of your time."

"What for? You know what I think."

"I know what you say you think, and like I said, you'd be first to hear if I thought I had something that could change that. I know you're pretty well-practiced in not giving me much of a chance at stuff, but I'm trying to be as ingratiable as I can because I think we're still friends even if you don't."

I don't say anything, but I peep my head out of the curtain again. Jo appears occupied and entertained with the townsfolk, but as I watch, her glance strays from the conversant faces besetting her and travels the room as though she has lost something unnecessary, but preferred. She's looking for me.

"How long will it take?" I ask, watching her pan the room in her rabbit suit. "I think I need to be with her."

"With who?" says Isidore. "And it won't be long. I got what it is in the van."

I lower myself from the window to the ground without saying anything, and follow him across the lawn and down the street until we reach the A.P.M. van parked beside a fire hydrant. Isidore slides open the side door, and hoists himself inside.

"Sorry there ain't no seats, had to take them out to fit the equipment. But it won't be long, like I said," he says, closing the door, and clearing a space for me amid the wires and soda cans on the floor. The interior is a muddle of cables, monitors, and A/V equipment, and smells like stomach gas, and overheated electronics. I rest my back against a tower of milk crates containing A.P.M t-shirts, and wait as Isidore plugs a laptop into a jack leading to a sequencer of some kind. He hands me a set of headphones, and I lower the hood of my rabbit suit, intending to put them on my head. But his hand touches my wrist.

"Hold on," he says. "Remember how I told you that P. left them recorders running at the house?"

"Sure do," I say, recalling the expression on Jo's face a moment earlier, searching for me, and wanting to return to it. "Go ahead and play whatever it is you want to share with me Isidore."

"I will. But you need to understand that this here was an accident. We caught it because that equipment was left on up the house all night, which just goes to show you that sometimes the things you're looking for are so hard to find because they been following you the entire time, and you just didn't turn around. I just thought it was…"

"That doesn't pertain to me," I say, donning the headphones. "Roll it, Izzy."

He looks disappointed at my halting his attempt to derive some adage from whatever he is about to play for me. But I'm impatient, because I know that I'm missed. I close my eyes, and lean my head against the crate of shirts bolstering me, reimaging the fall of the zipper between Jo's breasts, and her quiet embarrassment at the choice in costume, but more than this, the tilt of her head with the long ears extending from it as she searched the ballroom for me. The inchoate mythology of my life with her seems to be changing, and the first thing I need to do when I'm released from the van is call Denise, and convince her to abort whatever insanity she is about to perform on my behalf, for the sake of everyone involved, but mostly me. The time I spent hidden behind the curtain at the Herrenhof Inn may be the only moment I've had to consider what I actually want since the evening I spent in the town jail. I need more time to determine what exactly this might be before anything else complicates it.

But as someone begins to speak on the recording, I realize it's too late. I don't immediately recognize the voice as Jo's. The pitch is slightly off, and the tone muffled, as if the microphone were left face down on a cushion. She was probably standing in the hallway at the entrance to the living room, and speaking to Al in the kitchen, because his side of the conversation is completely inaudible.

"...I'm happy here...I have him, for now...That isn't what it's about, and...Well, why not?...It isn't a risk...Your 'tour company' was a risk, and you should be glad it got taken away from you before you sunk us both...I'm sure that's what he said. . . That's what I just said...So, we do agree on...You don't need a hobby, you need a woman...That's a terrible reason. Or a terrible excuse,

I should say. They're not scared of me, or they shouldn't be, and maybe they were scared of him, but he's...You're such a sally sometimes. I have the note, if we need it. But we won't, I don't think. Whenever they find him, it's just...I wish you wouldn't say 'Father' like that, you sound so starved for attention, or approval, yes, that's what I meant. You sound so starved for approval, it makes my skin crawl...No, my skin actually crawls when you whimper like ...This is why Dad, not Father, Dad hired him, because he isn't you, and doesn't scrape and cringe every time the pork shoulder or the fucking wine choice doesn't receive the right complement. Of course, I know I've had more time around him but...You can't blame me for that, Al. Lenore didn't ask you because you seemed happy cooking at that place in Montpelier and don't you think twins might have tipped him off?...Right, I know we were in diapers when we met him, but we all agreed it wasn't safe for you to come here with me!...Horseshit! What was the first thing I did after our wedding, Al? You remember? I called you! I said, 'Come, be a chef.' So, I'm sorry if you think he doesn't appreciate you, but I put in twenty years to make you comfortable here...Why do you think you have to prove something to him? He owes us!...and no, you're right, it wasn't entirely his fault. She didn't have to go with him out on the lake the first time, or any of the others, but she...Right, yes, fine, the first time was her choice. I don't know why she shared that with her children...But the rest of it, she didn't have to let him take her out again and again, but she did because she was fucking stupid. Mom was a stupid woman, and that's why she let herself be told what to do for her entire goddamn life here or in Randolph, or St. Dyer's or anywhere else, it didn't matter, don't you see that? Some people are born to be slaves, and some people are born to manage them, and I am a manager, just like Henry! No one

is taking me for any rides in the rowboat, or sending me anywhere I don't choose to go, and that's why I'm happy, because
I'm not a coward like her...Or you...Where are...If you meant
that, you would have said something to Huld already, because I
know you're not stupid enough to trust Blivet with...Wait! Come
back, it isn't..."

The voice fades to nothing as Jo pursues a retreating Aloysius away from the microphone. The argument continues, but
recorder only captures the distant sound of their entwined voices
sinking into the house.

"You shouldn't share this with her," I say to Isidore as I remove
the headphones.

"How can I?" he says, tapping the trackpad on his laptop to
stop the recording. "She's dead."

"What?"

"But I think she meant for me to hear all that. I don't pretend
to understand all of it, but she's saying everything for me. She's
happy. She doesn't want me to be scared. She knows about Releaf
Tours. I mean, she even said what you said. That I need a girlfriend. And all that boat talk, I wonder if it doesn't have something to do with the afterlife, you know? The river of sticks or
something like that? Like I said, some of it don't make no sense to
me. But ever since the night I saw her in my room, I was hoping
that wasn't the end. I wanted her to still be there, walking behind
me. And now I know she is."

"You think this is your mother," I say, amazed that Isidore
has entirely negated the import of the recording (though I'm still
trying to understand it).

"I don't think nothing," he says. "I know it's her."

"I believe you," I say, cautiously.

"You do? You're not just jerking me off about this?"

"Yes," I say. The ears attached to the hood of my costume brush the van's roof as I tug it back around my head. "You've convinced me. Do you have copies?"

"Uhyut. I made a few."

"I'd like one, please. For...to remind myself that ghosts are real."

"Well, sure. I can make you it right now, if you're willing to wait."

"I'll wait outside," I say, sliding the van's door open. "I need to make a phone call."

"I'm glad you know how it is now," says Isidore, touching my wrist as I step outside. "This could be a real career maker, but I only shared it with you and P. because I wouldn't feel right with anyone else knowing what I got walking with me. She doesn't need anyone more to know."

"I completely agree," I say. "I have to get my phone out of my car. I'll be back in five minutes."

"Thanks, Henry."

"Not necessary, Isidore."

He slides the door shut, and I walk back toward the hotel, passing small children and large adults in costume as they navigate an enfilade of carved pumpkins glimmering from yards along Loomis Street, the expressions of both child and parent mimicked in the illumined face of each burning gourd, but my own absent, or undiscovered, or perhaps spotted earlier, winking from my doorstep.

"A hamster!" says a very young child passing me as I stand by my car, listening to Denise' phone ring. "A hamster!"

"I think it's a gerbil," replies the chaperone. "Let's leave Mr. Gerbil to his phone call."

"Where are you?" I ask when she answers.

"At the house."

"Inside or outside?"

"Inside. It's cold out."

"I see. We need to hold on, please. Something came up. I can't get into it right now, but I need you to not do anything we discussed, and maybe leave. Does that make sense?"

"What should I do with Al?"

"That depends on what you have done with Al," I say, my naked body beneath the rabbit suit suddenly bathed in a moist jacket of sweat. "Is he alive?"

"Sure. I said I'd wait if you called, and you called. Now I'm waiting."

"But...that doesn't make sense..."

"I figured you would come up with some reason not to go through with it. Because I think I know what you want even if you don't."

"So...Why are you there?"

"I guess I was hoping there was a chance that it might not be that way," she says, sounding tired and disappointed. "Anyway, I'll see you when you get here."

"Does he know you're there?"

"Of course. He's sitting across the room in that weird outfit of his."

"I don't understand how you..."

"We had a conversation. I explained that I needed to wait in the house for a phone call, and why I needed to receive it. I think he's pretty relieved. Isn't that right, Al?" she says, raising her mouth from the receiver. I hear a murmur in the background. "I don't know why you were so worried about this guy. Most people just want to be told what to do, even if they don't want to do it. Anyway, I'll stay until you arrive in case something changes."

She hangs up, and I tuck the phone in my suit, and walk back to the van, feeling both anxious and relieved. But even as Isidore hands me the CD of the recording, I can't decide whether or not I'm still in a hurry.

"I listened to it again while you was making your call," says Isidore, climbing into the driver's seat of the van, and starting the engine. "The one thing that seemed strange to me was the rowboat. I always picture them ferrying those dead folks across the river in a sort canoe or kayak maybe, something a little more…I don't know, elegant, I guess. Not some old rowboat. It's like moving a coffin with Dad's old Ranger. But she's been there, and I ain't, so I suppose that's how it is. Anyway, I gotta get P. from A.P.M. Happy Halloween, Henry."

"And to you," I say, watching the taillights of the van recede and disappear at the corner. The rowboat. Where have I heard that before? The other details of the recording reconcile and confirm everything Wilbur said earlier. But he also mentioned something about being taken 'out on the lake,' so it seems that he and Jo's father shared the same boat (so to speak). But with whom did they share it? The identity of this naiad remains unknown, and will likely stay that way. I have enough information to even the pitch with Jo, or rid myself of her entirely, if that's what I choose.

And yet, as begin walking back toward the hotel, some memetic tug returns me to the question of the rowboat, or, more acutely, the fecund woman sharing this pleasure yacht with Wilbur Erlanger on the night Lenore was conceived. And returning to it (as Jo said on the recording) numerous times against her good judgment, with the man who likely fathered the twins. There is some ragged familiarity about this, but it remains just beyond my recollective ability. This is why I used a notebook. When memory fails, stories committed to the page return, and prevail. At least, that's how it's supposed to work. Would coloring the remaining limbs on an already gnarled family tree benefit me? I think not. Remaining ignorant is sometimes for the best.

But as I pause on the sidewalk outside the Herrenhof Inn, lingering in my caesura like an abandoned poem, I notice a leaflet affixed to the lightpole upon which I'm leaning, a flat white sheet with a colorless photograph of Dora beneath the legend 'LOST.' And beneath the photograph, handwritten instructions for what to do if she is found.

AMS/CORGI MIX, VERY FRIENDLY!!! MISSING SINCE MONDAY!
PLEASE HELP ME FIND BERYL! GENEROUS REWARD! IF FOUND, PLEASE RETURN TO JUNE BONES...

A telephone number, and the address of the apartments by the rec field follow this. But it is the dog's name, her real name, that I carry with me when as I enter the hotel, like one might carry a gift hidden beneath a coat, and cross the parquet dance floor to the opening pulse of 'The Burning' by Iron Curtain, the avian string band having pitched a roost at the bar for the time being. Like the boat in which she was conceived, I ply the costumed denizens of Acheron until I find Jo, dancing with a tipsy and disheveled Wilbur Erlanger beneath the rotating lantern at the center of the floor. He's wearing the same ill-fitting costume he deployed on the night he took me trick or treating, neither fully man nor beast, and as I draw alongside him, I touch the fur of his tunic, and raise the hand to my nostrils, inhaling the deep, lonely odor of his home, wood smoke, alcohol, and neglect. It takes him too long to recognize me, but when he does, he grabs the ears of my costume and yanks my head toward his mouth as though drawing me from a hutch, his lips moistening my ear through the furred hood as he shouts into it.

"I've been looking for you!" he bellows above the music. "Where is she? What has she done? You tell me! I know you know! Tell me!"

And from beneath my coat, I withdraw the gift, or the name that I did not learn from the poster, but from the last evening I spent with Mr, Castle on Mt. Abandon, the flier attached the lightpole having acted only as a sort of mnemonic guide, helping me remember what I did not realize I already knew. I pronounce the name into his ear, closer than he was to my own a moment ago (speaking quietly, lest Jo hear), and allowing him to divine the meaning less from the sound of the words, but the muscular movement of my mouth against his auditory canal as I empty the name from my throat, into his mind, where it has been since he was fifteen, unspoken until now.

By the time Jo separates us, he's already running toward the exit, fleeing through the field of gyrating neighbors like a man panicking in corn maze. Neither Jo nor I have any reason to pursue him, and her arms encircle my neck like a horse collar as she resumes moving with the music, the perfect shape of her body collapsing into my own as my hands join at her lower back. She doesn't feel pregnant, and I don't know if I love her. But when her mouth touches mine, warmly accommodating the words that I pronounce into it, the gift withdrawn from concealment, and deposited in this otherwise perfect moment, she doesn't parse the trail beaten a moment earlier by Wilbur. The character of her face is neither sad nor angry but relieved as it rises in a mezzaluna of partial light from a Jack O'Lantern lodged on a chair beside the dance floor. I remove my hands from her back, and touch them to either cheek, kissing her again, our first powerless kiss, to see how this feels, and finding the job-like satisfaction of information used well, the sensation I chased for a year while working for her husband, withdrawn beneath a pitiable affection for this harmless woman standing before me in a rabbit suit. The sandwich didn't mean what I thought it meant, but if Purvis hadn't eaten it, I might never have seen her like this, beautifully disarmed as the string band leaves the dovecote at the rear of the room, returning to their instruments, and striking the first note of 'Heaven's Airplane' as Jo presses the side of her face into my chest.

> *Oh, one of these days around twelve o'clock*
> *The whole wide world will reel and rock*
> *The sinner will tremble and cry for pain*
> *And the Lord will come in his airplane.*
> *All you thirsty of every tribe*
> *Get your tickets for an airplane ride*
> *Jesus our Savior is coming to reign*
> *And take you to glory in His airplane.*
> *Oh, talk of rides in automobiles*
> *Talk of fast times in motor wheels*
> *We'll break all records as we upwards fly*
> *For an airplane joyride in the sky.*
> *You must get ready if you take this ride*
> *Leave all your sins and humble your pride*
> *Furnish a lamp both bright and clean*
> *And a vessel of oil to run the machine.*
> *When our journey's over and we all sit down*
> *At the marriage supper with a robe and crown*
> *We'll blend our voices with a heavenly throng*
> *And praise our Savior as the years roll on.*

4.

AN HOUR LATER, we're sitting in my car outside her house, the windows of the dwelling dark because she is here with me, rather than inside, waiting for my arrival. Even this much has changed. The recording given to me by Isidore ended a moment ago. I didn't force her to listen, but asked if she would like to hear it. She didn't say anything. I played it anyway.

"He thinks it's a ghost," she says, locking her eyes on the isolated suggestion of a Jack O'Lantern resting beside the front door of her home. The candle has grown low within its damp gut, blurring the expression, and complicating its place in the silent world outside the car. "He thinks I'm a ghost."

"You were in his room," I say. "The night after she died."

"I thought he was asleep. Everyone had a headache that day. He took the aspirin to his room, and I was looking for it. If I just sat through the pain, we wouldn't be talking about this. Small motions."

"He isn't going to make it part of his pilot, if you're worried. He only told me because he wanted to show me I was wrong about everything."

"Fool," she mutters. "Not you. Him. You have to help me here because it can't be just me and him. I need you."

"Use Al. You already gave him my job."

"That was when you didn't have a choice. Now you have a choice, so I'm asking, because you can say no. I always wanted to ask you, but I was afraid of what you might say. When Al said he saw your car in the snow at the access, I panicked."

"Your brother is such a creep," I say, absently. "I thought I loved you tonight at the ball. I still think I do, but that isn't enough to want my job back."

"Do you? Love me, I mean."

"I'm deciding."

"Is it because I married him that you aren't sure, Henry?"

"No. That isn't why. Mr. Castle knows you're his kid," I say, resting a hand on the back of her neck as her head nods. "So he knows about me. Or us, even if he pretends not to see anything. He hired me for you, didn't he?"

"Not entirely," says Jo. "It was for your mother, too. And for himself. He doesn't trust Al, and Isidore is useless. But I'm not. I haven't worked for twenty years, but I know enough not waste his money looking for ghosts. And we figured marrying his wife's sister would look better than giving it all to some wayward daughter by a lady who drowned in a pond."

"He didn't kill her," I say, because I want it to be true. I can't imagine the gnomish cobbler that sat at the table calmly while his daughter obviously fondled me beneath it as a murderer.

"No, I never thought that," says Jo. "I saw him with her the last night. It didn't make sense. He just knew Al and I wouldn't say anything when they found her, because we didn't even know his name."

"But you saw him leave her in the water?" I ask.

"No. Just he and Mom walking through the field together, holding hands in the moonlight. It was cute. He bought her a house in Randolph with a pond in the woods out back for the boat. You couldn't really see it from my bedroom window. The pond, I mean. Beryl always put us to bed when he showed up. He wasn't interested."

"So he left you there. Alone."

"He said he panicked when he saw her like that. Maybe that's true. But yes, we were alone. When she didn't wake us up for school, Al and I watched game shows until we got hungry. Then we called Lenore."

"Nice of her to finish raising you."

"She did her best," says Jo, lowering the hood of her costume, and raking her fingers through her short blonde hair. The interior of the car smells like sweat. "She helped me get into Greatwood College, and got Al into the cooking school in Montpelier. And then she came here. I guess she had whatever Beryl had that made Jeremiah come for her years later. I don't know what it was, but I know I don't have it. I was only about six when Lenore looked her up. But I still remember Beryl saying to her, 'When you grow up, you're gonna marry that man, and never have to work again.' "

"She meant it," I say. "She didn't let Wilbur say anything."

"I didn't even realize he knew. Lenore said she didn't take Beryl seriously until after she came back in from the pond, and called the police. She didn't tell them about Jeremiah."

Jo fusses with the zipper beneath her chin, mulling some detail of the story, and her eyes catch and reflect the wavering glow from the pumpkin burning on the porch as she shakes her head.

"I still don't get it," she says. "I asked him once why he came all the way out to Randolph for a boat ride in the first place. He just said he left something unfinished."

"I think I know what that was."

"Tell me."

"I think you'd prefer I didn't."

"It doesn't matter. At a certain point, he and Lenore sort of grew into each other. I want that," says Jo, leaning her cheek into my hand. "I mean, it lasted twenty years. And they had Izzy. She must have started to like him after a while."

"Or she made room for him."

"I couldn't imagine doing what you do everyday," she says, touching the side of my face as if to make sure I haven't grown incorporeal while listening to her confession. "Getting up at 8AM and going to work...could anything be worse?"

"Marrying your dad might be."

"She had patience," says Jo, ignoring me. "They both did. Lenore and Mom. They could wait for what they wanted. I never learned how to do that. Neither did he."

"Are you even pregnant, Jo?"

"It doesn't matter now," she says, making a strange, unfriendly face at something behind me, which happens to be Denise standing outside the window. "What is she doing here?"

"No idea," I lie, lowering the window. Dora stands on her hind legs and lays both paws along the frame as a sort of greeting. Denise looks bored, and somewhat disappointed to find me camped out in the driveway with Jo, but not entirely surprised by it. "Thanks for waiting Denise."

"I'm finished waiting," she says, offering a bit of folded paper. "Al surrendered this."

"What did you do to him?" asks Jo.

"Use your imagination."

As I unfold the paper, Jo kisses my cheek and steps out of the car, leering at Denise across the hood.

"If he's hurt," she warns, "I'll make it hard for you to stay here."

"You don't have that power anymore," says Denise.

"You'll never have him," continues Jo, starting to walk toward the house. "He doesn't want you."

"He doesn't want you either, old woman," says Denise. "You're just part of the job."

"That's not nice," I say, but Jo may or may not hear this, because she's already reached the house. She closes the door and lights ignite within, prefiguring the house where there was only the implication a moment earlier. Denise crosses in front of my car, and gets in the passenger side after helping Dora into the back.

"Please take me home," she says. I don't respond. The note absorbs my attention. It's only a few lines, written in the wandering, nearly illegible hand of Mr. Castle.

This afternoon, I realized that I can no longer shit in the woods by myself, so this seems as good a time as any to call it quits. A man who has to spend his life chained to a toilet has no place between heaven and hell, so to speak. If you need me, I'll be in the woods, but I'd appreciate if you could give it some time before you come looking. Edward Abbey said something like "If I help a tree grow, or feed a buzzard, that's all I want, and all anyone deserves." I don't recall the exact quote, but I think you get the idea.

Consider it a last request, and if you don't believe me about the shitting thing, ask Henry. I owe him a drink, at the very least.

Wishing you kids the best in all your endeavors,

J.C.

"Do you think he wrote it?" asks Denise, as I start the car. "Al said he found it the night you stayed with me at the cabin."

"I no longer care," I say, backing out of the driveway to Castle Road for what I hope will be the last time.

5.

AFTER WILBUR FLED THE HOTEL, he must have spent the rest of the evening stuffing his fireplace, because by the time Denise and I arrive at his house, it is entirely consumed by flames. Past a cordon, firemen casually spray what seems like a nugatory stream of water into the gut of the inferno, the heat of which I feel on my face at the end of the street as Denise and I duck beneath the barrier.

"They look bored," I say, gesturing toward the men leaning on the engine. "I guess that means it's over. I'm sorry, Denise."

She walks beside me, either unmoved, or in shock, as we reach the semicircular crowd of neighbors in their pajamas and bathrobes watching her uncle's home burn.

"What the fuck are you looking at?" she asks them. I can't see the person to whom the question is directed, and several heads turn as she speaks.

"We're watching the fire, miss," says one of them candidly, as if nothing could be more normal. "It's a real rager."

"You're all guilty," she says, shaking my hand loose from her arm, but I take it again, and lead her away, toward the sidewalk. "Stop holding on to me, Henry. I know he isn't in there. And even if he was, I wouldn't dive into the flames to fish him out. Let go."

"I saw him at the ball," I say, releasing her. "But he left. I don't know if he came back here or not."

"Was he upset when he left?"

"Sort of," I say, leaning down to scratch Dora's coat so that Denise can't see my face. "I mean, does he ever seem happy?"

"It was only a matter of time," she says, staring at the burning house. "But it's just a house. I know he isn't in there."

"You said. But how do you know?"

"I'll show you," she says. "Follow me, if you like."

She walks between two of the houses, toward the woods abutting the street on the backside of Aornum Hill, the place where several days earlier, we deposited a pram with a necrotic doll for the benefit of the students we now pass skulking like ghouls at the treeline, bottles tipped in their mittened hands as they watch the fire.

Denise doesn't bother chastising them, but passes the cohort of costumed scholars as if they are part of the landscape into which we ascend, climbing the acclivity past smaller fires kindled and encircled by these same students, drinking and talking amid the cadavers.

Yes, the bodies. How could I forget them? The forest floor is laid like a residual plane of battle, with the frequency of dead thickening the deeper we travel into the woods They're hung from trees, of course, but also laid across the path and leaning against boulders, stuffed into crevices, and buried beneath piles of leaves. They sit in wheelchairs, on rocking horses, or loll from the slack maw of dilapidated pup tents, and, in one example of misapplied student ambition, are stuffed into the cab of a junked sedan somehow transported here for the purpose. The air is thick with the compound smoke from the islands of fire embarrassing the night, and the scent of rot. I've known the student population to stuff their decorations with meat or eggs, anything that will exude a malodor when left to spoil, and the scent becomes only more diffuse the further we go. Snatches of malevolent music ('Sucker Punch' by Savage Republic, followed by Siglo XX's 'Babies on a Battlefield') echo and fade with a kind of telegraphy, combining with the shouts of itinerant revelers touring this garden of the dead. They pass in pairs and groups, hooting and crowing as they fall upon one graphic tableau after the next, they're costumes uniformly animal in shape, but the character of each is obscured by the whiskered darkness left between fires. One of this retinue bumps my elbow as he passes, apologizes, and continues on in the opposite direction, but I stare back at him for too long, and have to run to catch up to Denise who hasn't stopped.

"I swear I just saw Rudolph Bones," I say as I reach her side. "You know who I mean. June's husband. He got killed in that hit and run out by the railroad tracks."

"Yes, it was him," says Denise, turning to me. But she is no longer Denise. She's aged, and grown less sharp, but still retains a commanding, familiar beauty and poise, the same attributes that made her such an excellent manager, and terrible parent.

"Hi, Mom," I say, as Winifred Hoffmann steps off the path, heading toward a fire burning in the center of a clearing, around which several people sit: Mr. Castle, Wilbur, and Lenore, drinking beer from a case dropped in the lap of a papier-mâché corpse leaning mordantly against a tree trunk. We exchange no greeting, but it seems I am expected.

As I drop down beside Lenore, Wilbur tears off the dummy's arm and tosses it on the fire. Mr. Castle toddles over to hand me a beer.

"I believe I owe you this," he says. "As per my note."

I take it blankly, and without thanks. Dora noses around the perimeter of the fire, squatting here and there. No one says anything.

"So you're ghosts now," I say, trying and failing to bridge the

358

abnormality of this moment with what I know to be true. "That makes sense."

"No. We're a search committee," says Mr. Castle, resettling across the fire, and watching me through the gold frames of his glasses. "Or a re-search committee, I should say. I guess Winifred wasn't sure it was clear, what with Jo acting up and confusing everything. The point is: you're the ideal candidate. You already know that. But we figured it was best to remind you."

"Jo needs your help," says my mother. "You need to go back to work."

"But you wanted me to kill her," I say. "Or, you wanted to kill her for me. I don't even remember which it was."

"That was Denise," says my mother, sipping primly from her bottle. "We're not the same person, as much as you might want that. Henry, I'm going to say this once: she isn't for you. You must have realized that when she wouldn't let you back out of the plan you two made. But you make sort of a carnival out of deceiving the townsfolk, so I don't think it's any surprise that you occasionally trick yourself. You're not good with people like her. Or any people really."

"You're not the first person to tell me that, Mom."

"Then it sounds like you somehow made a friend."

"We thought it would be fine for you to hate my sister," says Lenore, apparently trying to return the conversation to shoptalk. "And it may have been if Denise wasn't there to make you act on it. But apparently, all it took was seeing Jo in a rabbit costume to turn it around."

"Your mother used the word 'carnival,' " says Mr. Castle. "I think that's apt. Going forward, we need fewer sports, so to speak. Less pageantry. We don't need you to put on a show for the local dipsomaniacs, or harass the hired help. No more painting trees. No more scenes in the grocery store. And no more throwing independent contractors down the stairs when they won't let you dress them. Do your job."

"Norman tripped over Beryl," I say, gesturing at the dog.

"You've been hanging around Isidore too much," says Wilbur. "Ghosts don't exist, Henry."

"Aren't you dead, Wilbur?" I ask. "Didn't you perish when you're house burned down earlier this evening?"

"As much as I care to explain," he says, removing a package of graham crackers from a bag between his feet, as Lenore withdraws the toasted marshmallow from the flames. "S'more, Henry?"

"No thank you," I say, turning back to Mr. Castle and my mother. "So what are you offering me?"

"Offering you?" says my mother.

"Yes, mom. How do I know that if I go back to work, I won't be so bored that I'll have to really throw Norman down the stairs?"

"Well, Jo, for starters," says Lenore, skewering a marshmallow on the end of a branch and extending it over the fire. "You had one thing right. She loves you. And with that comes everything you might expect, the money, the property, the autonomy, and one thing more: what you thought you had with Denise that night at the cabin. There's no name for it, but I know you felt it when you saw Jo with Dora."

"How do you know about that, if you don't know about Norman and the stairs?" I ask. "And I don't know if I love her back. Is that important?"

"Not for our purposes," says Mr. Castle. "You might learn to, but if not, it's like I said that day on the mountain. She can't run things on her own. She needs your help."

360

"What about Isidore?" I say. "Is he beyond hope?"

"He isn't how we need him to be, and fixing him to be that way doesn't make sense when you're the best candidate," says my mother.

"Part of renegotiating your contract means that you keep him happy," says Mr. Castle. "That can sound either simple or complex, depending on how you define contentment. But I think you and Jo can figure it out."

"I don't understand why I need her," I say. "I like her. I may even love her. But why can't I just do what you're telling me without her there? Why must it be the two of us?"

"Because you are the hand, and she is the arm," says my mother. "Without her, you wouldn't be able to control people like Blivet, and without you, she wouldn't be able to use him properly. That's just the job."

"I controlled him because I knew what frightened him, Mom."

"No," says Mr. Castle. "You didn't know it. You represented it. You are its shadow. My daughter is the screen onto which you fall."

"Not to be a fussbudget," I say, trying not to look at my mother as I speak. "But what if I don't want the job? What if I would prefer to just …I don't know…serve coffee or something? Work at Sacred Grounds? Flirt with college girls for tips? Maybe bully Cornelius into giving me a master's degree? I could teach at the college. Get tenure. Come to work in my bathrobe. Marry a student half my age, and disappoint her. What I'm saying is that I think I have possibilities that we're not exploring."

"Consider that the sum of your possibilities still do not equal you leaving this town," says Wilbur through a mouthful of S'mores. "Isn't that Interesting?"

"What are you saying, Wilbur?"

"I think Wilbur means that even if you don't agree to the contract," says my mother, "you'll always be at work. And I don't think you'd be happy watching someone do your job. Remember how it felt to have Blivet hit you while Huld watched? Would you like to sit through that for the rest of your life?"

"They wouldn't let me quit either."

"You can't quit what you haven't started," says Lenore, "On that note, your new business cards will arrive here tomorrow. Or there, rather. We picked the title. You seemed like you were struggling with that choice. Although I liked 'Ambiguous Servant to the Doomed.' "

"Yes, that was good," agrees Wilbur. "So, you agree to go back to work, Henry?"

"Actually, I'm feeling sort of ambivalent about the whole thing, Wilbur."

"We're aiming beyond ambivalence, Henry," says my mother. "I didn't leave the hotel to watch you piss away your talent. You need to go to work."

"So...it's my destiny? Or fate, or something?"

"Didn't your mother just tell you that you have a choice?" says Lenore, offering me a S'more. "That's why we're negotiating. There is a vacancy, and we can always get someone else to fill the position. But you're the ideal candidate. Is it so hard for you to imagine that you're needed?"

"I know you want to be the lone wolf in all this beautiful order, Henry," says Wilbur. "But there's nothing to see, and no one is watching."

"Except you all," I say. My mother sighs across the fire.

"Maybe, Henry. But if you want to get rid of us, do your job," she says. "I need you to promise me you'll do your best."

"I'll try, mom," I say dolefully, as Lenore offers me a S'more.

362

I bite into it, chewing like a trash compactor, and watching my mother watch me across the fire. "And you promise that wasn't really your voice on Izzy's recording?"

"Of course not," she says, looking shocked. "There is no such thing as a ghost, Henry. No monsters or demons are required to make your work relevant. Cast a long shadow without drowning in it, if possible."

"I feel like new responsibilities keep appearing," I say.

"Since you're not going to try and kill her," says Mr. Castle, opening another beer. "Tell Jo you love her tomorrow. She'll want to hear that."

"My sister is still learning how to make herself happy," adds Lenore.

"Aren't we all," says my mother, looking at me, as Dora rests her head on my shoe. Crumbs of graham cracker fall from my mouth onto her muzzle as I wish everyone a Happy Halloween, but none of them return the blessing.

Sunday

"I only feel comfortable in church because it's the last place in town I expect to see my brother."
— Cornelius Castle, Phd., Dean of Acheron College and recent recipient of the Vermont Arts Council's sustainable design award

"Beware of Dog!"
— Handwritten sign taped to June Bones' apartment door

1.

THE NEXT MORNING, I'm awakened by a knocking on the front door of the house on Town Hill Road. Through an open window facing the street, I see Blivet's cruiser parked at the curb as I rise from the bare mattress on which I passed the night. A curtain missing from the rod above the pane is wrapped around my shoulders, and the remaining twin gestures into my mother's bedroom as a gust of arctic wind reaches the house from the broad shoulder of Mt. Abandon across the valley. I shiver, feeling misplaced and ashamed, as though I've tracked mud inside a temple. I own the house, but I don't own this room. I never will.

The knocking slackens when Blivet hears me descending the stairs from the other side of the door, and when I open it, the rictus fixed in the center of his jowls shifts to an expression of embarrassment, as if I've answered the door naked. But I'm not naked. I'm wearing the rabbit suit from the night before.

"Morning, Henry," he says cautiously, trying to avoid looking at the costume. "I just stopped by to talk for a minute…but if you're…in the middle of something…I can wait. Or come back."

"Now is fine. How did you know I was here?

"Well, your car is parked out front. I was just passing by, and I thought…"

"Right," I say, wondering why I don't remember parking it. "Why are you here?"

"Well, it's just that I been apprised of certain things, and I thought maybe the first thing I should do is pop over here and give you my sincerest apologies for...what I done to you, for starters"

"Knocking my tooth out."

"Yes, that'd be what I mean..."

"And saying you were going to wear it as a necklace."

"Well, sure. That too," he says, removing his hat, and running a khaki sleeve across his drizzling brow. "I'm awful sorry for... what happened, and I got no excuse other than my dander was up, and I can surely get mean when my work and family are involved, which is something I bet no man understands better than you and Mrs. Castle, and I'll say it straight as I felt it: you were threatening my boy, and I known Purvis ain't gonna cure syphilis or discover Atlantis, but, Henry, that's my boy, and I need to know he's safe, I gotta know that, you understand?"

"Personally," I begin, watching this sad, earnest lump of man occupy my porch as if it is the top step of saint's tomb, "I think the age of consent should be fourteen. Most everyone knows what they're doing when they're that old. I did. And you can't have people learning too old, otherwise you end up with a bunch of late fuckers, and we don't want that. I hope I didn't give you a scare, sheriff."

"Why...no, Henry," says Blivet slowly, looking over his shoulder toward the mailbox, as if to make sure he has the right house. "I never thought you would have done something to make a problem like that for me, because even when we were having our troubles, I always figured you for a reasonable fellow with his head in the right place, and I also wanted to mention that you don't need to worry about all that with Dennis, we..."

"All what with Dennis?"

"Well, his…the things he done…with them female athletes of his…" begins Blivet, obviously trying to find a way to frame the information without referring to my imprisonment. "Let me put it to you this way: my boy and Izzy happened to find some very clear evidence linking Dennis with those prowling reports I told you about, and what it looks to me is like he may have tried to hide all his…his perversities in that old house by Mt. Abandon, you know that one up by the…"

"The Sutpen House."

"That's the place! I guess they was bumping around there spook hunting last night, and Purvis put his foot through a loose floorboard, and whaddaya know? The rest was just good police work, though Dennis stashing a belt with his name on it sure made it simple, but at any rate, I just thought you'd want to know that he won't be messing around in anyone's rosebushes, or troubling you or me or anyone else for a while, I can promise you that, because…"

"You want to come in?" I say, backing onto the landing and leaving the door open. "I'm going to make some coffee if there is any."

"Why sure," says Blivet, definitely checking the house number again before he walks inside. "I've been known to take a cup from time to time, but only with the kind of people whose time I respect, and I must admit I'm curious to see inside of here, since I haven't been over since…well, you know when I was here last…"

"Yes, I remember, " I say absently, allowing him to bungle around the foyer while Dora and I walk toward the kitchen. But as we pass the entrance to the living room, she pauses, her tail beating against the floor. I stop, and join her in the doorway. "Is there something? What do you see?"

She pads into the room, amid the cloaked shapes of furniture I covered with sheets before moving out, and sniffs the edge of one draped over a love seat under the front window. Beneath it, the dormant form of a human body is apparent.

"Did I drag a corpse home from the woods?" I ask Dora aloud, as I tug back the sheet to reveal Denise, sleeping in a fetal position beneath it. Her breath is somber as the sound of church bell rung at the bottom of an ocean.

"You ask me something?" says Blivet from the hall, the hoof-like sound of his boots drawing closer to the living room.

"No, stay where you are!" I yell, recovering Denise as Dora begins sniffing at the back of her head. "I'll be right there."

Blivet is already most of the way up the hall when I intercept him and turn him back toward the front door.

"Sorry," I say. "There isn't any coffee, and it just occurred to me that I want to be alone. It's been some time since I was in this house, and I don't feel right about inviting anyone into it quite yet. As you know, a home is as both a shelter and a cenotaph. I'd like some time to unshroud the furniture and make it my own. I revoke my invitation. Please leave."

"Well, sure, like I said, I don't wanna intrude," he says, plodding through the door I left open, and out onto the porch. Despite all his apparent good will, he sounds relieved.

"You didn't say that exactly, sheriff. But I'm sure you don't."

"I suppose another time then," he says, extending the hand that knocked the tooth from my head several nights earlier. "In the meanwhile, no hard feelings about any of it."

"No," I say, staring at the mutinous paw without taking it. "See you at work."

I don't slam the door, but close it quickly enough to leave the sheriff with his arm still extended, as though offering something to the house. Through the sidelite, I watch him retract and pocket the hand I refused to shake as he walks slowly to his vehicle, and drives away toward town.

"What did he want?" asks Denise from behind me. She leans on the Newel post, rubbing her eyes and yawning, apparently still here, even after last night.

"To know that I won't punish him."

"So you said you would leave him alone?"

"For now."

"You're going back to her then," she says, reaching down to scratch Dora as the dog appears at her feet.

"I never left," I say, touching her shoulder in what I hope she will mistake for an affirmative, friendly gesture, though I'm actually checking to make sure she is corporeal. "Why are you here, Denise?"

"Well, the place where I was planning to sleep burnt to the ground, if you recall," she says, watching my face with a measure of concern. "Is that really the question you meant to ask?"

"So I invited you?"

"You said you didn't want to be alone. And that you were too tired to walk out the cabin."

"Did we have sex?"

"That isn't why I find you interesting. I thought you needed me. I was wrong."

"We both were," I say, probing her again as I walk toward the kitchen, and failing to disguise this as anything but what it is. She seems real enough. "Do you want coffee?"

"I thought there wasn't any," she says, passing me to remove the sheet from a mirror beside the door and check her reflection in it.

"There may not be. But I just said that to make him leave so he wouldn't see you."

"Because he might tell her."

"No. Because I wasn't sure who you were when I found you in the living room," I say, with my back to her as I fuss with a percolator at the kitchen sink. She doesn't respond, but I hear the scrape of chair drawn away from the table, and half expect to find my mother sitting in it when I turn around, beginning one of her working meals. But it's only Denise, her thin face grown nun-like with contrition during the time it took me to fill the pot and place it over a burner.

"So I invited you here," I begin, seating myself across from her, and trying to sound as casual as possible. "But before I did that, you didn't...become...something else, and take me to a meeting in the woods. Correct?"

"Why would I do that?"

"Well, to help me, I thought at first. But it became pretty clear it wasn't you. I just needed to ask."

"And what did I become, Henry?"

"...my mother."

"I see," she says. Her eyes look over my shoulder toward the door to the yard, probably trying to gauge whether or not it would be possible to reach in a hurry. "And what was the point of this meeting?"

"I think to remind me that I have a job instead of a destiny," I say. "I could decide to do something worse, but I'm the best candidate, apparently. What that means to me is I can do the best work for the shortest period of time, because how dull is it to watch yourself be competent all day? I mean, isn't that why I painted the trees?"

I pause here, looking to Denise for answer before I realize that she may not know what I'm talking about.

"Anyway," I continue, as Denise stands to attend the percolator whistling from its coil atop the range. "I guess they still think I'm the best candidate, because my contract was renegotiated, even though I don't understand what that means…"

"Who thinks that?"

"The search committee of people who died or didn't die or are alive but not available to us, Denise. Or, research committee as Mr. Castle said last night. In any case, I don't care anymore, because boredom is eternal, and having a job will always be water torture, even when I hold the bucket. Do you know the happiest I've been in the past year was while sitting in the jail cell beneath town hall? Why do you suppose that is?"

"Because you were uncertain," says Denise, setting a cup of coffee between my hands.

"Or I thought I was uncertain, because I thought I was free. But now Jo loves me, and I'm told we need each other. I'll take that, and the job, and the safety. This is what people want. Isn't it?"

"Do you love her?"

"I want to. I think that would make all of this easier. It's certainly the practical choice. I realized that after the night we spent in the cabin."

"Realized what?"

"That love is part of the comfort I need."

"I don't love you, Henry."

"No, I don't love you either. But we tried, and it nearly got the wrong people killed. And now I'm going to try with Jo."

"Coward."

"You helped me understand what I wanted, even if I didn't want it with you. I watched her become less like I thought she was, and you become more like I thought she was. I couldn't have seen what she was without seeing what you were. So I think I did need you."

"We are all your work. Goodbye, Henry."

She crosses the kitchen to the side door at which she was staring earlier, as if she can't stand to spend another moment alone with me in the house. Dora trails her out into the yard. Rather than following, I walk back through the house, and ambush them on the front walk, holding my car keys.

"Let me give you a ride. In fact, take the car. Keep it. She'll buy me another one," I say, nearly begging as I extend the keys, which she takes without much deliberation, as if collecting some sort of tariff.

"I'm taking Dora."

"Well, I'm afraid it isn't that simple," I say. "You see, her name is actually Beryl, and she has an owner. I know the woman. June Bones. Lost her husband recently."

"Take the car back," she says, but doesn't offer the keys. Another test.

"This isn't a trade, Denise. Beryl has a forever home whether or not you take the car. If you're willing to deprive a lonely widow of her animal companion, then perhaps it's not just me. Imagine that."

"Are you enjoying this?" she asks, kneeling to hug Dora, her mouth locked in portcullis of bitterness as she presses it to the dog's muzzle, while her eyes scour me for an answer. "I think you are."

"I'm not sure what you mean. Either way you get the car. No matter what, I get nothing. What am I supposed to enjoy?"

She doesn't answer, but walks stiffly toward the car. I call Dora and begin walking back to the house with her. The dog turns around at the sound of the engine (and 'Portugal' by Eleven Pond belting from the interior speakers), but I do not, and by the time we reach the porch, I can still hear the music, but Denise is gone.

"Don't be sad," I say to Dora, who continues to look toward the space at the curb from which Denise embarked. "Everyone likes you. You'll never be alone."

As I open the door, I notice an oblong box to the left of the welcome mat. It seems that sometime this morning, my business cards arrived, as Lenore promised. Since it's Sunday, the printer must have sent a courier. All other possibilities are too complicated to consider. I've cavorted along the edge of the abyss enough this morning, and if possible I'd like to retain a partial foothold in the semi-known world. And the sample card stapled to the box's short end is as fine a glue as I'm likely to find if I wish to cement my career on its former trajectory. In black ink on heavy white stock, the slightly raised script spells not only my name, but my title.

Henry Hoffmann
Vice President of Human Resources
Acheron Ventures, LLC

Not what I would have chosen for myself, and a bit under-whelming. But a title is as much a place to hide as the house I now reenter. And I'm pleased by the illustrations bracing either side of the script: Mercury (the crest of Acheron itself, I suppose), with his caduceus waving behind him as he fulfills some psychopomp office. But more than this, the artist has slyly added vestigial legs to the pair of serpents entwining the staff, making them not ser-pents at all, but lizards.

"I like this card," I say aloud, closing the door behind me, and setting the box on the floor. My phone beeps from within my costume, and when I unzip and remove it from its lodging beside my groin, I see a message from Jo.

"Of course, I'll bring dog," I say, touching the top of Dora's head with one hand as I use the other to remove my rabbit costume. It falls in a matted halo around my feet. "Why wouldn't I bring dog? You may go many places in life Dora, but you're certainly not going back to that dissolute third floor subsidized housing unit out by the rec field. June already has enough dogs for a sled team. She doesn't need one more, and besides..."

I step out of the costume, and remove one card from the box at my feet. Dora follows me, appearing to hang on my word as I wander through the rooms on the first floor of the house until I find a pen.

"Besides," I continue, bracing myself on the wall as I scribble on the back of the card. "She's as guilty as the rest. We know this. And if she tries to take you away from me, she will too. Here we are..."

I sit naked beside the dog on the carpet and hold the card between us so we can both see what's written on it.

" 'June B. 46. Female. 5'8'. 180 lbs. Brown hair. Brown eyes. Unemployed. Smoker.' "

And here, I set the card aside, and continue on from memory, recalling the appropriate entry in the immolated notebook, and mentally turning the lost pages until I arrive at J.

"Ugly. Alcoholic. Bad housekeeper. Lazy eye. Cuts hair herself. Waddles. Owner of between five and ten dogs, some of these appear ferocious/underfed. Litter of puppies confirmed accidentally by Tyler, her boyfriend, and likely co-conspirator in the hit and run murder of her husband, Rudolph 'Dude' Bones by Quim Crossing."

I close the revenant notebook, return the card to the box, and touch the top of the dog's head again, her witless expression fixed on my own, which I see reflected in the recently uncovered mirror beside the door. Aside from my nudity, I appear the same as I did on Monday morning. A young man, twenty-five years old, brown haired, hazel eyed, six feet tall, one hundred and seventy pounds, with a slim torso, broad shoulders, and a thin, high-boned face glaring at me ambiguously from the depth of the looking glass. A human gallows, more or less unchanged.

"And that, Dora," I say, standing and recovering the mirror, "is all we need to know."

Fomite

More novels from Fomite...

Joshua Amses — *During This, Our Nadir*
Joshua Amses — *Ghatsr*
Joshua Amses — *Raven or Crow*
Joshua Amses — *The Moment Before an Injury*
Charles Bell — *The Married Land*
Charles Bell — *The Half Gods*
Jaysinh Birjepatel — *Nothing Beside Remains*
Jaysinh Birjepatel — *The Good Muslim of Jackson Heights*
David Brizer — *Victor Rand*
L. M Brown — *Hinterland*
Paula Closson Buck — *Summer on the Cold War Planet*
Dan Chodorkoff — *Loisaida*
Dan Chodorkoff — *Sugaring Down*
David Adams Cleveland — *Time's Betrayal*
Paul Cody— *Sphyxia*
Jaimee Wriston Colbert — *Vanishing Acts*
Roger Coleman — *Skywreck Afternoons*
Stephen Downes — *The Hands of Pianists*
Marc Estrin — *Hyde*
Marc Estrin — *Kafka's Roach*
Marc Estrin — *Speckled Vanities*
Marc Estrin — *The Annotated Nose*
Zdravka Evtimova — *In the Town of Joy and Peace*
Zdravka Evtimova — *Sinfonia Bulgarica*
Zdravka Evtimova — *You Can Smile on Wednesdays*
Daniel Forbes — *Derail This Train Wreck*
Peter Fortunato — *Carnevale*
Greg Guma — *Dons of Time*
Richard Hawley — *The Three Lives of Jonathan Force*
Lamar Herrin — *Father Figure*
Michael Horner — *Damage Control*
Ron Jacobs — *All the Sinners Saints*
Ron Jacobs — *Short Order Frame Up*
Ron Jacobs — *The Co-conspirator's Tale*
Scott Archer Jones — *And Throw Away the Skins*
Scott Archer Jones — *A Rising Tide of People Swept Away*
Julie Justicz — *Degrees of Difficulty*
Maggie Kast — *A Free Unsullied Land*
Darrell Kastin — *Shadowboxing with Bukowski*
Coleen Kearon — *#triggerwarning*
Coleen Kearon — *Feminist on Fire*
Jan English Leary — *Thicker Than Blood*
Diane Lefer — *Confessions of a Carnivore*

Fomite

Diane Lefer — *Out of Place*
Rob Lenihan — *Born Speaking Lies*
Colin McGinnis — *Roadman*
Douglas W. Milliken — *Our Shadows' Voice*
Ilan Mochari — *Zinsky the Obscure*
Peter Nash — *Parsimony*
Peter Nash — *The Perfection of Things*
George Ovitt — *Stillpoint*
George Ovitt — *Tribunal*
Gregory Papadoyiannis — *The Baby Jazz*
Pelham — *The Walking Poor*
Andy Potok — *My Father's Keeper*
Frederick Ramey — *Comes A Time*
Joseph Rathgeber — *Mixedbloods*
Kathryn Roberts — *Companion Plants*
Robert Rosenberg — *Isles of the Blind*
Fred Russell — *Rafi's World*
Ron Savage — *Voyeur in Tangier*
David Schein — *The Adoption*
Lynn Sloan — *Principles of Navigation*
L.E. Smith — *The Consequence of Gesture*
L.E. Smith — *Travers' Inferno*
L.E. Smith — *Untimely RIPped*
Bob Sommer — *A Great Fullness*
Tom Walker — *A Day in the Life*
Susan V. Weiss — *My God, What Have We Done?*
Peter M. Wheelwright — *As It Is On Earth*
Suzie Wizowaty — *The Return of Jason Green*

More poetry from Fomite...

Anna Blackmer — *Hexagrams*
L. Brown — *Loopholes*
Sue D. Burton — *Little Steel*
Christine Butterworth-McDermott — *Evelyn As*
David Cavanagh— *Cycling in Plato's Cave*
James Connolly — *Picking Up the Bodies*
Greg Delanty — *Loosestrife*
Mason Drukman — *Drawing on Life*
J. C. Ellefson — *Foreign Tales of Exemplum and Woe*
Anna Faktorovich — *Improvisational Arguments*
Barry Goldensohn — *Snake in the Spine, Wolf in the Heart*
Barry Goldensohn — *The Hundred Yard Dash Man*
Barry Goldensohn — *The Listener Aspires to the Condition of Music*

Fomite

Barry Goldensohn — *Visitors Entrance*
R. L. Green — *When You Remember Deir Yassin*
KJ Hannah Greenberg — *Beast There—Don't That*
Gail Holst-Warhaft — *Lucky Country*
Judith Kerman — *Definitions*
Joseph Lamport — *Enlightenment*
Raymond Luczak — *A Babble of Objects*
Kate Magill — *Roadworthy Creature, Roadworthy Craft*
Tony Magistrale — *Entanglements*
Gary Mesick — *General Discharge*
Giorgio Mobili — *Sunken Boulevards*
Andreas Nolte — *Mascha: The Poems of Mascha Kaléko*
Sherry Olson — *Four-Way Stop*
Brett Ortler — *Lessons of the Dead*
David Polk — *Drinking the River*
Janice Miller Potter — *Meanwell*
Janice Miller Potter — *Thoreau's Umbrella*
Philip Ramp — *Arrivals and Departures*
Philip Ramp — *The Melancholy of a Life as the Joy of Living It Slowly Chills*
Joseph D. Reich — *A Case Study of Werewolves*
Joseph D. Reich — *Connecting the Dots to Shangrila*
Joseph D. Reich — *The Derivation of Cowboys and Indians*
Joseph D. Reich — *The Hole That Runs Through Utopia*
Joseph D. Reich — *The Housing Market*
Kenneth Rosen and Richard Wilson — *Gomorrah*
Fred Rosenblum — *Playing Chicken with an Iron Horse*
Fred Rosenblum — *Tramping Solo*
Fred Rosenblum — *Vietnumb*
David Schein — *My Murder and Other Local News*
Harold Schweizer — *Miriam's Book*
Scott T. Starbuck — *Carbonfish Blues*
Scott T. Starbuck — *Hawk on Wire*
Scott T. Starbuck — *Industrial Oz*
Seth Steinzor — *Among the Lost*
Seth Steinzor — *Once Was Lost*
Seth Steinzor — *To Join the Lost*
Susan Thomas — *In the Sadness Museum*
Susan Thomas — *Silent Acts of Public Indiscretion*
Susan Thomas — *The Empty Notebook Interrogates Itself*
Sharon Webster — *Everyone Lives Here*
Tony Whedon — *The Très Riches Heures*
Tony Whedon — *The Falkland Quartet*
Claire Zoghb — *Dispatches from Everest*

Dual Language

Fomite

Vito Bonito/Alison Grimaldi Donahue — *Soffiata Via/Blown Away*
Antonello Borra/Blossom Kirschenbaum — *Alfabestiario*
Antonello Borra/Blossom Kirschenbaum — *AlphaBetaBestiario*
Antonello Borra/Anis Memon — *Fabbrica delle idee/The Factory of Ideas*
Tina Escaja/Mark Eisner — *Caída Libre/Free Fall*
Luigi Fontanella/Giorgio Mobili — *L'adoescenza e la note/Adolescence and Night*
Aristea Papalexandrou/Philip Ramp — *Μας προσπερνά/It's Overtaking Us*
Katerina Anghelaki-Rooke//Philip Ramp — *Losing Appetite for Existence*
Jeannette Clariond/Lawrence Schimel — *Desert Memory*
Mikis Theodoraksi/Gail Holst-Warhaft — *The House with the Scorpions*
Paolo Valesio/Todd Portnowitz — *La Mezzanotte di Spoleto/Midnight in Spoleto*

More story collections from Fomite...

MaryEllen Beveridge — *After the Hunger*
MaryEllen Beveridge — *Permeable Boundaries*
Jay Boyer — *Flight*
L. M Brown — *Treading the Uneven Road*
L. M Brown — *Were We Awake*
Michael Cocchiarale — *Here Is Ware*
Michael Cocchiarale — *Still Time*
Neil Connelly — *In the Wake of Our Vows*
Catherine Zobal Dent — *Unfinished Stories of Girls*
Zdravka Evtimova —*Carts and Other Stories*
John Michael Flynn — *Off to the Next Wherever*
Derek Furr — *Semitones*
Derek Furr — *Suite for Three Voices*
Elizabeth Genovise — *Where There Are Two or More*
Andrei Guriuanu — *Body of Work*
Zeke Jarvis — *In A Family Way*
Arya Jenkins — *Blue Songs in an Open Key*
Bobby Johnston — *The Saint I Ain't*
Jan English Leary — *Skating on the Vertical*
Julia MacDonnell— *The Topography of Hidden Stories*
Marjorie Maddox — *What She Was Saying*
William Marquess — *Badtime Stories*
William Marquess — *Because Because Because Because Because*
William Marquess — *Boom-shacka-lacka*
William Marquess — *Things I Want You to Do*
Gary Miller — *Museum of the Americas*
Jennifer Anne Moses — *Visiting Hours*
Martin Ott — *Interrogations*
George Ovitt — *The Showcase*
Christopher Peterson — *Amoebic Simulacra*
Christopher Peterson — *Scratch the Itchy Teeth*

Fomite

Charles Phillips — *Dead South*
Jack Pulaski — *Love's Labours*
Charles Rafferty — *Saturday Night at Magellan's*
Joseph Rathgeber — *Bad Days on the Batso*
Mohsen Rezaei — *The Violet Needle*
Ron Savage — *What We Do For Love*
Vince Sgambati — *Undertow of Memory*
Fred Skolnik— *Americans and Other Stories*
Lynn Sloan — *This Far Is Not Far Enough*
L.E. Smith — *Views Cost Extra*
Caitlin Hamilton Summie — *To Lay To Rest Our Ghosts*
Susan Thomas — *Among Angelic Orders*
Tom Walker — *Signed Confessions*
Silas Dent Zobal — *The Inconvenience of the Wings*

More Odd Birds from Fomite...
Micheal Breiner — *the way none of this happened*
Bill Davis — *Cheap Gestures*
J. C. Ellefson — *Under the Influence: Shouting Out to Walt*
David Ross Gunn — *Cautionary Chronicles*
Andrei Guriuanu & Teknari — *The Darkest City*
Gail Holst-Warhaft — *The Fall of Athens*
Daniil Kharms — *Connections* (translator Roger Lebovitz, artitst Delia Robinson)
Roger Lebovitz — *A Guide to the Western Slopes and the Outlying Area*
Roger Lebovitz — *Twenty-two Instructions for Near Survival*
dug Nap— *Artsy Fartsy*
dug Nap— *Friends*
Delia Bell Robinson — *A Shirtwaist Story*
Claire Russell — *Dear Mr. Thoreau*
Peter Schumann — *A Child's Deprimer*
Peter Schumann — *All*
Peter Schumann — *All, Nothing, Nothing at All*
Peter Schumann — *Bedsheet Mitigations*
Peter Schumann — *Belligerent & Not So Belligerent Slogans from the Possibilitarian Arsenal*
Peter Schumann — *Bread & Sentences*
Peter Schumann — *Charlotte Salomon*
Peter Schumann — *Declaration of Light*
Peter Schumann — *Diagonal Man Theory + Praxis, Volumes One and Two*
Peter Schumann — *Faust 3*
Peter Schumann — *Handouts and Obligations*
Peter Schumann — *Planet Kasper, Volumes One and Two*
Peter Schumann — *We*

Fomite

More plays from Fomite...
Stephen Goldberg — *Screwed and Other Plays*
Michele Markarian — *Unborn Children of America*

More essays from Fomite...
William Benton — *Eye Contact: Writing on Art*
Robert Sommer — *Losing Francis: Essays on the Wars at Home*
George Ovitt & Peter Nash — *Trotsky's Sink: Ninety-Eight Short Essays on Literature*

Writing a review on social media sites for readers will help the progress of independent publishing. To submit a review, go to the book page on any of the sites and follow the links for reviews. Books from independent presses rely on reader-to-reader communications.

For more information or to order any of our books, visit:
http://www.fomitepress.com/our-books.html

* 9 7 8 1 9 3 7 6 7 7 7 1 8 *